WHITESPACE

Season Three

SEAN PLATT

DAVID WRIGHT

STERLING & STONE

WHITESPACE

Previously on Whitespace:
Season Two...

ORIGINS

In 1861, young Billy Conway and his father were duck hunting when their home and family were attacked by natives on the island. Billy managed to escape into a cave system but fell and broke his leg. Just when he thought he was going to die, a glowing orb appeared and saved him.

AFTERMATH **OF THE SHOOTINGS**

Following Roger Heller's shooting of his students, Blake Conway began to run tighter control over Conway Industries, threatening to shut down his son Warren's secret military project. Blake threatened Warren to clean up his mess, meaning to take care of the loose ends — namely Brock Houser and Roger Heller's family.

The Hellers planned to move to California to start over. Before departing, Alex hung out with his girlfriend, Katie, and his best friend, Milo, one last time. Milo seemed to be losing his mind, though, scratching at his arm and talking of conspiracies before leaving.

A couple of nights later, Bruce Henderson, the father of one of the slain students, was manipulated by Conway Industries' program into killing Alex Heller and his mother. Before Bruce could kill the baby, he realized what he'd done and killed himself.

THE CONSPIRACY

Milo was in contact with Don Bellows, a conspiracy theorist who said he had information about what was happening on the island. He told Milo that Roger Heller had been in contact with him and was going to give him a flash drive containing evidence. Don needed Milo to break into the house to find it.

While Milo was in the house, Paladin guards showed up. He overheard them talking about the murders and knew if they found him, he'll be next. Just as he was about to be discovered, their vehicles went up in flames. Milo ran from the house only to discover Jon Conway's private investigator, Brock Houser, waiting. Brock offered to help him escape, then questioned Milo about everything happening on the island. Afterward, Brock asked to meet Don Bellows.

Paladin's head of security, Carl Kaiser, managed to capture Brock Houser and interrogate him, during which it was revealed that Brock was implanted with nanobots during surgery after his car accident and Kaiser has complete and utter control of him. He forced Brock to reveal all he knew of what was going on, including information about Don and Milo.

Don met Milo and Houser in the woods but didn't trust Houser. He eventually revealed what he knew just as Paladin guards closed in on them. Houser, controlled by Paladin, pulled a gun on Milo, preventing him from escaping.

. . .

KEVIN BRADY

Hamilton Island Police Chief Kevin Brady and his family were still struggling over the disappearance of his daughter, Christina, six months ago. He was losing hope that she'd ever return home. His wife was slowly descending into an almost catatonic state. It was hard on both of them, and their son — the girl's twin brother.

When the body of a young girl was found at sea, he waited for the medical examiner to identify the body. While he hoped it wasn't his girl, part of him knew an identification would bring closure — and perhaps cure his wife's state.

It was, however, not Christina.

STARTING **OVER**

Jon Conway bought a new house to raise Emma in (when he had time with her). Eventually, as Cassidy and he got closer, he invited her to live there with them, like a makeshift family.

Everything was going well until Emma vanished one night and Houser was nowhere to be found.

Then Kevin Brady asked Jon and Cass to identify a body that had been found. They were devastated to see it was Emma.

When evidence pointed to Houser as the girl's killer, Cass wanted to murder him. But Jon refused to believe Houser was guilty. He and Cass were allowed to watch as Brady questioned Houser.

Houser didn't remember anything from the night of the disappearance, though. After the interrogation, he was arrested for Emma's murder.

WATCHING

Milo's father, Stephen Anderson, worked as a Watcher for

Conway Industries. He was tasked with secretly monitoring the optical feeds of some forty or so people in a secret program. Everything they saw and heard was broadcast to a secret watching station where Stephen monitored them.

When a new subject's feed showed up on his monitors, being interrogated by Carl Kaiser, Stephen was shocked to discover the subject was his son, Milo.

Stephen went after Kaiser, who told him his son was colluding with known "terrorists." Kaiser then told him Milo's memories would be wiped, and he would be monitored from then on by another Watcher.

Stephen knew there was nothing he could do. He'd already lost his second wife, Beatrice, to the program and feared losing his son, too.

SARAH HUGHES

Following Sarah's death in the school shooting, she woke in a space station where she learned she was part of the Conways' secret program. She met Blake Conway, who told her he was working on a project to better humanity — and she and Emma would play a very important role.

He then told her he brought Emma to the space station, too, as she was starting to remember too much and could've ruined the program had she stayed on Earth.

Sarah wanted off the space station but was grateful to have her daughter with her.

WARREN CONWAY

Warren, increasingly disillusioned with the things his father was doing, hatched a plan with his secret lover, Carl Kaiser, to kill Blake and take control of Conway Industries.

Kaiser planned to have someone shoot Blake at a ceremony.

At the ceremony, Warren succumbed to last minute guilt and called Kaiser, telling him to nix the plan. Kaiser said it was too late, and it was the right thing to do.

When Don Bellows appeared, brandishing a gun, he shot. But Blake wasn't his target. He shot Warren instead.

As Warren lay dying, Blake whispered something to him, revealing he'd been double-crossed by Kaiser.

KEVIN BRADY

Kevin couldn't sleep, thinking about Emma's death. He soon found himself driving to the station in the middle of the night to question Houser again, feeling like he was close to discovering something.

However, when he arrived at the station, two of his deputies were dead and Houser was gone.

JON

After the funeral, Jon and Cass found solace in one another. Jon told her he loved her. Still struggling with pain pills, she went to a Narcotics Anonymous meeting, more determined than ever to turn her life around.

One night while sleeping, Jon woke to find himself not in bed, but aboard a space station. And he saw both Sara and Emma still alive.

REVELATION

Blake met his father aboard the space station — Billy Conway, long believed to be dead, but still very much alive, thanks to the alien technology they were experimenting with.

They talked about Warren being a disappointment before opening a chamber and revealing a Warren clone poised to take his place.

Billy hoped this Warren would get things right.

AND NOW, THE CONCLUSION OF THE WHITESPACE SAGA...

Episode 13

Three months ago …

JON FOUND HIS FATHER, Blake, in the garage tooling with the engine of his Jaguar E-Type. "Dad, I need to ask you something."

Blake glanced up. When he saw the serious expression on his son's face, he immediately stood and gave him his full attention. "What is it?"

"Does Conway Industries have a space station?"

Blake's brows furrowed like they did when one of his sons said something so ridiculous that it edged the outlandish. And Blake Conway had little time for absurdity.

"What?"

"Do you have a space station? And more specifically, are Sarah and Emma on it?"

Blake set down his wrench and turned to Jon. "Are you okay, son?"

"Just answer the question, Dad."

"Do I even *need* to answer that? Of course, I don't have a

space station. Where would you even get such a ridiculous idea?"

"It's not important." Jon didn't want to tell him he was asking because of a dream — or worse, something that felt so real, he wondered if it really was just a dream — where the love of his life and his daughter were both still alive.

Blake put a hand on Jon's shoulder, an affection he almost never showed either son.

Jon's eyes started tearing immediately as the absurdity of his question became apparent. Of course, it couldn't have been real.

He felt stupid for even hoping such a thing, and even more so for asking his father. And he felt guilty, especially given his father's recent offers of financial assistance to Vivian Hughes in the aftermath of all that had happened to Sarah.

"Listen, son. I know the last few months have been stressful, what with Sarah dying, and then Emma, and with your brother being shot by that lunatic. It seems like the whole world is falling apart, doesn't it?"

He pulled Jon into a hug.

Jon couldn't remember the last time his father had embraced him. And so he bawled like a child.

Blake hugged him tighter.

And Jon was surprised by how much he needed this. How much comfort was in the arms of a man known more for his business acumen and icy reasoning than his warmth.

"It's going to be okay. I've got someone who can help you get through this."

Jon pulled out of the hug. "I don't need a shrink, Dad. I … I just need some time."

"There's no shame in getting professional help, Jon. I've used this doctor's services before. One hypnotherapy session, and I promise you'll feel like a new man."

"I dunno. I don't like the idea of someone rooting around in my head."

Blake shook his head and laughed. "Son, don't be so damned paranoid. I won't take no for an answer."

Jon said nothing.

"You've been through a lot. Through more than any man should have to go through alone. And you're not alone, son. You don't have to be. I'm here for you. And I've got the best people to help. But you need to let us. Will you let us help you, Jon?"

He wanted to get through this on willpower and the love of Cass alone, but the truth was that his pain felt infinite, and eventually it would overcome him. Poison everything if he didn't stop it.

And that meant getting help.

He nodded.

Blake hugged him again. "You won't regret this, son."

~

PROLOGUE TWO

THREE MONTHS LATER …

IT WAS the sort of Sunday at the Hamilton Island Outdoor Marketplace that Clair loved most. Cool, crisp, and perfectly clear. She was picking up some meat, cheeses, and wine, planning to go out on Chris's boat later that morning, the perfect way to start her vacation.

But despite the bright sun and morning solitude, Clair couldn't shake the feeling that something bad was going to happen.

She waited on the center pitch, a spacious grassy mound circled by benches, where kids threw Frisbees, families had picnics, and musicians — mostly guitarists and ukulelists —

performed with open cases or hats to collect donations from the crowd of couples and hipsters with disposable income. A few artists had set up on the pitch, painting either the landscape or taking commissions for caricatures.

It was like any other weekend at the Marketplace, and yet Clair felt as if the world around her were a piece of fabric with a loose thread waiting to be pulled by invisible forces.

Did I take my meds today?

She couldn't remember, and that wasn't a good thing. The last thing Clair needed was to have a panic attack out on the water with Chris. They'd only been dating for a few months, and he had no idea how bad her anxiety used to be. He was a successful investor, despite only being twenty-five and one year older than her. With his always calm demeanor, she wasn't sure how he'd handle her flipping the heck out on his boat. It would probably end their relationship.

Just relax. Nothing is wrong. Just find something to focus on.

Clair looked around, finding a young mother and her young son sitting on a blanket. She was handing the boy a giant apple to try. It practically looked like a honeydew in his hands. They were cute together.

A wistful pang stabbed her heart. Clair wondered if she'd ever have kids. For a long time, she opposed the idea of bringing a child into the world. Her own brood hadn't exactly been a role model for How To Be a Family. But lately, especially working at the restaurant, she saw more and more young moms and found herself envious. She wanted to have a child, to have someone look at her with that specific breed of love.

Did Chris even want kids? While he was a nice guy, warm and sweet, he could be incredibly self-centered and sometimes arrogant. She couldn't imagine him having the patience for children.

Clair turned her attention elsewhere, past a blue-haired teenage girl playing the uke to a few skater boys to a heavyset redheaded woman working at a flower cart. She smiled as she wrapped a bouquet of roses and handed them to a young blond who looked like he was late for his date. The woman's smile seemed so genuine. You could tell she cared about delivering a great experience, even if it was only in the purchase of a single rose. Clair imagined the woman asking the young man who the flowers were for, and the young man blushing as he told her about his girlfriend, or maybe a crush.

Do you think Chris could ever love someone like you? Damaged. He was supposed to meet you ten minutes ago. He's probably with that slut you saw him talking to last week.

Probably fucking her right now.

Clair wasn't sure where *that* thought came from, but looking at happy children and a young lovestruck man were obviously triggering her anxiety.

She closed her eyes, deciding to focus on the sounds around her — the laughter and conversation, the tinkling of glassware and utensils and the outdoor cafe, the musicians' songs slightly overlapping, gulls swooping over the nearby sea, the ocean breeze and lapping waves.

Plus all the static.

Static?

Clair opened her eyes trying to locate its source. The sound was barely there, seeming to come from the closest public address speaker high up on a pole to her left.

It sounded as if someone had accidentally left a detuned radio next to a microphone and that any minute someone would hear it, recognize the error, and correct it.

But, as Clair looked around, nobody else seemed to be paying attention to the sound. They either didn't hear it or were so absorbed in their activities that it didn't bother them.

The sound grew louder, hurting her ears.

The static was intermittent, small bursts, followed by seconds of silence before starting again.

It almost sounds like a signal.

She moved away from the speaker, heading over toward the flower stand, considering buying Chris a yellow daisy. She'd never bought flowers for a boy before.

And he's never bought you flowers, either. Fuck him.

Clair shook the negativity from her head, though it was getting hard to do as ugly flashes of Chris and that whore ran rampant through her mind.

She approached the flower cart. Up close, Clair realized it was actually a carriage, either drawn by horses more than a hundred years ago or made to look that way.

The woman was using a pair of scissors to cut the ends of the stems from some flowers before she placed them in her vase.

The static, somehow seemed to get louder, though Clair had gotten farther from the speakers. Now it seemed to be coming from a small radio the woman had playing classical music.

Isn't she bothered by the static? Why not change the station to something that came in better?

She looked up and smiled at Clair, setting the scissors down on the counter.

"Hi, how may I help you?" Her smile was deep and —

— *So fucking fake. It's a lying cunt smile. A whore's smile. I bet she's fucking Chris, too.*

Clair hated the horrible thoughts racing through her mind. While she was prone to depression and anxiety, she rarely had such angry, hateful thoughts, nor such vile words for people. Heck, she even thought in terms of "oh poop" or "what a jerk" rather than their more vulgar counterparts.

Where was this all coming from?

Clair wondered if she should head home and take her meds before things got worse.

"Ma'am?" The woman stared at Clair as if she'd been waiting for her to respond for several minutes. "How can I help you?"

The static grew louder still, enough that Clair wanted to scream to make it stop.

She could feel its vibration in her body.

"F… Fucking flowers."

The words that came out of her mouth shocked her. They weren't even close to the ones that were forming on her tongue.

The woman's eyebrows arched, "Pardon me?"

Clair tried to apologize, but "sorry" wouldn't come out. Instead, she said, "Slut! Slut, whore, cunt, fuck!"

The woman looked stunned, frozen, as if Clair had smacked her across the face.

And then, as if someone else had taken control of her body and all she could do was watch, Clair's hands grabbed the scissors.

What's happening?

Stop!

She tried to keep herself from doing the devil's work, but couldn't.

She could only watch as she plunged the sharp end of the scissors straight through the flower woman's right eye.

Clair screamed.

And it seemed as if the whole world screamed with her.

~

ADAM

AT HAMILTON'S OUTDOOR MARKETPLACE, Adam Foster worked the Tico's Taco Stand counter with his buddy, Rupert. When the static tickled his ear, he began to seriously question his life choices.

Between it, the sound of a crying baby further back in the long line, and the fat asses yammering at him about how he wasn't putting enough meat on their tacos, Adam wished he'd listened to his parents and gone to college.

But *nooooo*, he had to blow his money on partying and getting a job at Jerry's startup, thinking he had it made, fuck his parents and their old ways of thinking. College was for suckers. The new wealth belonged to those bold enough to say fuck the system and its ancient ways, and his friend was giving him an easy in.

But then Jerry took off with his investors' money and Adam was left looking for any gig he could get. That was how he wound up working with his stoner friend for the past five months.

He looked up and down the line. It was only eleven in the morning, why were so many people already starving for tacos? It might not have annoyed him so much if the tip jar wasn't stuffed with a whole lot of nothing.

Adam glared over at the pitch where a pair of gay dudes were dropping dollars into Heather's open guitar case. Heather was Rupert's girlfriend, and she routinely made more than both of them put together in tips every weekend. Made more playing songs, stoned out of her mind, than they made busting their asses and dealing with shitty customers.

Sometimes the world wasn't only unfair, it was downright fucking cruel.

He looked over at Rupert then nodded at Heather.

"Screw this shit. I should learn to play something."

"Yeah, they got rules against playing your skin flute in public," Rupert teased.

"Fuck you, asshole."

The static got even louder, and with it came a high-pitched ear-piercing that made his ears want to bleed.

He set the meat-filled spoon on the counter and clenched his teeth, trying to ride out the pain.

And then it was gone.

He looked up to find a fat couple in front of him. They ordered four tacos with lettuce and cheese. As he finished ladling the meat into the shells, the fat bitch said, "C'mon, don't be stingy."

Don't be stingy?

Adam wanted to tell her to fuck off, but he didn't make "Heather Money" so he needed whatever tips he could manage to get for his rent.

He put more meat into each taco, then looked up at the couple.

"This good?" It was twice as much as his boss had told him he was supposed to put in a taco, but fuck it, his boss wasn't here, and he just wanted the fat fucks gone.

"More, eh?" said the man, a fat Italian guy that looked, and sounded, like a retired mob boss and reeked of cigarettes.

Adam looked at them, then down at the tacos.

Whatever.

He grabbed the spoon and piled a giant glop right in the middle, enough to bury the shells.

Adam looked up and grinned. "That better?"

"You ruined it!" she said.

"What the fuck is your problem?" the guy asked.

The static came back, this time so loud, that Adam doubled over in pain, crying out, "Fuck!"

The obnoxious fat couple thought he was talking to them. The guy started to come around to Adam's side of the cart.

Rupert got between them. Though he was skinny and probably couldn't kick the wife's ass, let alone the guy's, he was loud and not easily intimidated.

"Hey, hey, calm down, man. What's the problem?"

The guy started to say something, but Adam could only hear static. He looked, wondering why nobody else was perking their ears. He stepped away from the stand, needing space to clear his thoughts.

Nausea roiled through his gut.

He ran toward the bushes and puked.

The static got louder.

Adam wiped the vomit from his mouth and turned back to the stand, noticing some people looking at him, probably wondering why he was puking, if he was drunk. But it was a few other people that drew his attention, three girls in the back of the line who all seemed agitated as well, shaking their heads, and squeezing their eyes shut.

They heard the static, too.

What the hell is happening?

Rupert was making tacos for the fat couple.

Something snapped in Adam.

One moment, he was glaring at the fat asses, hating that Rupert was going to cave into their demands, and the next, he was approaching the stand without even meaning to.

Fat Mob Dude looked at Adam and made a *fuck you* face.

Adam grabbed the knife off the counter, raced around it, and stabbed the fat fuck in his giant gut, fast and furiously, over and over.

The woman screamed, tried to pull Adam off her boyfriend, husband, or whatever the fuck he was.

Adam spun around, drove the knife right through her triple-jowled throat and out the back. He left the blade in her neck, laughing as she tried to pull it out, but couldn't.

A part of Adam was horrified by what he was doing, but that part of him was a passenger, loving this magic carpet ride to nowhere.

Adrenaline coursed through him. He felt good.

Indestructible.

Rupert screamed something, but Adam couldn't hear over the static and the woman's voice just underneath it.

Kill them. Kill them all.

He turned to find more victims, and saw the three girls attacking other people in line.

And then more people unleashing their monsters. All hell was breaking loose and goddamn it, this shit was a party.

Adam screamed as he turned and spotted Heather running away from a redheaded man with a knife.

He laughed and decided to join in the chase.

Prologue two

Three months later ...

IT WAS the sort of Sunday at the Hamilton Island Outdoor Marketplace that Clair loved most. Cool, crisp, and perfectly clear. She was picking up some meat, cheeses, and wine, planning to go out on Chris's boat later that morning, the perfect way to start her vacation.

But despite the bright sun and morning solitude, Clair couldn't shake the feeling that something bad was going to happen.

She waited on the center pitch, a spacious grassy mound circled by benches, where kids threw Frisbees, families had picnics, and musicians — mostly guitarists and ukulelists — performed with open cases or hats to collect donations from the crowd of couples and hipsters with disposable income. A few artists had set up on the pitch, painting either the landscape or taking commissions for caricatures.

It was like any other weekend at the Marketplace, and yet Clair felt as if the world around her were a piece of fabric with a loose thread waiting to be pulled by invisible forces.

Did I take my meds today?

She couldn't remember, and that wasn't a good thing. The last thing Clair needed was to have a panic attack out on the water with Chris. They'd only been dating for a few months, and he had no idea how bad her anxiety used to be. He was a successful investor, despite only being twenty-five and one year older than her. With his always calm demeanor, she wasn't sure how he'd handle her flipping the heck out on his boat. It would probably end their relationship.

Just relax. Nothing is wrong. Just find something to focus on.

Clair looked around, finding a young mother and her young son sitting on a blanket. She was handing the boy a giant apple to try. It practically looked like a honeydew in his hands. They were cute together.

A wistful pang stabbed her heart. Clair wondered if she'd ever have kids. For a long time, she opposed the idea of bringing a child into the world. Her own brood hadn't exactly been a role model for How To Be a Family. But lately, especially working at the restaurant, she saw more and more young moms and found herself envious. She wanted to have a child, to have someone look at her with that specific breed of love.

Did Chris even want kids? While he was a nice guy, warm and sweet, he could be incredibly self-centered and sometimes arrogant. She couldn't imagine him having the patience for children.

Clair turned her attention elsewhere, past a blue-haired teenage girl playing the uke to a few skater boys to a heavyset redheaded woman working at a flower cart. She smiled as she wrapped a bouquet of roses and handed them to a young blond who looked like he was late for his date. The woman's smile seemed so genuine. You could tell she cared about delivering a great experience, even if it was only in the purchase of a single rose. Clair imagined the woman asking the young man who the flowers were for, and the young man blushing as he told her about his girlfriend, or maybe a crush.

Do you think Chris could ever love someone like you? Damaged. He was supposed to meet you ten minutes ago. He's probably with that slut you saw him talking to last week.

Probably fucking her right now.

Clair wasn't sure where *that* thought came from, but looking at happy children and a young lovestruck man were obviously triggering her anxiety.

She closed her eyes, deciding to focus on the sounds around her — the laughter and conversation, the tinkling of glassware and utensils and the outdoor cafe, the musicians' songs slightly overlapping, gulls swooping over the nearby sea, the ocean breeze and lapping waves.

Plus all the static.

Static?

Clair opened her eyes trying to locate its source. The sound was barely there, seeming to come from the closest public address speaker high up on a pole to her left.

It sounded as if someone had accidentally left a detuned radio next to a microphone and that any minute someone would hear it, recognize the error, and correct it.

But, as Clair looked around, nobody else seemed to be paying attention to the sound. They either didn't hear it or were so absorbed in their activities that it didn't bother them.

The sound grew louder, hurting her ears.

The static was intermittent, small bursts, followed by seconds of silence before starting again.

It almost sounds like a signal.

She moved away from the speaker, heading over toward the flower stand, considering buying Chris a yellow daisy. She'd never bought flowers for a boy before.

And he's never bought you flowers, either. Fuck him.

Clair shook the negativity from her head, though it was

getting hard to do as ugly flashes of Chris and that whore ran rampant through her mind.

She approached the flower cart. Up close, Clair realized it was actually a carriage, either drawn by horses more than a hundred years ago or made to look that way.

The woman was using a pair of scissors to cut the ends of the stems from some flowers before she placed them in her vase.

The static, somehow seemed to get louder, though Clair had gotten farther from the speakers. Now it seemed to be coming from a small radio the woman had playing classical music.

Isn't she bothered by the static? Why not change the station to something that came in better?

She looked up and smiled at Clair, setting the scissors down on the counter.

"Hi, how may I help you?" Her smile was deep and —

— So fucking fake. It's a lying cunt smile. A whore's smile. I bet she's fucking Chris, too.

Clair hated the horrible thoughts racing through her mind. While she was prone to depression and anxiety, she rarely had such angry, hateful thoughts, nor such vile words for people. Heck, she even thought in terms of "oh poop" or "what a jerk" rather than their more vulgar counterparts.

Where was this all coming from?

Clair wondered if she should head home and take her meds before things got worse.

"Ma'am?" The woman stared at Clair as if she'd been waiting for her to respond for several minutes. "How can I help you?"

The static grew louder still, enough that Clair wanted to scream to make it stop.

She could feel its vibration in her body.

"F… Fucking flowers."

The words that came out of her mouth shocked her. They

weren't even close to the ones that were forming on her tongue.

The woman's eyebrows arched, "Pardon me?"

Clair tried to apologize, but "sorry" wouldn't come out. Instead, she said, "Slut! Slut, whore, cunt, fuck!"

The woman looked stunned, frozen, as if Clair had smacked her across the face.

And then, as if someone else had taken control of her body and all she could do was watch, Clair's hands grabbed the scissors.

What's happening?

Stop!

She tried to keep herself from doing the devil's work, but couldn't.

She could only watch as she plunged the sharp end of the scissors straight through the flower woman's right eye.

Clair screamed.

And it seemed as if the whole world screamed with her.

~

ADAM

AT HAMILTON'S OUTDOOR MARKETPLACE, Adam Foster worked the Tico's Taco Stand counter with his buddy, Rupert. When the static tickled his ear, he began to seriously question his life choices.

Between it, the sound of a crying baby further back in the long line, and the fat asses yammering at him about how he wasn't putting enough meat on their tacos, Adam wished he'd listened to his parents and gone to college.

But *nooooo*, he had to blow his money on partying and getting a job at Jerry's startup, thinking he had it made, fuck his parents and their old ways of thinking. College was for suckers. The new wealth belonged to those bold enough to say fuck the system and its ancient ways, and his friend was giving him an easy in.

But then Jerry took off with his investors' money and Adam was left looking for any gig he could get. That was how he wound up working with his stoner friend for the past five months.

He looked up and down the line. It was only eleven in the morning, why were so many people already starving for tacos? It might not have annoyed him so much if the tip jar wasn't stuffed with a whole lot of nothing.

Adam glared over at the pitch where a pair of gay dudes were dropping dollars into Heather's open guitar case. Heather was Rupert's girlfriend, and she routinely made more than both of them put together in tips every weekend. Made more playing songs, stoned out of her mind, than they made busting their asses and dealing with shitty customers.

Sometimes the world wasn't only unfair, it was downright fucking cruel.

He looked over at Rupert then nodded at Heather.

"Screw this shit. I should learn to play something."

"Yeah, they got rules against playing your skin flute in public," Rupert teased.

"Fuck you, asshole."

The static got even louder, and with it came a high-pitched ear-piercing that made his ears want to bleed.

He set the meat filled spoon on the counter and clenched his teeth, trying to ride out the pain.

And then it was gone.

He looked up to find a fat couple in front of him. They ordered four tacos with lettuce and cheese. As he finished ladling the meat into the shells, the fat bitch said, "C'mon, don't be stingy."

Don't be stingy?

Adam wanted to tell her to fuck off, but he didn't make

"Heather Money" so he needed whatever tips he could manage to get for his rent.

He put more meat into each taco, then looked up at the couple.

"This good?" It was twice as much as his boss had told him he was supposed to put in a taco, but fuck it, his boss wasn't here, and he just wanted the fat fucks gone.

"More, eh?" said the man, a fat Italian guy that looked, and sounded, like a retired mob boss and reeked of cigarettes.

Adam looked at them, then down at the tacos.

Whatever.

He grabbed the spoon and piled a giant glop right in the middle, enough to bury the shells.

Adam looked up and grinned. "That better?"

"You ruined it!" she said.

"What the fuck is your problem?" the guy asked.

The static came back, this time so loud, that Adam doubled over in pain, crying out, "Fuck!"

The obnoxious fat couple thought he was talking to them. The guy started to come around to Adam's side of the cart.

Rupert got between them. Though he was skinny and probably couldn't kick the wife's ass, let alone the guy's, he was loud and not easily intimidated.

"Hey, hey, calm down, man. What's the problem?"

The guy started to say something, but Adam could only hear static. He looked, wondering why nobody else was perking their ears. He stepped away from the stand, needing space to clear his thoughts.

Nausea roiled through his gut.

He ran toward the bushes and puked.

The static got louder.

Adam wiped the vomit from his mouth and turned back to the stand, noticing some people looking at him, probably wondering why he was puking, if he was drunk. But it was a few other people that drew his attention, three girls in the back of the line who all seemed agitated as well, shaking their heads, and squeezing their eyes shut.

They heard the static, too.

What the hell is happening?

Rupert was making tacos for the fat couple.

Something snapped in Adam.

One moment, he was glaring at the fat asses, hating that Rupert was going to cave into their demands, and the next, he was approaching the stand without even meaning to.

Fat Mob Dude looked at Adam and made a *fuck you* face.

Adam grabbed the knife off the counter, raced around it, and stabbed the fat fuck in his giant gut, fast and furiously, over and over.

The woman screamed, tried to pull Adam off her boyfriend, husband, or whatever the fuck he was.

Adam spun around, drove the knife right through her triple-jowled throat and out the back. He left the blade in her neck, laughing as she tried to pull it out, but couldn't.

A part of Adam was horrified by what he was doing, but that part of him was a passenger, loving this magic carpet ride to nowhere.

Adrenaline coursed through him. He felt good.

Indestructible.

Rupert screamed something, but Adam couldn't hear over the static and the woman's voice just underneath it.

Kill them. Kill them all.

He turned to find more victims, and saw the three girls attacking other people in line.

And then more people unleashing their monsters. All hell was breaking loose and goddamn it, this shit was a party.

Adam screamed as he turned and spotted Heather running away from a redheaded man with a knife.

He laughed and decided to join in the chase.

Chapter 1 - Kevin Brady

Hamilton Island Police Chief Kevin Brady's SUV screeched to a halt outside the perimeter established by Paladin Security outside Hamilton Island Outdoor Marketplace. He leapt out of his department truck and rushed toward the scene.

Sgt. Bill Franks, one of the Paladin officers working the perimeter, moved in to intercept. "This is ours, Chief. Holding it down until the Feds arrive."

"I don't give a damn about whose scene this is. I'm not working. My wife and son called. They're in there. Let me through."

Franks's eyes widened. "Sorry, Chief. Are they hurt?"

While territorial disputes were becoming ever more common on the island as Paladin's private force claimed more and more of the police work, the rank and file were decent people who always showed him respect in moments like this.

"No. Molly said she's with the witnesses, waiting to give statements. Where are they?"

"They're in the Welcome Center." Franks pointed back at the building Kevin had passed on his way in, just past the rows of ambulances and fire trucks on scene where victims were being treated.

"Thanks." He glanced past Franks into the marketplace, seeing the chaos of bodies, overturned carts, dropped bags and packages, and bloody makeshift weapons jutting from faces and chests. He could see at least twelve from his vantage, though he knew the number of victims was closer to forty. Men, women, and children who would never see another day. Lives rendered into corpses waiting to be photographed by evidence techs as their families grieved, wondering How and Why something like this could happen.

Hows and Whys that would be shut down by Paladin yet again.

Hows and Whys that the Feds would ignore because God forbid anyone question what the hell Conway Industries was really doing on the island.

Hows and Whys that would slowly fade from public view until the only people left asking were deemed too unimportant for attention — victims' families, fringe media, crackpots, and the easily ignored.

Outside of a memorial here and there, maybe an update on a survivor at the end of the news hour, most people would forget, as if nothing had ever happened. At least until the next tragedy.

Kevin's anger turned to heartache as he made his way into the Welcome Center and heard the sobs from those who had lost friends and loved ones — familiar faces that had been on the island forever. Some of them friends. Others, people he'd run into every now and then. And as he passed the grief-stricken people, Kevin looked at the ground, unable to meet a single eye.

What good was it being the chief of police when you couldn't help prevent such tragedies?

When you couldn't even work the scene and help the survivors?

And then he saw Molly, sitting against the wall, clutching their six-year-old son, Aidan.

Tears welled in his eyes as he approached her. "Molly."

He expected her to get up, to run to him, to cry on his chest, but she only stared. Her eyes and cheeks were red from crying, but she was out of tears.

Aidan leapt into his arms. "Daddy, it was so scary. Everybody was hurting each other. There was blood everywhere. They … they even killed a baby."

Kevin hugged his son tight, wishing he could somehow absorb the horrors, erase them from his child's mind. But there was no forgetting something like this. Brutality would haunt his memories and dreams forever. Violence might manifest in the same sort of post-traumatic stress disorder symptoms Molly had suffered since their daughter, Christina, vanished nine months ago.

"You're okay now," he whispered over and over, feeling his son's shuddering cheek against his as he looked down at Molly, still staring out into space.

"Molly?"

She didn't respond.

Kevin looked around and saw around two hundred plus people in the Welcome Center, but only three Paladin officers were interviewing the witnesses. These people would be here well into the night.

"Come on." He offered a hand to his wife.

She looked up at him as if he were speaking another language.

"Come on, honey. We're going home."

She took his hand. Her fingers were cold in his grasp as he pulled her up.

He tried to hug her, but she wasn't receptive. Just stood there in shock.

"Come." He carried Aidan as he led his wife toward the exit.

"Hey!" called one of the Paladins.

Kevin kept walking.

The officer ran up behind him, a young redhead, clearly a rookie. "You can't leave yet. We haven't interviewed them."

"You wanna talk to them, come to my office," Kevin said, tugging at the badge on his shirt pocket.

The kid looked confused, unsure of protocol. "Wait a second, I need to—"

"No. You all ought to have more than three fucking officers taking statements. I'm not waiting around for this bullshit."

He grabbed Molly's hand and led her out the doors. If the guard dared to stop him, Kevin would deck him, consequences be damned.

They made it to his truck without incident, though he could hear the redheaded rent-a-cop calling out to him, then shouting into his radio asking for someone to help.

Kevin laughed as he opened the passenger side door for Molly and Aidan, closed it, then went to the driver's side, got in, and started the truck.

"Hey!"

Kevin ignored the rent-a-cop as he backed out then tore away, spying the man's astonishment only in his rearview.

AN HOUR LATER, Molly was in bed resting while Kevin and Aidan sat on the couch watching cartoons.

Aidan eventually drifted into sleep on Kevin's chest.

He didn't want to get up or leave his son, but he couldn't just sit on the couch all day. Calls were mounting on his phone. Even though he wasn't working the case, it was blowing up with people wanting information, officials wanting statements, and media desperate for quotes. He would love to forward all the calls to Carl Kaiser, the head of Paladin Security, but he had an obligation to the people of Hamilton he couldn't just ignore.

Kevin grabbed a blanket off the laundry basket sitting on the recliner, unfolded it, and draped it over his son.

Then he went upstairs to see if Molly was awake or in need. He assumed she'd taken some pills to help her pass out, opened their bedroom door to confirm she was sleeping, then softly closed it.

Kevin pulled out his phone, went to his home office on the second floor, and sat at his desk. He was about to go through voicemail when a black Paladin SUV pulled into his driveway.

He slipped the phone back into his pocket and went downstairs to intercept the front door before whatever asshole was here to harass him could ring the bell and wake Aidan.

He opened the door to find Kaiser getting out of his truck. No matter how many times Kevin saw the six-foot-five bald man with the scarred face and prosthetic blue robotic eye, he could never be comfortable in his presence. It was like giving a rabid Pitbull robotic teeth to make him even scarier.

"Kevin." Kaiser nodded as he approached the front door. Using his name instead of calling him "Chief" was one of many ways the fucker tried to act like he was Kevin's superior.

Kevin closed the door behind him and crossed his arms. "To what do I owe the pleasure?"

"An officer told me your wife and son left the scene of a crime earlier. Is that true?"

"Yes, I took them out of there. You want a statement, you can get it from me right now."

Kaiser shook his head with a sigh. "Come on, Kevin, you know how important it is to get a statement immediately following the event in order to get things straight. Memory is a funny thing, ya' know. Witnesses aren't nearly as reliable after leaving a scene."

"Yes, I do know. Which is why I was surprised to see just three officers taking statements of what, two hundred people? Hell, I bet they're still taking them now, am I right?"

Kaiser nodded. "Obviously, resources are stretched thin in an event like that."

"Of course. So, why are you here?"

"I'd like to interview your wife and son now, if you don't mind."

"I do. They're both asleep, and I'm not waking them. You want an interview, *I'll* do it when they wake."

Kevin met Kaiser's gaze. He wondered what the bastard's electronic blue eye was doing — probably scanning Kevin's biometrics to determine if he was lying or how much of a fight he might raise. Hell, maybe he was trying to figure the best course of action, whatever might permit him to pull his gun and kill Kevin on his front porch. Then Paladin Security could make a case to close the already undermanned police department and gain total control over the island.

Kevin wished he'd not left his gun inside.

"You do realize I could compel them both to come down to the station right now?"

Kevin was tempted to go nuclear, to ask Kaiser how he'd feel if Kevin went to the State Attorney's Office with some information to remove Paladin's ability to investigate crimes which Conway Industries was responsible for. He would love to see the smug bastard's face go pale as he wondered what information Kevin might have, but doing so would put a target on his back. And his family's.

"You *really* want to go down that road, Carl? Pulling rank? Because we've been pretty cooperative with Paladin, and I'd hate to see a little misunderstanding get in the way of our working relationship."

Kaiser nodded. "Fine. But I want a statement tomorrow."

"I'll send it over in the morning."

Kaiser nodded then headed back to his truck.

But just as he was about to get inside, he stopped, turned back toward Kevin, and winked.

Chapter 2 - Jon Conway

Jon ordered another drink. There was no way he was getting through this meeting with his agent, Marty, and the Maris Brothers without dulling his frazzled nerves.

As he instructed the waiter to bring another Moscow Mule, Marty looked at him in his disapproving way, one of his bushy eyebrows raised like a caterpillar trying to leave his face and scurry back into his salt and pepper curly hair.

Jon was thankful that they were in a private room in the back of Chambray. The last thing he wanted was some groupie or the damned paparazzi snapping photos and video in the middle of his panic attack. Bad enough several of them had shoved cameras and phones in his face as they were entering the restaurant, asking if he had anything to say about the tragedy in his hometown. Fortunately, Marty was a bulldog, and he'd pushed past the parasites.

Jon held up his shaking hand. "Sorry, man, I need something to calm my nerves. And unless you've got something stronger, I'm gonna drink — a lot. I can't fucking shake it."

"You're sure you didn't have the TV on or something while you were sleeping? Maybe you heard the news and incorporated it into your dream. The mind is a tricky bitch."

"I didn't have the TV on. I dreamed it, Marty. Dreamed it either before it happened, or right as it was happening."

"And you're *sure* it was the outdoor market?"

Jon sighed. "Yes, I'm sure. And even though they haven't released names or photos, I'm damned positive I saw the people that did it. Like I was in their heads, man."

The waiter brought Jon his drink. "Can I get you anything else?"

Jon took the drink and resisted downing the whole thing at once, lest Marty's eyebrows flee his face entirely.

Marty answered, "No, our party should be here soon. Thank you."

The waiter nodded then left.

Jon continued drinking, his third drink since they sat.

"So," Marty began, "the Maris Brothers wanted to discuss your notes on Theo."

"They not like them?"

"No. Well, at least I don't think so. I think they wanted to explore your ideas further."

With principal photography starting soon, the Maris Brothers wouldn't want to go into major script revisions, but Jon felt like his interpretation of Theo was more nuanced than it showed in the script. A minor quibble, but one that Jon wanted to get out of the way before they started shooting.

But such a conversation seemed superfluous right now, like discussing a paint treatment in your house while riots were happening outside.

Jon finished his drink, waved the waiter down and ordered another.

Marty stared at him. "You going to be okay to get through this?"

"Sure," Jon said with a grin he wasn't feeling. "I'll just smile and nod a lot, tell them I'm sorry, I know nothing, and they're right. The Maris Brothers are *always* right. Yes? That work?"

Marty frowned. He didn't like this side of Jon, the contrarian provoking arguments. The kind of guy that proved a nightmare on-set.

"Relax," Jon said. "I'm just messing with you."

The waiter brought another drink. He was finally feeling a bit more relaxed, even if Marty was getting more anxious.

The brothers arrived.

No matter how many times Jon had seen them, it was still hard to reconcile the men with their art.

Reginald Maris, at forty-six, was the older brother, tall, and always dapper, dressed in styles that were at least a half-century behind. His long blond hair was always slicked back, and his piercing blue eyes were thin. He looked like he might break if someone were to tip him. He was also "the silent brother," known for rarely speaking. It was in an affected voice when he did, soft and with a strong but unidentifiable accent. The brothers were from New Jersey and rarely traveled abroad. Sometimes Jon wondered if Reginald's entire persona was some elaborate Andy Kaufman style trolling of the public.

Younger brother, Donovan, thirty-nine, more than made up for Reginald's silence and was almost always talking about something, usually at a speed about twice as fast as a normal person thought. Donovan was also a visual contrast to his brother, standing at about five foot eight, with dark hair and eyes. Stock. And he dressed like he was kidding, wearing track-suits, gold chains, and whatever else was criminally out of fashion. His accent was Jersey to the marrow.

It was hard to see them as brothers. The men looked like strangers. Yet the pair made magic together. They weren't just the most bankable directors in Hollywood, they did things their way, never compromising, even on a popcorn flick like *Black Nova*.

"Jonny!" Donovan said, thrusting his hand into Jon's, shaking it hard. "How the hell are ya', man?"

"Good, Donovan."

"Call me Donnie."

"Okay, Donnie," Jon said before going to shake Reginald's limp fingers.

"Good to see you, Jon," he said in almost a whisper. Today he was wearing eyeliner. Not a lot, just a subtle amount.

"You, as well," Jon said.

The two men sat opposite one another at the circular table and the waiter immediately headed over, asking what they were drinking. Reginald asked to see the wine list while Donnie ordered a beer, then turned to Jon and said, "So, what the hell's happening on Hamilton? You had that teacher shoot up his class and now a fucking flash mob of murders?"

Jon and Marty exchanged glances as if Marty was afraid Jon might go on and tell the biggest directors in Hollywood that he'd had psychic dreams about the massacre. They'd be wondering about Jon's stability the next second, maybe chasing down Court Embry or one of those other up-and-coming action star wannabes to step in. Marty had told Jon that Reginald had pressed for Court to get the role, but Donnie had been wanting to work with Jon forever.

Jon gave his agent an *I'm not gonna fuck this up* look then said, "I have no idea. Must be something in the water."

Did Donnie know he'd lost someone close in the Roger Heller incident? Didn't seem to, the way he was carrying on. After a few more minutes, Jon interrupted.

"So, about those script notes ..."

"You wanna get right to it, eh? I like that!" Donnie said. "No prancing around the bushes with this one."

He and Marty traded laughter.

Jon struggled to smile.

Reginald was pre-occupied with the wine list, which he was perusing as though he was about to order his last meal on Earth. He finally decided on a glass of 2005 Pavie.

Before the waiter left, Donnie told the man to get Jon and Marty another of whatever they were drinking.

The waiter nodded, took the wine list back from Reginald, then turned on his heel and was gone.

"So," Donnie said, "you had some concerns with Theo?"

"Nothing major. I just think the script missed a bit that was in the book, some of the sorrow Theo was feeling about his past. I mean, I know the story didn't really get into it until the second book, and it'll probably be the same with the movie, but I think we should hint at it … just a bit."

Donnie and Reginald traded glances.

For a moment, Jon wondered if he'd been too presumptuous. The Maris Brothers not only directed their movies, but wrote nearly all of them, including a treatment for *Black Nova* after infamously coming to blows with the writer of the series over *his* script.

Donnie smiled. "I agree. And *that's* why I'm glad that you took the role. That douche Court would never have suggested such a thing. Hell, he probably didn't even read the books. And don't get me started on Cooper Ford's antics."

Cooper Ford had been the actor pegged to do the *Black Nova* series until he got busted doing coke and hookers, which grated against his carefully cultivated image.

Jon relaxed, as did Marty, so when the drinks came, Marty tipped back with the rest of them.

As the lunch went, Donnie regaled Jon and Marty with behind-the-scenes stories of some of their biggest movies. He was an excellent storyteller, the sort of guy Jon always wished he could be in social situations. Though he was a movie star and had no problems in front of the camera, intimate settings often made him uneasy. Even today, after all his success, he sometimes felt like a fraud, awaiting discovery.

After a while, Jon was finally relaxed. Thoroughly shit-faced. His words slurred.

Fortunately, Donnie had a lot to drink as well, so Jon didn't feel like *too much* of an alcoholic. But he could feel both Reginald and Marty eyeing him with concern.

Donnie insisted on picking up the check, despite Jon and Marty's protest. In the end, you didn't refuse Donnie Maris, so they let him pay, then the foursome headed toward the exit and their cars.

Reginald and Marty were discussing something as they passed through the doors ahead of them.

Donnie was laughing as he attempted to tell a story Jon could barely follow, given the man's many tangents. A wave of men with cameras rushed toward them, coming between Marty and Reginald and them.

Jon could see his car and driver, twenty yards away, but a sea of photographers blocked his path.

Cameras clicked. Questions hurled so fast, Jon couldn't make out who said what, or to whom.

His head swam.

People were waves crashing on the shores of his body.

His chest tightened.

He and Donnie got separated by the sea of people.

Why are there so many fucking photographers?

Jon was dizzy, couldn't find his car.

Heard Marty calling out to him, but only barely.

Panic flooded him and he feared he'd never get to his ride.

He must've looked crazed to all the fucking paparazzi snapping photos. And that would only sell more papers, clicks, and views on TV.

Fucking parasites.

Someone was calling his name. Jon turned, thinking — hoping — it was Marty or one of the brothers.

Instead, it was a tall, fat, paparazzo with long dark hair dressed in a royal blue hoodie and jeans. "Hey, Jon! What do you have to say about the massacre on Hamilton Island?"

Jon stared at him, confused by the question. *What is there to say? It was horrible, obviously. But why the fuck ask me?*

Jon said nothing, shaking his head, then turning to find his car.

Then the man shouted something that made him turn around.

"Jon. Jon! Do you miss your daughter, Emma?"

"What the fuck kinda question is that?" Jon shouted, turning back and giving him the finger.

His gaze connected with the man for a moment. His eyes — brown, with dark circles under them — looked devoid of soul. The man's entire sad existence could be summed up in those empty sockets. Spending fifty or sixty hours a week chasing down photos of celebrities or whatever else the man clicked for cash, hoping for the best one, praying that he'd be able to sell it to some rag or online outlet, and that someone else didn't get a better, more perfect shot.

How many photos did this man shoot that never earned him a dime? Was he supporting a family? And for the slightest of moments, Jon imagined how hard his life must be. He almost felt sympathy for the devil.

But then something happened which set Jon off. The corners of the paparazzo's mouth turned up in the ever so slightest of smiles. The one that said, *gotcha.*

He'd set out to rile Jon. He mentioned Emma to get a reaction. And then got what he wanted.

Jon spun around, getting in the man's face.

The photographer raised his camera to catch the exchange.

Jon grabbed the camera by the lens, ripped it out of his hands, and threw it to the ground.

The man's eyes went wide. Then he smiled wider and taunted, "What? You gonna hit me, Conway? Come on. Do it. I dare ya'."

Marty grabbed at Jon. He could sense the Maris Brothers

watching their drunken star about to implode or explode. Probably both. The other paparazzi were aiming their cameras at him, all the clicking in unison, the hum of lenses focusing as the cameras recorded videos that might be online already.

The world was watching.

Jon's fists were balled, so much restrained rage begging to burst forth.

He wanted to punch the smug fuck in his fat face.

But the tax was too expensive.

He'd already get shit for tossing the man's camera, probably breaking it.

Instead of punching the man, Jon smiled, bent down, retrieved his camera from the ground, and checked to see if it was broken. The lens was cracked.

Jon handed it to the fucker.

Then he reached into his pocket, pulled out a money clip with two thousand dollars in cash, took the cash out, and tossed it at the man's feet. "Let me know if that doesn't cover it, ya' little bitch."

Then he turned and rejoined Marty and the Brothers.

Jon could feel their collective sighs as he left the tense escalation behind him.

Marty rushed him to the car, opened the rear door, and watched him sink behind the dark tint, glaring at the vultures still snapping photos.

"Take him to his hotel," Marty instructed the driver.

Jon rolled up the privacy window as the car pulled away, not wanting to see the driver, much less talk to him.

He sighed, remembering the photographer's smile. Jon wished he'd punched him in his fat, ugly face. Maybe knocked his teeth into the back of his throat.

But then he'd be fired from the movie.

He'd probably never get a job in Hollywood again, which

meant he'd never get the backing to make more of the indie movies that he'd been longing to make. Even if he could get financing, who the hell would see his finished films? The movies wouldn't even be about the stories in them anymore. They'd be all about, "Jon Conway, fallen star."

He'd become a cautionary tale to the next generation. A footnote in film.

A big fat bloated nothing.

He was already twisting the nipples of failure.

When his star rose fast, it also earned him enemies, people who wanted to see his star fall even faster. Funny thing about fame, sometimes the people who cheered you on most became your biggest haters. Jon tried not to take it personally, knowing it wasn't about him. It was because they identified with him when he was a rebel out to fuck The Man, regardless of the silver spoon he was born with. But blockbusters made Jon The Man. The rest of them were still pathetic losers looking for a new hero to worship, but now fuck Jon Conway because he was born rich to begin with.

So when his indies flopped, they were all too happy to pile on and declare him done and over with.

Black Nova would launch his star even higher. Fuck *all* the haters in their littlest holes.

And then he'd do what few in his position managed — earn respect back, and then truly do things his way with a bigger budget, this time, and with better, more personal stories to tell.

He'd lost too much already to also give up on whatever chance he had at a legacy. He couldn't let his losses of Sarah and Emma be in vain.

His phone rang. Caller ID showed it was his assistant, Alicia. Marty must've called her immediately and told her how he'd just about fucked everything up.

No point putting her off, so he answered .

"You okay?" Her nose sounded stuffy, her voice rough.

"Yes, I'm fine."

"I knew I should've come to lunch. I'm so sorry."

"It's fine. You've got the flu. Get some rest. I'll be okay."

"No. I should've come."

"Alicia, stop. It's all good. Besides, the last thing anyone wants is for you to spread the flu to the Brothers, and start some epidemic that wipes out half the crew."

"Yeah, but that paparazzi fuck face would've thought twice if *I'd* been there."

He laughed. Though Alicia was a tiny platinum blonde who looked too young and demure to handle herself, she was also a Pitbull. *She* probably would've decked the paparazzo. She'd lost her previous job as an assistant to a scumbag Hollywood producer who thought part of her job was to fuck him. She'd nearly castrated the man with a broken bottle. When said scumbag Hollywood producer tried to blackball her, Marty reached out and offered her a job — partly because he admired her take-no-bullshit ways, but also because he hated that particular producer.

"Okay, Jon. You need anything?"

"No. I'm good. Get some rest."

"All right. I'll see you tomorrow."

"No, you'll see me when you're better. I don't want your damned flu."

She laughed. "Yes, sir. Thank you."

"Goodnight, Alicia."

Jon hung up, opened the bar in the back of the limo, and poured himself some scotch.

His anger had soured to depression and loneliness, which, if it followed the usual path, would soon turn to self-loathing.

He wished he could've stayed on the phone with Alicia but was afraid of what he might say while drunk. He didn't want to blur the lines of professionalism. He wouldn't ever hit on her. He wasn't that kind of asshole. But he might have let her get too close, maybe become a friend. That could be just as disastrous as a sexual relationship given his highs and lows.

Jon trusted Alicia only second to Marty, but you never knew when someone might get pissed at you, then run off and write some book exposing all your deepest secrets. He was already the subject of a few unflattering biographies from people he'd thought were his friends. A few more from former lovers. He didn't need another one.

He thought about the last person he'd let get too close — Cassidy. And how things had ended after the last horrible words he'd said on his last night on Hamilton, terrible things that could never be taken back.

They'd not spoken a single word since.

And, riiiiiight on schedule, here comes the self-loathing.

He wasn't sure when he'd see her again. They were filming the first two movies back-to-back without a break, so he'd be in New Zealand at least half a year before he could leave.

A year was both nothing and an eternity.

And the tragedies that had taken Sarah and Emma only served to remind him nothing in life was guaranteed. He might never see Cassidy again. And the cost of his final words seemed so much heavier with that knowledge.

Fucking junkie.

He had to make things right. To at least apologize.

Jon called her number.

His heart raced as he wondered if she'd see his name and pick up, or let it go to voicemail. If she did answer, how would he start things? *I'm sorry* seemed like his best bet.

He wouldn't normally open up so boldly, but Jon was drunk, sad, and sentimental right now, so he may as well use it to his advantage, get past his normal barriers.

The call went to voicemail.

Was she truly not available, or was she avoiding him?

The latter hurt too much to consider, even if he'd been the one to leave. It wasn't as if she hadn't been pushing him away.

Hi, this is Cassidy. Leave a message. Or don't. Your choice.

Jon opened his mouth, but the words refused to leave him. So he hung up, then poured another shot of misery.

Chapter 3 - Cassidy Hughes

Cassidy pulled on her Shipwrecked T-shirt, wincing as her arms barely made it over her head.

Her back was killing her since she slipped and fell at work last week. But she wasn't about to go to a doctor's, not on this damned island. Every doctor here was beholden to the Conways and always pushing the latest in biotech.

No, thanks. Cassidy didn't need any nanobots crawling around in her system, even if that would make her feel better.

She gave herself a once over in the mirror to make sure she didn't look like a shipwreck, then went downstairs to get her purse.

"You going to eat something before work? You can't go to work on an empty stomach," Vivian said from the kitchen.

The television was on, news of a massacre at Hamilton Island Outdoor Marketplace grabbing her attention.

"What happened?"

"A bunch of crazy people just started attacking other people, then killed themselves. It was awful."

"Anyone we know get hurt?" With so many victims, undoubtedly Cass would know some of them. It was impossible to live on Hamilton and not know your neighbors, even more so when you worked at one of the most popular bars.

"They haven't released names yet."

"Jesus," Cass said.

Her mother turned off the TV and traded it for the radio, singing along to some awful pop song.

Cass looked at her mom, barely able to believe this was the same frail old woman she had to take care of just a few months ago. Not only was she dressed in a trendy blouse and matching blue dress, but she was always singing or dancing these days. She looked twenty years younger, no longer drank, and wasn't edging senility. Whatever she was having done at Conway Medical had worked wonders on her, and Cass was grateful the sketchy tech had helped to bring her mother back.

However, whatever medical magic had restored her mother's youth had also restored her more annoying qualities, such as being overbearing to the point of a pillow on Cassidy's face.

"I'll get something at work." Cass moved slowly, so Vivian wouldn't notice her pain. She'd not told her about her back, lest her mother have something else to go on about.

"Bah, that fried food'll kill you. Don't you even want to know what I'm making?"

"Smells like chicken, right?"

"It's Coq Au Vin," she said with a smile.

Woman takes a few cooking classes at the local school, then thinks she's Chef Louissa.

"Sounds good. But I've gotta head out." Cass pointed at the clock. 4:15. "Gotta be there by four-thirty."

Her mother frowned. "You can't just spend your days rotting away in your room and working at that godforsaken bar all night."

Here we go.

"Rotting away? You mean sleeping?"

"You get home around three or four? Why do you need to sleep so much of the day away?"

"Because I'm tired. Really not a mystery there, Mom. And as for my sinful employer, weren't you a drunk just a few months ago?"

Her mother frowned, then put her dish in the oven and turned back to Cass. "And getting healthy, I recognized my bad habits so that I could change."

"Yeah, it only took how many decades?"

Her mother's lips pursed.

Shit. That might have been too harsh.

"Why are you even staying here? You have that nice big place."

That Jon bought.

"I came here to take care of you."

"Well, no need for that now. I've never felt better!" Vivian waved her arms around like she was about to start dancing. She wasn't *just* better, she had the energy of a toddler after donuts. It was almost creepy.

"Clearly, you're better. Do you want me to go?"

"I'm not saying that, honey. I just hate seeing you throw your life away."

"Throw my life away? I work six or seven nights a week. I'm saving money and taking online business management courses. I don't party or have a social life of any kind. How exactly am I throwing my life away?"

She hadn't been keeping up with her classes, but Vivian didn't need to know that.

"You're going to make me say it, are you?"

"Say what?" Cass felt something coming, the thing that had been on the tip of her mother's tongue for a while. She had a feeling she knew what it was. And if Vivian said it, Cass might have to scream.

"You're obviously depressed. You lost your sister. And

Emma. Then Jon. You've got every right to be sad, but you can't wallow forever."

"*Wallow?* I'm moving on with my life. How is that *wallowing?*"

"You know what I mean."

"No, I don't, Mom. Tell me."

"I know you've been taking my pills."

And there it is!

"What? I have not been taking your fucking pills!"

"Please, Cass. I'm not stupid. I haven't needed my pain pills in months, and yet they keep disappearing from my bottle. Is the Pill Fairy taking them?"

"I haven't taken anything stronger than Tylenol in fifty-five days. And I've been going to meetings."

"Listen, I don't expect you to be honest with me, dear. But you need to be honest with yourself. That's the first step in—"

"You want *honesty*, Mom? Okay, here's some blunt truth for ya'. I liked you better as a drunk."

Cass didn't even bother to glance at her mother's reaction. Didn't need to. She already knew the clutching pearls look all too well.

She grabbed her purse off the kitchen counter, turned on her heel, and headed out the door, slamming it on her way out. When she got in her car, she grimaced as pain shot up her lower back.

Cassidy had to stay still for a moment, wait for the agony to ease. She imagined her mom looking out the window, maybe trying to see if Cass was digging into her illicit stash. Hell, Cass wished she had some pills right about now.

No. You don't need them.

She looked down at her phone and saw a missed call from Jon, and a voice mail.

Her heart started racing.

The part of her she'd been trying to push down, that part

that wanted Jon to return despite their bitter last words, was staring at the voicemail button, eager to press it.

Hope and Fear grabbed each other's hands and started their endless dance in her mind.

Hope that he'd come to his senses. That they could resume their life together. Yes, it would be without Emma, and that was a sadness neither of them could ever really recover from, but maybe together, they'd find something resembling family, or at least closer to normal.

Fear that he'd only called to further the distance between them, to say one last thing to signify that yes, it was really over.

Cassidy pressed the button then saw that the voicemail was only four seconds.

The flicker of hope inside her felt stupid, ashamed for daring to raise its head.

She pressed *PLAY* and heard an awful silence, followed by a terrible *click*.

"Coward." Cassidy dropped her phone on the seat, then tore out of her mother's driveway.

Chapter 4 - Kevin Brady

Kevin was in his home office staring at his tablet, watching the video of Aidan and Christina sitting at the breakfast nook on their fourth birthday. He was off-camera asking them questions, an "interview" he did each year to chart their changes as they grew.

"What do you want to be when you grow up?"

Aidan shouted, "I wanna be a ninja!" and burst into laughter.

Christina joined, giggling hysterically. "Me, too!"

"Girls can't be ninjas." Then Aidan looked at Kevin with his head tilted. "Can they?"

"Why not?" Kevin said, much to his son's surprise.

"Why aren't there any girl ninjas on Kid Ninja then?"

"Kid Ninja is a cartoon, not a documentary."

"What's a dock-you-menty?" Aidan asked.

"Documentilly, dummy!" Christina smacked him playfully.

Kevin laughed. "Documentary. It's a movie, but not made up. Like that one with the penguins we saw last year."

Christina said, "I want to be a penguin."

"You can't be a penguin, dummy!" Aidan was pleased

with himself for being able to retaliate with a "dummy" of his own so quickly.

"Daddy, Aidan called me the D-word."

Part of Kevin had been annoyed at the time that they'd completely gotten away from the interview, but another part of him, especially now watching it more than two years later, loved how it devolved. It showed them as they were, rather than some scripted Q&A.

A tear welled in his eye as he watched Christina giggle then compose herself for a serious answer.

"When *I* grow up, I want to be a police chief like Daddy. So I can protect people from the bad guys. And I want to be a mommy, like Mommy. Can I do both, Daddy?"

"Yes," Kevin said. "You can do anything you want."

"Except be a ninja," Aidan added. "You can't be a ninja *and* a police chief, right Daddy?"

"How do you know I'm not a ninja?" Kevin had asked, then ran around to their side of the table and launched a playful attack on them both.

Kevin was startled by movement behind him.

He clicked off the tablet and turned to see Molly standing there with tears in her eyes.

Shit.

"How often do you watch those old movies?"

He set the tablet on the desk, turned in his chair as his wife entered the room and closed the door behind her.

"I dunno. Every so often. Why?"

"I didn't think you thought about her."

"What? I think about her every day."

"Why don't you ever talk about her?" Molly was standing just inches away. This may have been the first time she'd met his gaze in the awful months of missing Christina, at least when their daughter was the subject.

"Because I don't want to make you sadder."

Molly sniffled and wiped at the tears running down her cheeks.

Seeing her cry made him want to sob, and he hated losing control, especially when she always seemed so close to that final downward spiral he'd never be able to pull her out of. "Because I don't have any answers. And every time you ask me if there's been any news and I have nothing, I feel like a failure. Like maybe you think I'm not looking hard enough. Or like I've given up."

"Have you?"

He'd be lying if he said no. But sometimes you needed a lie to hook the last of your hope.

"No."

Molly stepped forward.

He stood, staring into her eyes. "I'm sorry if you thought I had. We had so many false leads after she went missing. Every time I came home with some shred of hope, I saw how it brightened your eyes. And then, every time that lead led to nowhere, I saw the light die a little more. And I couldn't keep doing it to you. So, I had to keep those leads to myself. Absorb those dashed hopes for both of us."

She didn't say a word.

Instead, she collapsed into his chest, sobbing, loosing nine months of pent-up fear and sadness in an explosion, and all he could do was hold her tight and try to seem strong.

But as he held her tight, Kevin's tears betrayed him.

After what felt like an eternity of the two of them just standing there saying so much without a using a word, Molly broke the silence.

"I want to leave this place."

"What?" He pulled out of the hug, "I thought you wanted to stay here in case Christina came back."

"I can't keep living like this. This island is killing us. I don't know, there's just ... something here that feels so horrible. And if we stay, we're going to lose Aidan, too."

He wanted to reassure her that today's massacre was an anomaly, but he didn't have it in his heart to lie twice to her face in such a short span of time.

"You can find another job, can't you? I can go back to teaching, too, if we're worried about money. I don't *have* to homeschool Aidan. Not if we lived somewhere else, somewhere safer."

Kevin shook his head. "You won't need to go back to work. I'll find something. If you really want to leave."

"I do. Do you think if Christina came back she could still find us?"

"Yes. We know so many people. Someone would get in touch."

"What if Paladin found her?"

"They're not all assholes. Most of them are decent people working the only job they can get. Hell, as much as Kaiser hates me, I don't think it's personal. He sees me as a roadblock. Once I'm out of here, I imagine he'd actually feel indebted. Probably throw me a party."

Molly laughed.

It felt great to hear her music again.

"Can I see what you were watching?"

He pulled out the second chair at his desk, then they sat and watched the old movies together. And while Christina was still gone, for a moment, they *almost* felt whole again.

AFTER DINNER, Molly and Aidan sat together on the couch reading a story as Kevin retreated to his office. He listened to voicemails, writing a list of people to call back tonight or tomorrow. He'd ignore most of the calls, including dozens from reporters both on the island and networks on the mainland. Paladin and the Feds were running lead on the investigation. There was no room for him in the conversation, and he didn't want to be handed talking points. It was best to lay low.

Kevin glanced out his window and saw lights flashing at the end of his driveway.

At first, he thought it was a Paladin van, but as Kevin squinted, he realized it was a gray van he'd never seen.

He clicked on his tablet, bringing up his security cameras to make sure they were recording, then got up, grabbed his gun, and headed downstairs, passing Molly and Aidan on his way to the door. Though he hid his gun under his shirt, she could tell by the way he was walking that he was heading outside.

"Where you going?"

He held up his phone, "Just going to take a walk while I go through these damned voicemails."

"Okay." She smiled.

He wasn't sure if she was suspicious or not.

"Bye, Daddy," Aidan said before returning to reading out loud from his book.

Kevin closed his front door and locked it, then grabbed his gun, holding it just out of sight as he approached the strange vehicle.

He spotted two people in the front of the van, a dark-haired woman with thick black-framed glasses who looked vaguely familiar in the driver's seat, and a young black man with a red beret riding shotgun. They were both dressed in professional clothes and had a look he instantly read as journalists.

The woman rolled down the window as he approached.

He relaxed his grip on the gun and prepared to tell whoever they were that he wasn't interested in giving any quotes and didn't appreciate them showing up at his house uninvited, especially at night.

The woman spoke. "Chief Brady, my name is Judith

Deveroux. Sorry to bother you at home, but my partner wanted to speak to you in private."

The name was vaguely familiar. He remembered getting a call on his phone months ago from the woman, though he couldn't remember the context.

"Your partner?"

A man in the back leaned forward and out of the shadows. A face he'd seen on countless conspiracy theory videos over the past couple of years — Talbot Gray.

Talbot was a skinny man in his thirties with long platinum blond hair pulled back in a severe ponytail. He was wearing the same thing he wore in his videos all the time, his weird-ass camera glasses, a black hoodie and charcoal cargo pants.

"Take the glasses off." The last thing Kevin needed was being on one of Talbot's fucking conspiracy theory videos.

Talbot removed them, and slipped the pair of lenses into his pocket. Then he opened the side panel door and stepped out. "Pleased to meet you, Chief. I was hoping you'd indulge me with a conversation." He extended his hand.

Kevin didn't shake it, keeping his hand on the gun behind his back. "What do you want?"

"To expose the truth. Today's incident is proof that Conway Industries is still running a secret program. And I'm tired of the world ignoring it."

"Sorry," Kevin said. "I'm not interested in your conspiracy theory bullshit. I have *real work* to do."

He started to turn around, careful to keep his gun from view, particularly because they likely had other cameras on the van recording the conversation. The man and his group, Expose Them All, were known for ambushing public officials. Kevin didn't want to be all over the web advancing their stupid agenda.

"Did you ever wonder about the *real* reason Roger Heller's wife and son were killed?"

Kevin stopped, turned, and glared at Talbot. "They were

killed by a disgruntled man who blamed Roger for killing his son. Please, don't disgrace their memories."

"With all due respect, sir, I think we both know that's bullshit."

Kevin slipped the gun into his waistband and approached Talbot. "Listen, I know the game, okay. You all show up at places all around the country every time there's a mass killing, or some 'mysterious coverup.' It's all a ploy to get clicks, to make money. You're exploiting tragedy, real people's pain, and that makes you no better than the 'parasitical media' you all claim to abhor. Now, please, leave my property. I'm asking you nicely."

Talbot looked genuinely surprised by Kevin's response. But he wasn't launching into a defense, getting angry, or any of the other things he usually did in videos while trying to cause a scene. Instead, he seemed almost dejected.

"I thought you were one of the good ones, Chief. Someone who really wanted to know the truth."

"I'm a cop trying to do his job. Hell, I don't even run things around here. You want to talk to someone, talk to Paladin."

"Roger Heller reached out to us before he went on his spree," Talbot said. "He even sent us a video."

Kevin wondered if this group had fed into Roger's delusions. If maybe they were somehow responsible for him shooting up his classroom.

"I'm listening."

"Roger was convinced Conway Industries was experimenting on people. He said he had a flash drive full of evidence. I don't suppose you all happened to find said flash drive among his belongings?"

"I don't remember every detail of a closed case. What sort of evidence was on the drive?"

"I only know about the one video, Chief." Talbot reached

into his jacket pocket and handed Kevin a flash drive. "It's on there. The only bit of evidence left."

It looked like any other flash drive, but it felt like holding a loaded weapon that Talbot intended to aim directly at him.

"So, I'm just supposed to put some flash drive from you all into my computer? Maybe you've loaded it with spyware, wanting to get what's on my computer or network?"

Talbot turned to the van. "Gibson, give me a spare laptop."

The young black man reached behind him, pulled out a laptop, handed it to Judith, who passed it to Talbot, who then handed it to Kevin. "Fair enough. Use this. It can't go online, no hidden spyware, even the camera is taped. Completely safe."

Kevin said nothing, not wanting to appear interested.

"It won't hurt to look, Chief. Worse comes to worst, you're right. I'm a crackpot. But I think you'll clearly see otherwise once you look."

Kevin reached for the laptop.

Talbot handed it to him along with his card. "Call me if you want to talk further. I have a feeling you'll want to." Then he turned, got back in the van, and closed the door.

Judith nodded at Kevin as she backed out of the driveway.

Kevin looked toward his house to see if his wife or son had heard the van, but thankfully, no one was looking out any of the windows.

He got in his truck to see just what the hell was on this flash drive, besides *something important*. He hoped there was nothing on the flash drive, that it was as spurious as most of the group's other claims. But deep down, he feared that same dreadful something he'd been feeling for the last several months. That something deadly that was happening on the island. Nothing he could put his finger on, but something he felt deeply just the same.

Especially when Jon came back. It wasn't that Kevin felt

Jon was in trouble so much as that he was sure to bring it with him.

Again, Kevin didn't understand the sensation, but he'd been a cop too long to ignore his instincts. And every one inside him said that Jon was a magnet for trouble. It killed his little girl and got his brother shot.

Those same instincts told Kevin the flash drive would bring trouble to him. And his family.

But his curiosity was too strong.

Maybe whatever was on the flash drive might answer the question of what happened to his little girl.

He opened the laptop, turned it on, and noted that the camera was indeed taped over. That didn't mean that there wasn't a bug in the computer recording Kevin's audio. He could practically see Talbot's group posting a stupid "exposé" online.

Police Chief Watches Secret Recording They Don't Want You to See. PROOF of the Conspiracy!!!

He inserted the flash drive, saw the folder pop up with a filename: c-7913.mp4.

He pressed play.

The screen was black for a moment, then a loud sound like something rubbing against the mic. And finally, the screen revealed the shape of a copse in the darkness.

He heard a voice he recognized as belonging to Roger Heller's. "Just inside this cave."

Cave? On the north side of the island?

The screen went pitch-black again, then Kevin was staring at the inside of the cave, lit by whatever Roger was recording with.

"Just ahead," Roger whispered, as he made his way through a tunnel and into an opening.

"There they are." He aimed the camera into the darkness.

There's what?

As if Roger had heard Kevin, he moved closer to whatever he was filming.

The camera bounced between dark and light until it stopped and panned down onto two nude, adult male bodies lying face down.

Kevin practically gasped before reason told him Roger had found the remains of two suicides who had jumped from Tanner's Pass and washed into one of the caves.

Roger spoke again, and as he did, he turned the camera onto himself. In the bright light of the phone or camera's flash, he looked almost deathly, his eyes sunken, his hair a mess, and a nervousness in his expression. "My name is Roger Heller, and this is my proof that Conway Industries is behind a massive conspiracy to replace everyone on this island."

Roger gave the latitude and longitude of his location before, then set his camera onto the cave floor, walked over to the bodies, and bent down.

What the hell is he doing?

Roger turned the bodies over.

But Kevin couldn't see much of them thanks to the angle, distance, and darkness.

Roger returned, picked up the camera, and walked toward the bodies. He panned down.

Both bodies were, impossibly, also Roger Heller.

The video went dark.

Chapter 5 - Warren Conway

At Conway Industries ...

THE BOARDROOM FELT like a funeral as the four other members of The Circle waited for Blake Conway to enter for the special, and rare, Sunday meeting. He was just outside the room, pacing as he spoke to someone about the massacre on his phone.

The twelve killers from the Market Massacre were part of Project Raven, just as Roger Heller had been a part of Warren's project when he decided to shoot up his classroom three months ago. Warren had been on the phone all day, demanding answers from the scientists in control of Project Raven. And just like with Heller, nobody knew a goddamned thing.

Warren was starting to suspect somebody within the company was deliberately screwing with the subjects to sabotage the program. He called Kaiser, asking him to investigate all potential suspects, but he wasn't holding out hope that he'd find anything, at least not in time to satiate Blake's demand for answers.

Yet again, the blame would fall on Warren.

He braced himself, refusing to show any emotion, in front of The Circle, especially fear. They were the most entrusted members of Conway Industries. Spineless men and women who had no problem cashing in on Conway Industries technology when it suited them, but had no stomach for anything remotely bold. They had no problem partnering with the Department of Defense for secret projects, but at the first sign of trouble, they started throwing around terms like "moral obligations" and "legality," which only made Warren question their commitment to the science.

He wondered what today's tragedy would mean for the company. Stocks would take a hit in the morning, but he wasn't worried about that so much. Warren was more concerned with what sort of government oversight might follow today. Politicians would be looking to save their asses, as well. The public would start demanding answers and accountability. Politicians who backed the black ops projects would be just as cowardly as The Circle, looking to distance themselves from Conway Industries. But would this bleed over into the health and services side of the business?

Hamilton Island was the perfect model for public and private partnerships in biotech and medicine. The beginning of a new era in medical care, a model where Conway Industries' mission — to overhaul communities throughout the country, rebuild impoverished neighborhoods with the best in education and health — was slowly reshaping the country, and then the world, into something better than it had ever been. This was the second phase. It started with their private policing through Paladin, and was now in twenty-six cities throughout the country.

This fuck-up was just the sort of public relations disaster that could derail their plans, and erode public trust in Conway Industries. Blake would be looking for someone to blame, someone fall on his sword to protect the company.

Warren could practically feel the blade pressing into his gut already.

Blake entered the room, and every eye turned toward him.

Warren felt a sharp pain in his back, wanting to shift in his seat, but doing so would draw attention to him and might reveal his anxiety. He stayed still as Blake took his seat at the round table and folded his hands in front of him.

"That was the DOD on the phone. The projects we were phasing out are now on indefinite hold."

Warren flinched, even though he had figured as much.

"Meanwhile, I want an exhaustive report on every one of those people. I want to know what went wrong. I want all of their data. And I want data on each of their Watchers."

"Already working on that, sir," Warren said.

Blake ignored his son and rolled on. "This will not affect Project Phoenix. We've got more than enough in our Black Budget even without DOD funds for Raven. But for now, I am pulling all Raven feeds from the Watchers and putting my own people on them."

Nobody said a word.

"Warren, you will work with PR on a release for tomorrow morning. I've given them talking points. Depending how that goes, we may need to do some news rounds with a couple of the networks. Are you up to interviews?"

"Yes, sir."

Though Warren had been back to work only a month since the shooting, he'd never felt better — aside from the headaches and memory lapses, not that he was going to tell his father about those now. If Warren couldn't work point on this, what good was he to the company, to his father? If he performed well enough in the coming day, Father might finally see his true value.

"Does anyone have anything to say?"

Nobody did. Good. No blame to go around. No throwing Warren under the bus, yet.

This meeting was theater, for Blake to demonstrate his control of the company, even when things seemed to be at their worst.

"Dismissed."

Everybody else started to stand.

Warren waited like usual, figuring his father might want a word.

But once they were alone, Blake simply stood, turned, and left the room.

He felt the sting in the pit of his stomach, gathered his messenger bag, and got up from the table.

His father was already in the elevator, doors closing, looking down, without so much as a glance Warren's way.

NIGHT WAS FALLING as Warren pulled up beside the small private island house overlooking the beach and Puget Sound. The lights were on. His heart galloped as he got out and walked toward the door.

He flashed his thumb over the panel beside the door, unlocking it, then stepped inside.

Kaiser was in the kitchen cooking something that smelled delicious.

"You got away," he said.

"Took a while. Melinda had another headache, so she'll be out all night."

"Good." Carl poured Warren a glass of Patels.

Warren kissed Carl. Then he took the Cab and swirled it to let the bouquet rise before taking a deep drink.

"Rough day?"

"Blake is pissed, but what else is new?" He took a seat at the kitchen bar.

"Fuck him." Carl topped off Warren's glass. "Anyway, I'm making soft shell crab with Asian slaw."

"Smells great," Warren said. "So, how was *your* day?"

"Aside from the single biggest group mass murder in the United States? It was okay."

Warren laughed.

"Fucking Chief Brady pissed me off, though. Waltzes onto the scene and pulls his wife and kid out like he's the Goddamned King of the Island."

"Why?"

"I dunno. I think he's pissy because we've more or less made his department obsolete. He knows it's only a matter of time before Paladin absorbs the police in full. And then he'll lose the easiest job he's ever had. Fucking asshole."

Carl was really worked up.

Warren stood, came up behind him, and began to massage his shoulders. "Oh, you've got a big knot in there."

"No shit. I expect a full massage tonight."

"No problem." Warren smiled. Despite Carl's gruff asshole exterior, he was different when it was just the two of them. And Warren enjoyed being of service to the man, being needed — a role he hadn't felt in his business or marriage in years.

Warren kept rubbing at the knot with one hand and his arousal with the other. Maybe they had time for a quickie before dinner — unless Carl was too tired.

He was about to reach around to find out when Carl's phone rang.

Carl broke away from Warren, as if someone had walked into the room and caught them. He looked at his screen. "I need to take this." Then he strode outside.

Warren stared at the front door, wondering why Carl needed to take the call outside. He didn't have a wife to hide his affair from. And he was in the closet, so it was doubtful he had anyone else on the side. At least, not on the island.

But what if it's someone not on the island?

Warren was hit with a sudden anxiety he couldn't place. Something was off.

A flash of memory, a fight with Carl that he couldn't remember having. Ever since emerging from his coma after the shooting, Warren had moments where memories and dreams jumbled together. He was supposed to write down and keep track of these moments, so the doctor could adjust his medication. But Warren didn't dare tell the doctors just how often these moments were occurring, because that would call his fitness for work into question.

He suffered headaches, confusion, and sudden anxiety. But that was a small price to pay to stay in the game with his father.

Warren closed his eyes, inhaling and exhaling slowly, trying to focus on the present.

His private vacation home on the shore.

An excellent dinner about to be served, made by the man he loved — if he dared to think of their relationship in such a way.

Carl about to come back inside for a long night of good times.

Relax.

But he couldn't get the sensation out of his head, the feeling that he and Carl had had a blow-up over something big. Something lost with the coma.

No. It's just a side effect of the meds, or from the injury to my brain.

That's what Warren tried to tell himself. Tried to believe. But like always, it felt like a lie.

He went upstairs to the bedroom overlooking the front porch, where his lover paced as he talked on the phone. Warren couldn't see his expression in the dark, but Carl's tension was obvious in his hunched shoulders and ever-quickening strides.

Something is wrong. You need to find out what!

Warren unlatched the lock then palmed the window with both hands, lifting it slowly so as not to make too much noise.

God, if he catches me snooping on him, he'll be soooo *pissed.*

It took forever to pull the window up enough to hear the conversation.

"I don't know, sir. I don't know."

Sir? Is he talking to Father?

Warren supposed it could be some angry politician demanding answers about today's attack.

"Don't worry, I'll take care of the Brady problem."

Brady problem? Chief Brady?

"You've got nothing to worry about sir. He's as good as gone."

Chapter 6 - Cassidy Hughes

Cass was reaching for a bottle of Jack when her back seized up on her.

She froze, gritting her teeth through the pain.

"You okay?" Abby returned from the pool table with a tray of empties. She was the new manager, an older hippie chick that was dating the owner, Tom. The coolest boss Cass had ever worked for.

"No. Just pulled my back. Again." Cass hadn't made a big deal about slipping and hurting herself at work, figuring the pain would go away. Plus, she didn't want the bar to have to file injury paperwork or anything.

Abby set the tray down as she came around the bar. "Where's it hurt?"

She moved her hands down Cass's back.

Pain splintered at her touch. "Fuck!"

Abby withdrew her hands. "Why don't you take the rest of the night off. See a doctor in the morning."

"It'll be okay," Cass insisted. "Just need to sit for a moment, wait for it to pass."

"Don't be such a stubborn ass," Abby teased. "Go home.

What with the Marketplace incident, it's slow as hell in here. We can handle closing."

"You sure?" Cass asked.

"Yes," Abby assured her.

Cass went to the back, clocked out, and grabbed her purse, walking delicately the entire time. Every step sent spikes of pain from her lower back high into her skull.

She made her way outside and ran into the last person she wanted to see — her old dealer and former fuck buddy, Craig, standing in the parking lot talking with one of the regulars, a fifty-five-year-old failed musician named Skarr, who dressed like one of those eighties hair metal singers Cass had seen on cheesy old videos.

Skarr gave her the eye. "Hey. Leavin' early, darlin'?"

"Back is killing me." She hoped the look of agony on her face would prevent him from wanting to tell her one of his elaborate stories about a past where he could've been someone.

Craig approached her instead. "Hey, you need a ride?"

"I can manage." She pointed to her car.

"Catch ya' later, Skarr." Craig waved at the man and fell in step next to her. "What happened?"

"Nothing. Just slipped the other night. I'll be fine."

"You go to a doctor?"

"What? Are we suddenly best buddies? Please, Craig, let's not pretend you care. Just tell me what you want. Because if it's a hook-up, I'm not in the mood."

"What?" He looked astonished at the accusation. "I'm just seeing how you're doing. I care."

"Yeah." She laughed, wondering if he really believed that, or if he was just trying to see if he could get a handy in the parking lot. It's not like it hadn't happened before.

"For real, Cass. I've thought a lot about you since ... well, since everything with your niece. And then, after today, I dunno why, I just thought about you."

She stopped, looked him in the eye, and tried to determine if he was being sincere or bringing up Emma to hopefully fuck her. He seemed sincere. *Surprisingly* so. Upon closer inspection, he also seemed somehow different from the last time Cass had seen him, a bit less drunk and drug-addled. His hair was clean. And he looked healthy, well-dressed. Was taking care of himself or just so happened to be having a good night?

A small pang of guilt stung her for trying to blow him off. "Thanks. But I need to go home and rest."

Cassidy started walking again. She half expected him to keep following, trying different methods of smooth-talking her, but he was quiet. Maybe this was a new Craig.

When she reached her car, she got in with a grimace. After the pain subsided, she started to back out.

Then he waved her down.

Okay, here we go. His last attempt to woo me.

She stopped, hit the button to roll down her window, and looked up at him as he approached. "What?"

"Here." He handed her a bottle of pills.

She pulled her hands back as if he were handing her a dead animal he'd peeled off the road.

"What? You don't use anymore?"

"No. No, I don't."

"Okay, I can respect that. But, you're also in pain. A few won't kill you. Hell, the doctor would prescribe them anyway, right?"

"I don't need them," She started to back away.

He tossed the pills onto her empty passenger seat. They bounced once and rolled onto the floor. She considered stopping to grab the bottle to throw back at him, but bending over just might hurt enough to make her pass out. So, she started to drive away.

"You're welcome!" he shouted as she left.

"Asshole," Cassidy said under her breath as she put him and the bar into her rearview.

~

CASS PULLED up outside her mother's house but she wasn't ready to go inside.

Instead, she stared at the light coming from her mother's room. Was she still up, or had she fallen asleep watching TV like usual? Hell, the way Viv had been feeling lately, she was probably having a slumber party with friends, maybe dancing to golden oldies from the roaring nineties.

The thought of her mother dancing and having fun while she suffered annoyed her. Not that she didn't want her mom to feel good. But Cass was choosing agony over a relapse, while Vivian thought she was using, anyway.

"Fuck you." She gave her mother's window the bird.

She reached into her purse and pulled out her phone. Her finger hovered over Jon's number. She wanted to call him so damned bad, it hurt even more than her back.

How could things have gone so wrong between them?

Yes, Emma had died, and despite being there for one another right after, they each retreated to their own private hells. A ton of shit went down, a lot she couldn't even stand to think about. They were both guilty of detonating the relationship, each in their own ways. Even as it was burning around them, she held out some hope they'd find an escape from all this, find a way to keep things together. They loved each other, after all.

But then he'd said words that cut deeper than forgiveness. He'd called her a "fucking junkie."

And, just like that, shit went nuclear.

She wanted to press *CALL*, to hear his voice, to tell him she forgave him, at least a dozen times since he left. But each and every time, she flashed back on those words and that look in his eyes — a look she'd seen too often in her life to not recognize.

Hate.

Come on, Cass. Just call. He doesn't hate you. Things were rough after Emma, for both of you. Be the bigger person. Otherwise, you'll always wonder what-if?

But what if he's busy? What if he's on the set of his movie? The last thing he wants to see is me calling him.

Oh yeah, then why did he call you?

You mean call and hang up?

Still, it was a call. He was reaching out to you.

Yeah, well he fucking chickened out. Fuck that.

If he wanted to talk to me badly enough, he could've left a message.

Are you really going to be that petty? Really going to keep score like that?

You don't keep score with friends or lovers.

That was some sage advice Sarah had given her years ago. How would her sister handle this? She'd not dreamed of Sarah since Emma's vanishing. Nor had she experienced any of those weird moments where she felt like Sarah was there.

Was it because Sarah was in heaven with Emma and no longer had time to be her guardian angel or whatever she might've been doing? Assuming that hadn't all been in her fucked-up mind.

Cass stared at Jon's name.

She thought of his sweet face, his beautiful eyes.

The way he smiled at her, a way no man ever had before. A smile that beamed with love.

Love for Sarah, not you, Twin!

She growled at her inner addict's shit-talking.

"Fuck you. I *am* going to call him."

Cassidy pressed *CALL* then listened as the phone rang without any answer.

Before his voicemail message played, she hung up, dropped the phone on the seat, and cried.

Chapter 7 - Jon Conway

Jon's head swam as he stepped off the dance floor with the Russian, stunning despite — or because of — her neon purple-hair.

She took him by the hand, leading him to the VIP section in the rear of the club, where he crashed onto the sofa, still laughing his ass off.

"What did you give me?" he asked her over the throbbing electronica.

He looked around to make sure nobody else was watching. They were the only ones in this corner. The other parties seemed to be having their own fun, not paying attention to the movie star and ... well, whatever this girl was.

A model? An actress? A club girl? A prostitute?

Jon didn't know, didn't care.

She laughed. "You like?"

"Damn, yes." He pulled her down on top of him.

She straddled him, her white leather dress hiked up revealing perfectly tanned thighs under her white fishnets. See-through underwear tight against her crotch. He wasn't sure where to look — her slit, her thighs, or the cleavage pouring from her top to tease him.

Maybe her beautiful blue eyes.

She wasn't just stunning. She was fun, with a purse full of pills he'd never tried. He'd met her at the bar about twenty, maybe thirty minutes ago, and she'd pulled him onto the dance floor.

Jon wasn't one to get down, not unless he was properly fucked up, which he was.

And she'd made it worth his while. Now she grinded against his crotch, rhythm like a lap dancer. Her fingers played with the zipper on his pants.

Jon closed his eyes, enjoying the sensation of her warmth against his erection.

He would stop her if she tried to fuck him, but anything else was fair game.

She began to grind faster, and she reached into his pants, squeezing the tip of his dick beneath his underwear.

His phone buzzed against his hip.

There were very few numbers that weren't set to hit voice-mail. This had to be important.

He pulled out his phone, then glanced at the screen.

Cassidy.

A flush of shame as he glanced up at the woman riding him. He held up a finger.

"I need to take this."

She slid off of him with a sigh.

He got up, rushing out of the VIP room and through the club, trying to reach the exit, away from the loud noise, where it was quiet enough to answer.

Everything was a dizzy blur, though, and he couldn't find the exit.

He bumped against someone, many someones. Then he was shoved.

"Watch out!"

Jon turned to apologize, but as he turned, he fell to the ground, his phone slipping away.

Fuck!

He crawled on all fours, lost in a chaos of legs, pulsating light and darkness. Bass pounding loud enough to neatly split his mind in two.

He'd gone from amazing to shit in minutes, and now he couldn't find his damned phone.

His heart raced. He scurried around, reached out. Fumbled in the darkness as people stepped on his fingers. He cried out, retracting his hand, pain shooting through his hand.

Jon tried to find the fucker that stepped on him, but there were too many people. Then he spotted his phone, the screen still lit, beckoning him with Cassidy's name.

He raced toward the phone, seized it, then saw the exit sign in the darkness.

Another push forward, bumping past person after person until he was outside in the fresh evening air.

He brought the phone up but it was too late.

Jon had missed her call.

Fuck!

He slid his fingers across the screen, then he swiped through his contacts list until he found her name.

But before he could return her call, his stomach heaved. Everything he'd drunk in the past hour or so, along with his food, came screaming out of his mouth in a violent explosion.

Jon staggered around the parking lot, puking and spitting, trying to clear his mouth of vomit enough to call Cassidy back. Then he leaned against a wall, and the world came crashing in around him.

~

JON WAS on his hands and knees, cold dirt pressed into his fingernails, surrounded by the darkness and fog rolling around him.

Where am I?

A woman said, "None of this can hurt you once you put it in the hole."

He looked around but couldn't see the source of the voice, though she sounded familiar.

That's when he saw the chain around his ankles, tied to the ancient wooden chest.

"Take the chest full of your pain and your memories, and throw it down the hole."

"I can't," some former version of himself cried as if he was hearing a recording, or a ghost from the past.

"You can. You must. Before the fire consumes you."

The fog was replaced by fire, its brightness a flash that illuminated a hole in the ground, a few feet away.

"Hurry, before the fire comes."

Jon could feel its warmth burning his skin. While he knew he was dreaming, it didn't lessen the panic rising in his chest.

"Hurry, Jon!" she said.

He got up, pulled at the chain.

The box was heavy. The chain hot, blistering his hands.

"Come on, Jon, you can do it."

He pulled harder.

The fire grew closer, hot flames erupting on his jacket.

He tried to drop the chain to extinguish the fire, but the woman scolded him, "There's no time. Throw the box into the hole, Jon."

He jerked the chain again, and the box suddenly budged.

"Yes!" she cried.

He pulled harder, faster, as fire spread up his arms. It was hot, but not yet hurting. If he could just get the box into the hole, he would be safe. Jon pulled harder still, every tug an effort that strained his muscles taut.

"Pull!" she yelled.

The box was finally in his hands even as the fire spread down onto his pants and upward toward his face.

"Throw it in the hole."

For reasons Jon couldn't make sense of, he couldn't.

"I can't!"

"If you don't, the fire will kill you, Jon. Throw it in the hole."

He stood at the precipice of the hole, staring down into its impenetrable darkness.

So far down.

He couldn't just let go.

He had to keep the box and everything in it. Even if it killed him.

"I can't!" he cried out again.

"Throw it!"

And then he felt the fire searing into his flesh, all at once and everywhere.

He screamed and dropped the box into the hole.

Only then did he remember his ankle was chained to it.

Too late.

The box dragged him down.

JON WOKE to the Russian riding him in a hotel room that wasn't his.

"Oh, Jon, fuck me!" She moaned, pinching her nipples, gyrating faster. "Yes, yes, cum inside me!"

His head was still swimming, and nothing made sense.

How did he get here?

And why was she riding him and screaming like she was in a porno when he wasn't even aroused?

Something was off.

She collapsed against him. "Oh, you were so good."

Then she stood and began to get dressed.

Jon tried to talk, to ask her what was happening, but no words would come out. He could barely even move. The room kept spinning.

He closed his eyes to at least shut off the visuals of the world turning on its head, even if his insides felt like he was on a Tilt-a-Whirl times twenty.

"Thank you," she said.

Thank you, for what?

He opened his eyes and saw her taking cash off the nightstand.

What the fuck? Is she robbing me?

He tried to raise his hand to object, but his arms refused to follow his orders. He turned his head and watched as she approached a dresser to his right.

Then he saw the reason for her performance.

She picked up a phone she'd been using to record the whole thing. After turning off the video, she said, "Thanks again." Then she smiled.

What the hell is she doing? Why did she record us?

Then things started adding up in his head. The cash on the dresser, her over-the-top theatrics. She was likely a prostitute, or posing as one, and just made a sex tape that she was surely planning on selling to a tabloid or porn site.

No! No! No!

Jon tried to call out to stop her.

But he blacked out instead.

Epilogue

Kevin drove along the dark, winding dirt road, cutting a path through the forested hills with his lights off.

He was just south of the giant fence that Conway Industries used to lock away the northernmost section of the island. He checked the digital map on his tablet. Just south of Heller's location.

He was near one of the few cave entrances on the south side of the fence, one he didn't think too many people knew about.

Oh, yeah? Then how did Roger get over there? Surely Conway Industries knows about it. Hell, the family has been on the island longer than anyone.

The interior of his truck was preternaturally quiet. Kevin couldn't help but feel like someone was watching him, even though he was far from the main road and didn't think that Paladin had any cameras up here.

What the hell are you doing, Kevin?

This is Conway Industries private property, and you do not have a warrant.

This is insane.

Yet he couldn't just turn away. He had to find the bodies

that Roger Heller had discovered in the cave and determine the truth.

Assuming you do find the bodies, what are you going to do, Kev? Call the Feds and explain why the hell you went onto Conway property without a warrant?

He was going to get one, but the Conways were the island's biggest economic engine, meaning the county judges were all in their pocket. Even if he got a warrant, someone would notify Conway Industries or Paladin so they could scrub it up first.

The only way he'd get to the truth was to find it himself.

What if they already moved the bodies? If they got a hold of Roger's flash drive and the cave recording was on it, then maybe they already took care of whatever they were trying to hide. In which case, Kevin was risking his life *and* wasting his time.

Yet, he had to know what Roger found.

He got out of the truck, grabbed his backpack — filled with an expandable crowbar and some other supplies — then locked the truck and looked down the hill where the cave entrance loomed in the darkness, covered by trees. At least he hoped it was still there.

Years ago, trying to keep kids from hanging out in the caves, cops erected a wooden barrier just inside the tunnel. But anyone with a crowbar could get past it.

Maybe Paladin blocked the whole damned thing off with cement.

A cold breeze brought fat drops of rain.

Shit.

Kevin hurried down the incline, boots kicking up dirt as he somehow managed to stay on two feet and not land face first into a swath of nasty underbrush.

He half expected cameras or a security detail and was pleasantly surprised to find neither as he approached the cave.

His heart pounded. He hadn't explored these caves since

he was a teenager, back when he and his friends would use "exploring" as an excuse to drink and smoke and try to scare the shit out of each other. Kevin never startled easily. At least, not back then.

But now, even though he was an adult — a police chief with a badge and a gun, no less — he hesitated, drawing slowly closer to the impenetrable darkness of the cave's mouth.

He sensed a sudden electricity in the air, felt and heard a low humming sound. But he couldn't place where it was coming from or even if it was just some trick of his ears.

A wave of vertigo hit him hard, causing him to stumble back.

He shook his head, trying to reorient himself.

What the hell?

The humming continued, a low vibration. A cross between static and a droning low musical note.

What is *that?*

He stepped closer to the cave.

The tone grew louder. The hairs on his arm and neck stood on end.

Curiosity pushed him forward.

He stepped inside and clicked on his flashlight, training it on the tunnel ahead. Long forgotten memories flooded his system, as if the cave itself were coaxing them from his youth.

There was the time he and Jerry McRichards came up here and drank a twelve-pack of some godawful bargain basement beer that Jerry's dad had bought.

Another time when he came here with Melanie Sanchez, hoping to make out. But she was so freaked out by the cave that she threw up the second she set foot inside it.

Then another time he, Jon, and the Hughes twins had come here for some party. But the cops came and scared everyone off before they made it inside. That was before the barricade, and probably the reason it was raised.

He took another few steps toward the tunnel's gaping maw.

Just inside the cave, his flashlight made a *tink-tink* sound before going dark.

Fuck!

He banged it into his cupped palm, trying to get the beam back.

Something brushed against his elbow.

Kevin spun around, swinging the flashlight as a weapon, but it connected with nothing.

He dropped the useless torch, grabbed his gun, and readied it. His heart pounded. Adrenaline coursed through him. Every nerve tensed, and he braced for what he couldn't see.

What the fuck was that?

He didn't think it was a person. Maybe a deer? A bear? Something big enough to reach his elbow, that was for certain.

He froze, trying to pierce the darkness for any shapes that stood out.

Saw nothing.

Listened intently.

Heard nothing.

Nothing … except the hum.

The flashlight flickered on and off with that same *tink-tink*, and he saw something in his peripheral vision. What, he couldn't make out. Just a dark shape moving into the tunnel.

He spun with the gun aimed in case it came back toward him.

If this is a fucking bear den, you do not want to go in there.

Just back out and go away.

Find another way to the spot where Roger found the bodies.

No.

I didn't come all this way just to be scared off by shadows.

Your Glock22 ain't gonna do shit if a bear comes at you fast enough, buddy.

Kevin bent, retrieved the flashlight with his left hand and trained it on the tunnel, scanning for movement.

Found none.

He continued toward the tunnel, light moving across any crevice a bear might be hiding.

The hum grew louder.

And with it, he heard … voices behind the static, like some distant transmission.

He strained to hear what they were saying.

It sounded like … numbers.

"Twelve… fourteen … eleven …"

But then there was other stuff he could barely make out, words that didn't appear to be English.

Every fiber of his being screamed, *Get out of here!*

Something is wrong.

Something bad is about to happen.

Get out get out get out GET OUT!

A low growl rolled out from inside the tunnel.

Fuck.

He turned, quickly, and ran toward the exit.

Something slammed into Kevin, knocking him face down into the wet mud just outside the cave. Footsteps pounded past him, back toward the cave.

He rolled over, raised his gun. Looked for whatever might be coming to finish him off.

His gaze darted toward the cave, then in every direction, but Kevin saw nothing in the darkness.

Get in your truck and get the fuck out!

He was shaking and more scared than he'd ever been. Not just of whatever might have knocked him down, but of something else, something he recognized in his primal brain, a part just under his consciousness.

Get out!

He ran to the truck, opened the door, scrambled inside.

His shallow breathing echoed in the cabin.

Kevin could hear his heart pounding beneath the sound of rain hitting his roof. And beneath that damned hum.

He flicked on his headlights, turned on the ignition.

Just go.

Go.

Instead, he drove toward the cave, blasting his high beams.

Where the hell are you?

He blasted his horn, not even caring what attention he might draw. He needed to see what knocked him down.

The lights pierced the cave to light the darkness on one far wall, but there were too many places out of the path where something might hide in the shadows.

Come on, you fuck.

Something moved in the cave, just to the right of the entrance.

He waited, sitting in silence.

Come on.

He honked again.

Come on.

The hum grew louder as rain fell harder.

His heart hammered so loud it might as well have been thunder.

He watched the spot he'd seen something move, gun aimed through his windshield.

Come on, come on, come on.

The rain stopped as if Mother Nature hit the *off* switch. One second a downpour, then nothing.

The hum ended just as fast.

Now there was only silence and his hammering heart.

Come on, come on, come on.

Hot steam plumed from whatever was hiding just out of sight.

Something was there, waiting.

He eased up on the brake, ready to coast inside the cave. He had to see what it was.

The truck rolled forward.

His phone rang.

The sound startled Kevin so much that he both slammed on his brakes and nearly fired his weapon.

He stopped, looked down at his phone, then pressed a button to answer the call via Bluetooth.

"Molly? Everything okay?"

He could tell she was crying.

Oh, God. Something happened to Aidan.

Oh, God, no.

"Molly?"

She finally spoke. "She's back."

"Who's back?"

"Our daughter is here. She's come home."

Episode 14

Prologue

Three months ago

JUDITH PEERED at the raised hood of her stalled car, looking down at the engine with her best look of confused frustration.

Her car was stopped in the middle of the narrow road, making passage difficult.

"Come on, come on." She stared into the night, waiting to see headlights approaching.

Nothing yet.

"Did they take a different route?" she asked into the hidden mic on her jacket.

Gibson responded, "No. Target is still en route."

She patted at the taser gun at her left, in a belt pouch concealed by her duster. Then she patted her right side, where she kept the gun.

"Target acquired. Turning onto your road."

"Copy." Judith stepped back in front of her car, returning to her role as *stranded motorist*.

Light silhouetted the upturned hood.

Showtime.

She forced tears by thinking of the thing that always got her to cry — her brother Keiran's suicide.

Tears streaming down her face, she came out from around the car, stepping in front of the van before it could go around her on the left.

The black Paladin van braked suddenly.

She couldn't see the driver, and likely passenger, beyond the headlights, so she hoped they hadn't recognized her as a threat.

"Help!" she shouted. "My car won't start." Then discreetly into her mic, "They're stopped."

The van went dead. Their engine and electronics cut off by Gibson remotely.

The officer in the passenger seat looked up at Judith, instantly seeing the trap.

He went for his piece.

Judith wouldn't be able to taze him through a windshield. So she raised her pistol.

"Get out, hands up!"

She hoped he would obey, so she wouldn't have to fire. Despite years of training, Judith had never taken a life. That was the one line she hoped never to cross. Conway Industries cost Keiran his existence, and she wanted to see them all punished. But killing workers wasn't part of the plan.

Plans changed, however, when shit went down.

The man on the passenger's side was going to fire.

She had no choice.

Judith put a bullet in his brain.

She stared, momentarily frozen.

There's two ways this can go now. You either give in to emotion and get yourself killed, or push it down and do what you came here to do.

She aimed her gun at the driver and shouted, "Get out!"

He did.

"Drop your weapons." She approached, her gun trained on him.

The man shook. Dropped a pistol.

He wasn't much older than her brother had been.

"Is that everything?"

"Y-yeah, that's it," he said.

"Unlock the rear door."

"I … I can't. They'll … they'll fire me."

"And if you don't open it, you'll join your partner." Her voice was void of emotion, even though the cruelty of her threat stung her heart.

No. No room for sympathy. He'd put a bullet in me if given a chance.

But as she looked at his innocent face, Judith wondered if he could. This wasn't some hardened Paladin veteran responsible for years of coverups, dirty deeds, and who knew how many deaths. This was an hourly wage kid, trying to get through a shift.

"Open it." She stepped closer, but not near enough to give him a chance at her gun.

He nodded. "Okay, okay. Please, just don't shoot. I've got a baby on the way."

Judith wasn't sure if he was telling the truth, but damn it if her emotions weren't starting bubbling up.

She pushed them down again, telling herself Keiran had been a baby once, too.

We're all babies once. Then we make our choices and pay the price.

"Open it!"

But he wasn't opening the door.

She knew from the planning of the operation that unlike the front doors, the engine, and the radio, that the van's rear doors couldn't be opened remotely. You needed the key.

The driver started fidgeting with his keys, then dropped them. He started crying. "Sorry."

"Pick them up," she demanded.

He bent down, searching in the grass.

Suddenly, dirt was flying in her face, and the Paladin officer was charging at her.

Judith fired, squeezing off the rest of her ammo.

The boy fell to the ground, moaning.

"Why?" she asked, tears stinging her eyes. "All you had to do was open the fucking door."

Blood poured from his dying body.

She went to where he'd dropped the keys, picked them up, then went to the van's rear door and opened it.

Her target was inside. The six-foot-five muscle-bound detective with the robotic leg.

Chapter 1 - Brock Houser

Upstairs, in an unused bedroom, Houser picked up the scent of paint and noticed the fresh patch of yellow on the wall behind the large bookcase. Drywall dusted the carpet.

Houser reached behind the bookcase, touched the wall, then looked at his fingertip. Sure enough, it was yellow.

"Get up here!" he shouted, then pulled it to the floor, sending volumes pouring from the shelves and into a pile.

A large, wet paint spot barely concealed a bad plastering job, covering a wide hole in the wall. Houser knocked twice.

"Hello?"

A muffled cry behind the wall.

Oh, God.

He'd found Cecilia, and she was still alive!

His heart pounded as officers poured into the room. Houser punched high where the wet spot started, straight through the quickly crumbling drywall, then tore at it, throwing chunks to the ground.

Inside the wall, he found the girl.

But it wasn't Cecilia.

It was Emma.

What?

"Houser?" She looked up at him with groggy eyes. "What's happening?"

Suddenly, they were no longer in the house.

They were in a dark field, the only light spilling out from his open trunk.

"Houser?" Emma called behind him.

He turned, confused. Emma was now Cecilia, the missing girl.

But she died.

How can she be here?

"What happened?" she cried, looking around, terrified. "Where did you bring me?"

"I … I didn't bring you anywhere." He looked around, no memory of driving there or taking her out of the trunk.

Suddenly, she was a wide-eyed Emma. "Uh-oh."

"What?"

She pointed up at the sky.

"They're coming."

"Who's coming?" He couldn't see anything above, other than clouds concealing most of the moon.

A light appeared above them, so bright and so wide, it seemed to swallow the sky.

"Help!" Emma shouted.

Houser looked down to see her reaching out for him.

He raced toward her.

And then she was gone.

~

HOUSER SCREAMED HIMSELF INTO WAKING.

Bright lights above him.

He tried to move, but his hands were restrained.

As his eyes adjusted to the brightness, Houser found himself in what looked like a hospital room, with its equipment and utilitarian appearance. But the camera and prison-style siding, and the door with a lone window that was probably locked, told him that this wasn't a regular hospital.

He pulled at the cuffs and was shocked for his efforts.

HOUSER WOKE UP AGAIN, but this time he wasn't alone.

A dark-haired woman with glasses stared at him, expressionless. "You're awake."

He eyed her up and down, trying to figure out what she was. His doctor? His guard? His warden? She wore jeans, a red blouse, and a black duster. Not exactly a prison outfit, or a doctor's.

"Where am I? Why am I cuffed?"

"For your safety, and ours. How much do you remember?"

"Not much. I was in the jail one minute then here the next. This a prison hospital?"

"No." She looked at a laptop next to him, maybe checking his vitals. Several wires ran to pads stuck into his chest. An IV tube ran into his arm.

"Was I hurt?"

"You've been in a coma for almost three months."

"Three months? What happened?"

"Paladin was going to kill you. We stopped them. Someone will be along to tell you more soon." She turned to leave.

"Wait," he called out.

But she didn't. Just as well. Brock wasn't sure what he would've asked. His mind raced with too many questions, most of them a fog, as he tried to make sense of the information.

In a coma for three months, and Paladin was going to kill him.

He vaguely remembered Kaiser telling him he was under their control because of nanobots implanted in him when he'd lost his leg. Nanobots that controlled him. Nanobots that forced him to tell the man things he didn't want to and couldn't remember now.

He was about to pull at the cuffs again, but then he remembered the shock.

Who are these people? Why save me? Why shock me?

The door slid open again.

A man stepped through. Slim and in his thirties with long silver and white hair pulled back in a ponytail, wearing a black hoodie and dark cargo pants.

"Hello, Mr. Houser. My name is Talbot Gray." He approached the bed, holding keys. "Before I set you free, just a warning. We've disabled Paladin's nanobots. They can no longer track, control, or monitor you. However, our good doctor has installed a kill switch. If you do anything stupid, we *will* put you down."

Houser glared at him. "So, you're not truly setting me free?"

Gray smiled. "You're free once you leave here. We won't keep you. And the switch will deactivate once you're out of range. But we hope you will hear us out and want to help us."

Houser wasn't interested in helping anyone just yet. But they had saved him from whatever Paladin had planned for him. And it wasn't as if Houser had anywhere else to go. He was still a suspect in Emma's murder. And her father was his employer, and only real friend. So, where would he go? He nodded. "Okay."

Gray slid the keys in, uncuffed Houser's right arm, then his left.

He rubbed at the lines in his wrist, then sat up, feeling tingles run through his spine. His head spun.

Gray seemed to notice. "You might want to take it easy. Doc put some nanobots in you to counter you being in the coma, but still, you'll take a bit of time to get back into fighting shape."

"*Fighting,*" Houser said dismissively. All he wanted was to find out who killed Emma and make them pay. Only then could he find Jon and apologize for his part in her death. He did take her out of the house and hand her to someone. But who had he given her to? The answer would only be found by getting to Paladin, since they were the people who had been controlling him. And if this Talbot guy could help, then Houser would play ball. For now.

"Come, I want to introduce you to some people."

Houser followed Talbot out of the room, through a narrow hallway until they reached a dark long wide room with a low ceiling, just a few inches higher than Houser. It looked like a control center with work stations, each with several monitors showing closed-circuit camera feeds, news feeds, or dark screens. Several whiteboards and pin-boards lined the walls showing charts of organizations and photographs of men and women, most wearing suits. At the top of one of the larger charts he saw the familiar face of Blake Conway. It looked like an undercover operation to topple organized crime.

"This is the Bunker," Talbot said, waving his hand across the room. "Our underground headquarters where we run Expose Them All."

"Where are we?" Houser asked. "Hamilton Island?"

"No. God, no. We couldn't keep this hidden under their nose. We're on Lopez Island, a short ferry or boat ride away." He nodded toward a young black man in a black leather jacket and black Seahawks beanie, typing away at a computer. "These are the heart and soul of ETA. This young man is Gibson." Gibson looked up at Houser, nodded, then returned to his screen.

"Judith, you've met already," Talbot said, nodding toward the woman who had greeted him as he entered. She was at a desk opposite Gibson, also typing away, but not looking up at Houser.

"And then there's Doc Jackson." He pointed toward the

far corner of the room, toward a closed door. A large dry erase board hung on it, and giant red letters were scrawled on it.

DOC ONLY. NOBODY ELSE.

"Hey, Doc, our visitor is awake!" Talbot shouted.

The door opened, and a tall, older black man with a wild bushy gray mane and thick glasses stepped out.

"Ah, Brock Houser, alive and awake!" he exclaimed in a deep voice as he came over. He crossed his hands in front of his chest, looked Houser up and down, blinking repeatedly as if he had a nervous tic or maybe obsessive compulsive disorder. "How are you feeling? Any headaches, vertigo, sickness? How's your vision? Any trouble walking?"

"Feeling good, more or less, Doc. Bit of a headache, bit dizzy when I got up. And memory is foggy. But other than, not bad."

"Good. Memories may come back, I don't know. They had some scrubbers in there, along with remote manipulation and a kill switch. Standard shadow soldier setup."

"Shadow soldier?"

"One of Conway's early DOD projects. I was back there at the start. They used some of my research and discoveries to turn it from theory to practice, unfortunately."

Talbot said, "Doc knows Conway Industries better than anyone out there. One of their best, but then he started asking too many questions and voicing concerns about some of their projects. So they tried to buy his silence. When that didn't work, they coerced him. Then they killed his wife and made the authorities think he did it. He's been on the run ever since."

"Fuck," Houser said. Just a few months ago, he might not have believed such a wild conspiracy theory — usually when a husband was accused of murdering his wife, ninety-nine times out of a hundred he did it — but that was before Houser was set up to take the fall for Emma's disappearance and murder.

"Fuck indeed," Doc said with a sigh.

Talbot continued, "We believe the recent murders, including the massacre, are all part of a massive mind control program being developed with the Department of Defense."

"Recent massacre? What happened?"

"Gibson, pull up the video footage of the Outdoor Market massacre."

Gibson grabbed a tablet, pulled up a video, walked over to Houser, and handed it to him.

Talbot narrated as the horror unfolded.

"Eleven random people go mad and start murdering people before taking their own lives, all at the exact same moment. We managed to get a hold of CCTV footage from thirty different angles before Paladin scrubbed the lot of it. They're trying to paint this as a 'terrorist plot' or something, but we know better. And we're hoping you can help us prove it."

Despite what had happened to him, the suspicions around Roger Heller's mysterious spree, and what happened after that, Houser still found it difficult to think all these people were being controlled by Paladin.

"Okay, one or two people snap, I get it. But why have all these people do this if you're trying to keep the experiments *hidden?* It doesn't make any sense. And even *if* Conway Industries is behind it, how do you expect to prove it?"

Doc's blinking got worse, as if he hated Houser's skepticism enough to push his compulsion buttons.

"We don't start with the hard stuff." Talbot raised a finger. "We start with the tip of the iceberg."

"What's that?"

Talbot turned to Doc, who was squeezing his eyes tight and silently counting to five.

He opened them and looked up at Houser. "Conway Industries is running a massive surveillance program. Not just the cameras all over the island, but hidden ones in most buildings, and … inside subjects as part of an optic nerve implant. They were rolling out the second phase when I was forced out."

Talbot stepped in before Houser could ask anything. "We prove that, it's the thread that unravels the rest."

"If you have evidence, why not just go public?"

"Because A, the good doc here is in hiding and exposing him is not an option, and B, nobody's going to believe him, or us, if we speak out. But … we get someone who is part of the program, like a Watcher, then we can exploit them to get proof."

"A *Watcher?*"

Doc nodded. "Conway Industries spent years identifying people with hyper-focused attention to detail, the kind of people who could count fallen matchsticks, find the needle in a haystack, and identify how many bees were in a swarm — at the same time. They amped up their abilities, put them on monitors overseeing people in their programs. These people spend entire shifts doing nothing but watching the subjects."

"Okay, so how do we find one of these Watchers?"

"We have one who I think might be sympathetic to our cause. His name's Stephen Anderson. His wife, Bea, was institutionalized after she drove through the front of a grocery store a few months ago. His son was in contact with a member of a conspiracy group that Roger Heller had been talking to, then that man just so happened to shoot Warren Conway before being put down. Around the same time, Milo disappeared."

"Milo?" Houser closed his eyes trying to remember how he knew that name. Then it came back. "I helped him get away from some Paladin goons. Maybe I could talk to him?"

"Well, you can't get to him. I have a feeling he's been compromised," Talbot said. "Probably have him loaded up with nanobots or optic relays."

"And you don't think Stephen is being monitored by a Watcher?"

"No. That's one of the flaws of their system," Doc said. "They can't use the optic relays on the Watchers. Their brain interferes with the spy kit somehow. But they probably have cameras in his house and car. Getting to him without drawing attention will be tricky, but not impossible."

"We've got jammers that'll scramble any monitoring they've got," Gibson said. "At least long enough for you to speak to him. Or … extract him."

Talbot met Houser's gaze. "It's a lot to take in, and you're only just waking, but I need to know. Are you in?"

Houser looked at the group. Four people in a basement taking on Paladin and Conway Industries seemed like a war they couldn't possibly win. But there was something about the look in each of their eyes, even Blinky Doc's, that told Houser if any group could expose what was happening on Hamilton Island, it was them.

He looked them each in the eyes then nodded. "I'm in."

Chapter 2 - Kevin Brady

Kevin raced home, his wife's voice kept playing back in his head as he wondered one thing on repeat. *How?*

She's back … our daughter is back.

And there were too many other questions.

Who had been holding her?

Did they hurt her?

Was she okay?

Molly hadn't said much after that other than Christina was dazed but looked physically fine. The rest of her words devolved into tears, other than *Please, come home!*

Physically fine.

Well, that was something. But what *psychological* hell had Christina gone through? What had she suffered at some monster's hand?

For so long, he'd imagined what monster, or monsters, had taken her. Being a cop, he'd seen enough to fear predators and murderers. Hamilton had very few sexual offenders, so it didn't take long to check out all of their alibis following Christina's disappearance. After that, the net grew to the surrounding islands and then to the mainland.

He'd imagined some predator coming via ferry, or hell,

even taking a boat, and scoping out the area, searching for his prey. Paladin had at least been helpful enough to share all the closed-circuit footage near Kevin's house, near the marina, and other spots someone might have taken Christina in order to flee the island. And still, nothing.

Kevin had other theories, too. In some, his daughter had sleepwalked out of the house, wandered to the ocean, and fell in, her body never to be found. Enough people had died from falling or jumping from Tanner's Pass to consider that an option, too, even if it was a hell of a walk for a six-year-old.

Other times, he considered someone else took his daughter. Not necessarily a predator, but maybe someone who couldn't have a kid of their own. But that was unlikely. Usually, when you heard about stories like that, it was someone taking a baby or toddler. A six-year-old, not so much.

But anything was possible.

And, at times, Kevin hoped that was the case. That someone nice had taken her and was treating her well. Maybe someday they might return her.

Is that what happened?

Did they finally decide to do the right thing?

It had to be something like that. A rapist or killer, even a first-timer, wouldn't risk returning a child who had seen his face. No matter the level of guilt or remorse, self-preservation would kick in, preventing such a risk of being identified.

Right?

Nearly home, it was all Kevin could do to keep the tears inside. Tears of joy, tears of sadness to come once he found out what happened to Christina. He had to keep them all bottled for now. Had to get his family through this. Had to get Christina through the process of answering questions and going to the hospital to be checked out. Get through all the things she'd have to do, all the questions they'd be assailed with from both officials and the press once word got out she was back.

Their daughter had returned, and the only thing they would want to do is protect her from the outside world, but for now he would have to be strong enough to get them all through it.

Kevin steeled himself as he pulled up to his driveway.

He leapt from the truck, raced to the front door, dashed inside.

There, in the living room, Kevin saw his daughter on the couch between Molly and Aidan.

He lost every tear he'd been holding.

"Daddy." She hopped off the couch and ran into his arms.

He lifted her, hugged her, and kept right on crying, hardly able to believe that day was finally here. He was holding Christina. His family was whole once again.

As they hugged, Molly and Aidan joined the embrace, all of them standing there, hugging each other as they sobbed.

AFTER DROPPING Aidan off at a neighbor's for the night, Kevin and Molly drove Christina to Conway Medical where they waited for Christina to be seen.

"Am I gonna get a shot?"

"I don't think so, honey," Molly said. "They just want to look you over to make sure you're not hurt."

"I'm not hurt."

"To make sure you weren't hurt." Then, as if realizing where the conversation might lead, she pivoted. "And to make sure you're not sick or anything. You've been gone a while."

"Oh," she said.

Though Kevin had already asked a few different ways, he tried again. "You don't remember anything from the past six months? Nothing at all? Not even the house you were in?"

"I already told you, no." Frustration laced Christina's words.

"What about coming home? Do you remember who brought you to the house?"

"No. I only remember waking up in the front yard, looking up and seeing the door, and knowing I was home."

"And before that? The last thing you remember was going to sleep in your own bed? And you thought it was yesterday?"

Christina nodded.

Kevin thought back to how she jumped off the couch and ran to him, it was as if she'd missed him. If she had no idea how much time had passed, why did she miss him so much? Of his twins, she was usually the one who didn't make a commotion when he came home from work. Aidan usually ran up to greet him, but more often than not, Christina was playing with her toys or drawing pictures, barely noticing him until she was ready. Yet the way she responded tonight meant some part of her knew time had passed, some part of her had missed her family.

Some part of her had to know she was gone for a long while.

Whoever had taken her had obviously used drugs to mess with her memory. While people could block things out, especially victims of post-traumatic stress, it seemed highly unlikely she'd repressed so much on her own, especially the events of earlier today. A blood test would likely show some drug in her system.

Then would begin the work of recovering her memories.

That would be the hard part. He wanted to catch whoever took her, but at the same time, he didn't want to hurt Christina. And recovering memories could be painful. It could take years of therapy. They might never get the answers they were looking for.

Why can't you just be glad she's home?

Stop overthinking all this.

He looked at her lying in the hospital bed as they continued to wait for the doctor.

She met his gaze and smiled. Faint, but there nonetheless.

He held her hand. "I love you, honey."

"I love you too, Daddy."

Daddy. It felt so good to hear her say that again.

His phone buzzed. He glanced down, saw that it was Officer Henry. Given the hour, Henry wouldn't be calling unless it was important.

"Gotta take this," he said to Molly as he stood and left the room. "Yeah?" Kevin answered, walking toward the end of the hall and looking out at the stormy night. Lightning flashed, illuminating the lot below. He glanced down at the news vans set up outside, waiting for word on those who'd been injured in the massacre.

"Sorry to bother you, Chief, but I wasn't sure what to do."

"What is it?"

"Dispatch has been getting calls all night, people claiming they saw a UFO. They want to file reports, show us some burnt grass or something they claim is proof."

"How many calls?"

"More than forty. I dunno if it's prank calls or people just plain lost their damned minds after the killings. Do I need to go out to all these calls? Lori isn't sure if it's bullshit or not, said I ought to treat them all real."

"No. If it's not an emergency, just have Lori get their info and we'll call them tomorrow."

"Thanks, boss. Sorry to wake you."

Kevin thought about telling him that he didn't, but that would just draw the conversation out, and he wasn't ready to tell anyone else about his baby girl's return. The world would know soon enough. All he wanted for the moment was to get back in the room with his Christina and find out if she was okay.

He said goodnight, hung up, and was about to head back

to his daughter's room when the elevator doors dinged open to reveal Blake Conway. He stepped off and headed toward Kevin. Even though it was his hospital, the man was a rare sight these days, especially at such a late hour.

"Hello, Chief," Blake said extending his hand to shake.

Kevin shook it and nodded. "Mr. Conway."

"I heard about your daughter," Blake said, further surprising Kevin. "I just want to let you know she'll have the best treatment available. I've already put in a call to a specialist, a doctor who has helped many children recover from kidnappings and other trauma. She'll be on the first flight in the morning, at no expense to you, of course."

Kevin wasn't sure what to say. While the Conways had provided free basic medical to everyone on the island, this sort of service was above and beyond the norm, and he couldn't imagine there weren't strings attached.

Yet, who was he to say no to the best help available for his daughter?

"Thank you," Kevin said. "I appreciate it."

"No problem at all. And please, give my best to Molly."

Kevin nodded as Blake headed back to the elevator, got on. The doors closed and the down arrow lit.

Had the old man specifically come to the hospital to see him, or had he been here already, heard Kevin was around, and decided to stop by and greet him?

Either way, Kevin glanced at the ever-present cameras at either end of the hall, and felt that familiar sense of being observed.

And he hated it like always.

Chapter 3 - Stephen Anderson

The Sunday of the massacre ...

STEPHEN SAT in the dark room staring at the monitors, watching as his subjects scurried about their lives. He was one of few people on the planet with a talent for being able to monitor twenty feeds at once, following not only what the test subjects were doing, but also tending to twenty distinct conversations at once. This was partly because of the way his brain worked, but also thanks to nanobot enhancements that Conway Industries had installed in his body.

Today, four of the twenty screens were blank. As he viewed the lives of his other sixteen subjects through the view offered by their secret optic implants, Stephen wondered where the other four subjects were. It was mid-day, and none of them were known for sleeping in late or taking naps.

He looked down at the tablet on his desk, punched in the subject numbers, and checked to see if any of them were scheduled for maintenance, tests, or doctor's visits. When patients were involved in the highly secretive tests or at their doctors, their feeds went dark, as Watchers were supposed to be kept in the black about the nature of their subjects' partici-pation in any of Conway Industries secret projects — whether they be biomedical in nature or secret military shit for DARPA.

But whenever a subject was considered offline, a note was in their file. And none of these subjects had notes.

He considered calling his boss, but it was the weekend, and Hank Weeks was a bit of an asshole when you "bothered" him on the weekend. So Stephen made notes in each of their files and put in a request to check each person's house feeds on the off chance that any of them had discovered the implants and were trying to hide their activities from whomever they suspected might be watching.

Stephen watched Subject C10910, an attractive young brunette, as she stared in the dressing room mirror, posing in a new bra before buying it. He'd been a Watcher long enough to usually ignore his subjects' nudity. He often felt a little ashamed watching them go about their more private activities. But every now and then, he'd get one that he was really attracted to, someone he'd come to care about more than he should. And Subject C10910 was adorable.

Her name was Natasha Drovcik, a first-grade teacher, who'd recently moved to Hamilton when her mother got sick and needed someone to care for her. He wasn't sure what program she was involved in for Conway Industries, but Stephen hoped it wasn't one of the questionable drug trials that would screw with her health. She'd been through a lot in the two months he'd been watching her.

She removed the bra.

Stephen admired her breasts in the dressing room mirror, then, as her eyes seemed to almost meet his, he looked away, red-faced.

It had been a long time since he'd had sex. His wife, Bea, had been institutionalized for more than three months, and she didn't even recognize him when he visited her. There was emptiness in her eyes, no spark of recognition. Nothing of the woman he'd fallen so hard for. But hell, there hadn't been much of her before that, either.

Piece by piece, Conway Industries had robbed Bea of her memories in one procedure after another.

And he'd just watched it happen.

And now they'd put implants in his son, to track his movements, and spy on him. They'd also erased whatever it was he'd seen a couple of months ago. If the boy screwed up again, looking in places he shouldn't be looking, talking to people he shouldn't be talking to, Kaiser had made it clear Milo would be put in one of the programs, a guinea pig for Conway Industries.

And there was nothing Stephen could do.

How the hell had he gotten here?

He'd gift wrapped his life for this organization.

Growing up, he'd been ostracized for his autism. But then, thanks to an experimental program by Conway Industries, Stephen could change a perceived weakness into a strength. He blossomed, not only fitting in with his peers, but excelling at everything he put his mind to. After university, he'd come to work for the program that saved his life, and he thought he'd been doing good. He believed that Conway Industries was changing the world.

Had he been blind to their terrible deeds?

Stephen turned his gaze to another subject, trying not to pay attention to C10910 slipping into a flimsy camisole. Trying to ignore his erection.

Suddenly, one of the four black screens went live.

Subject C10920's camera, a young redheaded man who worked at a bike rental shop, showed him walking through Hamilton Island Outdoor Marketplace. He was alone, and his gait was off, as though confused. Subjects' phones were fitted with apps that allowed Watchers to listen in on them at any time. Stephen heard bursts of static, with something he couldn't quite make out beneath the hissing.

Words, though he could barely register them. At first, he thought it was a man's voice, then he heard what was clearly a woman saying … *something*.

The garbled sounds reminded him of when he was a kid and his father would listen to shortwave radio. His father liked to listen to shows around the world. Stephen always found it more interesting to hear the signals that were barely coming through — catching snippets of music or words, rarely in English, always under the static. It was like listening to some far-off signal he wasn't meant to hear, and he felt like a spy trying to decode the secret signals.

The static stopped.

And so did Subject C10920.

Through his eyes, Stephen saw that he was stopped in front of a bent-over old man, tying a toddler's shoes.

Subject C10920 looked down at his hand. A knife shook in his grip.

What the hell is he doing?

Stephen leaned forward.

Subject C10920 leapt at the man and plunged the knife into his neck.

"What the fuck?" Stephen yelled as he jumped out of his seat, staring.

Subject C10920 turned to the child, a little boy wearing a blue tee with a cartoon character on the front.

No, no, don't do it. Put the knife away.

He then looked at the knife, coated with blood.

The boy stared, his face starting to contort into a cry.

No, no, no.

The sound of static again, so loud that it hurt Stephen's ears.

Subject C10920 screamed as he brought the knife down into the boy's neck.

Stephen screamed.

Then, as he backed away from the monitor, his hand reaching for the phone to call Paladin, chaos spread to the other screens. Five of the other subjects stabbing, clawing, biting, or trying to get away from others.

What the hell is happening?

He called Paladin. "We've got a problem."

After explaining what he'd seen, Stephen hung up and started the preservation protocol, to back up all data on the streams to a remote location then delete local storage, on the off chance an investigation team not under Paladin influence were to get ahold of their footage.

As Stephen entered instructions onto a screen, a thought stuck out like a tiny thread threatening to unravel an exquisite fabric print.

That idea turned into compulsion as he brought up Subject C10920's feed and rewound through it, prior to the black screen just before his attack on the old man and the child.

Stephen kept rewinding as fast as it would allow him to go, at twenty-four times normal speed.

He didn't need to slow the feed down to take in all he saw. He need only watch it once, then could later recall and break it down in his mind. He kept going, trying to take in as much as he could before the Subject's feed was forever dumped off-site and he could never bring it up again.

He wasn't sure what exactly he was looking for. He already knew Conway Industries had been behind horrible events on the island, and Paladin had done its part in covering those things up. Was he looking for something he could use against them, to get out from under their thumb? Or simply looking for something to ensure Milo's safety, maybe get Bea back to a normal life, if that was possible.

Stephen wasn't sure. All he knew is that he was looking for something.

Then he saw it. And he couldn't believe his eyes. Because what he saw was impossible.

He was about to rewind when his entire room went dark and a red light came on, indicating his superiors were on the job now and he was locked out of the system.

He wondered if they saw the same thing.

If so, how long before he got a visit from Kaiser, or worse, wound up dead, his body floating beneath Tanner's Pass.

The door to his office clicked open and the AI voice instructed him, "Please take the rest of the day off, Mr. Anderson. We'll see you in the morning."

He left the room, shaking.

And the entire walk from his room to his locker and then to his car, Stephen kept waiting for someone to stop him.

Somehow, he escaped the facility without event.

But how long before Kaiser came calling?

Chapter 4 - Milo Anderson

Monday morning ...

"MILO. MILO, WAKE UP."

Alex?

Milo woke, startled to hear his dead best friend's voice, calling to him.

But then he realized that he'd been sleeping.

And the weight of reality came crashing down on him yet again.

He glanced at the clock on his nightstand.

It was 10:11 in the morning. He'd gotten to sleep in since school closed following yesterday's tragedy. Milo wondered if that was because of the students who had lost their lives or loved ones, or because school officials were afraid there might be a copycat something or other today.

He reached for the anxiety pills, the ones that were messing with his emotions, sometimes making Milo feel worse than he did before, other times making him numb.

"You have to take these," the doctor had said. "Or you could have a complete breakdown."

He hoped he'd not have to be on them forever. He hated the rollercoaster, though Milo supposed it was preferable to losing his mind completely.

He took a pill, washed it down with a swig of bottled water, then got out of bed.

The house was empty, yet again, his father already at work. Milo headed downstairs, turned on the TV, and ate cereal as he flipped around news channels listening to people who knew nothing about the tragedy offer their theories and condemnations.

His head buzzed, a weird sense of déjà vu that he couldn't quite place.

He watched as two panelists on the news program were talking about how a growing number of people were calling yesterday's incident the act of a "killer flash mob." Many were culling the suspects' social media for reasons why they might have chosen their victims. Why attack Hamilton Island? Both panelists agreed it seemed like these people had voiced anti-transhumanism resentment.

He flipped the channel and found some blowhard conspiracy asshole bloviating about how the whole thing was part of a plan to make the Expose Them All group led by Talbot Gray look responsible. That it was a plot by Conway Industries, or its proxies, to end the group.

The whole conversation made Milo sick. He had no opinions one way or another on what these people were saying. But people were discussing the deaths of people he knew, who lived in his hometown. Using them as pawns in their argument.

He turned off his TV as the names of nine schoolmates crawled across the screen yet again.

He thought about the shooting a few months ago. It had taken the lives of his friends, a teacher, and the girl he liked. A shooting, which inevitably led to the loss of his best friend, Alex Heller, and his mom through retaliatory murders.

He missed Alex. What he would say about this bullshit on TV? While they were both big fans of anything even remotely sci-fi, they were also frightened of some of the darker themes of transhumanism, such as AI and body modifications which gave companies unparalleled access to, and control over, people.

"Soon, Conway Industries is going to control when we shit," Milo had once joked. And while neither of them had really ever considered Conway Industries an evil company capable of the things that Truth Manifesto claimed, there were times when Milo felt like something was going on, and that something might have been linked to the first shooting. Maybe this killing spree, too.

Milo wasn't sure why he thought this. He didn't usually believe wacky conspiracy theory websites. Especially not Truth Manifesto, which tended to serve up some of the weirder shit that couldn't possibly be true, the kind of clickbait that seemed more interested in generating ad revenue than exposing *the truth*.

Just another player in the bullshit game of manipulation, as far as Milo was concerned.

As he finished his cereal, he wondered what the hell he'd do with the day since school was canceled.

He didn't want to sit home all day. But it wasn't as if he had many friends left. He'd withdrawn after Alex died. He also spent some time in Conway Psychiatric after his father found him collapsed on the floor, having suffered what the doctors called "mental exhaustion." Then there was the little incident where his stepmother, Bea, drove through the front of that store, with Milo in the front seat beside her.

He'd gotten a few texts from friends following his release from the hospital, but there was little follow-up. And, after a while, nobody texted him about anything. In person, old friends gave him wide berth or made the smallest of talk. Hell, even Alex's girlfriend, Katie, barely spoke to him anymore. They'd been good friends before. And he thought they'd stay friends after Alex died. But that was before he went to the nuthouse. Maybe she'd never really liked him at all.

He grabbed his phone off the counter and pulled up his contacts. Alex's name, photo, email, and number were all still there. Sometimes, Milo would almost text him about something cool before remembering Alex was gone. Forever.

He scrolled down to Katie's photo, smiling. That was back during happier times.

His thumb hovered over her picture.

He was bored. And worse than that, lonely. Yet, if she didn't like him anymore, or if she found it too hard to talk to him without missing Alex, then he didn't want to call her. Didn't want to add to her stress or sadness. Didn't want her obligated to talk out of pity.

Don't call her. Find something else to do.

There's always porn.

But Milo was too sad to jerk off.

So he pressed her face and dialed.

As the phone rang twice, then three times, he figured she was ignoring his call, going to let it go through to voice mail. If she did that, he'd hang up. No way he wanted her to hear his desperation.

But then she picked up. "Hello?"

"Katie? Um, hi."

"Hi, Milo." A long pause, then, "How's it going?"

Although he'd wanted to talk to her, he had no idea what the hell to say now that she was on the other line.

Shit, this was a bad idea!

"You okay?"

And he didn't know what to say to that. Not in the least fucking bit. Tears welled in his eyes, and he felt like a big giant pussy.

He couldn't let her hear him crying.

He had to get off the phone, but how the hell could he do that when he'd just called?

Think of something, stupid ass!

"Do you wanna get lunch? Catch up?"

Another long pause, and he imagined her shaking her head.

Of course, I don't wanna get lunch with you, dork. Hell, I never even liked you. I only talked to you because you were Alex's best friend. Get the hint.

"I've got this thing —"

"It's okay. We can meet another time," Milo said, eager to hang up.

"I can meet after that, though. Where you wanna go? Burgerbakers?"

Milo *was* in the mood for a burger.

"Yeah, that sounds good."

"Want me to pick you up?"

Milo looked outside. It was nice, so far, anyway. "No, I'll bike over. What time?"

"I should be able to meet you around one. Just get a booth in the back if you're there first, okay?"

"Cool. See ya then."

Milo hung up, grinning like an idiot. It had been forever since he'd hung out with anyone, let alone Katie. He hoped it would be like hanging out with Alex, if only a little.

THE WIND FELT great in his hair. Same for the sun on his skin, zipping through the island's streets as Milo made his way downtown toward Burgerbakers, a place he hadn't been to since he, Alex, Katie, and Manny had gone there for lunch last summer.

He tried not to think about Alex and Manny being dead.

It was time to put the pain and past behind him, to live

again. At least that's what his father said at dinner a few nights ago.

He passed by Hamilton Island Outdoor Marketplace. The place was still closed and populated with Paladin security cars along with several dark sedans Milo figured were Feds. More than two dozen news vans were stationed at the far end of the parking lot, where they'd probably stay for the next month as the tragedy played out, then they'd cover the aftermath as people tried to put their lives back together and resuscitate their businesses.

Returning to school after Roger Heller shot up his classroom was one thing. They had to go back eventually. But how did businesses attract people after a massacre? He imagined the Marketplace would be tarnished by the deaths forever, but maybe people would be more resilient. After all, it wasn't like people could just stop shopping.

He continued along until he reached the Burgerbakers' plaza.

The parking lot was packed, probably because the Marketplace, and the restaurants within it, were all closed. The nearby workers, along with the influx of media and law enforcement, needed *somewhere* to eat.

Shit. We'll be lucky to get a table, let alone a booth in the back like Katie wanted.

He parked his bike in the front, not bothering to lock it since Burgerbakers didn't have a rack. He scanned the lot, but it was so packed, he couldn't tell if Katie's car was there. And Milo didn't want to waste time looking as even more cars pulled up.

Inside, he found at least a dozen people waiting in the vestibule, some seated, most standing, as if that would somehow mean a reduced time, and his heart sank at the thought of them having to wait forever to get a table. He didn't have anywhere else to be, but he and Katie would be forced to stand or sit in the vestibule with all these people around, making what promised to be an awkward conversation that much more difficult to start.

His chest tightened with anxiety.

Milo approached the hostess and was surprised to see it was someone he went to school with last year, a cute brunette named Emily. She smiled. "Oh, hi, Milo."

He was surprised she remembered his name. They'd been in exactly one class, History, and had spoken maybe twice as many words.

"Um, hi, Emily. How are you?"

"Good. Katie's waiting for you in the back."

"Oh," Milo said, surprised and relieved that Katie had already nabbed a table. "Thanks."

He waved nervously and headed toward the back where Katie was sitting at their old spot.

She smiled, got up, and hugged him tight. "It's soooo good to see you. How's it going?"

"Good." Milo sat across from her. As she started updating him on the latest, he found himself surprised by how much she genuinely seemed to enjoy his presence. He felt almost guilty for thinking she'd been avoiding him.

They talked through appetizers and lunch, about old times, laughing a lot more than he expected. It felt great.

Halfway through the main course, Katie sobered and stared at him intently. "Do you ever see Alex?"

Milo laughed, thinking she was kidding, but her face said otherwise. "*See* him? Like in a dream?"

"No. See him. Every now and then I see him in a crowd, or in class, just out of the corner of my eye. And then he's gone. I know he's not really there, but sometimes it feels like he is, for a moment at least. He only vanishes once I turn and see him."

"Like a ghost?"

"Maybe. I dunno."

"Sometimes I dream about him, about all of us, Manny

and Jessica, hanging out like in the old days. Then I wake up, and for a minute I forget that they're gone. But no, I don't think I've ever seen him."

Katie fell silent, as though she'd said too much. He needed to say something, otherwise she might stop talking and want to go. He'd been without friends too long to let her just leave.

There was one thing he could mention, a recent occurrence he felt silly even raising, but maybe it would make things less awkward. Or, at the very least, she'd feel less stupid for thinking she was seeing a ghost.

"Sometimes when I'm drifting off to sleep, or just waking up, I hear him talking to me."

Katie leaned forward. "What do you mean?"

"Like, I hear him say my name. Or he'll say 'wake up' or something else. And, for a minute, I feel like he's right there, but then I figure it's just remnants of some dream.

"Maybe it's not, though." Katie's eyes laser-focused on Milo like *this* was what she had been waiting to discuss. "What if there's some part of him trying to talk to us, to tell us something."

"Like 'wake up?'" Milo laughed.

Katie frowned.

"Sorry. I mean, he might very well be trying to contact you, but I think if he was trying to talk to me, he'd say something other than 'wake up' or—"

"Maybe 'wake up' means something else."

The way Katie was leaning forward and looking at him concerned him. He'd seen that crazed expression before. He tried to remember, it felt so recent, like a memory on the tip of his tongue, but … he couldn't recall it.

Katie was still staring at him, waiting for him to speak, but what could he say that wouldn't give away his fear that she'd lost her mind? Or that she was sad enough to believe fantastical things. Milo was a writer, or wanted to be when he grew up, but that didn't mean he believed in ghosts.

"Be right back. Gotta use the bathroom."

Milo stood, went to the restroom, and took a piss.

As he walked toward the sink, he heard a voice behind him call out, "Milo."

He turned, but there was nobody in there with him.

And it wasn't just *a voice*. It was Alex's.

He'd never heard it while wide awake. It only came on the edges of sleep.

What the hell? Maybe Katie's crazy is contagious.

He went to the sink to wash his hands.

An ear-piercing screech caused him to double over in pain. He braced the sink so as to avoid falling to the ground.

The sound was LOUD, like someone had set off an alarm, but at one constant pitch, and it was pressing on his skull from all sides, trying to crush it.

He felt it through his head, in waves that radiated down into his gut.

His eyes burned.

And then he felt his lunch bubbling up.

He gritted his teeth, trying to keep it down, but lost the battle as puke sprayed from his mouth to cover the floor.

And then the sound was gone as suddenly as it had started.

His face and eyes were burning.

Tears streamed down his cheeks.

He looked down at the mess on the floor, chunks of the food he'd just eaten and felt pure, undiluted embarrassment.

Couldn't even puke in the trash can or the sink.

Milo straightened himself dand looked in the bathroom mirror to see if he'd gotten any vomit on his clothes.

But his reflection was suddenly gone.

What the hell?

He stared at the impossibility. The entire bathroom was looking back from the mirror without him.

He squeezed his eyes shut tight to recalibrate, certain that normal would resume when he opened them.

What if it's not? What if I'm losing my mind?

He flashed back to a fuzzy memory of Bea, staring at the static on TV.

But that memory didn't make any sense.

He gripped the sink tight to anchor himself in reality and opened his eyes.

His reflection had returned, but it was askew. Mirror Milo was to his left, arms folded across his chest, staring at him.

Not staring. Glaring.

Milo turned around, half expecting his mirror self to be there in front of the bathroom stall.

But there was nothing.

He turned back to the mirror to find his reflection as it should be.

He blinked through tears.

What the …?

He stared at himself in the mirror and had the uncanny sense that he wasn't looking at his reflection, but rather at another being studying him from behind the glass. A weird being from another world, watching him, fucking with him.

He leaned closer, half expecting Mirror Milo to do something different. But he matched his every move.

He closed his eyes again, trying to shake this off.

The pills were messing with him. Nothing else would explain the weirdness. And it if was the pills, then it wasn't real. It could be corrected with a change in medication.

He scooped water into his mouth, gargled, then spit into the sink. He grabbed a stick of gum, then another, and popped them into his mouth, hoping to mask the smell of vomit before returning to Katie.

He was about to leave the bathroom before someone saw his mess, but a sudden flash of light stopped Milo in his tracks.

It was brief, barely there. Hell, maybe not even there.

But it was the source of the flash that drew his attention.

He leaned closer to the mirror, looking at his eyes. They looked completely normal.

But then he leaned in closer. Saw another flash, a bright red light. There and gone in less than a second.

Milo backed away from the mirror.

"What the fuck?"

He leaned in again, and this time seeing something that stopped his heart.

Just under his iris, a flash of light, but this time he saw that it had a shape, like a tiny worm.

A worm with lights in it.

In his fucking eye.

What the …?

His heart was a kick drum.

Adrenaline coursed through him, mixed with a rising panic — whatever was in him was going to burrow deeper, straight into his brain.

He had to get it out.

Now.

Milo reached into his pocket, found his keys.

No time to think. Or second guess.

He gripped the largest of his keys into a blade and brought it to his eye.

But he froze before he could gouge out his eye.

He heard Alex say, "No."

And then Milo fell to the ground.

Chapter 5 - Kevin Brady

Kevin woke up embarrassingly late.

It was quarter after one, and he was lying on Christina's bedroom floor.

Her bed was empty.

He stood quickly, worried that she was gone again or the past twelve hours had been a dream. He raced out of her room then relaxed once he heard a sound that the last nine months had reduced to a memory — his children laughing in front of a movie.

He stopped at the top of the stairs, listening to the joy. He thought about what the doctor had said last night. Christina was physically healthy. No signs of physical damage or abuse. He also found no drugs in her system, so he couldn't find a reason for her memory loss. But he couldn't rule out psychological trauma. The next few months might be difficult. It could be a while before she was back to normal. Even longer before she regained any memories. Maybe never.

That might not be so bad.

They'd given her an IV to help with her dehydration, but beyond that, Christina was as good as the day she'd left.

After getting her diagnosis and driving home, he spent the

better part of the rest of the night calling everyone involved, updating them on the investigation, telling them he'd write up statements and such. He also called Kaiser's voicemail and left a message asking if Paladin could pull closed-circuit footage of his street. Maybe they could find the person who dropped her off.

He'd waited too long to call for the ferry to the mainland to stop, so if it was someone from off-island, they were in the wind by now.

A part of Kevin was pissed that he'd not thought to close the island immediately, and had probably missed his window to catch the bastard. But another part of him didn't care. The most important thing was that his daughter was back and seemingly in good health.

He stayed at the top of the stairs a while longer, listening to Molly laugh with their children. God, it felt great to hear her laughing again. She hadn't smiled this much in a lifetime. Lately, he'd wondered too often if he might not come home to find his wife dead from an overdose.

But now his family was back.

Things were normal again.

He took a shower.

While getting dressed, he heard the doorbell ring. Hoped it wasn't Talbot peddling more of his conspiracy shit. Then he remembered the earlier half of last night, how he'd been on Conway property, snooping in the cave, searching for bodies.

And how someone, or something, had been there with him.

His throat knotted as the doorbell rang again.

It's Paladin. They saw you last night, and now they've come to ask questions.

He had no idea what he would say, or how much trouble he might be in.

He tried to relax as he went to the window to see whose

car was in his driveway. It wasn't Kaiser or another Paladin vehicle. No, it was an ancient Jag.

Blake Conway's car.

He thought about Blake's offer last night. Had he come to reiterate? Or had he come to ask why Kevin had been snooping around his land?

He swallowed past the lump and went downstairs.

His wife beat him to the door. "Why, hello, Mr. Conway," Molly said with surprise in her voice. "How are you doing?"

"I'm fine, Mrs. Brady. And yourself?"

"Good. No, great. Our daughter is back."

"Yes, I heard last night. I ran into your husband at the hospital."

"Ah." She turned to Kevin as he descended the stairs.

"I hope you don't mind my interrupting, I just came to pick your husband's brain about something. Won't be but a few minutes."

"No problem at all. Would you like a drink or anything?"

"No, thank you, ma'am."

She turned to Kevin. "You want me to keep the kids busy?"

"No, that's not necessary," Blake said. "We can talk outside."

Kevin nodded then led the old man onto the porch.

Molly said, "It was nice seeing you, Mr. Conway."

"You, too. Take care."

Kevin stepped outside, the lump growing bigger in his throat. In all the years he'd been police chief, never once had Blake Conway appeared at his doorstep. This was important.

He followed Conway out to his car. The driver sat dutifully awaiting his boss.

Blake's eyes were serious when he finally turned them on Kevin. "I'm not going to ask why you're talking to Talbot Gray."

Shit.

"Nor am I going to ask what you were doing last night before your daughter returned."

Shit. Fuck.

Still, Kevin said nothing. While Blake was an intimidating man, Kevin rarely allowed someone to back him into a defensive position. Better to say nothing than hem or haw. The man might own the island, and the private police department which ridiculously outmanned his, but Kevin was the chief of police, and that still carried some weight.

"Paladin will be absorbing your police department."

"What?"

"Yes. The Hamilton Island City Council will be voting on the matter in a couple of months. And I can assure you, they'll be voting to shut you down."

Kevin still held his silence. Now it was more to keep from giving in to his rising anger.

"But I'm here with an offer."

Blake reached into his pocket, withdrew a cashier's check, and handed it to Kevin.

He looked at the number — a half-million dollars — and tried not to gasp.

"Consider it a down payment on your retirement. Pay off your home, or move somewhere you've always wanted to go. I'll give you another check in six months. In any event, all I ask is that you not stand in the way of the takeover. To please go with grace and not make a scene. Perhaps even agree publicly that it's the best thing for the residents of Hamilton Island."

Kevin knew this wasn't *just about* taking over the police force, though he'd long figured it would only be a matter of time before Paladin made the move. This was Blake trying to buy his silence over recent events, or prevent Kevin from interfering with the official investigation.

He offered the check back to Blake. "With all due respect, I don't need your money, Mr. Conway."

Blake backed away toward his car, leaving the check in Kevin's hand.

"No, you hold onto it. Consider my offer more carefully, and what it could mean for your family. You've been given a second chance, Chief Brady. I don't think you realize how lucky you are to have such a thing, especially in a world that can be so very cruel. I only ask that you retire, and you stop speaking to Talbot Gray. That man, and his organization, are trouble, and I'd hate to see you get caught up in all this." He nodded, then got into the back of his car.

As the Jag sped away, Kevin stared down at the check. It was generous, but he couldn't interpret Blake's message as anything other than a threat. The only question was how far he would go if Kevin were to reject him.

He shoved the check into his back pocket and as he turned back to the house, found Molly looking out the front window.

But he couldn't tell her why Blake had come. Not until he'd made up his mind.

Chapter 6 - Stephen Anderson

Stephen woke to a text from Kaiser asking him to report to the office of Internal Investigations. The Watching Station was closed for the next few days while a Paladin team conducted an investigation into the massacre.

Stephen was told to report to Conway Industries rather than his usual building.

He arrived just before nine. Before he entered the building, Stephen pressed a button on his private phone, tucked inside his jacket. It initiated a failsafe protocol to warn Milo if Stephen didn't deactivate the button within an hour. A protocol that would send a message to his son's phone, computer, and tablet, along with the television, telling Milo to grab the go-bag under Stephen's bed then get out of the house, run far and fast, and never look back.

He prayed he wouldn't need to trigger it.

Prayed even more that he could if he had to. That Conway Industries wouldn't have signal jammers set up in the room, or confiscate his phone. If they did and attempted to access it, it would also trigger the protocol — assuming it could get a signal out.

His throat was dry and his nerves on edge as he made his

way past security and rode the elevator to the top floor of Conway Industries corporate headquarters where he was greeted by Melody Denham, the head of internal investigations.

She was in her early thirties, short, with dark hair, severe bangs, and black eyeliner that only made her pale blue eyes seem even more icy. Every time he'd seen her, which was rarely, she'd always been dressed in the same thing — a black dress with some red embellishment or another. Today it was a red bracelet, the woman's only hint of warmth.

Melody greeted him with a curt nod and asked him to follow her to the interview room down the hall.

In their few prior interactions, she spoke in a clipped British accent that suggested she had neither the time nor the desire to exchange anything beyond the bare minimum with him.

Stephen wanted to make the interview take as long as possible by drawing out every word like an anthropomorphic sloth. But he didn't have time to screw around if he expected to cancel the failsafe.

She led him to a small room, all black — from the carpet to the walls to the ceiling. The only things not black were two matching chairs at a brown table and the red box sitting on it.

"Please, have a seat."

He tried not to look at the box as he sat, though he couldn't help but wonder what was inside. Was it evidence they had on him? Had they reviewed his review of Subject C10920?

Had they seen the same thing that he had?

And if so, were they going to let him leave this building alive?

A horrible thought hit Stephen with wallop. What if Kaiser, or one of his minions, grabbed Milo during this interview?

Fuck.

He tried to push the thought out of his mind, but it was difficult with that damned red box and Melody's intense glare.

She sat opposite him and pressed a button on her tablet. A red light on the video camera blinked on in the corner of the room. Melody opened the box and retrieved a glove with wires and lights all along the outside. He'd never seen it, but had a feeling he knew its purpose when she asked him to put it on.

"What is this?"

"A biometric scanner to … a lie detector, basically."

Stephen considered joking to lighten the mood, but doing so would only make things worse between them. She had the humor of a four-foot coffin.

"Take off your jacket, roll up your left sleeve and give me your hand."

He set the jacket on the back of his chair, feeling the weight of the phone calling attention to its bulk, then sat and followed her instructions.

She slid the glove onto his hand, fastened a black metal cuff around the wrist, then let go and turned her attention to her tablet, where she opened up a display to control the glove.

The cuff tightened.

Stephen swallowed, trying to stay calm.

"State your name, please."

"Stephen Anderson."

She asked more basic questions to establish a baseline. He tried not to overthink things. To remove all emotion from his answers. When he inevitably lied, maybe it would be devoid of feeling, too.

After a couple of minutes, the questions changed. "When was the last time you had sex?"

"What does that have to do with anything?"

"Answer the question please."

"I don't know. Six months?"

No expression as she went into the next question. "Do you trust Conway Industries?"

"Yes," he lied.

Still no expression.

"Tell me about the incident at Hamilton Island Outdoor Market on Sunday."

He began telling her the truth up until the part where he enacted the preservation protocol.

"And what did you do afterward?"

"I called it in, then the room went dark, and I was asked to leave. Went home, had a sandwich, and watched TV."

"Before you called it in. Did you go back and rewind any of your feeds?"

They have to know, right?

May as well give them something.

"I don't know why. I just figured maybe I'd see something that led up to it, some explanation."

"Are you an investigator now?"

He fought the urge to glare at her.

"No."

"Then why did you rewind the subject?"

"I don't know."

"And what did you see?"

"I don't know. Nothing out of the ordinary."

The cuff on his wrist tightened. He grasped at the bracelet surrounding the top of the glove.

"Don't resist. It'll only get worse."

Melody stared down at her laptop, the screen at an angle that kept him from seeing it. "What did you see?"

The bracelet continued to tighten until a piercing pain ripped through his fingertips, like tiny electric eels pulsing from digits to wrist.

He screamed, tried to stand. Couldn't move anything from his neck down. "Make it stop!"

The glove stopped tightening, and the pain suddenly paused.

Stephen was able to move again, though he stayed in his chair.

She regarded the screen without meeting his gaze. "Tell the truth, Mr. Anderson. What did you see?"

He couldn't tell them.

If he did, they might not let him leave. They might grab Milo and kill them both.

"Nothing. I swear."

The glove tightened. Pain pierced his fingertips. He clenched his teeth, trying to ride it out.

Agony crept through his fingers and into his palm. Crossing his wrist, it intensified, then spread in several directions at once.

And that's when he saw them — the shapes beneath his skin, like tiny worms, burrowing, swimming up his arms, bringing fiery pain as they traveled through him.

"I can't be responsible for what happens once they reach your heart."

Stephen tried to get up again, but his body refused.

The worms raced across his biceps, his entire arm on fire, muscles twitching in hideous pain.

What would happen once they reached his heart? Would they stop it? That must've been what she meant. "Please!"

"Tell me what you saw."

The worms crossed from his arm and into his shoulder.

Pain intensified as they began to trail downward, toward his heart.

No, no, no!

He couldn't tell them.

Could not risk it.

Are they actually going to kill me?

Conway Industries was ruthless, but would they actually murder him for something they thought he saw?

The worms stopped just over his heart.

And then the pain got even worse.

Stephen screamed. Bellowed. Broke his voice box in two.

"Tell me, Mr. Anderson, and it'll stop."

"I saw him!"

"Saw who?"

"I saw Roger Heller!"

The pain stopped.

His entire body shook.

Tears streamed from his eyes.

He'd failed his son. Endangered them both.

Melody looked at him. "Saw Roger Heller? The teacher who killed himself?"

"Yes," Stephen said, because he had no more lies inside him.

Chapter 7- Milo Anderson

Milo woke with the world racing by in a blur.

It took a moment for him to realize he was in a car. Another moment to see Katie was driving. His head spun. "What's happening?"

"You fainted at the restaurant. I'm taking you to the medical center."

He wasn't sure why, but fear flooded his system. He tried to remember what he'd seen before passing out, but the world was still fuzzy. No matter what, Milo couldn't let her take him to the hospital.

"No."

"What?"

"I'm fine. Just … take me home. Please."

"No, you're *not* fine. You look like a ghost."

"Katie." He struggled to sit up, then fixed his gaze on her. "I'm fine. It happens sometimes. No big deal. Just please, take me home."

She stared at him for a moment before turning her attention to the road. "What do you mean *it happens sometimes?* What's wrong with you?"

"Just not getting much sleep. I'm okay. I promise. See?" He gave her a big, goofy smile.

She looked at him again. "Okay, but I'm staying with you until your dad gets home from work."

"If you really wanna punish yourself," he teased.

She laughed. Truth was, he was glad for the company. On the other hand, he was afraid he might see things again, maybe pass out, and then she would definitely take him where she thought he needed to go.

As she turned the car around, he wondered why the hell he was so afraid of going to the hospital.

Because they put it in you.

Because they'll put something else in you.

Then his mind flashed on the light worm in his eye.

He yanked down the passenger side visor, opened his eyes wide, and leaned in close to the mirror.

"What's wrong?"

He ignored Katie's question, concentrating, searching, moving his head around, blinking.

He turned to her. "Is there anything in my eyes?"

She looked at him like he was crazy.

"Never mind." He might very well scare her into taking him to the medical center. Milo turned back to the mirror, blinked a couple of times, then leaned back, trying to look calm.

She kept driving, but he felt her nervous gaze all over him.

He flashed back to his reflection, the one that wasn't there, then reappeared out of place — Mirror Milo.

No way that was real. It had to have been a hallucination. Which meant that the light worm was, as well. He remembered one time when he'd been sick as a child and had a really high fever and had thought he'd seen monsters above his bed.

This has to be a fever.

He resisted the urge to look in the mirror.

~

"WANT SOMETHING TO DRINK?" Milo looked in the fridge. "Got Coke, water, tea, or some weird-ass juice my dad drinks."

"I think I'll pass on the ass juice," she joked. "I'll have a Coke."

He grabbed two cans, brought them to the living room, and sat next to her on the couch.

She flipped on the TV as she started drinking. The news was full of stories about the killings.

Katie turned to him. "Do you ever think something weird is going on?"

"What do you mean?"

"Did Alex ever tell you about what happened with Jake and Ray?"

"Um … I can't remember. A lot of my memories from that time are fuzzy."

"Mine, too." Katie's eyes widened. "One day, Alex and I were skipping class, meeting at the racquetball courts, and we ran into those assholes, Jake and Ray. They used to bully Alex when they were younger, and this time was going to be worse. They were pissed at Alex because his father killed Eddie Tarroza, and they wanted payback, even if it was against Alex instead of Mr. Heller. Anyway, Jake came at Alex with a knife. He managed to avoid getting stabbed, but slammed Jake's head into the wall. Jake dropped. We thought he was dead. And Ray freaked out, got on top of Alex and was probably going to kill him. And then something happened."

"What?"

"I grabbed Ray and threw him off of Alex. But not *just* threw him. He went like ten feet. I don't know how, but I had … this power inside me. Nothing I've ever done before or since. It was … just there.

"After that, we took off into the woods. And Alex was

freaking out, thinking he'd killed Jake. He was totally losing it. Then it started storming, bad, and we found refuge in a cave. And … *something* happened, but I can't remember what. Just that … something happened. One minute we were … well, having sex, then I was falling asleep in his arms. Next thing I knew, I was in my bedroom. I don't know how I got there. Alex told me when he woke up, I was gone. He thought something had happened to me."

"And you don't remember?"

"No. And then I remember what you said that day you came over to the house acting all weird. About Bea zoning out in front of the TV before driving through the front of Jordy's supermarket. Mrs. Hawthorne saying something in a Survivor's Meeting about how Alex's dad had been seen doing the same thing."

Milo shook his head. "I said that? When?"

"The last time all three of us were together. Then you were scratching your arms and ran off. Next time I saw you was at the funeral service for Alex and his mom."

"I … I don't remember any of that."

"And you said something about some guy, Cody, who you'd been talking to about weird things happening on the island. What else did Cody say?"

"Cody? I … I don't know anyone named Cody."

Even as he said it, there was some familiarity with the name, a memory just past the edges. Milo closed his eyes, trying to dig deep into his foggy thoughts for anything to do with a Cody. He felt the memory, or memories, just past a darkness too black to see through.

"Fuck. I … I can't remember. They've had me on these drugs, and everything is a haze."

"What are they giving you?"

"Hold on." Milo got up, ran upstairs, grabbed the bottles from his bathroom vanity, then ran back down. He handed them to Katie.

She set down her Coke and began looking over the labels.

"Well, these are for anxiety and depression." She set three bottles aside. "But I've never heard of these two."

She grabbed her phone and searched for the names.

"I'm not seeing anything for either of these pills."

"*Nothing?*"

"Nothing." She showed him her search results, which suggested alternate spellings that weren't even close to either pill.

He picked up the bottles, dumped one of each into his hands and read off the letters and numbers on the pills, asking her to search for those.

"Nothing. Those pills don't exist."

"What the fuck am I taking?"

They stared at each other in silence. Milo couldn't help but feel like they were on the verge of some discovery, maybe something to do with his hallucinations. Or with whatever the hell was happening on the island.

He felt something on the periphery of his memories starting to reveal itself — a piece of paper.

A list with names.

He closed his eyes trying to see it better. To remember what was on it.

Names.

Names on a list.

Whose names?

He saw it in his mind's eye as clear as if it were in his hands right now, except for the fuzzy letters.

And then a name slowly took form.

His phone buzzed in his pocket, startling him and eroding his focus.

He grabbed it, his heart racing, and saw his father's name.

"Hello?" He tried not to sound as spooked as he was.

"How's it going?" His father almost never called during a workday. And he seemed ... *off.*

"Okay," Milo said, concerned, but not wanting to ask anything. It might be his paranoia. And that would only give Dad more reason for worry. "Katie came over to hang out."

"And … everything's okay?"

"Yeah. Why wouldn't it be?"

"No reason. Just checking in. How's Katie?"

"Good. Wanna talk to her?"

"Nah, that's okay. You two have fun. I'll see you later."

"Okay, see ya later, Dad."

"Milo?"

"Yes?"

"I love you, son."

His father almost never said he loved him. Milo fought the urge to ask if something was wrong. Instead, he said, "I love you, too."

His father hung up.

Katie stared at Milo. "What's wrong?"

"I don't know, but definitely *something*."

Chapter 8 - Stephen Anderson

Getting drunk was the last thing Stephen should've done after leaving the interrogation, but damn it if he didn't need a drink or five to calm his frazzled nerves.

He sat at the Shipwrecked bar, tossing back his third whiskey as he thought about his morning.

After telling Melody he saw Roger Heller, alive and well, through Subject C10920's eyes, he was ushered into another room where he waited, half-certain he wouldn't live to see his son again.

Kaiser came in, asked him to review what he'd seen. Afterward, Kaiser reminded him of three things. First, he'd signed confidentiality agreements. Second, they had his wife, Bea, in the mental facility and if he ever wanted to see her again, he'd best play ball. And last, Milo could be in a room next to her.

"And, Kaiser said, "just in case none of those things motivates you, remember, nobody asks questions when a body is found to have leapt from Tanner's Pass. Do we have an understanding?"

"You don't need to threaten me. Why would I jeopardize my career, not to mention my family, to harm the company I owe my life to, over something that doesn't even make sense?"

"Good," Kaiser had said. "You're free to go."

His heart had raced the entire time as he walked to his car, certain someone would grab him at any moment, put a black bag over his head, and make him disappear.

It wasn't until he'd gotten a half-mile away that he pulled over, vomited into the dirt, then turned off the failsafe before it sent Milo a message to get out of the house and run.

He called his son to make sure things were okay. Milo had Katie, Alex's ex-girlfriend, over. Stephen knew Milo once had a thing for Katie but wasn't sure if anything had come of it. He hoped something good, something normal, could come out of them spending time together. Milo deserved a childhood, not an adolescence under a microscope where he watched his friends die and his stepmother nearly kill them both. Where his mind had been wiped.

Stephen had cried for nearly fifteen minutes after talking to his son. Then he'd headed to Shipwrecked. And now he sat, trying to drown his sorrows.

"Another Jack?" Cassidy asked.

"Yes, please."

She filled his glass to the brim. "Rough day?"

Stephen laughed as he took a gulp. "Yeah, you could say that."

"Anything you wanna talk about?"

Stephen looked up at her. Her eyes were so kind. He'd known of her from the bar and that she was twin sister to the teacher who had been killed in Roger Heller's shooting. Knew she'd briefly dated Jon Conway. Things fell apart after his daughter, Emma, died. He'd also heard rumors about drugs.

But none of those things made her eyes any less kind.

"Not if I wanna live," he said, immediately regretting his bluntness.

She picked up on his tension. "Ah, running from the mob, eh? What is it? Into them for gambling debt? No, wait … you were in the mob then ratted them out, right? Need somewhere to hide? I've got a shotgun under the bar and can get at least two of 'em before they've even drawn their guns."

"Two, huh?" He played along.

"Two, maybe three. Six if I've got my pistol. But it's in my purse in my locker."

"Wow, I guess it's my lucky day to run into the reincarnation of Annie Oakley."

"Why's it gotta be a woman? Maybe I was Billy the Kid or Wyatt Earp. In a past life, I could've been anyone. Right?" She smiled coyly.

"Fair enough." He raised his glass as if toasting her. "To Billy the Kid." He kicked the drink back then set his glass on the bar.

She didn't rush to refill it. Nor did he ask. He hadn't eaten anything, so he asked her for a menu. "How are the burgers here?"

Cassidy smirked. "They won't kill you."

"Wow, that's a ringing endorsement."

She laughed. "They're all right, for a bar."

"Okay, I'll have a cheeseburger, well-done, and fries. With a Coke."

"Sure thing, pardner," she teased.

He took his time eating over small talk with Cass, which she said she liked better than Cassidy. After about an hour, he wasn't sure if it was the whiskey or her company, but he was feeling a little less anxious.

Truth was, he didn't want to leave. It had been a while since he'd had a normal adult conversation, especially one with a beautiful woman. He felt a bit guilty thinking about someone else with Bea in the mental facility, but she was far enough gone that she wasn't ever coming back.

He'd lost her. Just like his first wife, Lisa, who'd just vanished without a word five years ago. He'd loved them each dearly, and they were both gone, one way or another.

And he was alone, struggling to raise a son whose life he barely felt able to protect.

He was desperate for conversation, something resembling normal. Cassidy's humor and kindness lifted him. She was safe to talk to. Drug addiction made a horrible candidate for any of Conway Industries' secret programs, and she wasn't being monitored.

A part of him wanted to talk to her all night, to tell her, to tell someone, what he'd seen. *Roger Heller is alive!*

But he couldn't endanger her. Just because she wasn't being monitored didn't mean that everyone else in the bar was safe. He looked around, wondering if anyone was being watched, or hell, was maybe an undercover or off-duty Paladin officer, following him, spying on him.

And saying anything would get Cassidy killed.

Still, he didn't want to leave.

But he couldn't drink any more, nor could he eat another bite. No, he had to head home.

"Thanks." He paid his bill and left a generous tip.

"Anytime you want crappy burgers and heartburn, we're here."

He smiled. "All right, Billy. See ya next time."

Stephen left the bar, engaged the Autodrive, and closed his eyes as it drove him home.

IT WAS NEARLY DINNER, so Stephen wasn't exactly surprised when he went inside to find Milo and Katie eating pizza on the couch, watching a movie and sitting *close*.

He wondered if Milo had ever kissed a girl. A father ought to know these things, and yet he didn't. And then he thought how awful it would be if something were to happen to his son before he had that first kiss or date.

Stephen felt a sting of sadness and made a mental note to ask Milo if he'd ever kissed a girl.

Or, maybe not. It'll only embarrass him.

He thought of Kaiser's threat — were he and Milo safe? They'd let him walk out of Conway Industries. Would they have let him walk out if they planned to kill him? Or might they reconsider, decide it was an error, and come for them later?

His sadness turned to anxiety, tightening his chest.

He looked at the windows and his wide-open curtains. A sniper could fire on them at any moment. He grabbed his phone and pressed a button to close the curtains in every room, then locked the front and back doors. He engaged the security, knowing all of this was a joke if Paladin *really* wanted him.

"Hey, kids, how's it going?" he asked from the kitchen, setting his phone and keys on the island, keeping his distance lest they smell the shots on his breath.

"Good, Mr. Anderson. Want some pizza? It's still hot."

"Maybe after I shower." Then he made his way upstairs. He went into his bedroom, closed and locked the door. In the bathroom, Stephen turned on the shower. As the water warmed, he bent down, opened the cabinet under the sink, pulled out bottles of cleaning sprays and a few folded hand towels, then reached into a recess in the corner of the cabinet floor. He pulled up the wood and set it aside.

Then he reached into the hidden space and retrieved what he was looking for — a Ruger SP101 and a full box of ammo.

Episode 15

Prologue

Three months ago …

ROGER HELLER WAS WORKING on Deck 3, teaching class for the eleven children aboard the space station, when he felt a flush of rage from nowhere.

It was what Doctor Hanz Engel had often referred to as a cross-stream, picking up a random memory or emotion from the man he was cloned from, the original Roger Heller down on Earth.

Something was wrong with the other Roger, his mind a cacophony of dark and scary emotions as he was walking toward his classroom.

What's wrong?

What are you doing?

Clone Roger had had many moments of cross streaming with Earth Roger since he'd *come online,* as Hanz referred to his first days two years ago. Most of the cross streams had been pleasant moments with Roger's family, or mundane moments at work. Every now and then, an anxiety or worry that Earth

Roger was experiencing would be felt by Clone Roger in the heavens above.

But lately, the streams had come less often. Clone Roger wondered if someone had somehow severed their connection.

But now, this … anguish and confusion was all too much.

A sudden pain sent him to the ground, clutching at his skull to keep it from exploding.

He could hear alarm in his students' voices as the youngest among them began to cry and others asked if he was okay. He couldn't respond. The pain was too intense. He could only suffer through it, wait for it to pass.

And then he saw a flash of Earth Roger taking the gun out of his briefcase.

What are you doing?

The man answered by taking aim at his class and opening fire.

Clone Roger was now fully connected, seeing everything through Earth Roger's eyes. A passenger inside Earth Roger, feeling and seeing everything with him, even smelling the blood, piss, and fear like a fog in the room.

"No!" Roger cried, as if he could appeal to Earth Roger and keep him from killing anybody else.

And then Roger was looking down at one of his students. A boy named Manny.

He leaned down, stared at the boy. Clone Roger could feel his doppelgänger's loathing for the child. He didn't view what he'd done as murder, even as the boy's blood leaked to the last drop from his body.

Earth Roger didn't think of Manny as human. Instead, he viewed him as some alien creature that needed to die.

He bent down and whispered to the boy, "Tell them my mind is my own."

Clone Roger wasn't sure *what* he meant by that.

Earth Roger turned around and looked down at another child, one that Clone Roger remembered from prior memories. His son's friend, Milo. They'd gone to a minor league baseball game last summer, a fond memory that Clone Roger enjoyed.

No. No. No. Do not kill Milo!

"Please, don't kill me," Milo cried. "I'm friends with Alex. You know me!"

Earth Roger's certainty fell apart.

He stared down at the boy, realized he wasn't an alien. He was, in fact, human. Milo Anderson, Alex's best friend.

And when Roger thought of his son, tears streamed down his cheeks.

What the hell have I done?

He looked around the classroom, at the bodies on the floor. None of them aliens. All of them very human.

God, no.

Then he looked at the whiteboard, pointed at the word he'd written —*Eleven.*

Oh, God. What have I done?

He raised the pistol, put it in his mouth, and fired.

Clone Roger screamed as his mind kicked violently out of Earth Roger's body and back into his own.

He looked around his classroom, half expecting to see dead children. But they were all alive, cowering in back of the class.

"Are you okay?" asked a girl whose name escaped him.

Roger Heller shook his head. No, he absolutely was not.

Chapter 1 - Sarah Hughes

Sarah longed to stay beneath her silken sheets.

She and Emma shared a large bed in a spacious suite that looked like a decent-sized city apartment, located in the Employee Living Quarters section of the space station.

It was, "Grandpa Billy" assured her, the best accommodations afforded any of the subjects. Because, he liked to remind her, she and Emma weren't just any subjects. They were *family*.

Billy was far kinder to her than Blake had ever been, though she didn't trust him a single molecule more. Whatever they were doing up here started with Billy, not Blake. And both of the Conway men were responsible for her and Emma's imprisonment.

Family.

Family didn't kidnap you and keep you aboard a space station to run weird scientific experiments on you.

Family didn't spend decades abducting you in the middle of the night then erasing your memories.

Family didn't allow your loved ones on Earth to think you were dead.

Yet, Billy had promised to help make her and Emma's lives as close to what they were before Roger Heller had ended her old life with a stray bullet. He arranged for them to be in better housing. He ensured Emma went to school with the other kids aboard the station and didn't subject her to any of the harrowing experiments that Sarah endured when she first arrived, tests she only remembered in glimpses that occasionally turned her dreams into nightmares. These days the experiments were more mundane.

She should be thankful for that much. Surprisingly, she and Emma were growing accustomed to this new normal.

Emma woke up and popped out of bed, practically singing, "Good morning, Mommy. What do you want for breakfast?"

"Sleep," Sarah joked as she turned over in the bed and pulled the covers up over her head. Then she peeked at Emma.

Her daughter laughed, then bounded off to the kitchen with so much energy that Sarah wished *she* could go back to being nine.

"Want oatmeal?" Emma called out from the kitchen.

"Okay," Sarah said, though she didn't care much for the space station's version of healthy cereal, a flavorless, way too crunchy mix of grains that failed to be anywhere near as good as the oatmeal she was used to, with cream and honey or sugar.

Nothing sweet on the space station, save for the strains of bananas, apples, and oranges grown in the greenhouses.

"Take your shower, Mommy." Emma placed ingredients in the glass bowl then into the microwave.

Sarah climbed out of bed, undressed, then got into the shower, scrubbing up quickly and enjoying the brief allowance of water.

She brushed her teeth and looked at the dark circles under her eyes, then brushed her hair.

After getting dressed, she met Emma at the small circular table in the kitchen where breakfast was waiting.

Emma was already dressed in her favorite white dress, ready for school.

"I sliced banana for yours," Emma said, smiling.

"Thank you, Em."

"No problem." She said eating hers, filled with raisins and cinnamon.

"So, what are you doing in class today?"

"We're going to be tested on science. And then I think Doctor Engel is going to have us compete again."

"You haven't told anyone about Daddy, have you?" Sarah whispered, just in case they were being monitored, which she assumed they always were.

"No."

"Good."

Emma had been trying to reach Jon when he slept. Just as Sarah could sometimes reach Cassidy, knowing what she was feeling and even thinking, Emma had a similar link to her father.

She'd told Sarah some rather vivid descriptions of him talking with his agent, Marty, or his assistant, Alicia. She'd also seen him with Cassidy, though not for a while since they had broken up. And when Jon was asleep, she could engage him. She'd even brought him into one of her dreams, inviting him to the garden, telling him that they were alive and trapped on the space station, and to please help them.

But help never came. Sarah had to assume that he'd forgotten, or dismissed it as a dream that was too wild for him to lasso.

Sarah told Emma to keep trying to reach him, to tell him about the portal in his father's office, to contact the authorities, God knew who, and tell them.

"It has to be our secret, Emma. Okay? We can't trust anyone else up here. Nobody, no matter how nice. Do you understand?"

Emma nodded, but Sarah wasn't sure she got the message.

The girl loved being praised by her teacher and the doctor, and anyone else who would compliment her for doing cool things that nobody else could do. For using "her powers," as she called them. Sarah feared she'd let it slip during one of her tests that she'd also been able to communicate with her father. If that happened, they would put a permanent end to it, for sure.

Sarah urged her to keep this one power to herself, or else they might separate them forever.

"What did the doctor have you do last week?"

"He had us passing messages to each other using just our minds."

"And how did you do?"

"Best in the class," Emma beamed. "Even better than Kaylee."

Kaylee was the most popular girl on the ship, having been the newest kid prior to Emma's arrival. But her status changed once Emma's appeared, and she'd been taking it out on her ever since.

"You didn't say anything to make her feel bad, did you?"

"No. Though some of the kids did. I felt bad for her. But then she was just mean, so whatever."

"It's okay. Just give her some time. Eventually, you two might be best of friends."

"No way. She's mean. I like Christina more. I don't need any other friends."

"There are only eight other children up here. You'll need all the friends you can get, kid."

"No, I don't," Emma said self-assuredly. "Besides, we're going to go home, anyway."

"We don't know when we're going home, so don't get your hopes up."

Sarah didn't want her to start talking about the attempts at communication with Jon out loud. She gave her a subtle wink.

Emma, thankfully, caught it then changed the subject. "What are you doing today?"

"I'm not sure. I have an appointment with Dr. Engel."

"I'm sorry."

"Why are you sorry? It's okay."

"No, you're never *you* after your tests."

"What do you mean?"

"I dunno. You're just not you. You're different somehow. Hard to say."

Sarah hadn't noticed any difference in herself after those tests, though Emma's bringing it up made her wonder if they weren't in fact still subjecting her to the bad tests and removing her memories.

Of all the things she hated about being up here, that might have been the worst — not knowing her own mind and having her most precious of memories subject to alteration. Billy had promised no more "memory wipes" after a particularly bad panic attack a month or so ago.

Had he been lying?

A computerized voice spoke: "You have a visitor name Roger Heller. Shall I open the door?"

Sarah looked at the clock on the wall. Roger picked up Emma each school morning promptly at 7:45 on his way to teach her class, but today he was ten minutes early.

"Yes, let him in," Sarah said.

The door unlocked and slid open.

Roger usually came with a couple of the other kids whose parents were already working, but today he entered alone. "Hi."

"Hi, Mr. Roger." Emma hopped out of her chair to hug him.

He looked past Emma and met Sarah's gaze with sad eyes.

"Hi, Roger. What's going on?"

Roger was the closest thing to a friend she had on the ship.

Yes, he wasn't her Roger, whom she'd been good friends with before he'd lost his mind. Rather, he was one of the clones. But he shared so many of Roger's qualities and memories, it was hard not to enjoy his presence.

"I wanted to come tell you the news before class, Emma."

Her brow furrowed. Something unpleasant was coming. She bit her bottom lip.

"Your friend, Christina won't be in class anymore."

"What?"

"She went back home."

"*Home?*"

"Yes. She's all done up here. She was ready to go back."

Emma's lip began to tremble and her eyes filled with tears.

She ran to her bed, threw herself on it, and started bawling.

Roger looked at Sarah, "I'm sorry."

"It's okay, honey." Sarah went to the bed and rubbed Emma's back.

"She was my only friend! I want to go home, too."

"We will, baby. Someday."

"I want to go now!"

"I know, Emma. So do I."

Roger wiped at the corners of his eyes. "I know it'll be hard, but I promise we'll have fun today. We can all tell our favorite stories about Christina. Do you have any stories about her that you'd like to share? I know you two spent a lot of time together, playing in the recreation area and reading books together in the library."

"I dunno," Emma said, wiping at her snot.

Sarah handed her some napkins then told her to blow her nose. "I'm sure you've got something you can say. How about that time that you and Christina drew those funny animals, and kept trying to make even more ridiculous ones? Or ... what about that time you were in the cafeteria and you made her laugh so hard, pudding came out of her nose?"

Emma laughed.

"See," Roger said. "We can all tell our favorite Christina stories. And we'll do some fun stuff before testing. But I need your help today, Emma. I know the other kids are gonna be sad, too. It's always hard when one of them leaves. I need your help in making the other kids feel a little less sad. Can you do that?"

"How can I do that when I'm sad?"

"Well, that's the thing about helping to make other people smile. When you spread joy to others, it grows in you."

Emma smiled.

"He's right," Sarah said. "And I think the fact that Mr. Roger is asking you to help him shows he thinks you're probably very capable of spreading joy."

"Just like your mother," Roger said, meeting her eyes, reminding her so much of her friendly exchanges with the other Roger that it only made her sad for the tragedy that had ended his life. Nobody on the ship would talk much about it, but she had the distinct feeling that Roger going crazy had to be tied to something they'd done to him. Maybe they'd brought him aboard the space station, too. She wasn't sure if he had a twin, and they tended to test mostly though not exclusively on twins.

"You need a few more minutes?" Roger asked Emma.

She shook her head. "No, I'm ready."

Sarah hugged and kissed Emma goodbye, same as she always did, but even a little more so today. "I'm so proud of you."

"Do I have to spread joy to Kaylee?" Emma whispered in her ear.

"Especially Kaylee," Sarah said with a smile.

"Ugh," Emma said with a long and exaggerated sigh.

Roger laughed.

Emma headed out the door. Sarah walked them out. As they reached the threshold, Roger surprised her with a hug.

While they'd talked a lot, he had always maintained his distance and remained somewhat reserved.

He slipped something into her dress pocket.

"Take care, Sarah." He met her gaze as if to confirm she knew he'd passed her a secret.

"Take care," she said with a nod.

They left, and the door slid shut.

Sarah took the bowls to the kitchen sink, set them inside, then made her way to the bathroom.

Safe where Billy promised there were no cameras, she reached into her pocket and palmed the piece of paper.

She still didn't completely trust that the bathroom was entirely safe, she was careful in unfolding the note, never showing it to a mirror that might be a snitch.

She opened the letter just enough to read the message scrawled inside.

NEED TO TALK WHEN I DROP EMMA OFF. IMPORTANT.

Chapter 2 - Jon Conway

Marty paced in Jon's hotel room. Alicia sat in a chair opposite him.

Jon was too numb to move and could barely stare at the video playing on his tablet.

"Fuck, fuck, FUCK!" Marty said, for maybe the tenth time, "how could you let this happen?"

"I didn't know she was recording me!"

"I know a fixer. He can take care of this," Alicia said.

Jon wished Houser was still around. *He* would know how to handle this.

"Get him on the phone," Marty said.

Alicia was already dialing.

Jon stared at the screen, then clicked back to the email which demanded one million dollars in cryptocurrency. If they didn't pay in forty-eight hours, the video would be leaked online. And once that happened, Jon would be fucked. The media would run with the story of how just months after his daughter's death, he's back to his drunken, drugged, partying ways, fucking women on the set of his new movie. The very sorts of things that he was trying to get away from as he rehabilitated his image.

The violation was even worse.

He'd been drugged. He'd been set up. And someone had filmed him in the most intimate of acts.

Oh, God. Cassidy. When she saw …

Whatever slim chance they had of ever getting back together, it was now destroyed.

Marty was talking, though Jon wasn't sure if it was to reassure him or himself. "Okay, this isn't the end of the world if it does get out. The first *Black Nova* movie won't be out for another two and half years, right? We'll spin the fuck out of this. Tell the press how you are the victim here, not the asshole."

"Yeah, but after the Cooper Ford incident, the Maris Brothers would be crazy not to let me go."

"Maybe this goes away and the Maris Brothers never find out," Marty said, rarely ever optimistic about anything, let alone man's inclination not to fuck over his fellow man.

"But what if it doesn't go away? What if these scumbags take their money and go but then leak it anyway?"

"Let's just hope it happens far enough into production that they can't fire you without having to do a ton of reshoots."

Jon shook his head. "I dunno. Maybe we should just go to them and explain what happened?"

"No." Marty shook his head. "That is exactly not the thing we will do. We'll see what Alicia's fixer suggests."

They both looked at Alicia, on the phone talking in a hushed voice.

Jon hated that his future was in the hands of fucking criminals. He was dying for a drink.

He got up, went to the bar, and poured himself a whiskey.

Marty and Alicia shared a disapproving glance.

He ignored them both and downed the glass, then set it on the kitchenette counter as if to show his restraint and that he only needed one to take the edge off.

Alicia hung up. "Okay, my guy is on it."

"Who is your guy?" Marty asked.

"Darius Salton, one of the best. I'm sending him the email we got. He'll get what he can on them, see if we can't turn this around, put a scare into them."

"And if we can't?" Marty asked.

"Then we probably pay and hope for the best. But let's see what Salton says."

Jon closed his eyes. Now his future was in the hands of unknown criminals and a fixer.

Goddammit, he needed another drink.

WHILE ALICIA WAITED to hear back from the fixer, she spent much of the morning monitoring social media for any mention of Jon's name — waiting for the dreadful "porn tape" to drop.

"It doesn't make it easy to monitor your name after that shit with the photographer," she scolded.

"Hey, not my fault you were out with the flu and not there to protect me," he joked.

She gave him a look, then went back to scrolling through mentions. "Between that and the Conway Illuminati conspiracy theorists saying your family engineered the incident on Hamilton, you're all over the Internet this week!"

"Yay?" Jon kicked back another shot of whiskey.

Marty had some errands to run, which Jon took to mean he was going to go out with Sharon and the kids. He'd brought them along for the first few months while he stayed with Jon to make sure everything was going okay.

He spent the next hour and a half on the phone talking to both Maris Brothers about changes to the script. They'd incorporated all of his notes, even the ones he thought they might push back on, and were going to send over revisions in the morning.

They confirmed production would start in just two more weeks.

It was hard talking to them, hearing the joy in their voices as they looked forward to doing *Black Nova* with him, when he couldn't help but wonder when the bombshell would drop.

It would be a long two weeks, waiting to see if his world would fall apart. It would be hard to focus on anything. Hell to get through without drinking, a lot.

Their phone call ended just before lunchtime, and Jon had already emptied so many glasses, he'd forgotten how much he'd drank. But he was feeling good enough. At least for now.

Alicia set her tablet aside and looked at him. "So, I was going to ask if you want to go to lunch, but you look like shit."

"Thanks!" He lifted his glass with a giggle. "I'm good. You go."

"You sure?"

"Yeah. I'm gonna catch up on my social media. Maybe post some things."

"Um, no. You are forbidden from reading or posting to your social media."

"Fine. I'll take a nap. Didn't sleep much last night, anyway."

"Okay. After lunch, I'll be in my room if you need anything."

She was staying at the same hotel as Jon and Marty. Per custom, they rented the entire top floor.

"Gotcha." He poured himself another drink.

"Please tell me that's the last one for now?"

He looked up with a smile. "It's the last drink ... for now."

She shook her head. "You're incorrigible."

He winked at her.

She turned and left.

While Jon was exhausted, he needed something for his mind, so he decided to lie in bed and look for a movie. He flipped through the selection, finally settling on an indie horror flick he'd missed in the theaters.

His eyes grew tired as it started, then they closed.

It was pitch black when he woke, except for the TV, which was all static and white noise.

He reached for the remote to turn it off, but it had gone missing from the nightstand.

Groggy, still half asleep and fully hungover, Jon leaned over to see if the remote had fallen and was maybe under the bed. He reached underneath, now on his stomach, fingers fumbling blindly.

The static flickered. White noise punctuated by a vaguely familiar clicking.

His hand still groped the carpet as he turned toward the TV to see if something had come on-screen.

Still static.

His fingers felt the tip of the remote.

He tried to grab it, but only pushed it farther under the bed.

"Fuck." He nudged himself more toward the edge of the bed so he could extend his reach.

But his fingers found nothing.

"Damn it." He got out of bed then knelt, his back to the TV as he leaned down to look under the bed.

The TV died and cast the room into darkness.

Great!

He reached under the bed, into the black, figuring the remote couldn't have gotten too far, and finally his fingers brushed against it.

Gotcha!

He grabbed it, but the thing was sticky.

What the hell?

He considered leaving the remote where it was. God only knew what was on it. Maybe he'd puked or something, though his mouth didn't taste like vomit.

The TV came back on behind him. The white noise was louder.

He grabbed the remote, sat up and looked down at it, trying to discern what the dark goo might be.

It wasn't puke. Or blood. It looked like thick oil or something.

He brought it to his nose to smell it and was overwhelmed with a strong, bitter stench unlike anything he'd ever smelled.

He dropped the remote.

And then, out of the corner of his eye, saw a shadow on the wall in front of him.

Someone was behind him, standing in front of the TV.

Jon tried to turn around to see who it was, but his body was frozen.

What the hell?

Dread gripped his throat, tightened around his chest, dripped down his back.

He heard breathing.

Was it that Russian woman? Did she drug him again? Or maybe it was whomever she was working with.

He tried to speak, to ask who it was, to plead for them to leave, but his mouth was stuck open, his vocal chords frozen taut.

The shadow grew closer.

Footsteps on the carpet behind him.

What the hell is happening?

All he could do was stare at the shadow on the wall, trying to discern identity from darkness.

Cracks and pops interrupted the white noise, like some sort of ancient signal being broadcast from millions of light-years away.

The breathing was right behind him.

He could feel the warmth on his neck.

Again, he tried to speak, to beg whoever was behind him

to please not hurt him. And again, his body failed to obey the screaming in his mind.

He braced himself for all the horrible things that might happen to him so far from home. A gunshot to the back of the head, a knife slitting his throat, a …

Hand on his shoulder.

Jon pissed himself.

The white noise grew louder, the clicks and pops more pronounced.

And the breath behind him, now in his ear. "Daddy?"

A girl's voice. No, not *a* girl. *Emma.*

"What's in the hole?" she asked.

The hole?

He turned around …

JON'S EYES SHOT OPEN.

He was kneeling on the floor, his pants wet with hot piss.

And the remote was in his hand, though it wasn't sticky.

He whipped toward the TV.

The set was off, and there was no sign of his daughter. And he had the oddest sense of déjà vu.

Chapter 3 - Cassidy Hughes

Thunder rolled outside, rain pelting the windows and the roof of their bedroom.

Happiness spread its warmth through Cassidy's body as Jon kissed her, then pulled the covers over them both, as if to say goodbye to the world outside.

It was just them.

The way it should be.

The only thing that had ever felt right in her life.

His warm skin against hers felt like home.

His kisses along her neck were a familiar song that belonged only to them.

Everything was perfect in this moment. She wanted to seal it in a bottle impervious to the cruelties of time. Cling to this moment forever and let it play in an endless loop.

Just her and him.

The only person she'd ever let inside. The only person she'd ever loved.

Just them.

She closed her eyes as his kisses trailed downward. Though his lovemaking was familiar and comforting, there was still enough mystery to give flight to her butterflies.

Where might he touch her next? What pleasures would unfold?

Perfection.

Forever.

Thunder rolled again.

Except it wasn't thunder.

It was the sound of muffled knocking on their bedroom door.

He pulled away, about to get out of bed.

She called out, "No. Just leave it."

But he was already up and floating over.

Lightning lit the walls.

The butterflies all drowned in an acid anxiety.

He opened the door.

It was her sister, Sarah.

And Emma.

Both of them dead, yet alive.

Sarah pointed at Cass and cried out, "How could you?"

Emma turned her head that funny way she did when confused, except this time it wasn't funny, and Cass shook her head, crying. "It's not what you think."

Emma's head rolled off her shoulders and then onto the floor.

Cassidy woke up screaming.

"I knew it!" Vivian yelled.

"What?" Cass said, confused as the dream world crashed into her waking one — if this was, in fact, the real world and not another dream.

"How could you?" Vivian shook the bottle of pills that Craig had thrown into her car last night.

Shit!

Did she bring them in? Did she take any?

She couldn't remember, and that scared her.

"I knew you took my pills, you lying shit!"

Lying shit?

Cass shot up. "Those aren't your pills!"

"Yeah, who's are they? Yours?"

"No, some asshole at the bar slipped them into my pocket last night. I didn't even notice until I was getting in the car. Where did you even find them? Did you go through my car?"

"I have every right to go through your stuff if you're staying at my house! How long?"

"How long what?" Cass said, getting up, still wearing the clothes she wore to work last night. She must've passed straight out.

God, she hoped she didn't take any pills. She didn't feel that hungover, so she was probably good.

"How long have you been using?"

"I'm not using! I swear!"

"Ha! If I had a dollar for every time you swore you weren't." Viv laughed, shaking her head. "I don't even know why I bother. You'll never change."

Tears burned at the corners of Cassidy's eyes. It was one thing to be accused of doing drugs when she was actually doing them, but she'd been clean ever since that night Jon left, and damn it, why couldn't her own mother give her the benefit of the doubt? Why couldn't she see that she was doing better?

"You know, Mom, I'm not using. But if I were, I'd expect you, of all people, to show some damned compassion. How long did I take care of you when you were a fucking drunk? How many years when I was a teenager did I have to make sure you didn't leave a cigarette burning after you passed out? How many times did I have to clean up your messes? How many times did I have to lie to cover your ass? And you stand here accusing *me* of something I didn't even do?"

Cass's voice hit that high-pitched whine she hated hearing out of her own mouth.

Vivian stared at her, eyes glaring, face turning so red it was on the verge of purple, as she built up whatever was going to explode out of her yell hole.

And then Viv let her have it.

"You took care of me? *You* took care of me? Ha! Is that what you tell yourself when you're going to sleep, that it was *you* and not Sarah that took care of me? Yes, I was a drunk for far too long, and I wish I could take back all those years, but you were barely home. It was your sister who looked after me while you were out whoring around, being a pathetic junkie!"

Cass slapped her mother across the face.

And then time froze.

Vivian stared in shock. Cass looked down at her hand, unable to believe that she'd hit her mother.

But she couldn't apologize. Not after Viv called her *that word*, the same word Jon had used on her that last night. Viv had no idea Jon had called her that, but still, it hurt.

Viv continued glaring, her eyes watering. Then she finally spoke. "Get out."

"Fine!" Cass grabbed her bag off the floor, threw clothes into it, got her shit together as fast as she could while Viv stared her down.

Then her mother stomped downstairs as Cass grabbed her essentials and stuffed them into her overnight bag.

It was too full to zip.

"Fuck it." She grabbed the bag, hefted it off the bed, and carried it out of the room, not even caring that stuff was falling out.

Viv was in the kitchen, slamming cupboards as she did God only knew what. Maybe she was looking for a hidden bottle of alcohol?

Good, get drunk, you hypocrite!

"Where you going to go?" Viv asked from the kitchen. "You're too damned proud to live in the house that Jon got for you both!"

Cass didn't bother to explain it had nothing to do with

pride, but rather the painful memories inside the place. Where they lost Emma. Where he broke her heart and she his. Viv would never understand.

Cass stormed out of the house, practically knocking the door off its hinges as she shoved it open. She dropped her bag the passenger side of her car, then slammed the door.

Neighbors were outside, looking at her like the nosey gossip-hungry fucks they were. She considered saying something for their benefit, but instead she got in her car, started the engine, then threw it in reverse.

Viv was in the rearview mirror, standing there.

Cass slammed on the brakes, almost running her mother over.

"What the fuck?" Cass screamed, tears streaming down her cheeks.

Her mother walked around to the passenger side and yanked it open.

Was she getting inside? Was she going to give her one last talking to or I Told You So?

She threw the bottle of pills into the car, just as Craig had, and yelled, "Don't forget your fucking pills!"

Then she slammed the door.

Cass hit the gas, leaving Viv and the nosey fucking neighbors in her trail, screaming as the rubber burned behind her.

Chapter 4 - Emma Hughes

After lunch, Mr. Roger told Emma it was time for her testing.

Emma hoped it wasn't that creepy Doctor Engel, and smiled when she saw instead that it was Great Grandpa Billy.

"Grandpa!" She ran into his arms.

He picked her up into a big, warm hug. "How's my Emma Bear?"

"Good, Grandpa. How are you?"

"Still kickin' and tickin'." He smiled as he thumped at his chest. "You ready for a fun one today?"

"Yeah!"

Grandpa Billy led her to the gardens, which was Emma's favorite place on the station. Not only because of all the pretty flowers, but because of the animals. The gardens were huge, and if you were especially quiet, you'd see birds, squirrels, and sometimes even a fox.

Grandpa sat her down on the bench. "You really like the gardens, don't you?"

"Yes. They're beautiful."

He went to a bush, picked a blue flower, then put it behind her ear. "A cornflower. Beautiful like you, my child."

She smiled. Grandpa Billy was nice, even if Mommy said not to trust him one hundred percent.

"When I was a kid, there were these beautiful gardens on Hamilton Island. I'm not sure who originally put them there, but I loved going there to find myself. You know what I mean?"

Emma wasn't sure if she did, but she nodded because she wanted Grandpa Billy to think her smart.

"So, when I got a bit older, I went to the spot where the garden was only to find that men had knocked them down and built some small homes. I bought those homes, knocked them all down, and built my new home there, Conway Gardens. I was never able to fully create the gardens. And your grandfather, Blake, eventually knocked down almost all of it to put in a tennis court and larger pool. So, I guess these days Conway Gardens is a garden only in name. Anyway, when I came up here, this was the first thing they let me bring with me, or at least recreate."

"Who are *they?* You keep talking about them, but why haven't we ever met them? Are they aliens?"

"They're not from our world, no. They call themselves *The Ones,* an ancient civilization who spread out across the stars a very long time ago."

"And they're on the space station?"

"This is their space station, honey. There's only one of them on the ship, though. I met it as a child."

"It?"

"They're not male or female like us. They're something altogether different."

"When can I meet it?"

"They're very private, honey. They know most people aren't ready to see them, and they don't want to interfere with the progress happening up here. They are getting us ready for the next step in evolution, and that means not scaring us by showing themselves."

"You saw it, though. Were *you* scared?"

"That was a bit different. I was much younger, and I was running from people who wanted to kill me. I fell down a deep hole. It saved me. So, no, I wasn't afraid. But most people aren't ready."

She frowned. Usually, when she did this, adults would give in.

But Grandpa Billy shook his head. "Nice try, kiddo. No guilt-tripping me. But I will say this, of all the people I've met, I think you are most ready to meet them. You've come very far in your lessons and tests."

"Thank you."

"Speaking of which, do you know why I brought you here today instead of the testing chambers?"

"No. Why?"

"Because this is the only place on the ship where we have privacy. No cameras, nobody watching or listening to us. You can tell me anything here. Do you have anything to tell me?"

She felt bad lying to Grandpa Billy about trying to contact her dad. But she had to trust her mother's warning.

As nice as Grandpa Billy is, he wants us up here. He doesn't want us to leave. So we can't tell him.

"Like what?" Emma asked, smiling, hoping he couldn't tell she was lying.

"I dunno. Anything you haven't been able to tell anyone else? Things you worry about? Maybe things you miss from home?"

"Like my dad?"

"Yes, like him. Do you miss him a lot?"

"Yes. Do you think he'll ever come up here?"

"Yes, someday. When he's ready. Like I said, some people are ready before others. Anything else that you miss? Does your mother miss anyone?"

"She doesn't talk about missing anyone. I think she's happy just to have me here."

"You don't think she wants to go home?"

A part of Emma wanted to say yes, that they both wanted to go home, because maybe Grandpa Billy didn't know they wanted to go home. And maybe if he did know, he'd let them leave.

But she kept up with the lie. "No, I think she's happy here."

"Are you?"

"Yes," Emma said.

"But you have to miss something, right? It's okay to miss things from home. I missed my gardens, and they let me make new ones here. Is there anything you miss?"

"Well, one thing. My friend Mr. Houser had a teddy bear named Ted E. Bear that I wish I could hold again."

"Good. Do you remember the pear test we did?"

"Yes." How could she forget?

"You didn't tell anyone else about it, did you?"

"No, of course not."

"Good. Because Grandpa Blake might not be happy me teaching you all of these things so early."

"So, why are you teaching me?"

"Because Blake holds a cynical view of people whereas mine is optimistic. I believe in you, Emma."

She smiled, warm inside.

"Anyway, this is a bit different than the pear test. Instead of taking the pear from behind my back, I want you to take the teddy bear and bring it up here."

"What? How can I do that? I have no idea where the bear is."

"You don't need to know exactly where it is. Do you remember what you felt about the bear?"

"Yes, I loved him because I loved Mr. Houser. He was so kind and funny. And he'd make Ted E. Bear say funny things to me."

"Good. I want you to close your eyes and focus on Ted,

remember as much as you can about him. And when I say 'go' I want you to hold out your hands and make him appear."

"Can I really do it?"

He smiled. "I guess we're gonna find out."

She closed her eyes, and imagined the bear in her fingers, its soft fluffy belly, its big brown eyes staring up at her. The bear's fur was worn thin in a few spots, probably because it was so old.

"Go," Grandpa Billy said.

Emma remembered how she made the pear disappear from behind his back and then reappear in her hands. It was a focus, a pinching in her mind, and then imagining a shift in space. It took several tries, but when she did it, Emma practically squealed in delight.

She did the same thing now, then opened her eyes, expecting to see the bear.

But it wasn't in her hands.

"I tried."

"Then let's do it again. Remember, it took several tries to get it right with the pear. We've got time."

They tried, another seven times.

Each time Emma imagined the bear in such vivid detail that she fully expected to make it appear. She even did the pinch thing in her mind.

But nothing.

Frustrated, she threw her hands over her chest. "I can't do it! I stink."

Grandpa Billy opened his arms. "Come here, child."

He hugged her. "When you think about the bear, what are you thinking about?"

"I'm imagining him as good as I remember him. His big brown eyes, the worn patches, his soft, fluffy belly. His smile."

"And what are you missing in that equation?"

"What do you mean?"

"With the pear, you didn't just visualize the pear, which I'd asked you to see and hold, but you also imagined tasting it, right, and how it would make you feel when you finally got it."

She smiled as she realized what he was saying. "So, I need to imagine how Ted E. Bear would feel?"

"No, imagine how he made you feel back then, the emotions he stirred in you. Obviously, he stirred something. He was the first thing you thought of when I asked what you missed, other than family."

"Ah, okay."

"Let's try again."

She closed her eyes.

Emma remembered bringing the stuffed bear to Mr. Houser in the hospital after he got in the accident. He was so happy to see it, smiling like a giant child.

And how much she wanted to hug him right then, because despite being such a tough guy, he was very much a teddy bear to her.

She smiled thinking of him.

And then she felt Ted E. Bear in her hands.

Emma opened her eyes, and he was there. "Oh my gosh!"

"You did it!" He reached out to touch the bear himself. "You actually did it."

She squeezed the bear to her chest. "Ted E.!"

"Okay, now you need to send it back."

"Why? I want to keep him here with me."

"Because if he stays here, then someone will see him and people will start asking questions. We can't let anyone know you can do this, do you understand?"

"Not even my mom?"

"No. Not yet."

"Why not?"

"Because you should always keep an ace up your sleeve."

"What does that mean?"

"Hundreds of years ago, there were card sharks — people who would rely on skill and deception to win at card games.

Often these people would tuck an ace up their sleeve to give themselves a hidden advantage."

"So, it was cheating? Isn't cheating bad?"

"It's all relative, Emma. In this case, it's not cheating. You are merely hiding a talent you may need at some point."

"But hiding it from my mom?"

"Not your mother so much as everyone else. There are people on this ship who don't want the same things I do. They think they're smarter than me, and those people may have gained influence over my son. And if that's true, then we cannot trust them. And I need you to be the ace up my sleeve."

"I'm your ace?"

"That you are, Emma."

He smiled and pinched her nose. "Now you have to send Ted E. Bear back before anyone finds him."

She hugged the bear goodbye, then said, "If you see Mr. Houser, tell him I don't blame him for what happened. And I still love him."

Then Emma focused, as she had with the pear, and sent it back .

Chapter 5 - Sarah Hughes

Doctor Hanz Engel greeted Sarah with a smile as he entered the exam room where she was sitting on the table, waiting.

He was tall, heavy, and almost ghostly, with red-rimmed pale blue eyes, and white short-cropped hair. His teeth were too big and rectangular, like Chiclets, not that he ever smiled. He wore a white lab coat, and was, so far as she knew, the station's chief doctor and scientist. There were two others in the office, one woman and one man, both younger, but she'd only seen them a couple of times, and they'd never worked with her.

"How are you today?" His German accent was thick. He looked to be in his early fifties, but something about him seemed far older, much like how Billy Conway seemed to look much younger than his one hundred seventy-plus years.

As Dr. Engel spoke, she often wondered if he was some Nazi doctor that Blake or Billy somehow got up on the space station.

"I'm good," she answered.

"Please disrobe."

Sarah did, same as she had for each of the weekly sessions,

dropping the gown and standing before him in only her underwear.

He held a small glass box that he used to scan her each week. The glass had a small circle inside it, glowing bright green, and sometimes blue, as he waved it over her body, head to toe.

She could feel its vibrations as it went.

Sarah had once asked what it did, but the doctor said, "It's above your understanding."

Like the arrogant ass he was.

"Good, good," he said, reaching her feet. "Seems you are doing fine on your regimen. Any new pains or symptoms to report this week?"

"No, doctor."

"Good."

"Get dressed." Engel went to the table next to the door and typed into a standing glass tablet.

Sarah picked up her bra and slipped it on, wondering what today's experiment would entail. Last week's had her looking at the back of cards, to see if she could pick up the numbers or letters printed on the other side.

She'd gotten nearly half of them. Surprising to her, but seemingly a disappointment to him.

The week before that she was sat opposite another subject, an old woman named Marjorie, and tasked to connect with her psychically, then get her to take a bite of an apple. She did this without any problem. But after that, she was asked to have the woman reach her hand into a tank with a crawling taran-tula. The woman had arachnophobia. Sarah had to calm her, which she first tried to do by talking to the woman, telling her that the spider wasn't dangerous. They would never endanger her. Just trust her. This tactic didn't work.

So Dr. Engel spoke into Sarah's mind and said, *"Lie to her."*

Sarah thought back to him, *"What do you mean lie? She can see the spider!"*

"Then show her what she wants to see."

Sarah projected something else into the woman's mind, making it appear that the spider was a fluffy bunny.

And *that* had worked.

Sarah finished getting dressed as the memory ended.

"Okay, let us go to the test chambers." Engel headed out the door.

She followed him down the hall from the medical bay to the elevator. It was cylindrical and all glass, with half of it revealing the Earth below, looming large, so close, yet so impossibly far.

Engel pressed a button on the glass panel and the elevator descended.

"Do you miss it?"

"Miss what?"

"Earth?"

"Yes." Sarah saw no point in lying. It wasn't as if she had any legitimate means of escape.

After he said nothing in return, she asked, "Do you?"

"Not in the least."

"Why not?"

"Because it is filled with vermin who don't deserve the wonder of it all."

"Alrighty then," she said, wishing she'd never engaged him.

The elevator opened, mercifully ending the conversation.

The more comfortable test chambers were all to the right. White rooms, usually with a table in the center and mirrored walls. To the left were the other chambers, the ones she didn't like. Where they did the tests Billy promised they wouldn't do anymore.

They turned left.

Sarah's heart fell into her gut.

Why are we turning left?

They passed a few armed guards dressed all in black that

reminded her of the Paladin guards on Hamilton. Perhaps that's where they sourced them from.

They passed several black doors, all of them looked rubber. They stopped at the last one.

Dr. Engel waved his hand over a panel outside the door and it rolled up revealing the test chamber — a long all-black room with more roll-up doors in the rear and a glass observation booth in the front where Engel would sit and conduct his test.

She found it hard to breathe, her chest tight enough to choke her. "Why are we in these chambers? I thought I wasn't doing any more of this sort."

"Oh, and who said that?" He led her into the room.

"William Conway. He said that we were done with these."

"Not to worry, dear. We're only using this chamber because it's larger and we required the space. It's not like the other tests."

Sarah tried to relax.

She considered demanding to see Billy but didn't want to push her luck. She was getting better treatment than before, probably better than any of the other subjects on the ship, whom she rarely saw outside of the rare social hour in the cafeteria. And she had Emma, which was more than ever before.

"Please, don't keep us waiting." Dr. Engel waved to the door leading through to the test chamber.

A cold chill ran down Sarah's spine.

It's okay. He said they only needed the large room for space. They're not going to hit you with another torture simulation.

She couldn't even remember the bad tests, only glimpses of emotions she'd felt, which were more than enough.

She passed through the observation booth door and out into the cold chamber, her footsteps echoing off the shiny black floor.

Dr. Engel's voice came over an intercom. "Today we are doing things a bit different."

Sarah didn't like the sound of that.

The two doors at the opposite end of the room, about forty yards away, started to roll up.

Her pulse quickened. Hair stood on her neck and arms.

Through the door on her right, came a group of six armed men in black, pistols in hands, and blindfolded. Each of them wore giant headphones.

Through the door on the left, came six men and women wearing blindfolds, patient's hospital gowns, and headphones. A few of them she'd recognized as subjects, though she didn't really know any of them.

A dozen people marched forward in almost perfect unison until Dr. Engel said, "Stop."

What the hell is going on?

Sarah felt their nerves, palpable in both groups. Fear, neither of them knowing what was about to happen.

"Now, Sarah," Engel said. "I need you to connect with the armed men. Get into their heads please."

"All six of them? I've never gotten into more than one person's head."

"One, six, twenty. If you can do it with one, you can do it with six. I have faith in you."

Sarah focused on the six men with guns. Correction, five men, one woman. Julia. Sarah gleaned her name as she made the shockingly simple connection.

She heard the woman's voice in her head. *"What's happening?"*

"Just relax."

"Who is this? What are you doing in my head?"

My name is Sarah Hughes. Dr. Engel asked me to connect with you and your other officers. Okay?

"Yes, ma'am."

Sarah then *knocked* on the next man's head. But he wasn't

letting her in. He was too distracted, and his apprehension levels were leaping off the scale. His finger tight on the trigger, feeling like he was being thrust into something dangerous, testing his skills.

She'd have to come back.

She knocked on the next man, Clarence.

Suddenly, Engel was there in her mind, *"Thirty seconds counting down."*

The black wall to the right showed giant neon red numbers reading 30, then 29.

Thirty seconds to what?

"Thirty seconds to get them to put their guns down. Twenty-four, twenty-three."

What are they going to — No! I can't!

"Nineteen"

Sarah yelled into Julia's head. *Drop the gun. Now!*

Julia did as instructed.

Fifteen. Fourteen.

She focused on all of them, *You have to put down your guns! Dr. Engel commands you to put down your guns!*

Ten…

A couple of voices asked, "Why? Who is this?"

She didn't have time. The clock was down to *seven, six…*

She screamed into their heads, "Drop the guns! Now!"

Two more dropped. Three still had theirs.

Two…

One.

Engel's voice boomed throughout the room, and in her head, "Raise and fire."

Sarah screamed, "No!" unable to stop as the three officers raised their pistols and fired repeatedly.

Sarah fell to her knees, mouth agape as the guards emptied their guns.

All six patients fell to the ground in a bloody heap.

Lights blinked on and off.

The guards were instructed to turn and leave the way they came, and to leave their blindfolds on until they were told to remove them.

They did as instructed. Obedient. Though Sarah could feel the three she connected with sobbing as they realized what had happened.

Julia spoke in her head, *"Oh, my God. What did we do?"*

You didn't know, was all Sarah could say.

As the guards disappeared beyond the closing door, Sarah turned and glared up at Dr. Engel.

She raced toward the door, threw it open and pointed at him. "What the hell was that?"

He stared at her with no emotion. As if he had slaughtered targets made of wood, rather than people with histories forever erased.

"A test, which you failed."

"What do you mean I failed? You gave me thirty seconds to get into the heads of six people. How was I supposed to do that?"

"You don't see it, do you?"

"See what?" Hot tears licked her face.

"You didn't need to get into six heads. Just one, which you did. And you should've had her shoot the other guards."

Sarah felt as if she'd been smacked across the face with both an obvious, monstrous, solution.

"I was supposed to have her kill the guards?"

"Well, if you wanted to spare the people. This was a test to see how you perform under stress, and how quickly you can adapt. And, as I stated before, you failed."

"It was a test I couldn't win! Someone was going to die no matter what I did."

"Maybe. Maybe not. Maybe there was another solution."

"What?"

"If you can't see it, I can't possibly illuminate it for you. Let us go."

"People are dead."

"And your point is?"

"Don't you care? You're all up here trying to better humanity, right? Trying to evolve our species into something better? Yet you don't give a damn if your subjects or guards even die!"

Dr. Engel got up in her face, looking down on Sarah, eyes boring into hers. "First, you do not raise your voice to me. Second, these people, both the guards and the subjects, are beneath us. They are vermin, and you should not despair their loss. Because I guarantee you, they are animals and would not think twice about killing you if it meant saving themselves."

On that, he turned, and left.

"Come," he instructed.

Sarah followed.

Obedient, just like everyone else.

Chapter 6 - Jon Conway

Jon and Alicia sat in the hotel's restaurant eating dinner as she waited to hear from the fixer, Darius Salton.

He was hungover, feeling like shit, missing Emma and Cassidy, and craving a drink.

He looked at Alicia. "C'mon, just one?"

"No, you're meeting with the brothers and Yuna Matsui tomorrow, and you need to look like the star you are. Not some drunk hobo."

"Hoboes are criminally frowned upon," Jon joked. "Some of my best friends have been hoboes."

"Well, *Black Nova* doesn't want a hobo starring opposite *the* Yuna Matsui."

Yuna was the hot new It Girl out of Japan, a nineteen-year-old actress with perfect English. She did most of her own stunts and made Jon feel ancient in comparison.

The character he was playing in the books was in his early twenties, as was Matsui's. It was one thing to cast him, in his early thirties, as Theo, since he still looked young and was a damned good actor with box office appeal. But casting a much younger actress made Jon worry he'd look significantly older in comparison.

Maybe it would make the chemistry seem off or their relationship forced. What if he looked like a lecherous old dude instead of the young hero he was supposed to be? All of these things would be fingered by critics and would call into question his suitability for the role. And if Jon became The Thing wrong with the series, he would shoulder all the blame if it tanked.

And his attempts at a comeback would crash in a fiery ball.

"You're not worried I look like a hobo. You think she makes me look old, don't you?"

"Well, she *is* nineteen. Hell, she looks *sixteen*."

"Stop," Jon said. "Just … stop."

Alicia laughed. "Feeling self-conscious about your age, *grandpa?*"

He flipped her off.

"Relax. I hear the Maris Brothers hire the best FX people. They'll make you look at least twenty-five. But, you might want to lay off the drinking and partying until the movie is wrapped. Or, until after *all* the movies are wrapped. Not like you'll be any younger in the sequels."

"Or maybe I take her out to party, get her to prematurely age so she catches up a bit?"

"Yeah, good luck with that. From what I hear, she already parties hard and it's done nothing to her."

"Maybe she's a vampire. In which case, I can realize my dream of eternal youth."

"Youth? I think you missed that boat."

They continued joking around as they ate, anything to not talk about either the looming threat of a "sex tape" or his sorrow over Emma and Cassidy.

As they talked, Jon realized he'd never really gotten to know Alicia outside of the job and a few of the stories she told about her time working for that scumbag producer.

"So, what did you want to be when you were a kid?"

She looked startled by the question. He half expected her to point out that it was the first time he'd ever asked her anything personal. But she was, thankfully, too polite to do so.

"I wanted to be a writer."

"Oh? And … do you write?"

"A little here and there. But the more I see behind the scenes, the less hopeful I am of ever writing something that'll take off."

"Even with all your contacts? All my contacts? You still don't think you can make a hit?"

"I don't want to use my contacts, or yours, thank you. I want the book to succeed on its own merit."

"Well, that's noble. Though a bit stupid, too."

"Stupid?"

"Yeah. Using your available resources isn't cheating."

"I don't know. It just feels wrong. I think the best way to explain it is how you hate when people bring up the Conway wealth. You wanted to succeed on your own, without being tied to your family name."

"Ah, that I *do* understand. But … if there's ever anything I can do, even if you only want a pair of eyes to look at it, just ask."

"Thank you," she said, then a silence settled between them.

Maybe this was why he didn't ask for personal details, because some relationships were better suited to small talk and laughter.

The phone rang, ending the awkward moment while threatening a worse one.

Alicia answered and nodded to Jon, indicating it was her fixer.

Jon shifted in his chair, took a drink of water — wishing it was whiskey — and watched her face, trying to divine the details of their conversation.

"I see," she said as it wound down. "Okay, let me know if anything happens."

And after a moment, "Yes, thank you."

Alicia hung up.

"Well?"

"Well, first off, the blackmailers used an anonymous service to send you the email, which isn't much of a surprise, but it means we can't track them yet. He emailed them back, and the only response he got was to pay up or else."

"So, we're fucked?"

"He's flying in tomorrow morning. He's reaching out to some people who might be able to track down the girl that drugged you. If she's still around and we can squeeze her, maybe this all goes away."

"*If* she's still around."

"Right. Let's hope."

"I'd feel a bit more hopeful if I could get a drink."

She shook her head. "Well, I can't babysit you all night, *grandpa*, but I'm hoping you can at least go the night without getting trashed, just until after your lunch tomorrow. Okay?"

"Fine. But keep calling me grandpa, and you're gonna give me gray hairs."

After dinner, Jon went to his hotel room, opened his fridge, and found it restocked.

"Thank you, hotel staff." He grabbed bottles from the fridge, carried them to his bed, and flipped on the television.

He had a flashback of his dream as he reached for the controller, half expecting it to be coated in oil. But he wasn't about to let a nightmare stop him from zoning out.

Jon passed by the indie horror movie he'd started watching earlier and found a documentary on ancient Greece.

Then he cracked open the first bottle, a good old-fashioned American Budweiser, and smiled as he saluted Alicia, in a room down the hall, unable to see him being naughty.

He sighed, thinking about their conversation and how she

admitted that he was way too old to be co-starring with Yuna Matsui. He was only thirty-one. While he certainly wouldn't *date* a nineteen-year-old, Jon didn't think he looked *that* much older onscreen.

But maybe he did. Maybe this was the decline of his stardom. He thought about all the young leading men who stayed well past their primes, and how many looked foolish with love interests played by girls so much younger than them. It was difficult to watch, and he prayed he'd have the sense to walk away before it happened to him.

But was it already too late?

He wanted to age gracefully as an actor, taking more mature roles rather than trying to play the young man's game past his prime. Hell, he didn't even want to do *Black Nova*, except that after a few failed indie movies, he needed a few hits to raise his stock and give him the cache he needed to choose his path forward.

As he drank, he became more convinced that he'd fucked things up, that doing these movies was a mistake. That he should've just stayed in Hamilton and tried to repair his relationship with Cass.

But no, I had to run away.

Just like I did with Sarah.

Fuck.

He opened another bottle.

Then an idea hit him. Probably an awful one.

He went downstairs and had the concierge call him a cab.

IT TOOK fifteen minutes until they found the club where Jon had partied hard the night before.

"Thanks." He paid for the cab with a swipe of his phone, then got out.

He was wearing a baseball cap, shades, and a jacket,

which he hoped would camouflage him enough without drawing attention to the disguise.

Inside the club, Jon ordered a drink, then leaned casually against the bar, scanning the crowd for a purple-haired Russian.

In his hazy memories from last night, the club had been so exotic — full of beautiful people, fantastic drinks, and the sort of architecture and lighting he'd only seen in some of the world's hottest clubs.

But the place was less appealing when he wasn't fucked up. The people less beautiful. The mystique was worn thin, with jagged edges of desperation seeping through. At least the drinks were still good.

He walked around, skirting the edges of the dance floor. Then he made his way upstairs, where most of the seating was located, and the VIP section. He walked around, steering clear of the many bouncers and anyone else that looked like they might be trouble, blending in to the crowd.

It was a long shot that she'd be here, of course. Hell, it was probably stupid to assume she'd come back the next night. And the more Jon thought about it, the less sense it made. The woman, or the people she worked with or for, would have to be stupid to come back. Or supremely arrogant.

He hoped to affect a look of aloof arrogance as he walked around, getting a lay of the land, seeing social mechanisms in play that he'd not seen last night while wasted — the desperate guys trying to impress their date or just get laid, the rich and powerful men who ordered everyone around and barely deigned to look at the women they wore like arm candy, and the women searching for easy marks. Marks like he'd been. He spotted a couple that seemed to be working the crowd, looking for just the right men, and sat back, observing.

Jon went back downstairs and walked through the undulating throng. A couple of young women tried to dance with him. He played along enough to avoid any unwanted attention, then held up his glass indicating he needed a refill and made his way to the bar. There he faux-flirted with the bartender just long enough to disappear, and ordered a second drink.

He sat, using the mirror behind the bar to scope out the dance floor, searching.

And then he spotted a familiar face sitting, at the bar on the other side of the dance floor.

He didn't turn, just kept using the mirror, gaze locked on the woman. Her hair was red rather than purple, but her makeup and dress were exactly the same.

She was seated with a group of wealthy-looking men, flirting and laughing at their every word.

Oh, I got you now.

He set his glass down, left a tip, then headed across the dance floor, making his way toward the opposite bar slowly enough as to deny all attention.

Jon was halfway across when she turned and saw him.

Her eyes widened. Not much, and only for a split second, indicating she was a pro and used to extracting herself from situations like this at a glance.

She stood, touched the closest man's shoulder, and said something before leaving. Didn't turn to look at Jon. Perfectly casual on her way to the stairs.

He had to catch her before she reached the VIP area and all the bouncers.

Jon had no plan beyond finding her. What had he hoped to do — grab her and make her confess, tell him where her co-conspirators were?

What if they were in the club? They were probably organized crime types that were more prepared for a fight than he was. Jon was an action star, trained in several martial arts, so he was confident enough in his fighting skills. But if they were packing, his odds went to shit.

He sped up his gait, gaining distance on her as she neared the stairway.

If he didn't run, he'd miss her.

Jon ran.

He felt eyes on him. Including hers as she turned.

And started running.

Fuck!

Jon gave chase, feeling eyes and bodies turning toward him. Shit was already well on its way to the fan.

She was at the foot of the stairs.

He kept running.

She was halfway up when he reached the bottom.

He vaulted several steps, almost running straight into two dudes, dodging out of the way at the last second.

She was three-fourths of the way up, looking back at him.

How long before bouncers saw him and pegged him as some psycho chasing a woman through their club, then descended with fists and clubs?

He pressed on, closing the gap as she hit the top step.

He grabbed her by the elbow and spun the woman around.

She screamed, swinging at Jon with her free hand.

He ducked, then punched her in the chest, knocking the air from her lungs and sending her to the ground.

He leapt on top of her, gripped her by the throat, and yelled, "Who are you working with?"

Two barrel-chested men in black suits, one bald, one with a man-bun, were heading toward him, shouting, "Hey! Get off of her!"

"Call the police," Jon shouted as he got off her and slowly stood with his hands raised. "She drugged me."

Jon whipped off his hat and shades, hoping they recognized him.

They did, and stopped in their tracks, confused. But they

weren't the only ones to recognize him. So did half the club who had their phones out, recording video of the incident.

Fuck.

"What's going on?" Man-Bun asked.

The Russian tried to speak, but she was still catching her breath, and could only gasp.

"Please, just call the police," Jon said.

The woman finally caught her breath and cried out, "It wasn't my idea. They forced me."

"Who forced you?"

"I'll tell you whatever you want to know, but please, don't call the police. I've got a kid back home to support."

Jon traded glances with the guards, then asked, "You got a room where we can all talk in private?"

The men nodded.

As the bald man helped the Russian to her feet, Jon heard people calling his name, asking what was happening, asking if this was part of his movie, why he attacked the woman, and what she had done.

And as they walked toward the rear of the club, Jon wondered if he had merely traded one public relations disaster for another.

They reached a red metal door in the rear of the club with a sign that read, *EMPLOYEES ONLY.*

The bald guard opened it to reveal a dimly lit hallway with several doors to offices behind it.

The Russian went through first.

Jon followed.

As he crossed the threshold, one of the men grabbed him in a chokehold.

Then shoved a wet rag over his nose and mouth.

Chapter 7 - Cassidy Hughes

Shipwrecked was slow, and Cass was wondering if she might get cut before happy hour was over.

Most nights she wouldn't have minded, but tonight she had no home to go home to … unless she went back to Jon's. Or crawled back to Vivian.

And no way in hell she was doing that.

Cassidy should have just rented an apartment after leaving Jon's. But she didn't have a lot of money and figured she could stash some cash by staying with her mom. Who knew she'd turn into an even more difficult person *after* she quit drinking?

Jon tried to send her money and help out, but Cass always refunded the deposits when they came through. He eventually stopped.

Was Viv right? Was she being too damned proud and stubborn by not taking Jon's money or staying in his house, the place that was to be *their home?*

Why couldn't her mother understand that it no longer felt like hers? Now it was a house haunted by ghosts of what might have been.

Despite trying, they fell into old ways of coping after Emma's death, closing off and self-medicating. Jon's mood darkened, and she could feel his loathing, even if she wasn't sure why he hated her. Was she a reminder of the life he could have had with her twin?

It sure as hell felt like it, even if she'd never asked him. He'd never admit such a thing, of course. To her or himself.

Cass was wiping down the bar when she spotted Craig at the pool tables, arriving with two other regulars who always brought their own sticks and chalk. As they set up, Craig flirted with Trudy while he gave her his order.

He popped his credit card into the jukebox, which meant the random pop songs she had been enjoying were about to be replaced by some crappy classic rock.

What abomination would he choose this time? Craig thought he was being cute playing bad classic rock because he knew she hated so many of the songs. She probably wouldn't care at all if she didn't have to listen to them day in and day out while the drunks shot pool, got into fights, and hit on Cass without mercy.

One night, he spent ungodly sums playing "Werewolves of London" on repeat for hours after she mistakenly told him it was the worst song ever made. After the fifth play, people started to get annoyed, but by the end of the fourth hour, people were singing along and howling like it was one big hilarious prank at her expense.

Cassidy was surprised she didn't murder everyone in the bar that night.

Craig looked at her and winked.

Oh, God, not more "Werewolves of London." Please, anything but that.

She ignored him, pretending to be busy. Then "Sweet Home Alabama" started playing, the only song she hated more than "Werewolves."

She kept a straight face, showing no sign of annoyance that might let him know he'd found a song to piss her off. She turned to Stan, one of her regulars.

"Another beer?"

"Thanks." Sam slid the empty her way.

She filled the mug, then went into the back to refill her ice bucket. As she carried it to the front, her back wanted to break, and she wished she'd gotten one of the barbacks to fill the bucket.

She set it down and sighed as a familiar face came toward the bar. Stephen Anderson.

"Hey, there." She smiled, trying to hide a wince as she turned her attention to him when he sat at the bar. "What can I get you?"

He looked troubled, but she didn't want to pry, so she didn't mention anything, yet.

"Surprise me."

"Okay." Cassidy set down a coaster then grabbed a frosty mug and filled it with a new craft on tap.

"Here ya' go. Something trendy."

He thanked her and was taking a drink when Craig sauntered up. "Hey, bartender, can I get a pale ale?"

Trudy was working his area near the pool tables, but she was busy with another couple who'd just come in. Cass grabbed a bottle, cracked it open, and handed it to him. She hoped he'd take it and leave, afraid he was going to flirt with her again, or worse, ask about the pills. Maybe see if she needed a refill.

Fuck him and his damned pills!

He was about to hand her cash, but she held up a hand. "I'll tell Trudy to add it to your tab."

He nodded just as "Sweet Home Alabama" started again.

She glared at him. "How many times did you put this damned song on, Craig?"

His stupid grin was taking up half his idiot face. "Oh, you better settle in, darlin'. It's gonna be a looooooong night. The South shall rise again. Yee-haw!"

Cassidy flipped him off.

He turned on his heel, rejoining the two guys he was playing pool with.

Stephen smiled. "Friend of yours?"

"No."

He laughed.

"So, how's it going?" She made her way to the ice bucket, contemplating if she wanted to reach down and lift it to fill the cooler. She decided to wait. Marco was heading her way.

"Hey, Marco, can you get the ice?"

The bar back was young, handsome, and built, with a tight black tee stretching across his biceps as he lifted the bucket without effort and dumped it into the cooler. "Need more?"

"Would you?"

"Sure thing." He headed into the back.

"My son is out with his friend, maybe girlfriend, I'm not sure. So I figured I'd come here for dinner."

"Oh?" Cass raised her eyebrows. "You liked the burger that much?"

"Best I've had in a while."

"Now that's just sad, Stephen. Is it Stephen or Steve?"

"Whatever."

"I like Stephen," she said, not intending to flirt so much as lift the man's spirits. She did find him attractive, though, in a professorial sort of way. And she sensed a sadness, just under the surface, that made her want to treat his wounds.

Stop it, Cass. The last thing you need now is a hookup.

Yet, feeling as alone as she did, she couldn't help but wonder what he was doing later. It would also solve her lodging problem, if he took her home for the night.

Stop it! He's a married man!

Marco came back with another bucket, and then a third, filling the cooler.

"Thanks," she said.

"Need anything else?" He flashed a boyish smile.

"Nah, I think Tom might, though." She pointed to the opposite end of the bar where Tom was starting to get busy.

Marco left.

She made small talk with Stephen, avoiding movement, lest her back pain flare-up too much, while "Sweet Home Fucking Alabama" kept grating on repeat. Each time the song started again, Craig would shout "Woohoo!"

Some in the bar started groaning, while others sang along. Craig was right, it was going to be an awfully long night. And since the bar was suddenly busy, no chance Cass would get cut without asking to leave, which she didn't want to do.

At least she had some pleasant company.

~

AN HOUR LATER, and who knows how many more "Sweet Home Alabamas," her back was throbbing too hard for Cass to finish her shift.

She got permission to leave, with Trudy taking her spot behind the bar, then told Stephen she'd see him around and that she wasn't feeling well. Cassidy went to the back, clocked out, grabbed her bag, and headed outside to the parking lot.

She made it to her car only to find Craig standing there, waiting with his stupid smile.

"What do you want, Craig?"

"Shit, is that any way to talk to the only friend you got left on the island?"

"What are you talking about?" She reached the car and got in his face, hoping he'd back down and leave her the hell alone.

"Heard you and your mom had a big fight. Thought I'd invite you to my place to crash."

"How the hell ...? You know what, never mind. I don't care. No, thank you. I don't need a place to crash."

"Oh, yeah, you got that big cozy Conway place. I forgot."

The way he looked at her, the way he was grinning, she wasn't sure what he was insinuating, but was sure enough that he was calling her a gold digger with his eyes. "How about you bring me back to your place, then?"

"No, I don't think so. If you don't mind, I'd like to get in my car, please."

"What? You too good for me now?" His voice had found the angry drunk tone she'd heard a thousand times too many at both the bar and in her life.

"Craig, please. I've had a shit day, my back is killing me, and I just want to go to bed."

"Now we're talking." He reached toward her crotch.

Cass sidestepped his awkward grope, though it sent a splinter of pain up her back. She glared at him, her fists balled. "Craig, stop fucking around, or I will deck you."

Plenty of people on the island were afraid of Craig, but Cass wasn't among them. And he knew it. That made him more dangerous on a night when she didn't feel much like fighting.

"Come on." He put on his best smile. "Okay, I'm *sorry*. I'm really not trying to be an asshole. I just miss you, is all."

"Yeah, well give me a call sometime. Right now, I just want to go."

He didn't budge. "Kiss me first."

"Craig!"

Another voice from behind her. A man saying, "There a problem here?"

She turned to see Stephen Anderson heading toward them.

Fuck. This was the last thing she needed.

"This ain't none of your business, Anderson," Craig said. "So just move along, son."

Stephen didn't back down. He came up to them and asked her, "You okay?" even though his eyes never left the enemy's.

"Yeah. Craig here was just about to move out of my way and let me go home. Right, Craig?"

Craig glared at Stephen. "What, you fucking her now?" He vented a pitiful laugh.

Stephen took a swing, hitting Craig square in the jaw and knocking him back.

Craig bounced back quickly, whipping out a knife, much to Stephen's surprise.

Craig smiled. "Yeah, let's go."

"Stop it!" Cass shouted.

Neither man would back down, both holding their stand-off. If she didn't do something, someone was gonna get hurt. Maybe killed.

She swung, punching Craig's hand, causing the knife to fly out of his grasp and onto the pavement. The other half of that move was a kick to the balls, but she spared him that indignity, as she seemed to have nabbed his attention.

He stared at her in shock. "What the fuck? Why you going all Kung Fu on me, bitch? I wasn't gonna *really* stab him!"

"Leave, Craig. We'll chalk this up to you being drunk and not an asshole, okay?"

"Fine," he said, slinking away. If he had a tail, it would've been between his legs. Despite his backing down, he still gave a glare at Stephen, showing who was the alpha in this contest. Well, at least between the two of them.

She looked at Stephen, not sure if she was insulted that he didn't think she could handle herself or flattered by his rescue. She hated being a damsel in distress even more than "Were-wolves of London" and "Sweet Home Fucking Alabama" combined, but Stephen didn't seem like the kind of guy who looked down on women or was in search of one to rescue. He was doing something nice, in either ignorance or defiance of the fact that Craig could probably kick his ass twice as hard in half the time.

As Craig went back inside, her adrenaline surrendered to pain.

"Fuck, I *really* shouldn't have done that." She hunched over.

"Where does it hurt?"

She pointed at the small of her back.

"I used to be a massage therapist, when I first got out of school. May I?"

"Really?"

"I wasn't always a boring analyst."

"Yeah, go ahead if you think it'll help."

He pressed into her back at just the right spot, and she closed her eyes as he went to work.

"Wow, that does help."

"I could do better if you were lying down."

She looked at him.

He went red with embarrassment. "That ... that wasn't a proposition."

"Too bad," she grinned.

His eyebrows arched. "Um, I just meant if you wanted to come back to my place, I could give you a proper massage."

"Okay, *Stephen*. I'd like that."

Chapter 8 - Sarah Hughes

When Emma got home, Sarah raced to the door, picked her up, and hugged her tight, never wanting to let her daughter go.

"Are you okay, Mommy?"

Sarah was crying and didn't even bother to try and hide it.

Roger stared at her, wanting to talk. She wondered if he knew something about the test she was made to do and had been planning to warn her.

Sarah turned to Emma. "Honey, I need you to make something for us to eat."

"What do you want?"

"I want you to surprise us, okay. Just go find something in the fridge or cupboard. Your choice!"

"Okay. Did something happen?"

"No, baby. Momma's just happy to see you."

"Okay," she repeated, then turned to the kitchen.

Sarah grabbed Roger by his tie and pulled him into the bathroom.

She shut the door, hoping Emma wouldn't notice or ask what they were doing in there together.

Once inside, she looked up at him, "Can they hear us in here?"

"No. I don't think so."

"What did you want to tell me?"

"I know you've been able to connect with your sister. Is … is Emma able to connect with either Cassidy or her father?"

"Why do you ask?"

"Just something she said the other day."

"What did she say?"

"Just something about her father looking sad. I don't think any of the other students made anything of it, but I need to know … can she really do that?"

Sarah wanted to trust Roger, wanted to tell him yes, she can, and maybe it might be their ticket off this station. But he was a clone. God only knew where his allegiance lay.

"No, she dreamed about him, but I don't think she connected with him."

He grabbed her hands. "What happened to you today?"

She had to tell someone, and Sarah sure as hell couldn't tell Emma. So she told him about the test, about the dead subjects, and how callous Dr. Engel was afterward.

"My God. I'm so sorry."

And then he hugged her. She burst into tears, not realizing how much she'd missed having a shoulder to cry on.

Once calmer, she pulled away. "I'm sorry. You don't need this on your head."

He shook his head, "It's okay, Sarah. I'm here for you. And the reason I asked about Emma is because if she can contact her father, then maybe she can tell him we're up here."

She stared at him, hoping to God her expression didn't betray the ignorance she was aiming to portray. "What?"

"I want to get off this ship. My baby girl is down there, living with God knows who as her parents. Aubrey is my child, Sarah. *I* should be raising her."

Sarah didn't bother to correct him, to remind him that Aubrey wasn't his daughter, but rather Roger's. The line between them was so blurred, sometimes she even forgot he wasn't *her* Roger. Still, she had to say something to get the crazy idea out of his head before he risked his life and did something stupid, or got someone thinking that she and Emma were attempting escape.

"But the world thinks you're dead, Roger. You can't just go down there."

"The world thinks you and Emma are dead, too. But if we all go down there, we can expose this thing. We can get these other people home. No more tests. No more deaths."

She wanted to tell him now more than ever. To have one more confidant, to help her plan this right. That might make the difference between escaping this station and dying on it. Yet, as she considered Emma's safety, she couldn't take the chance of trusting him.

"Listen, Roger. I've been connecting to Cassidy for months, and while I've seen bits of her day-to-day, and even felt her emotions and seen through her eyes, I've yet to actually have a conversation. And she's my twin, someone I should be able to easily connect with. If I can't get word to her, what hope do you have in Emma connecting with a man she hardly knows?"

He looked at her for a long time as if trying to read her eyes for truth, or maybe hoping to see some ray of hope for him. But she couldn't show him anything. Yet.

"Come on, we've gotta get out there."

Sarah opened the door, not giving him a chance to continue the conversation because she wasn't sure she could maintain her resolve much longer.

They ate dinner together, chicken and rice, mostly in silence, the gravity of Roger's disappointment and her tragic day weighing over the meal. Emma was quiet, trapped in the shadows of their mood. They engaged in small talk about

Emma's day, but it was a long volley of perfunctory back-and-forths.

After dinner, Roger tried his best smile. "I'll see you tomorrow, Emma."

"See you tomorrow, Mr. Roger," she said, with a smile that Sarah had never seen.

As Roger left and the door closed, her smile vanished. Sarah was surprised to see that Emma had mastered a fake. It might've been the first time she'd ever seen it.

"I'm gonna take a bath, Mommy. Will you put bubbles in it?"

She went to the bathroom without waiting for a yes.

Sarah followed, a weird sensation rolling through her gut. Something was going on with her daughter.

Once in the bathroom, Emma closed the door and met her mother's eyes.

She whispered, "Something is wrong with Daddy."

"What?"

"Something is going to happen, and we need to help him."

"What are you talking about?"

"We need to go to the garden, Mommy. Now."

Chapter 9 - Jon Conway

Jon was jostled awake to find himself in the back of a dark van, riding along a bumpy road.

Confused and groggy, it took a moment to remember how he got here. He'd followed the Russian woman into the back of the club, with the pair of bouncers behind him.

One of them grabbed Jon, likely chloroformed him.

And now what?

His hands were tied behind his back. His mouth was gagged, taped shut.

In the front he heard two men with thick New Zealand accents arguing about him. Probably the bouncers, but Jon couldn't be sure.

"This is a bad idea, mate." one of them said to the other.

"Well, it's not my decision, so stop yer whining."

Jon couldn't see them through the curtained partition, so they couldn't see him. He was free to do whatever he could to escape, so long as he did so silently.

He pulled at the bindings, hoping they were plastic or rope, but they were metal cuffs.

What the hell are they doing?

Judging from the bumpy roads, and his being bound, Jon deduced that these fuckers were about to get rid of him.

He looked around the van for anything that might offer escape.

His gaze seized the handle of the van's back doors. If he could get over to it, he might be able to open the doors and drop out.

He'd get hurt, and they might even hear him, but at the moment, it seemed like his only shot at escape.

Jon sat up, his head spinning and stomach lurching. He felt a lot like he had last night while waking to find the grinding Russian making her movie. Had they used the same drugs on him again?

He made his way to the doors just as the van hit a hole or bump or something and he bounced into the doors, hitting his head.

Shit! So much for not making noise.

He quickly went prone, closing his eyes, in case someone peeked back.

A moment later one of the men said, "No, he's still out."

Jon waited through a few more bumps, then got to his knees and made his way back to the door.

He turned, hands fumbling for the handle, praying the doors weren't locked.

His eyes were bolted to the curtain, knowing for certain it would open at any second and one of the men would see his attempt to escape. Then shit would go south fast.

He pulled at the handle.

Nothing.

He pulled again.

Fuck.

It was locked.

The van stopped.

Shit.

Jon froze, his back to the doors.

He heard two doors open and the front of the van go slightly up as it was relieved of their weight. Then the men walked on either side of the van, coming to the rear.

His mind raced between options — run forward and try to scramble out the front, or turn and face them head-on, maybe take the men by surprise.

They were closing in on the rear door. Jon had no time to make an escape through the front. They'd catch him for sure.

He turned and waited for the doors to unlock.

The soft click was followed by the doors starting to open.

Jon fell onto his back, kicked out his legs with all the force he could muster, and slammed the doors into the men, knocking them both down.

He leapt into the night and raced along the dirt mountain road, his head down.

With the moon barely out, or concealed behind clouds, he could barely see anything or make out his surroundings. All he knew was he was on a forested mountain road and couldn't see anything past trees. No streetlights or homes. Just a whole lot of nothing. And his captors.

Jon's legs were pins and needles, and tied, offered him limited mobility. His arms bound behind him kept him off balance. Top speed was impossible.

"Hey!" one of the men shouted.

"Fucker!" yelled the other.

Jon didn't need to turn around to know they were getting to their feet and about to chase him.

And he didn't need to see how far ahead he was of them to know they would be on him in seconds.

He turned off the dirt road and thrust himself through the darkness, swallowed by thick brush and trees scratching at his face.

Jon cursed as he stumbled and hopped his way forward into the darkness, his momentum carrying him too far, too fast and without any care.

His heart raced as he kept falling forward, out of control.

And then he saw something that stopped his heart cold. The ground stopped a few yards away, plummeting into a deep ravine he could barely make out below.

He would tumble right off the mountain and drop to his death if he didn't stop.

Jon was at such an angle, he couldn't just put on the brakes. He had to fall to halt his momentum.

He hit the ground violently, bouncing and up, rolling forward to his horror.

Without being able to spread his arms, he had little control over his tumbling body.

Death would be immediate.

All he could do was brace and hope it was quick.

And then, somehow, he stopped, just at the lip of the drop. He looked down.

The drop was far. He couldn't even see where the ground began again in the darkness below.

He breathed a deep sigh through his nostrils.

And then he heard footfalls coming fast. Branches breaking.

He got to his knees.

The men closed in. It was Man-Bun and Baldie. The bouncers and the Russian were in on the little extortion attempt. And judging from their conversation, someone else was above them. They answered to someone who paid them. And that meant maybe Jon could negotiate his way out of this — if they'd take off his gag.

Man-Bun aimed a pistol at him. "Why the fuck did you run?"

Jon widened his eyes so they could see their whites, then looked down at the gag in his mouth, signaling to take it off and hand them their answers.

The bald bouncer came and ripped off his gag.

"Listen, I don't care what sorta thing you've got going on

at the club. You want money, fine. I'll get you twice what you asked for. Just … let me go."

Baldy exchanged a look with Man-Bun.

Man-Bun shook his head. "Nah. I think we'll stick with our current employment arrangement."

Jon upped his price. "Three million. Three million dollars, for you to split however the hell you want. You gonna make that much working for whoever it is you're working for?"

They exchanged looks again. Baldy seemed willing to hear Jon out, but Man-Bun kept shaking his head. Unfortunately, he also held the pistol, so it wasn't like Jon could turn the two men against each other without getting shot for his efforts.

"Okay, five million. Come on. That would be insane to refuse. Five million, *tonight*. You just take me back to the hotel, and we all go our separate ways." He didn't even bother asking them to destroy the video, as that might have been something they couldn't negotiate. And Jon wasn't particularly worried about that in the face of his imminent death.

Man-Bun kept his gun trained on Jon. "Undo him."

"Thank you," Jon said.

Baldy cut the ropes from his feet then instructed him to turn around.

"You won't regret this," Jon said as the man removed his cuffs.

He turned back around and realized his error. They weren't letting him go at all.

Man-Bun said, "Do it."

Then Baldy pushed Jon off the cliff.

Epilogue

Jon woke in an indoor garden, wondering why he wasn't in pain.

The garden felt familiar, even though he didn't think he'd ever been in it before.

The place was filled with pinks and purples, petals in lavenders and whites, greens and reds and blues. Vacant stone benches were surrounded by lilacs and roses.

He looked around, but couldn't see anyone else. Not even a door beyond the tall rows of bushes surrounding him.

Where am I?

How did I get here?

One minute he'd been falling through the darkness, and the next, he was here in this garden.

Is this Heaven?

It didn't feel like what he thought Heaven might be like. It felt too terrestrial, yet, oddly not in a way he couldn't explain.

Something was different about this garden. Was it the glass dome above that showed a bright blue sky that felt artificial? Was it something about the air that felt off?

And yet, all so familiar.

It can't be Heaven.

But what else could explain the lack of pain, and the weird garden that couldn't possibly be anywhere near the mountain he'd fallen off of? Nor did it explain how he woke up here?

That's it, dumbass, you didn't *wake up. You're dreaming.*

Or maybe this is your brain's final dream as your body slips into death. One last show before you hit the road. Neurons firing in a dying engine, making sense of the senseless one last time.

But it felt like something else entirely, something he'd never felt.

Something he had no words for.

Something …

"Daddy?"

He turned around and saw the impossible standing in front of a hedgerow.

Emma, standing there in a white dress, a blue flower in her hair. Cassidy was standing behind her.

No, not Cassidy.

Sarah.

Chapter 8 - Jon Conway

Prologue

Three months ago…

ROGER HELLER WAS SITTING at his desk, watching his students reading their books when the violent wave came to claim him.

He grabbed the scissors on his desk and felt a compulsion to drive the sharp end through one of his students' heads. Not one in particular, just the closest one.

His eyes settled on Karina, the twelve-year-old brunette in the front row.

She's evil. She's part of their plan. Kill her.

He closed his eyes, the scissors shaking in one hand as the other held it in check, riding out the urge.

After a terrifyingly long moment, it passed.

He set the scissors back in the cup on his desk and looked at his class, just to make sure he hadn't blacked out and killed anyone.

They were all still alive.

Karina looked up at him, smiled, then returned to her book.

He smiled back, then looked down, ashamed for the hateful violence inside him, even though it belonged to an echo of Earth Roger's rampage from a couple weeks ago.

Days like this, days when Roger was tired after waking up from horrible nightmares, teaching was difficult.

But he was the only teacher aboard the space station, and he couldn't let the kids down. Class time was the closest thing they had to a normal routine. And the closest thing Roger had to a normal life.

But these kids were anything but normal. From what he knew of the program, they represented the next step in human evolution, each of them chosen for their special abilities, engineered into them at birth, sometimes for the second generation.

While they were supposed to keep their powers in check during their daily lives, every now and then one would slip up or play a prank — a bit of telepathy here, a dash of telekinesis there, and sometimes they demonstrated things Roger didn't know if there were even names for.

They were a special group of kids, and he loved them all. He could never imagine killing any of them, even as he picked up on reverb from the other Roger's occasional thoughts.

After Earth Roger shot the kids, Clone Roger was pulled from duty for more than a week while Dr. Engel and Billy Conway each interviewed him to ensure he didn't have any residual memories from Roger that might trigger a violent act.

He assured them he did not. If they knew of the violent urges, they might not let him teach ever again. They might decide that he served no purpose then do whatever they did to clones who no longer had value. Maybe put him on ice.

Maybe worse.

While he had few memories of his time before activation, aside from those born of his connection to Earth Roger, he had no intention of being decommissioned.

He loved his life, even if it wasn't his to begin with. He hoped the Conways would eventually bring his wife, Liz, his son, Alex, and his baby girl, Aubrey. Then they could all be a family.

They'd never been an actual family. Earth Roger's life did not belong to him, but Alex and Aubrey had been brought up here for the project. So maybe someday.

"No, no," Karina said, drawing Roger's attention.

She was holding her hand under her nose, blood spurting all over her book, desk, and dress.

Roger leapt from his seat, grabbed some paper towels, and handed them over, helping her through the nose bleed.

After a few minutes of keeping pressure on it, she asked Roger if he could take her to the restroom connected to the classroom.

He brought her in.

She closed the door behind them and he wet some of the paper towels and helped clean her up.

"Are you okay?"

"Yeah," she said, "I had a vision."

"Okay, I'll call the doctor, and you can document it."

"No, he doesn't need to know." Her eyes serious. And … frightened.

"What do you mean? You're supposed to report any visions to Dr. Engel."

"Your family is in danger, Mr. Heller."

"What?"

"I just had a vision. A man is going to kill your family tonight."

Roger stared at her, thinking it had to be some sort of joke. But Karina was a kind girl, not prone to pranks or cruelty.

"How?"

"A man named Bruce Henderson is going to kill them. He's … not right. Someone has control of him."

"Who?"

"I ... I don't know." Her nose started to bleed again.

He handed her more paper towels, though his mind was racing, unsure of what he could do, how he could warn his family.

"When is it going to happen?" Roger asked as he realized he had no idea about the hour on Hamilton, or what time was based on here.

Roger was shaking as he left the bathroom and told the kids he'd be right back.

He got his radio and called the dispatcher onboard. "I need you to connect me to Billy Conway."

ROGER SAT in the bright white chamber at a table along with Tommy, the sixteen-year-old remote viewer, and Billy. Mirrors on either side made the room seem even larger than it was, as if stretched to infinity.

Dr. Hanz Engel sat in the observation booth, speaking to them over the intercom. "Are you ready, Tommy?"

"Yes," said the boy.

"What do I do?" Roger asked.

Billy said, "He will knock on your head. Not literally, but a mental knock. You let him in, and then he will search your memories, or rather the other Roger Heller's memories, for Liz. Once he finds her, he should be able to connect to her, though I can't make any promises.

Roger wished Billy would just call the police and warn them about Henderson. But Billy said they couldn't just make a call like that and keep everything secret. Roger suggested something anonymous, but Billy said nothing was anonymous these days, and they couldn't take any chances.

So it was a wing and a prayer of the untested psychic abilities of a sixteen-year-old.

Roger felt the knock. And then a circle floating in his mind space.

"Just open your mind, Mr. Heller," Tommy said. "Imagine opening the hole I'm placing there."

Roger reached out and opened it.

Tommy was inside his head, darkness surrounding the two of them.

"I need you to go to your home. Imagine us there."

Roger imagined his home, or rather Earth Roger's, piecing it together from scraps of memories, hoping he was close.

Suddenly, they were in a nursery.

The room was dark, walls shifting between paper and paint, the window moving from one wall to another, as if the entire room was in-flux.

"You don't need to be exact," Tommy said. "Just relax."

Roger did.

The walls then on the wallpaper's pattern.

And then he saw Aubrey lying, asleep in the crib.

He approached, "Is … is that really her? Are we here?"

"Yes," Tommy said. "Now we need to find your wife's room."

Roger went to the door, but it refused to open, the knob refused to turn.

"What's wrong?"

"I don't know," Tommy said. "Imagine it open."

Roger let go of the knob and it vanished.

"What the hell?"

And then the door wasn't there.

All four walls became mirrors, shaking.

"Stop it or you're going to bounce us out," Tommy said. "Find something to focus on, one thing, and only stay focused on that."

Roger looked back down at Aubrey, who was looking up at him.

"Da-da."

His heart melted. "She sees me!"

Roger wanted to pick her up, but he was terrified he might vanish and drop her to the ground. The world felt ephemeral, like the slightest distraction might blow it to shreds and send them back into the chamber.

"What's that?" Tommy pointed at the baby monitor.

"A monitor." And then he had an idea. If they were truly there, then he could call Liz into the room.

"Liz," he said, his voice tentative.

"Louder," Tommy said.

"Liz!" he screamed at the top of his lungs.

He heard footsteps approaching.

It worked!

He watched as the door opened, and Liz stormed into the room. She stopped when she saw him.

Her eyes widened in shock.

Static came over the baby monitor, causing both the room and everybody in it to flicker. Roger feared it was all going to collapse before he could warn her.

He didn't have time to explain what was happening, not that she was asking. He needed to get them out of the house.

"Get out! You have to get the kids and get out. Bruce Henderson is going to kill you!"

"What?"

He wasn't sure if she was having trouble hearing him or was swimming in disbelief. Maybe she thought it was a dream.

Roger kept yelling his warning, but she kept looking at him, not hearing and not moving.

She approached, reaching out to touch him, as if to see whether he was there.

As her fingers touched him, his body fluttered as if a wave coursed through it.

More static.

The room flickered.

He screamed, "Liz! Get the kids and get out! Now!"

"What?" she cried.

Aubrey was crying too.

"Get OUT!"

And then a thunderous explosion downstairs.

No. No. It's too late.

He's here!

No!

"What's happening?" Liz cried and ran to the window to look outside.

She turned to Roger, her wide eyes now even wider.

"What is it?" he asked, but then he was gone.

He heard her scream, "Don't leave!"

But they were back in the white room, and Tommy was staring at Roger with wide-open eyes.

"What happened?" Billy asked.

"We need to go back!" Roger screamed.

"It's too late," Tommy said. "He's there."

"We can still do something."

Tommy shook his head. "No. I can't do anything. Neither of us can."

"Damn it!" Roger bellowed, reaching across the table and grabbing both of Tommy's wrists. "Come on, Tommy. Please."

"You don't have to do anything, Tommy," Dr. Engel said over the speakers.

"It's not too late," Roger pled. "Please. Just try."

Tommy looked at Billy.

Billy said, "Well, Bruce can't hurt either of you, so if you think you can return, try."

Tommy nodded. "Okay, Mr. Heller. Let's go back."

But it was already too late.

Liz's body beneath the window.

Same for Henderson's, but his with a gunshot to the face.

And Alex lying dead, cradling his crying baby sister in one last attempt to protect her.

Roger screamed.

He was back in the chamber.

Helpless and dead inside.

Chapter 1 - Jon Conway

Jon was certain he was dreaming as Sarah and Emma approached him.

"How … how did you get here?" Sarah asked as she stared.

"What do you mean?"

"I did it, Mommy. I knew something was going to happen to Daddy, and I brought him here."

Jon stood, and while this still felt like a dream, he was slowly starting to believe it wasn't. A feeling in his gut. And … flashes of memories he'd somehow been here before — with them. "Is this real? Am I really here? Are you?"

Emma ran up to him, threw her arms open, and jumped into his embrace.

The déjà vu was overpowering, and suddenly Jon saw himself sitting in the shrink's office, the one his father made him go to, the hypnotherapist.

He could hear her voice in his head.

When you wake up, you will forget the things we placed in the hole.

He remembered the dream, the box, the chain, the fire, and the hole.

Only it wasn't a dream, but something the shrink did to him to make him forget.

And now he remembered his previous visit to the space station, remembered asking Blake about it, his father feigning ignorance, insisting that he see the shrink.

Emma squeezed him tight, crying. "I did it! I did it!"

Sarah looked at him, and he was transported back in time to any number of times he looked into her eyes and felt that same love.

"Sarah? What's happening? Are we dead?"

"No. We're not dead, Jon. Your father did something and brought us up here. We're on a space station. And your grandfather, Billy Conway is up here, too. Still alive."

"What?" Jon shook his head. "Billy?"

It all felt so familiar. "Have I been here before?"

"I think we've all been here, as kids. They experimented on us, gave us … *powers.*"

He reached out to touch Sarah's face. Her skin warm against his fingertips. "You're still alive."

He hugged her, with Emma between them, tears streaming down his cheeks, "I thought you were both dead."

"I tried to tell you in the dream, Daddy. Don't you remember?"

He shook his head. "I'm sorry. I … I think the doctor made me forget."

Emma's eyes went wide. "I think someone's coming. I need to send him back before they find him and hurt him."

"Send me back? No! I want to stay here with you."

Sarah looked around, then at Jon, her eyes urgent. "Listen, Jon. Please, listen. You have to go back and bring someone to save us. Your father has a portal he uses to come up here. It's in his office at the house. You have to find it then bring help. Please, Jon, you're our only hope for coming home."

"What is he doing to you up here?" Jon stared at Sarah. "Why are you here?"

"Just please, can you get us. Where are you?"

"I'm in New Zealand, filming a movie. But I can go home. I'm on the next plane. I'll find the portal. I promise."

Sarah opened her mouth to say something, but then she, Emma, and the garden were gone.

Or rather, he was.

Jon woke in the darkness, flashlights bouncing toward him.

"Jon!" Alicia screamed his name. "There he is! There he is!"

He was surrounded by a confusing mix of police and paramedics, asking if he was okay and how he got there. He didn't answer a single question. He couldn't speak.

All he could think about was Sarah and Emma. His daughter begging him to save them. Had that really happened? Or had he passed out and dreamed the whole thing?

As more lights cut into the darkness and vehicles approached, Jon realized he was at the bottom of the mountain.

He'd been pushed off, and yet, as he looked down at himself, he had nary a scratch.

Impossible. Unless Emma had really somehow brought him aboard the space station.

Which meant it was real.

That she and Sarah were still alive.

And that he had to save them.

A paramedic asked if he was okay to stand. Jon found his voice. "Yes. Yes, I'm fine."

He stood, shaky at first, but then okay.

"What happened?" an officer asked.

Jon told them everything leading up to him being shoved off the mountain. No need to tell them that part. Nor did he mention the space station or his family.

He gave all the details he could remember, then was led

into the back of an ambulance where a short brunette paramedic introduced herself as Jillian and said she'd be looking him over.

"Can you bring us back to the hotel, Jillian?" he asked her and the paramedic in the driver's seat, just out of his view. "I need to get my stuff."

"What do you mean *get your stuff?*" Alicia asked, after joining them in the back.

"I'm going home."

"What?"

"I can't explain now. But I need to go home, for at least a couple of weeks."

"What?" Alicia turned to Jillian, "Can you check to see if he bumped his head or anything?"

Jillian felt along his head.

"I didn't bump my head," he said, irritated as she pressed on his skull and asked him if anything hurt.

Are you in pain? Do you need medication?

Christ.

"I'm good. I don't need anything, except to get back to the hotel. Just please drive," he said to the paramedic up front.

The guy looked back and spoke to Jillian. "Is he okay to go back to the hotel?"

Jon looked at the woman, hoping she wasn't going to say no. He'd have to get out of the ambulance and walk back to the damned hotel if she did.

Jillian shrugged. "Seems okay."

The paramedic started driving.

Alicia looked at Jon, confused. "What's going on?"

"I can't explain. I just need to go home, back to Hamilton."

"I need to call Marty." She reached for her purse.

"No." He put his hand on hers. "I don't need either one of you trying to talk me out of this. It's not gonna happen.

I've made up my mind. I need to go home. Production can wait. They'll have to find someone else if they can't."

She stared at him, silent for perhaps the first time since she'd met him.

Then he found himself wondering, so he asked, "How did you find me?"

"When you got drunk earlier, I sneaked into your room and chipped all your shoes and jackets."

"You put tracking chips on me?" He might have been mad under other circumstances, but right now he was grateful, even if he wasn't going to thank her outright.

"Yeah. After that girl drugged you, I figured someone ought to look after you when you went out on your next drunken escapade."

He sat silently, thinking about Sarah and Emma, wondering how long it would take to get a flight back home, then catch a ferry to the island.

"What happened out there? What did they do to you? What did they threaten you with?"

"I don't give a damn about some stupid sex tape." He was unsure if Jillian or the driver had been following along, nor did he care. But he needed to say something to get Alicia off his case. "It's Cass. She needs me."

"Cass? What's wrong? We can have someone help her."

"No, it has to be me."

"Okay, maybe we can push principal photography back a bit? Just go, take care of whatever you need to, and then come back. You can do *that*, can't you?"

"I guess," he lied.

Jon wasn't thinking about the movie. He couldn't think about that while knowing that his family was alive. Or with the alternative — that he'd finally lost his fucking mind. And really, it could be either.

As Jillian continued looking him over, Jon sat in silence, trying to sort through things, fighting the doubt as it crept in at the edges, insisting he'd dreamt it all, was suffering effects from the drugs, or was in such denial about Emma's death, his mind had concocted some bullshit to convince him she was breathing. And she just so happened to bring Sarah back as well.

All of those were possibilities. But they didn't feel right.

He could almost imagine Marty's voice if he told him.

So, what, you're just gonna ruin this movie and all these people counting on you because you had a fucking dream?

He knew how stupid it would sound. How stupid he might very well be to follow this, but then he thought of holding Emma and Sarah, and how real they felt.

Hell, he could still smell them both.

Yeah, but what if it's not real?

What if you go home and there is no portal?

What then, Jonny Boy?

He didn't want to consider that horrible possibility.

Because that was a dark road which ended with him suffering a lunatic's descent into madness. The sort that either got you thrown in the looney bin for good, or ended only when you found the courage to shove the business end of a pistol into your mouth.

Chapter 2 - Sarah Hughes

Sarah was in the garden, holding Emma after Jon disappeared, when she heard a gasp behind her.

She turned to see Roger standing there, looking as if he'd seen a ghost.

Had he seen Jon?

"Was that … Jon?"

Shit.

Sarah let go of Emma and swiftly approached him. "You can't tell anyone."

"H … *How* did he get up here?"

Emma piped up. "I did it, Mr. Roger. I saw he was in danger, and I brought him up."

He looked wide-eyed at Emma. "Oh, my God. How did you do it?"

"I've been practicing. Um … never mind. I'm not supposed to talk about it."

Sarah wanted to ask more, but not here, not in front of Roger. She'd have to wait until later.

Emma said, "It's okay, we can talk here. They don't record anything in the gardens. Grandpa Billy told me so."

Roger asked, "Does this mean she can get us back to Earth?"

Sarah looked at Emma. "Can you do that? Can you send us there?"

"I don't know. I don't think so. I haven't tried it. So far the only thing I've been able to move are a pear, Ted E. Bear, and now Daddy. But I brought those things to me. I … I don't think I can send us somewhere else."

Roger asked, "Who taught you to do this?"

"I … I can't say. I promised."

"It's okay." Sarah would press for answers when they were alone.

Roger looked deep in thought.

"What are you thinking?" Sarah asked.

He shook his head, appearing defeated. "Even if she did manage to send us home, what's to stop them from zipping us right back up? We can't stop them." Then he turned to Sarah. "What did you tell him? Does he know everything?"

This wasn't the Roger she knew on Earth, and therefore she had no allegiance to him, but he was her friend, and the only one she had up here. He missed *his* baby fiercely. He would want to know if there was hope, that maybe they could escape. Maybe he'd see *his* baby girl again.

"We told him to get help."

"You did? How is he going to help us?"

"He's going to Hamilton. To find the portal. We're going home."

"Daddy is going to save us, Mr. Roger!"

"Oh, my God," Roger said, still stunned.

"You can't tell *anyone*," Sarah said, first to Roger, then to her daughter. "Neither of you."

"Mum's the word," Roger said, zipping his lips. "Did he say when he'd be coming?"

"He's in New Zealand. Not sure how long it'll take to fly back, but I'm guessing at least a day. So hang tight."

"How does he expect to save us? Just waltz in here and ask his father to let us go?"

"I don't know, but if anyone can talk sense into Blake, it's Jon. He can be *very* persuasive."

"Let's hope," Roger said.

Chapter 3 - Stephen Anderson

Stephen woke up to the alarm telling him it was time to get ready for work.

And, unlike every other morning since Bea went away, this time he wasn't alone.

Cassidy was lying beside him, naked under the comforter.

He hit the clock to stop its incessant whine.

Cass turned over, but stayed asleep.

He stared at her in the dim morning light bleeding through his curtains. She was beautiful. Even in the morning with messy hair and smeared makeup she'd forgotten to take off, she was still something else.

Last night had started innocently enough. He invited her home for a massage. And because he'd heard from someone in the bar after she left that her mother had kicked her out.

They talked as he massaged her. Yeah, he was horny the whole time, but he hadn't planned to take things any further than he did. Especially after conversation dipped into a deeper discussion about what happened to her sister, and then her recurring nightmares. She told him about the fight with her mother that morning. He asked about Craig, and she told him of their sordid history and how he used to be her dealer.

As she talked, a part of him wanted to tell her he saw Roger Heller, still alive.

But if he did that, he'd put her in danger. Plus, he didn't know if it was something she'd *want* to know. Right now, she might have some small comfort in thinking the man who'd killed her sister and his students was dead. Why rob her of that?

When she asked what was on his mind, he had to lie, so he said he confessed to missing his wife. Which led to a conversation about Bea. Of course, he couldn't tell her the truth, that Conway Industries had wiped her brain so many times that she'd lost her mind and drove through a store-front in an apparent suicide attempt which could've killed Milo as well.

Cassidy asked if she'd ever come back, and he said no, she was too far gone. And that was the truth. He talked about the nebulous realm where he mourned her while she was still very much alive. He'd gone to visit her, but she didn't even recognize him and screamed for security to take him away. He described how awful he felt driving home then because a part of him would prefer her to be dead than in this state.

He admitted how helpless he felt about it all.

She asked about his first wife, Lisa, who'd gone missing, one of the more famous cases on the island five years ago, and then asked him if he thought Lisa might be out there somewhere alive, even though she'd been declared dead long ago.

That choked him up.

Cassidy sat up, not bothering to cover her bare breasts. Then she hugged him, which led to a kiss, which led to them making love.

It felt odd and wrong to go from discussing two women he loved to sleeping with Cass, especially with the clarity of hindsight in the morning light.

Last night was likely a mistake, but at the same time, it seemed perhaps mistakes were all either of them had. She calmed him in a way nobody else could. He wasn't sure if it was her tough exterior or some inner serenity. But being with her made him feel like a different man, one that hadn't fucked up his life, one that might not be trapped by circumstances and working for Conway Industries. Like he might actually be able to do something to change his situation.

And she seemed to enjoy his company. He'd made her laugh several times on the way to his house. And she looked at him in a sweet way that reminded him of Lisa.

Maybe they could help one another through difficult times. He enjoyed their conversation and liked how she wasn't like most people he ran into on the island, another cog in the Conway Machine. No, she was different. Complicated. Didn't give two fucks about anything was and fiercely independent, having a strength that he only wished for.

Yeah, but what do I offer her?

As he looked at her in the early light, feeling woefully inadequate. A needy man trying to render a one night stand into a relationship. And he hated feeling needy.

Her eyes opened.

His face went flush as he turned away.

"Morning," she said, stretching, the sheets and comforter falling off of her breasts.

Stephen wanted to look but didn't.

She pulled the covers over her body.

He stood. "I've gotta shower and take my son to school."

"Oh, yeah, school starts back up today, doesn't it?" She got up and started dressing. "Okay, I'll head out."

"No," he said, too fast.

She looked at him as she pulled her shirt over her head. "Everything okay?"

"Um, well, I'm not sure how my son would react to seeing you come out of my room. I mean, he didn't care much for Bea, so maybe it wouldn't bother him, but I have to get a feel for where he is."

While that was part of the reason, he also knew Milo was

being monitored. Anything Milo saw or heard, someone, another Watcher, was recording. If Conway Industries saw Cass spending the night, he could be exposing her to a life of monitoring endangering her.

Cass's face was frozen in a blank expression before she nodded. "Ah, gotcha. So, um, do you want me to hang out in here and wait until you leave, then sneak out?"

He wasn't sure if she was being sarcastic, testing him, or serious in her offer. "No, I have a better idea. Why not stay here until you've gotta go to work?"

"Why would I stay here when you're not around?"

"Well, I just figured since you didn't have anywhere else to go …"

"I have places I can go." Cassidy glared at him. "I don't *need* to stay here."

"Hey, I didn't mean anything by it."

"You don't think I slept with you because I didn't have anywhere else to go, did you?"

"No, I didn't think anything like that."

"Good." She reached down to grab her bag, then went to his bedroom window, looked outside, shoved it open.

"What are you doing?"

Cassidy pulled out his screen and set it on the floor.

"You said you don't want your son seeing me. So I'm going out the window."

"It's a two-story drop! Don't be stupid. If you want to meet my son, fine. I'm sorry if I offended you."

"It's all good." She hopped out the window.

He ran to the ledge in time to see her land on her feet and start walking toward the street.

"Wait. I drove last night! You need a ride to get your car."

"Got it." She held up her phone. "Bye, Stephen."

He stared at her as she walked away, wondering what the fuck he did to piss her off. Then he wondered if she thought he was ashamed of her, hiding her from Milo like that. Maybe she was only a one night stand to him. But it was his offer of a place to stay that really seemed to get her going, and why she'd be pissed at that, he had no idea.

As he placed the screen back in the window, Stephen wondered if he should try and talk to her, work to smooth things out, or if this was a warning sign of worse things to come. Maybe it was a bad idea, sleeping with someone so volatile.

Drama was the last thing he needed.

STEPHEN SHOWERED, then got dressed and headed out to the living room.

Milo was standing like a statue, staring at a television that wasn't even on.

"Milo?"

He didn't respond.

Anxiety tightened his chest. Stephen had seen this behavior before, subjects zoning out in front of TVs or other electronics. Sometimes there was static, others, like now, silence.

He wasn't sure what caused it. If it was the subjects realizing that something was off, that there was something, and someone, monitoring them, or if it was some side effect of the nanobots and spyware loaded into their bodies. Or maybe just a random glitch.

Perhaps it was data being downloaded, or maybe it was going the other way.

What if it was instructions.

Like kill, kill, kill!

"Milo!" Stephen reached out and touched his shoulder.

Milo turned around, startled.

"You okay?"

"Yeah, sorry." Milo blinked a few times. "Just drifting off waiting for you."

He smiled, and Stephen saw his son was just busting his balls for being late, something he routinely did to Milo.

"Sheesh, I thought you were never coming," Milo said.

"Sorry. Had some calls to take care of. You got your lunch card?"

"Yes, and my tablet, and everything else." Milo held up his backpack.

As they walked out to the car, Stephen asked him if he was nervous going back to school. "It's okay if you are."

"No, I'm good," he said matter-of-factly, getting in on the passenger side.

The news had been saturated the past couple of days about how security would be tight at the school following the Marketplace incident, an additional increase since the shooting back in September. For all their supposed attempts to calm the public, they may as well have screamed, "There might be another shooting!"

And Stephen wouldn't have blamed his son if he was nervous heading back. But he certainly didn't want to put the fear in his head if he wasn't already afraid. Because the way Stephen figured, the safest place for Milo, if Kaiser decided to make a move on him, was in school.

They're not going to come after you or Milo.

You're safe.

They're watching him, and they know you'd be stupid to do anything.

You're fine. And so is Milo.

And Cass.

As Stephen drove he noticed Milo was busier than usual on his phone. "Whatcha doing?"

"Texting Kate."

"Ah. So?"

"So, what?"

"How are things going between you two? Does she like you?"

"Dad!" His face turned red.

"What? It's a fair question. I just want to know how things are going, I'm not asking for dirty details."

"*Dad!* There are no *dirty details!*"

"*That's* not what I meant," Stephen said, feeling like he was fumbling this conversation as badly as this morning's with Cass.

What the hell is wrong with me today?

"I only meant, I wasn't trying to pry. Just want to make sure everything's okay."

"Everything is fine," Milo said.

The drive after that was painfully quiet, but still Stephen found comfort in the normalcy.

Almost.

Stephen dropped Milo off in front of the school, said goodbye, then started toward work. He was halfway there, along a lonely stretch of tree-lined roads, when his car died.

"Fuck."

He tried to start the car but got no response, not even the tell-tale clicking of a dead battery.

After pulling the trunk release, he got out of the car then popped the hood.

As he studied the engine, brakes squealed behind him.

He turned around as the rear doors of a black van exploded open. A large black man in a black trench coat had a gun in his face. "Get in."

Stephen turned to run, to get back in the car and grab his phone to warn Milo Paladin was coming.

But the big man caught then held him in a chokehold. And before he passed out, Stephen heard a woman's voice.

"Let's get out of here," it said.

Chapter 4 - Jon Conway

Jon shoved his clothes and tablet into his bag, grabbed it, then made his way out of his hotel room.

He barely got twenty feet toward the elevator when Marty called out, "Hey! What's going on?"

He was standing there with Alicia. Of course, she'd ratted him out. "What the hell, Alicia? You told him? You're *my* assistant, not his."

She just stood there, staring at him, refusing to look guilty as she should be feeling.

"What's going on, Jon? Alicia just told me what happened, that those men tried to kill you. I know you're probably freaking out, but—"

"I don't want to talk about it, Marty. I'm going home. And there's nothing you can say to stop me."

Marty shook his head. "Listen, you need some time to clear your head, I get it. I'll talk to the brothers. We'll push production back. It's not a problem."

"I don't care about *Black Nova*. I'm done."

"Done? With the movie?"

"Yeah, Marty. Done with the movie. I need to go home." Jon was thinking he meant done with *all movies*, but he didn't bother telling Marty that, or else the conversation would only yawn longer.

Marty's eyes were wide. His face pale. "You're not thinking clearly, Jon. Why don't we go down to the bar, pour some stiff drinks, and talk this over?"

Jon shook his head. "Stop, Marty. I'm not in the mood to talk."

He supposed he should say something to mollify his agent. Maybe tell him he would think about it, that yes, maybe he would come back to the set. But Jon didn't feel like lying. He was exhausted and on the verge of either saving Sarah and Emma or losing his damned mind. In either event, nothing else mattered, including Marty's feelings.

His agent put on his salesman's smile. "C'mon, Jonny. Don't do this to me. You know what hell I went through to get you this role? And now you're gonna piss it all away? Sorry, pal. I know you've had a crazy couple of nights, and I wouldn't blame you for needing to take some time, but you can't just walk away from this project. Nobody will ever want to work with you again. Your career will be over."

"Good. I don't care."

Jon pushed his way past Marty, bumping into him as he went.

"Damn it, Jon. Stop being such a selfish cunt."

He spun around. "What?"

"You never could appreciate a good thing, could you? You were always too good for the popcorn movies, wanting to do these stupid money-losing indie projects, doing everything you could do to kill the good name *we* built for you. The drugs, the women, the flops. You kept fucking up, and *I* kept fixing your name. *I* kept begging people to put you in their movies. *I* kept the worst of the gossip out of the rags, keeping you from being the laughingstock they wanted to turn you into. *I* made your life easier. *You* aren't Jon Conway, *we* are Jon Conway.

You and me, partners. And *this* is how you repay me? By fucking up the best deal ever?"

"This about your commission, Marty? You already spend it on vacation? Or did the wife make you go and get a bigger house you can't really afford? Let me know how much I owe you, and I'll cut you a check when I get back. So then I can go back to being me and you can go back to being a —"

"Fuck you, Jon. You know it's not about the money."

"No, Marty. I *don't* know. All I know is right now, my head is not in a good place, and you're not listening to what I want or need. And I can't have an agent, or an assistant" — he made a point to glare at Alicia because she had failed him and he needed her to know it — "who don't have my interests top of mind."

"So, what? You're firing us?" Marty asked incredulously.

"Yes," Jon said. "Goodbye."

"Wait," Alicia called out.

Jon turned and headed toward the elevator, knowing he'd thrown a grenade at the only bridge back to his old life.

And he didn't give a damn.

Fuck the movies.

Fuck his legacy.

And fuck anyone who stood in his way.

Chapter 5 - Kevin Brady

It had been a day like they used to have, a nice breakfast with the kids and now a picnic by the sea at Waterfront Park. The air was cool and salty, blowing through Molly's hair in a way that reminded him past family outings, before the last year had taken its toll.

Aidan and Christina were flying a kite, running across the grass on the fenced-in cliffside, laughing like they used to.

Molly was watching them, smiling.

The sandwiches were a bit stale, but everything else about the picnic was perfect, from the basket to the blanket to the sliced fruit to the drinks. Hell, they could've been eating dirt as far as Kevin was concerned. It didn't matter, so long as they were together. It was the sort of day he thought his family would never see again, and now there was no reason to think they couldn't have forever after.

All he had to do was quit his job and take Blake's money.

He'd been holding off on telling Molly about the offer until the time felt right. And, as she laughed at the kids skipping and screaming like happy little monkeys, now seemed as right a time as any.

"Blake Conway offered me a lot of money to quit."

"What?" She turned to him, her eyebrows furrowed.

He handed her the check that was in his shirt pocket. "That's half."

"Oh, my God. *Half?*"

"Yes. The other half in six months."

"Why does he want you to quit?"

"He's going to get our department shut down and make Paladin the exclusive provider of police services on Hamilton. He has the council votes already. I think he's worried that I'll put up a stink, and because so many residents and business owners like me, I'll get them to push to keep the police department open."

She stared at the check. "This is a lot of money, honey."

"I know."

"What's he really buying?"

While Molly had been in a haze since Christina disappeared, she wasn't a dummy. She knew men like Blake Conway didn't overspend when they didn't need to. They did it to make their problems go away.

"Is this about what happened at the Market?"

"I think so, among other things."

Molly nodded and looked around, maybe checking to see if anyone was listening. She whispered, "Does Conway Industries have anything to do with it? Some drug trial or something?"

"Probably." No need to delve into other suspicions.

"What do *you* want to do?"

"I don't know. I've always done the right thing. But what if the *right thing* endangers you and the kids?"

Her eyes widened. "Did he threaten you?"

"Not in so many words, but … the head of Paladin, Carl Kaiser, has made no secret that he'd love to find a reason to screw with me."

Molly folded her arms across her chest as if a sudden chill had taken over her. "I don't know what to tell you. I want you to do the right thing, of course. But … not if it comes at the cost of something happening to them." She looked out at their children, her eyes tearing up.

He wished he'd never brought this up, never posed this question to her and caused her reason for concern. "I'm taking the offer."

"What?" Molly turned back to him, surprised.

"We just got Christina back. Just got our lives back. And, way I see it, Conway Industries doesn't lose. Ever. I only have this job because they've allowed it. I'm outmanned. They've got the federal government beholden to them. And hell, I don't have any proof of what I think they're doing. So it'd be me against them, their lawyers, *and* the Feds. What chance does the truth have in that situation?"

"I'm sorry. I know how rough this must be for you."

"Not as rough as I thought. Frankly, I've done the right thing for so long, and where has it gotten us? I say we take the money, move far away. Maybe find a place on the east coast. Like Maine? You always wanted to go there, right?"

She nodded, staring at the children.

"Then Maine it is."

Molly handed him the check.

He put it back in his pocket, grabbed his phone, and called Blake Conway to tell him that yes, he'd take the offer.

Blake said, "I knew you'd do the right thing."

The right thing.

His choice of words sent a chill through every part of Kevin's body.

Chapter 6 - Stephen Anderson

Stephen woke up in what felt like a basement, tied to a chair, bright lights in his face and a video camera aimed at him. The last thing he remembered was being choked out.

This is it. Paladin has come to erase me.

And his phone, the one he needed to warn Milo, was still in his car.

Hell, they might already have him.

"Where's my son?" he asked his unseen captors, wherever they were watching from.

The room was small enough to bounce his voice against the walls.

He turned his neck to try and see behind him, but there were only more lights blasting into his eyes.

"I'll do whatever you want, just leave my son out of this."

A voice bleated from an ear-piece in his left ear. "Well, that's very nice of you, Mr. Anderson. We'd like you to begin by stating your name for the camera."

The red light came on.

Stephen wondered why they'd film his execution. Wondered why he was still alive at all. Why not just kill him? Why go through all this — whatever *this* was?

Something was off.

"Who are you?"

"We're asking the questions here. If you want to see Milo, you will answer them."

"Do you have him?"

"He is safe," said the man. "For now. Just please, answer the questions. State your name."

"My name is Stephen Anderson."

"Good. And who do you work for?"

"I work for Conway Industries."

"And your job title?"

"I'm an analyst."

"Your real job title, Mr. Anderson."

That feeling of things not adding up was only getting worse. At first, he thought Paladin had taken him to kill him. But maybe this was a test, to see how much he would spill if questioned. Just the sort of thing Paladin would do, kidnap him to see if he'd talk, and if he did, then they'd kill them for sure.

"I'm an analyst," he repeated.

"You mean you're a Watcher."

"I don't know what you mean."

"Don't lie, Mr. Anderson."

"I'm *not* lying. I don't know what a Watcher is. I'm an analyst for Conway Industries. Who the hell are *you?*"

The red light on the camera went off.

A door opened behind him, echoing in the small chamber, and he felt a hand grab the back of his head, tightly.

He couldn't turn around to see who had him, but his money was on the big black dude.

The man leaned in, "Answer the questions, or we take out your silence on Milo."

The man shoved his head forward, then the door slammed shut again.

The red light on the camera came back on.

The voice in his earpiece asked, "What is your job?"

Even though he was terrified that he might be wrong, that someone else was holding him and playing stupid would get Milo hurt, or worse, he had to go with what seemed most likely — that this was a test. He had to stay the course.

"I'm an analyst. I don't know what more you want to know. I told you, I don't know what a Watcher is. You've got the wrong guy."

Silence in his earpiece.

And then a voice. "Do you want us to kill your son, Mr. Anderson. Is that what you want?"

"I don't know what to tell you! You've got the wrong person. Why don't you come in here and talk to me face-to-face. Maybe we can figure out what the hell is going on together?"

Stephen didn't know everyone, but he had an excellent memory for faces. He doubted there was anyone on the island he'd not seen at least once.

And then he thought about the big man who'd taken him at gunpoint. He'd seen him somewhere not too long ago. Flashes of news clips flooded his mind. Memories unspooled around the face, and gave him a name without context.

Brock Houser, the private detective wanted for Emma Hughes's death.

And suddenly Stephen was terrified that he was wrong about his captors' identity and motivation. He was more in the dark than even before.

The camera's red light died.

The door opened behind him.

Footsteps echoed behind him.

He swallowed as fear trickled down his spine and leaked into his gut.

Brock Houser stepped into view, looking at him with his head titled. "Okay, let's talk."

"You're Brock Houser, aren't you?"

Brock looked surprised for a moment, but then he nodded. "Yes."

"Do you work for Paladin?"

"No, I most certainly do not."

"Why did you take me?"

"We want information on the Watcher program. We want to expose Conway Industries and Paladin so the world will know what's happening on Hamilton Island."

"Who is this 'we' you're talking about?"

More footsteps behind him.

Two more people entered. A woman he didn't recognize, and a man he most certainly did — Talbot Gray, head of the conspiracy theory outfit that called itself Expose Them All.

What the hell is Talbot Gray doing with Brock Houser?

"You know me?" Talbot said, a twinkle in his eye as he positioned himself in front of Stephen.

"Yeah, you're the head of Expose Them All."

"Yes. Then I guess you can figure out what we're doing. We want your help in exposing them."

Stephen shook his head. "No. You are going to let me go. This is illegal. You've kidnapped me and are threatening my son!"

"I'm afraid I can't let you go until you tell me what I need to know. I was hoping you'd play nice, as I didn't really want to have to employ any harsher tactics."

"Fuck you," Stephen said through gritted teeth. "Paladin tracks all Conway Industries employees. The moment they find you've got me, you're all fucked. And you," he said, looking at Houser, "your ass is going back to jail for killing that poor girl."

"I didn't kill Emma."

"Then why'd you kill those cops and flee?"

"Paladin framed me. And they were going to kill me next. Talbot and his people saved my life, much as we're trying to do for you."

"*You* are trying to save *me?* From what?"

Talbot said, "We know they've got your wife locked in the institution. And they're monitoring your son. I can't imagine you're feeling very safe."

Stephen stared at Talbot. Up close, he didn't seem nearly as flamboyant or over-the-top insane as he did in his videos. The man seemed perfectly reasonable. That he knew about the Watcher program, Bea, and Milo, all made him wonder what else they had.

Did they pose a threat to Conway Industries? Probably not too big of a threat, otherwise they wouldn't have taken him. They would've gone up the chain, to someone who knew a lot more shit.

The woman spoke, "We just need you to tell us what you know, so we can get a fire started under the right politicians, the right people, to blow up their secret programs."

Stephen glanced at the camera to make sure it was still off. A part of him wondered if Talbot Gray and his people were some elaborate part of Paladin, all of this a test to see if he would crack. It was far-fetched, particularly given how long Expose Them All had been around, and how vocal they had been in their criticism of the company, others like it, and government entities in general. But Stephen didn't put anything off the table when it came to Paladin or Carl Kaiser.

Way Stephen saw it, he had nothing to lose by keeping his mouth shut. They were, ostensibly, a do-gooder organization. They weren't going to torture him or murder his son. They were trying to scare him. And if they were part of Paladin, then he'd score bonus points by keeping quiet like a good little soldier.

"I'm just an analyst. I don't know anything about any Watchers or any secret programs. I swear."

"I had really hoped you'd keep this simple." Talbot nodded to Houser.

The man approached him as he reached into his coat pocket.

Stephen glared at him, not wanting to show any fear. There was, after all, no way they were going to hurt him.

Houser walked behind him.

Stephen resisted turning around to see what he was doing, even though it was hell keeping himself in the dark. His gaze locked onto Talbot. "If you hurt me, they will destroy all of you. You know that, don't you?"

Something pinched his neck, then he realized they weren't going to torture him after all.

They were drugging him instead.

Fuck.

~

STEPHEN WAS ALONE in the room again. It had been more than ten minutes since they drugged him, and he was feeling happy and co-operative, even as he tried to hold onto the fear.

Again, the voice spoke in his ear. "Mr. Anderson, please state your name again for the record."

The camera's red light came on.

Stephen stared at it, trying to fight the effects of the drug, but all resistance was melting into something warm and gooey. Same for his fear.

"Please state your name for the record, Mr. Anderson." the voice urged again.

"My name is Stephen Anderson."

"And what do you do for Conway Industries?"

Must fight it. Don't tell them.

If this is a test, they will kill you and Milo both.

Probably Bea, as well.

Stephen had to tell them. Whatever they gave him was *forcing* him to speak.

His mouth opened.

He bit his tongue, pain intense, the iron taste of blood flooding his mouth.

He clenched his teeth.

Don't do it. Don't tell them.

"What do you do for Conway Industries?"

Stephen shook his head again and bit his tongue harder.

Blood poured past his lips.

He heard the door open behind him again. The woman came in, shaking her head, "Jesus Christ. Open your mouth."

He did as instructed.

"Okay, he didn't bite it off. We can continue."

Stephen violently shook his head. "No."

She looked at him for a while before she opened her mouth. "Why are you being so stubborn? Just tell us what you know. Help us, and we'll help you get out from under them."

"They'll kill them if I talk."

She looked at him, her annoyance seeming to soften. Then she reached into her jacket, pulled out her phone, and showed him a photo. A man who looked familiar to Stephen ... Keiran Sullivan, one of the scientists who worked for Conway Industries. He'd killed himself a few years ago.

Why was she showing him his photo?

"You recognize him, yes?"

Stephen nodded.

"That is my brother, Keiran Sullivan. He worked for Conway, helping them create medicine. He was a brilliant man who wanted to save the world. He believed in what they were doing. At first. But he fell apart at the end. Started to talk about how they were doing something awful. And he wanted to expose their lies. You know what happened next, right?"

She pulled up a video of Keiran crying, saying, "I don't know what's happening. I can't take it anymore. It's ... it's all falling apart. There's nothing I can do. I'm sorry. I thought I was ... never mind."

He composed himself and looked right into the camera. "Goodbye, sis. I'll see you on the other side."

Then he leapt from Tanner's Pass.

"His body was found the next day, washed up on the eastern shore of Hamilton Island. Conway Industries must pay. Please, help me."

Stephen was crying as he thought of Bea and Milo, how neither of them had signed up for this hell. How they were suffering at the cost of his career. How long before Milo would prove too dangerous for them? What hope did his son have of leading a normal life, leaving the island, going to a university?

They'd never let him go.

They'd never escape the shadow of Conway Industries or the island's atrocities.

Not unless he took a stand against them.

Not unless he told the truth.

But what if this is a set-up? What if Paladin is testing me?

But as he looked at Keiran's sister, Stephen could see from the pain in her eyes that this was indeed a test, but only of his humanity. And he could no longer stay silent.

"Okay," he nodded. "I'll talk."

She thanked him, put a hand on his shoulder, and left the room.

Then Stephen told them everything.

Chapter 7 - Roger Heller

Roger slowed his steps as he left the garden, walked down the hall, and made his way to the elevator. He could barely contain his excitement as he got inside it. Things had worked out perfectly. He, like Earth Roger, tried not to dwell on the negative, but sometimes it was hard to keep the faith.

For months he thought he might never see his baby again.

But somehow, things had worked out perfectly.

He stepped into the elevator, nodded at the scientists on board who were in deep discussion about something. They nodded back, then kept talking in hushed tones about the recent results from one test or another.

They seemed excited about their discovery, but their excitement could not possibly exceed, let alone match, what Roger held inside.

He got off on the floor with the Science Labs and walked down the long hall, still trying not to let his joy show. Not yet. Not until Aubrey was back in his hands.

Outside the laboratories, one of the guards stopped him and asked him to state his business.

Roger told him who he'd come to meet.

The guard checked on the radio, then said, "Follow me, sir."

He led Roger down a hall with several windows looking in on scientists working. He brought him to the last door, an office without a window, and waved his hand over the plate beside it.

The door slid open.

Roger entered the room and the guard left.

Dr. Hanz Engel looked up at him from behind his messy desk, stacked high with papers and notebooks, charts he'd drawn out, and ancient yellowed texts filled with arcane knowledge that Roger could only guess at. "You have something for me?"

"Is your offer still good? That you'll bring Aubrey up here to live with me?"

"That depends. What do you have for me?"

"You were right, Emma was in contact with Jon. But it gets better. She somehow brought Jon onto the station. And he's coming back to rescue Sarah and Emma."

"How did this happen?"

Roger spilled every detail as the doctor leaned forward, hanging on every word.

He felt awful selling out Sarah and Emma. Truly, truly terrible. Especially since he felt like he may have put the seed in Sarah's mind to try to contact Jon. But at the same time, he couldn't pass up the chance to have what was left of his family aboard the space station. It was the only thing keeping him going day in and day out in this place, knowing that someday they'd be reunited.

He asked if Emma had been in contact with Jon. Sarah obviously had. If she'd told him the truth then, maybe he wouldn't be turning on her now.

But Roger had to go with the plan that seemed most likely to succeed. Sarah and Emma's was half-baked at best. They had no idea what Jon would do once he arrived, and he'd likely wind up a prisoner just like the rest of them.

This was Roger's one chance to provide valuable information to make this trade with Dr. Engel, and he'd be a fool not to take it.

Still, after seeing the doctor's smile, Roger felt unease creeping through his gut. "You're not going to hurt them, are you?"

"Heaven's no. They are too valuable for that. If Jon wants to come up here, we'll reunite him with his family. But anyone else he brings? Well, I can't promise *their* safety."

Roger swallowed. "But Sarah and Emma, they will be safe? You promise."

"I promise, Mr. Heller. Now, come. I believe it's time to deliver what I promised you. Follow me."

"She's here?"

"Oh, yes, she's been in the nursery since last month. I knew you'd come through for me."

Roger's heart swelled with joy as he imagined holding Aubrey in his arms.

"After you," Dr. Engel said as he waved towards the open door. "I'll follow you to the elevator."

Roger turned and headed out the door, unable to keep a wide smile from his lips as they started down the hall.

He turned when he felt a pinch in the back of his neck, confused as his body started to fall.

Doctor Engel caught him. "There, there, Roger, sleepy time."

What did you do to me?

Chatper 8 - Jon Conway

Jon was in a window seat, second to back row of first-class, thankful nobody else had the seat beside him. The only other people flying first class were a Korean couple three rows up.

It was a long flight, and in order to make sure he got some sleep, Jon ordered drinks from the raven-haired brown-eyed flight attendant named Kari who told him she was a "huge fan."

His exhaustion was finally catching up with him, so he leaned his seat back, closed his eyes, and waited for sleep to claim him. Unfortunately, the moment he shut his eyes, his mind decided to race over the last twenty-four hours.

The further he was away from his appearance on the space station with Sarah and Emma, the less real it felt. The more he wondered if he had, in fact, dreamed the whole damned thing. And if it *had* been a dream, how long before regret sank in for ruining his career?

He had a job that most anyone else on Earth would kill for. Not only was he an actor, but he was among the Hollywood elite. He'd been blessed with the right blend of good looks, talent, and the right roles at the right times to launch him into the tier that made you for life. Ensured you'd never starve, not that he needed to worry about that, with the Conway fortune. But still, he'd made it in the biggest of possible ways. And more or less on his own.

Now he was about to burn it all to the ground.

But if Sarah and Emma were alive, it was a sacrifice he'd make a million times over.

If …

Despite his fears, Jon found himself examining things he'd not thought about in years. Growing up, Blake Conway was the very definition of an absent father. Gone for days, weeks, and months at a time, and yet, sometimes, he'd just appear as if he'd been in the house the entire time. In fact, Jon couldn't remember a single time seeing his father arrive in a car, as one would do following a trip.

He always just showed up somewhere in the house.

Almost as if there were a portal.

Jon thought again about Blake's locked office, his father's most private of places. And how he had guessed the password to the locked room as EMMA a few months ago before sneaking inside.

It was a tiny office, and there was certainly no portal out in plain sight. But, now that Jon thought more about it, the office seemed almost too small, especially for a man who enjoyed extravagant homes, vehicles, and businesses. Blake Conway never thought small, so the office must have had some hidden passageway to another room.

Maybe it was behind the bookcases that lined the far wall?

And that's where the portal lived?

It's the only thing that made sense.

Only because you're trying to untangle the crazy.

You need to give up. They're dead.

Get used to it. Don't get your hopes up.

He tried to shake off the dark thoughts. To hold out hope that when he arrived on the island, he would find what he was looking for and finally be reunited with Sarah and his daughter.

As he thought about Sarah, he couldn't help but think of Cass. What would become of his relationship with her once Sarah came home? Did she still love him? Did she even want to be a family? How would Sarah react once she found out that he and Cassidy had fallen in love?

And that begged the question circling his mind for some time, the question that he didn't dare ponder, lest it unravel him. Did he truly love Cass?

Or had she always been a proxy for Sarah?

It sure as hell felt like love, or at least the closest thing he'd felt to it since Sarah, but was it truly *love?*

Despite their similarities, the twins were very different people. As opposite as twins could be. Sarah was sweet, laid back, thoughtful, and creative. They'd spent most of their teen years lying in the grass staring up at stars pondering life's Big Questions.

Cass was more rambunctious, a go-getter who always spoke her mind, not giving a damn what anyone thought. He loved that about her. She was witty and hilarious. But she was also more self-absorbed. Her higher heights crashed to much deeper depths.

While Sarah was a steadier relationship, a calm sea with few waves, it lacked the excitement of his time with Cass. She was full blast, the good and the bad.

They were both adrenaline junkies, so they fed off of each other. But when things went bad after Emma's death, they ate at each other like vultures.

He remembered their big fight. The one that ended everything.

If there was blame to be handed out, he deserved the most for initiating The End.

It started innocuously enough.

They were living together in their big new house, the one

where they were planning to raise Emma together. But the ghosts of what might have been weighed on him heavily.

He'd started having trouble sleeping, and he'd leave the bedroom to go work on an idea he had for a script. A mother grieving for her child who comes back as a ghost. His way of dealing with the pain of losing Sarah and Emma.

The more he got into it, the more he shut her out.

So Cass went back to work, even though she didn't need the money. He tried to get her to stay home but couldn't argue when she said she didn't have anything else to occupy her time. She needed something that felt like normal, if only for a little bit to get through the aftermath of losing Emma.

Jon didn't fight it.

He was, after all, busy with his writing. Having her out of the house gave him more time to work without guilt.

But then she started coming home later and later, and drunker and drunker. And then she'd sleep in later and later. And he thought for sure she was using again.

One night, he asked her.

She flipped out.

He said he wasn't being judgmental. He even offered to get her help.

"Like your family got for me? No, thanks. I don't need your charity."

Then she went to work, angry.

He went to the Shipwreck, spying on her. Saw her talking to Craig, her old dealer. Jealousy flooded through him, angered him enough to approach them. He got in Craig's face and told him to stay the fuck away.

There was some pushing and shoving. Cass got pissed and took Jon out to the parking lot. "I don't need another mother."

"Why are you being so defensive of Craig? Are you sleeping with him?" He wasn't sure where that bit of insecurity came from, and he hated the words, and the weakness they implied, the moment they left his mouth.

That was like pressing the button.

She got in his face. "Well, at least Craig doesn't tell me what to do or follow me around, spying on me!"

And that's when Jon said the thing he wished he'd never said.

"Yeah, why don't you go be with Craig, then. Two junkies, fucking perfect for each other."

Time froze long enough for Jon to realize his fuck-up. Enough to see the look in her eyes, the hurt he wished he could take back. But he was too much in the moment and in his own ego to retract.

And, of course, it gave her enough time to cock back her hand and slap him straight across the face.

And that was the end.

Jon had hated himself ever since that moment.

She never came back home. Or returned his calls.

He had never felt more alone. So when Marty called with the offer back on the table for *Black Nova*, Jon saw it as an escape. A chance to bury himself in his work, and maybe finally get his shit together. Eventually, he'd return to Hamilton and patch things up with Cass.

Because he really did love her.

Was it possible to love them both?

Didn't loving one person preclude you from loving another? He'd always thought it did, but … maybe not.

Shaking the thoughts from his head — or trying to — he ordered another drink. After downing it, he turned in his seat and pushed his face into the pillow, hoping sleep would move his mind away from these thoughts.

He was dreaming of Sarah when he heard the sound of static coming over the television on the seatback in front of him. He opened his eyes and noticed that the sound wasn't just coming from his television, but from *every set* in sight.

The screens were flashing, flipping through movies erratically, static erupting in staccato bursts.

At first Jon thought it was some sort of weird interference, but something felt oddly familiar.

He looked three rows up to the Koreans and noticed that they were staring at the screens, just as confused as he was. Not just staring, but frozen.

What the fuck?

He was about to call out to them, to ask if they were okay. Then he felt someone standing beside him. It was Kari, looking down at him with that same blank stare the couple had been wearing.

"You okay?" he asked.

Then he saw the knife in her hand, coming straight at his face.

Jon dodged forward as she sank the blade into the seat cushion.

"What the fuck?" He bolted up, barely avoiding a second attack.

Her eyes were blank, but her movement was not. Swift, and not at all in a daze.

"What are you doing?" Jon yelled, knocking the blade from her hand and onto the ground.

Kari said nothing, immediately clawing at his face.

In any other situation, Jon would have defended himself, but something told him she wasn't in her right mind, and he didn't want to hurt her. He just needed to get away, maybe call back past the curtain that separated first class from the rest of the passengers, yell for an air marshal, someone who could apprehend the woman without harming her.

He shoved her backwards and she fell into the other row of seats, momentarily stunned.

Jon was about to head through the curtain when the Korean man rushed him, his hands claws around his neck, choking him.

What the fuck is happening?

Jon fell back, using the window as leverage to raise his foot and kick the man in his chest, propelling both him and the woman Jon assumed to be his wife, backward into the flight attendant.

The static grew louder, now coming over the speakers, as the light strobed with an effect that felt oddly familiar to Jon.

He flashed back to when Brock Houser was being questioned about Emma's death in the police station. The lights had flickered then, as well. And the static had been there, right before Houser tried to slit his own throat. Afterward, Brock had seemed utterly confused.

Whatever got to him is getting to these people.

Fear was a vice clamping down on his chest. Jon needed to get away from these people before one of them killed him. He looked around for the knife, but didn't see it.

His three attackers were struggling to get up, eyes still vacant, yet on him as their target.

"Stay down!"

He considered kicking the man, who was on top of the pile, but like the flight attendant, he seemed out of it, and Jon didn't want to seriously hurt anyone. They were like feral animals.

And the static had something to do with it.

He pushed through the curtain, calling out, "Is there an air marshal here?"

And then he saw another twenty or so passengers standing, staring at him with that same blank gaze.

"Oh, fuck."

Hands seized him as the lights went off, casting the entire plane into darkness.

Epilogue

Roger woke up strapped to a chair in a dark room, bright lights in his eyes.

Where am I?

What happened?

He was groggy, confused, his head pounding.

Then he remembered Dr. Engel behind him, something in his hand — an injector.

Anger thickened his blood. "What did you do to me?"

"There, there," Dr. Engel said, just out of sight. "Don't get yourself all worked up. This will all be a distant memory soon enough."

The doctor circled around and stood in front of Roger.

"Wait. You're not bringing Aubrey to me?"

"Oh, heaven's no. She's happy with her new family. What kind of life would you provide her here?"

"*We're* family."

"No, idiot," he said pressing his finger hard into Roger's chest. "You are not Roger Heller. You are an inferior copy."

Roger was angry, but more than that, he was hurt. Tears streamed down his face. "Please, I'll do anything you want. Just let me see Aubrey."

"Oh, I know you'll do whatever I want, and no, you can't see her."

"You lied!"

"Scream all you want, nobody will hear you." Dr. Engel opened his mouth and yelled, waving his hands up and down as if conducting some macabre orchestra of pain. "Nobody hears you, and, more importantly, nobody cares."

He went to a table in the corner and retrieved a large hypodermic with a glass vial attached. Inside was a glowing violet serum with tiny blinking lights.

"What is that? What are you going to do?"

"This is a nano-serum to erase what I want from your memory so that you can go back to being a useful tool."

"No. Don't. I … just want my daughter." He was bawling. "Please."

Dr. Engel laughed. "Jesus, you're pitiful. I'll make it a bit easier on you by making you forget your daughter. How about I do the same for your dead wife and son? Forget them all, then things'll be easier for everyone."

"No! Don't make me forget. I did what you asked. I gave you the information you wanted! You lied!"

"You're right. I lied. And you were too stupid to see I was doing so. What kind of father would you be to that child, unable to protect her because your brain is too limited? Oh, and while we're at it, I lied about *two* things."

Roger felt like his heart might burst. What else could this monster have lied about? How could this get any worse.

"Don't you want to know what?" Dr. Engel asked, taking a lot of joy out of teasing him.

"What?"

"Sarah and Emma are not safe. In fact, they are very much in my way. Nighty night."

And then the doctor injected his neck.

Episode 17

Prologue

1992

IN BLAKE'S DREAMS, Anastasia was always alive. They were together in Conway Gardens, sitting on the bench he'd made for her as a Valentine's Day present years ago. It felt good, talking to her again. He'd had so much to tell her since her death two months ago giving birth to Jon.

When he woke, his wife was still gone.

Her side of the bed still empty.

And the pain was still fresh.

Blake didn't let many people get close to him. He felt that showing emotions too readily armed your enemies, and even those close to you, with weapons to wield against you. Why hand them the means to harm you?

Ana was the only one he'd allowed into his heart.

The only one he could drop his guard in front of.

The only person he could not live without.

And now she was gone due to cardiac failure as she gave birth to Jon, a child Blake would have to raise alone — without her.

He was not a good father in that namby-pamby way of modern fathers, being "emotionally available" and other bullshit. And he was fine with that.

Blake would rather follow his father's example. Now that was a man. You did your job, which in this case was building Conway Industries. That advanced the world through science, while continuing to provide enormous wealth that would be passed down to his children someday.

There was no quarter given, nor expected. Even though Blake was Billy's son and heir apparent to the family business and fortune, Blake wasn't above screwing up. Or paying for his mistakes. He remembered one time he'd messed up in his late twenties, and his father temporarily fired him, telling him not to take it personal. It was only business.

And that was how Blake fathered — as a business. And his main jobs were to prepare his children for the world that waited for them, to make sure they did everything they were capable of doing, and to provide them the tools to realize their abilities.

He'd always left the other stuff, the stuff he wasn't good at — like love and emotions — to Ana. Between them, things would work out. He'd have smart, self-determined children who would also be kind and loving, like her.

But now, he felt like a boat unmoored, lost at seas he wasn't equipped to navigate.

"What am I supposed to do now?" he asked the place where she should be.

Of course, there was no answer. She was dead, and despite having the best medical care in the United States, somehow Ana's rare heart condition had gone unnoticed by every doctor she'd ever seen.

When Blake came back to Hamilton Island, he fired every physician who had ever treated his wife. If he could have had them shot, he probably would have. He had to settle for ruining their careers.

Then he hired a live-in nanny to help Madge with the kids.

And finally, he started drinking again. While he usually waited until after dinner, on this particular morning, he felt the urge to start early.

He left his bedroom, made his way to his library bar, and poured himself a glass of Glenlivet. He was going to sit and relax before the kids woke up, but then went to his office to work instead.

On the way, he grabbed the bottle of scotch and his glass.

Upstairs, he heard the baby crying.

The sound of Jon gave him a headache.

He went to his office, closed the door, and was thankful not to have to answer the child's every cry. He couldn't look at the bastard without blaming it for Anastasia's death.

It was wrong. Ana would hate him for blaming the baby for her death, but he couldn't help how he felt.

Emotions were a weakness, sometimes beyond even his control.

He sat at his desk. As he waited for his computer to turn on, Blake went to the fax machine and yanked his waiting faxes. The only one of any interest to him was the latest report by the head of the pharmaceutical arm of Conway Industries. He hoped to see good news on their recent trial of a new anti-depressant.

Halfway through the summary, he saw there was nothing good to report, so he tossed all the pages to the ground and deeply sighed. Then he fell into his chair and poured another drink, listening to the obnoxious dial up as his computer connected to the net.

He was about to check his email when he heard a knock on his door.

"Dad?"

"What is it, Warren?" he asked, annoyed.

"Can I come in?"

He let out another sigh, set his scotch down hard on the desk. "Yes. Make it quick. I'm working."

Warren came in with red eyes. He'd been crying. Probably had bad dreams about his mother again. While a part of Blake wanted to hug him and let him know it was okay, his instincts told him not to — the only way through grief was to face it head-on and not have anyone sugarcoat the truth. Life sucked, get over it.

"Dad? Can I go to a party this Sunday?"

"A party? Whose party?"

"Melinda Peterson. It's her birthday and I … well, I'd like to go. But I also know I'm supposed to help take care of Jon."

"You know the nanny can't be here on Sundays. Why are you even asking?"

"Well, …" he trailed off, looking at the tiled floor.

"If you can't speak your reason, why on Earth should I let you go. No."

Warren started to cry, but then caught himself. He knew better. Blake would find a way to make whatever he was sad about even worse until he learned to just suck it up and stop the damned whining.

"Yes, sir," Warren said, turning around to leave the office.

Blake almost let him, glad to return to his drink and work. But he was too curious to release him just yet. "Warren."

"Yes, father?"

"What was your reason for wanting to go? You were going to say something, tell me."

"Well, I don't know if you'll find it a *good* reason is all. And I don't want to make you mad."

Blake wished he'd not asked, but in for a penny …

"Go ahead, son."

"Well, I really like Melinda."

"*Like* her? Like or love, son?"

"Love?" Warren said.

"Love? Why so much of a question in the statement. You either love her or you don't. So, which is it? Love or like?"

"Love."

Blake nodded.

"What time is it?"

"Noon. At the community center."

Blake rolled his eyes. Melinda's parents had money. Why were they having the party at the community center instead of renting out a hall or restaurant. "Okay, then. You can go to the party. We'll find arrangements for the baby."

"Thank you, Father," Warren said, with a goofy grin that almost warmed his heart.

"You're welcome. Now let me get back to work before I change my mind."

"Yes, sir," Warren said, closing the door.

Blake could hear him running down the hall, excited.

He pulled up the email on his screen when his phone rang.

Caller ID showed that it was Hanz Engel, the doctor who had worked with his father right up to his retirement in his nineties. A no-nonsense man, like Blake. If he was calling him at home, especially this morning, it must be damned important.

He picked up the phone. "Yes?"

"Mr. Conway?"

"Yes, Dr. Engel, how can I help you?"

"I need to discuss something very important with you."

"What is it?"

"We need to meet in person. Please be here at exactly ten-fifty."

Blake didn't press him by asking why. The man was intelligent, and likely had news that he didn't want to deliver over lines which could be tapped by the Feds. Perhaps something illegal they'd all someday want to claim ignorance of knowing.

The doctor told him to meet him at an old warehouse on

the west end of the island. And to come alone, to not even use a driver.

Now Blake was doubly curious.

He said okay, then hung up, his curiosity piqued, though he was annoyed at the highly specific time.

He got in his Jaguar and drove.

~

BLAKE WAS SURPRISED to find an armed guard and a gate surrounding the warehouse. It was his property, and he had no recollection of anything going on here, let alone it being fenced off or any security stationed.

Was this something the board did without his approval? Was it a legacy project from his father's years? His father had been dead for more than a decade, so that seemed unlikely.

He had many questions for Dr. Engel.

Blake showed his credentials to the armed guard stationed outside of the warehouse and was waved through.

He got out of his car and passed another two guards.

When he stepped through the entrance, he didn't find the dilapidated building he'd expected. The place was giant and clean, the laboratory brightly-lit. A couple of scientists he recognized as his top people were there. Computers lined the walls, and the entire center space was cleared.

A large red X was painted on the floor in the center, surrounded by a red circle.

"Good afternoon, Doctor." He shook the man's hand.

Engel's grip was tight and firm. "Good afternoon, Mr. Conway. I've been waiting for this day for a long time."

"What is it?"

"It's time to give you a peek behind the curtains."

"What are you talking about?" Blake didn't like the smile on Dr. Engel's face. Same for the scientists. They all knew something he didn't, and that annoyed him. Maybe infuriated him. They were *his* employees. Whatever bullshit pet project they were working on had better impress the hell out of him, or they'd be on the chopping block.

"It's better to just show you." Doctor Engel walked toward the center of the room, stopping just outside a circle.

He put out his hand. "Don't go past the circle until I tell you it's safe."

The doctor pointed to a giant digital clock display on the far wall. *11:05 AM.*

"Just six more minutes. Everybody, make sure you've backed up your work."

"What's in six minutes?" Blake asked.

The scientists rushed to a pair of computers to save their progress.

Doctor Engel said, "At the eleventh minute of each hour, the veil is thinnest."

"What *veil?*"

"You'll see." He grinned like an idiot kid teasing about the thing behind his back. He'd never seen the man even smile, let alone look this ridiculously happy. And frankly, Blake was starting to wonder if the doctor had finally lost his mind.

He was old, though Blake had no idea how old, since most of his file was redacted. His father had brought him in during the seventies, saying Engel was in a federal witness program and most of his information, including his real name, was confidential. An ideal scientist for what they were working on.

Because Billy Conway trusted the doctor, Blake had as well. But now, as he watched the man bordering on lunacy, he might have to seriously reconsider the man's value to the company.

As the clock struck 11:10, the doctor took a couple of steps back, then looked at Blake. "Are you ready?"

The air around them crackled with blue light.

Lights flickered.

Then the computers all died, static crackling from their speakers.

The room went dark.

Blake was growing increasingly annoyed at the theatrics and was about to ask what the hell was going on, when a blue circle appeared, hovering over the red X.

"What the hell is that?"

"It is a portal, Mr. Conway. A portal to somewhere very special."

The portal was flat, not three dimensional, as if someone had just drawn a ring on the world, colored it with some blue light, and opened it.

On the other side, he saw movement — a dark shape, blurred, growing closer.

Someone was coming from the other side.

His heart raced. It wasn't fear so much as a wonder he'd not felt in forever.

The shape stepped through the portal.

Billy Conway, very much alive and breathing.

"Jesus!" Blake said.

Billy smiled, "Not quite, son. But close."

Chapter 1 - Jon Conway

One moment Jon was in the grip of the mob, clawing, scratching, and trying to murder him. Another, he somehow slipped through, back into first-class, running face-first into the Korean man with the knife.

He took a swing at Jon, cutting him across his arm.

Jon screamed, then headbutted the man in his nose.

The man fell back into the seat, blood spraying everywhere. The flight attendant dove for the fallen knife. Jon vaulted over her, moving toward the front of the plane.

The static and flickering lights had reached a fever pitch, turning the entire cabin into a hellish display of light and sound, making it impossible to see or hear anything clearly. Their madness was seeping into his skull, and he wanted to plunge the knife into his head to halt the chaos.

More movement behind him. The mob of crazies shoved their way through the plane, spilling into first-class in an unending wave of death and destruction. Bodies fell beneath them, trampled on, bleeding, very likely dying.

Even if Jon could get the knife, he couldn't fend them all off. The mass yielded to nothing, moving forward as one.

And he certainly couldn't kill a plane full of people. Who

the hell would ever believe that he'd been attacked by them all? This would be splashed over every screen, newspaper, and magazine in the world, *Movie Star Jon Conway Goes on Airborne Killing Spree!*

He seized on the only possible refuge, the bathroom, and raced toward it.

The Korean woman came at him, fast, teeth gnashing, eager to bite him. Jon used her momentum, ducking, running his shoulder into her body, upending then dropping the woman on her head behind him as he continued forward and flew into the bathroom, pulling the door closed and locking it.

Screams as bodies hit the door. First they beat on it, then they started clawing.

Jon watched in horror as the door rattled on its hinges while more bodies gathered around the door. The screams kept coming, though no words anywhere close to intelligible — mostly grunts and wailing.

His heart raced as he stood, legs on either side of the toilet, watching the door, convinced at any moment it would be yanked off its hinges and he'd be dragged out and shredded.

But the door held.

After several minutes, Jon noticed blood soaking his entire right shirt sleeve.

He took his shirt off, assessed the cut as not too deep, then ripped the other sleeve, tearing a makeshift bandage. He cleaned the wound using soap and water from the sink, then wrapped the torn shirt sleeve around the cut.

Outside, noises faded. Same for the banging. Were the crazed people out of their daze? He didn't dare open the door to find out.

Did the effect wear off?

And if so, what next?

Had life just returned to normal?

And then, as if answering his question, he heard screams

and cries as the people suddenly became aware of the injured, and likely dead, people lying trampled in the aisle.

Jon stayed put, terrified to open the door.

As he sat in the bathroom, he started thinking again about Sarah and Emma being alive. How could Blake pull off two phony deaths? Jon had seen Emma's body, and even identified her corpse. It was too convincing to have been a fake.

Jon had been around enough special effects to know the difference between a prop and a corpse. He had no doubt whatsoever. The body had been real.

So, whose was it?

How did his father, brother, or whoever the hell was pulling the strings of this conspiracy, manage to find a dead child who looked exactly like Emma?

But did she look like his daughter or a bloated corpse fished out of the sea?

Suddenly, Jon couldn't remember what her body had looked like. In his mind, it had been her, but grayer. But there was no way that was possible, being found dead in the ocean like she'd been.

He remembered her wide-open eyes, staring up at nothing the way they'd once stared at him. Eyes that he'd never see looking back at him again.

But was it her?

Memory was a tricky thing, and maybe that was what Conway Industries was counting on.

After a while, he was sitting on the toilet, going stir crazy being stuck in the tiny bathroom, when someone knocked on the door. A normal knock.

"Occupied."

After a while longer, another knock.

"Occupied," he repeated.

"Sir," a woman said, "we're about to land in Sydney. We need you to take your seat."

It had to be the same flight attendant that tried to murder

him. But instead of sounding murdery, now she sounded downright pleasant.

He peeked out the door.

She smiled, as if she hadn't tried to shove a knife through his head. "Are you okay, sir?"

He glanced at the Korean couple, who looked like they'd been in a tussle, the man's face blooming with a pair of ugly bruises. But neither of them looked at him as anything more than a fellow passenger.

Jon cautiously left the bathroom then slowly returned to his seat. Everything looked normal. No static, no zombie-like people trying to murder him. He might've thought he'd hallucinated the whole thing if not for the knife mark in the seat. And his arm.

He sat down and prayed that the rest of the flight would be free of static.

When they landed, the captain reminded everyone that there would be a lengthy delay until the flight resumed its course to LAX and then finally Seattle.

Feel free to enjoy some of the fine dining at Sydney's airport restaurants, and thank you again for flying with Qantas.

As Jon got off the plane, the flight attendant winked at him. It was all he could do to stifle a laugh.

Chapter 2 - Sarah Hughes

Sarah and Emma were settling down to dinner when their door opened and the men in black stormed in.

"What's going on?" Sarah got up from the table.

"Come with us." A woman approached her with open cuffs.

"What's going on?" Sarah repeated as a man strode toward her daughter. She stepped between them, "Do *not* touch her!"

The man dropped his cuffs, and stared at her blankly. And that's when she realized she'd commanded him, same as she'd commanded the guards to drop their guns in Dr. Engel's sick experiment.

"Leave us!" she shouted, hoping to force them all out.

The woman shoved Sarah forward, knocking her to the ground, then fell on top of her, knee in her back, forcing the cuff around one of her wrists.

Sarah kicked out, trying to push the woman off her.

"Help me cuff her," the guard yelled.

Another body was on her, grabbing her arm.

"Get off of my Mom!" Emma screamed.

Sarah turned to see one of the guards cuffing Emma, pulling her toward the door.

"Leave her alone!" Sarah screamed.

"Shut up!" The woman punched Sarah in the back of her head.

Darkness flooded the edges of her vision. She tried to stay conscious.

But failed as darkness won.

~

SARAH WOKE in a tiny cell with bright white walls and harsh lights burning overhead. A big glass door separated her from the hall beyond. Across the way was another cell, though it was dark and she couldn't tell if it was occupied.

When she sat up, a wave of dizziness crashed over her. There was a throbbing lump on the back of her head.

She was sitting on a foam matt on a slab of metal that served as a bed. The only other thing in the cell was a metal toilet and sink.

Someone had dressed her in white scrubs, the same kind the subjects shot dead by the guards had been wearing.

Sarah got up, the polished white floor cold on her bare feet.

She went to the door and could only see three other cells, all of them dark, from her vantage point.

She pressed against the door, tried to push then slide it. But the thing wouldn't budge.

"Hello!"

No response.

Sarah pounded on the door, timid at first, and then repeatedly, loud and annoying.

"Hey! I want to talk to Billy Conway!"

A woman's voice boomed over the speaker inside her cell. "Please step back from the door."

"No! I want to see Billy Conway."

"Please step back from the door."

Sarah was sick and tired of playing by their rules, only to be locked up like some damned criminal. She crossed her arms over her chest and glared up at the camera.

And then came the shocks, from where she didn't know.

~

SARAH WOKE to someone looking down at her.

Blake Conway.

She sat up. "What the hell is happening?"

"I might ask you the same. I've been told that Emma brought my son aboard the ship and you asked him to rescue you both."

Roger!

She glared in silence.

He stood there, hands in his pockets, completely at ease, his face unfazed by her steady gaze, or the situation.

"How can you be so damned calm when you're imprisoning people? When your doctor had guards shoot test subjects? I want off this damned station!"

"But our work is not yet done."

"I don't give a damn about your work."

"That's obvious by your disdain for our rules."

Sarah felt a rush of Cassidy inside of her. "Fuck your rules."

His eyes finally registered an emotion — surprise.

"I'll come back and talk to you when you're calmer."

"I'm sorry." She didn't want him to leave. Not yet. "Where is Emma?"

"She's in the cell across from you, sleeping."

"Why can't she be in here?"

"There's not enough room for two people." He looked at

her as if it should be obvious. "Besides, I don't think you want her getting shocked for your bad behavior."

She wanted to punch him in his smug face. But she resisted the urge. "Why do we have to be up here?"

"I already told you. The world thinks you're dead. Besides, you and Emma are providing us a lot of excellent data which is helping with our research."

"Your plans to evolve humanity?"

"Yes." He folded his hands in front of him.

"Looks to me like you're creating super soldiers or something up here. So are you doing this to advance humanity, or to sell the Department of Defense?"

He smiled. "Ah, I always pegged you as the optimistic one. I think perhaps you spent too much time with your sister. While the DOD would love our advancements, and we have certainly given them some of our technology, we've saved the best for us. And no, we're not creating super soldiers. This isn't some comic book, dear. What we're doing is something you can't even comprehend."

"Try me."

He looked at her for a long time, then said, "No. You're not ready. But I think Emma will be soon."

"Don't you dare do anything to my daughter. I swear to God, I will kill you."

"Why do you insist on being so adversarial, Sarah? Can't you see I'm trying to help you? I'm trying to help everyone. And yet, you think of me as what? Some awful monster locking you and your child away?"

"You really see yourself as the hero in all of this, don't you? You have a mad scientist killing people, and you're conducting tests on people completely unaware of what you're doing. And … don't even get me started on the clones. You aren't the hero, Blake. You are the crazy villain, and if you can't see that, there is no hope for you."

"I have sacrificed more than you know, more than *anyone*

can possibly know, in the name of science, for the betterment of humanity. I don't expect you to understand … yet. But you will. Soon, everyone will see I was right." He turned to leave. "Guards, open the door."

The door slid open, then he turned to her. "Please don't try to escape again, or I will put Emma somewhere you can't see her. Perhaps in Doctor Engel's chambers."

He left.

The door slid shut.

Sarah wanted to murder him.

Chapter 3 - Cassidy Hughes

After the driver dropped Cass off at the Shipwrecked parking lot, she got into her car and punched the steering wheel, wondering why the hell she'd overreacted this morning with Stephen.

It was as if she was destined to find a way to fuck up everything she touched.

She wished she'd not gone home with him. That she'd not been so weak, that she hadn't needed the distraction from the shit show her life had become.

It wasn't that she regretted sleeping with him. He was a nice enough guy, not a scumbag like Craig and so many of her regulars. And she enjoyed his company. But when she woke up in a room that he'd shared with his wife just a couple of months ago — a wife who was now in the looney bin — and saw how he'd reacted at the notion of his son seeing her, Cassidy realized her error.

She not only slept with a married man, but one who felt guilt and shame for his actions. The last thing she wanted was to be somebody's guilty fling. But those weren't the things that set her off. It was the pitiful way he'd looked at her when he asked if she wanted to stay at his place.

That look — like she was a fuck-up incapable of taking care of herself. She hated pity, especially from someone she didn't know, or from someone she thought hadn't pitied her. That was one of the things she'd liked about him. He didn't seem to know her. Wasn't aware of her baggage. Sure, he knew about Emma and Jon and all that, but he didn't know about all of her fuck-ups or her drug history.

Except maybe he did.

It was hard to keep anything quiet on this godforsaken island.

She looked at her phone to see how many hours she had before Shipwrecked opened for lunch.

Still at least three hours before she could clock in, assuming they let her grab an extra shift.

Cassidy wished she'd not been in such a rush to get out of his house, that she'd at least taken a shower before leaving. She smelled like last night and felt even worse.

You could go to Jon's house.

She hated that idea. For one, Jon's security system recorded all entrances and exits to the house and sent them to his phone. So he would know.

And that was almost as bad as going back to Vivian's. Maybe worse.

She could rent a hotel room, but Cassidy didn't have a ton of money, and she had to work at four anyway, so it would be a waste to check in now.

Come on. Just go to Jon's. He's probably too busy to even notice who is coming and going.

Maybe. But what if she ran into the cleaning crew that came however often he had them coming? They would know she was there, that she'd gone crawling back to the Conway house.

She sighed, resigning herself to heading back there. Chances were he wouldn't call, anyway, given how he'd been ignoring her attempts to reach him.

And if he *did* call, well then, maybe she'd talk to him. Maybe she'd even let him apologize. Hell, maybe she would say sorry for all the things she'd done, some of which he didn't even know.

It wasn't that his calling her a drug addict had hurt her, though it certainly did. The last thing she wanted was confirmation that he, someone who meant so much to her, had seen her the same as every other fucking Conway had.

One of the things she'd loved about Jon was that he didn't eye her in that judgmental *I'm better than you* way like the rest of his asshole family. And half the fucking island.

It wasn't the words that hurt so much as their truth.

She had been using. And, something he didn't know and she could never tell him — she'd fucked Craig in his van one night when she was "working late."

And the more she thought about her actions, the more she recognized them for what they were — an attempt to sabotage her happiness. As if she didn't deserve the good things that had been happening.

She deserved to suffer, and if Jon wasn't going to hurt her, then she'd make him.

God, how fucked up am I?

She looked at the bottle of pills still on her seat where her mother had thrown them. She was a bit surprised someone hadn't spotted them and broken into her car for a fix.

She picked them up, hating them more than anything she'd ever loathed in her life. How could something that promised so much pleasure bring so much pain?

And right now, the pleasure was calling to her, her inner addict begging, *Come on, Cass. Just one to get through the day. One won't hurt.*

"Fuck you." She threw the pills at the floorboard. "Actually, you know what?"

She leaned over, grabbed the pills, and got out of her car.

She made a beeline toward the trash can next to the front door of Shipwrecked.

Fuck the pills.

Fuck Craig.

Fuck the temptation.

She went to toss them into the trash when the Addict whispered into her ears.

I wouldn't do it.

You never know when you might need them. What if your back acts up again? Can't go get a massage from Stephen now, can ya?

And you have to work. Just try and get through a shift with that pain. Go ahead, I dare you.

She stared at the pills, squeezing the bottle tight enough to turn her knuckles white.

Just throw them away. Do it now and you won't have to worry about the temptation. Just do it.

But the Addict answered, *You can't do it. You need it. You can pretend to be strong, but we all know deep down inside that you're not.*

Jon was right — once an addict, always an addict.

Fuck you! I'm not an addict.

Then throw 'em away. Go ahead.

The bottle shook in her hands as she held the pills just inside the trash can lid.

Then pulled her hand out, bottle still in it.

She went back to the car.

See, you're not an idiot. You know you need them. No shame in that.

She opened her door, threw the pills at the passenger side floorboard, got in, then slammed it shut.

Correction. The pills weren't the thing she hated more than anything else.

It was herself.

She started driving, winding up in Jon's neighborhood, trying to summon the strength to go back inside the house that was meant to be their home, the place where she was going to have a normal family for the first time in her life.

And then she saw the flashing lights behind her — a Paladin SUV.

Chapter 4 - Milo Anderson

Milo waited a moment after his father dropped him off in front of the school, then he high tailed it to the corner store where Katie was waiting in her car.

"Any problems getting away?" Katie asked as Milo climbed inside.

He smiled. "Nope."

"Good," she said, pulling out of the parking spot. "You ready?"

"Yes."

"You sure you can find the cave again?"

"I think so."

They were going to find the cave where she and Alex took refuge during the storm. She was convinced something had been calling to her ever since that day. Something that might help explain all the weird shit on the island, and maybe trigger memories of what happened when she vanished after making love to Alex.

Milo wasn't as confident that they'd find anything, but he kept his doubts to himself. Spending time with Katie was bringing back fragments of his memories, so it couldn't hurt to spend more time together. Plus, it felt great to hang with an old friend. Or hell, *any* friend. Milo had spent the past couple of months in solitude, even in school. He was often a ghost among the living, barely interacting, walking in a constant drugged daze.

But today, Milo hadn't taken his pills.

He wanted to see clearly. To feel again, even if today only brought back painful memories of Alex or his life before the shootings. He longed to feel something, to remember anything of his old life.

And Katie was the key.

If she was nervous, he couldn't tell. She was in good spirits, singing along loudly to the radio, searching back roads along the woods, looking for a spot close to where she thought the cave might be.

She eventually drove down an old dirt access road, overgrown with vegetation, and parked.

"You sure we won't get towed?"

"I dunno." She didn't sound overly worried. Even though Katie was troubled by missing memories and haunted by Alex's death same as Milo, she hadn't closed herself off to the rest of the world. She still knew how to enjoy life. Milo hoped he could figure out how to follow her example.

They got out of the car.

She went to the trunk and grabbed a backpack. "Got some food and water in case we get lost."

Milo offered to hold it — the gentlemanly thing to do.

She stopped in the middle of the road, looked around as if trying to gather her bearings.

"You remember which way it is, right?" Milo asked.

"Uh-huh." She pointed north. "That way."

Her tone inspired no confidence.

~

THEY'D BEEN WALKING for what felt like an hour when a cold wind blew in, shaking the trees and branches. It felt as if they'd walked in one giant circle.

"You sure you know which way?" he asked.

"Um, yeah."

"*Um, yeah?*" Milo repeated. "Awesome!"

"Relax, Milo. I'm sure we'll find it."

Thunder rolled overhead. Then the first fat drops of rain splashed down on them. Katie burst into laughter.

"What are you laughing at?"

"Reminds me of when Alex and I found the cave. How rain forced us to look for cover. Oh, my God."

"What?" he asked, looking around.

Then he saw what she was looking at, half-buried beneath brush and grass growing atop of it, nearly concealing the entrance.

"Is that it?"

It seemed much smaller and more forbidding than he'd imagined. More like the kind of hole you wouldn't go in for fear it would collapse on you. Or the sort a bear might have made its home.

"I don't think so, but …" She approached it, anyway.

"What are you doing if that's not it?"

"Can't you feel it?"

"Feel what?"

She stopped and turned to him, holding out her shaking hands. "The vibration."

He looked down at his own hands, perfectly still. Then back at hers, trembling as if an invisible current pulsed under her skin.

"It's in there!" A smile split her face as she ran toward the cave.

"Wait! Don't you want to talk about—"

Too late. Katie ran into the darkness.

Milo looked around, getting one last look at the topside

before he left to follow his friend into the subterranean depths below Hamilton Island.

~

THE SMALL ENTRANCE led them deeper, eventually opening into a spacious cavern that seemed impossibly large and surprisingly warm. The sound of dripping water drew his flashlight to an underground pool with rising stalagmites.

Milo was fascinated by the structures and how alien the cave felt, as if they'd crossed over from Earth to some bizarre landscape on some other planet. He felt anxiousness taking root in his head, threatening to spread its tendrils. Impossibly far from the world. They could get lost here and never be found.

Yet, another part of Milo was too fascinated by his surroundings to turn back.

He swept his flashlight ahead and stopped when he saw movement, something dark moving fast.

"Fuck!"

Katie spun around. "What?"

He searched for whatever he'd spotted, then froze in horror as his flashlight illuminated thousands of bats clinging to the ceiling.

"Oh, fuck this." He swept the light back and forth. Most of the bats seemed to be asleep, though a few were flying erratically around.

Milo could imagine them all waking at once and descending, their sharp teeth burrowing into his flesh. How many would it take to eat both he and Katie, to leave nothing but their clothing and bones, piles of things that were once human, to be discovered years, maybe decades, later by unfortunate explorers.

His heart was frozen, and his chest tight.

He needed to get out, now.

"Relax, they won't hurt you," Katie said.

"What? Are you a bat expert now?"

"No. But they're hibernating."

"That's just another word for sleeping. They can wake up any second. We're in their home. We've gotta get out of here."

She put her hands on his shoulders and squeezed, meeting his gaze. "Relax, Milo. They're bats."

"Are they carnivores?" His stunning gap of bat knowledge made him feel ignorant. He had almost encyclopedic knowledge of the *Dungeons & Dragons Monster Manual*, yet he didn't even know if bats ate flesh.

"As long as you don't corner them, you'll be fine."

"Are you s-s-sure?"

"Yes, Milo. I'm sure. Look." Katie pointed toward a tunnel leading further into the cave. Red vines crept up the wall. Glowing crimson, pulsating between a bright and dark glow, like a heartbeat.

"The vibration. It's coming from that way."

Katie started walking.

"I dunno if this is a good idea," Milo protested, but she ignored him as she headed toward the passageway.

Damn it.

He quickly followed, making sure to keep quiet. He didn't want to wake the winged beasts above.

"You might want to watch your step." She trained her flashlight down at what looked like a river of black sludge frozen in place to their left. "That's bat shit. Oh, and one more thing, while they won't eat you, they *do* transmit rabies."

"Awesome."

She giggled.

As Katie headed through the tunnel, a dark shape dove straight into Milo.

He yelped and he dropped the flashlight, then crouched on the ground, swatting at his head to make sure the furry fucker wasn't attached.

Milo hunched over, waiting for either another dive-bombing or for Katie to call after him, teasing him when she saw that he was cowering in fear. The light lay on the ground, practically teasing him as it shined straight ahead into the tunnel where he should be headed.

When neither attack nor insult arrived, Milo grabbed the light and treaded carefully forward, bracing for attack.

He stepped into the tunnel. It grew even warmer as he followed its winding curvature. Vines followed the passageway, growing thicker and brighter as he progressed.

He followed the path around a bend, flashlight bobbing frantically on the lookout for threats.

"Katie," he called out, hoping she hadn't gotten too far ahead. He rounded the corner, and the vines' reddish glow intensified. A humming drone vibrated in his bones.

The anxiety that had nested in some deep recess of his brain was now spreading, infecting every part of Milo's mind.

Get out.

Now.

Run.

It will devour you both.

But he couldn't leave without Katie.

He called out to her.

No response.

Fuck.

"Katie!"

He heard only his racing heart and that infernal hum. The vibration intensified. The hairs on his arms stood on end.

"Katie!"

Leave without her!

Go.

Now, Milo.

Now!

But he couldn't leave her.

Milo had to find her and get her to come with him. Why

wasn't she responding? Had she gotten too far ahead, so deep in the cave that she could no longer hear?

He ran forward, calling out to her as he went.

The farther he got into the cave, the louder the hum, and the faster he ran, eager to find Katie.

The flashlight's beam bounced as he ran, though the red glow was so bright, he no longer needed a light source.

Milo ran faster, no longer afraid of waking bats or slipping in shit. Desperation spurred him on.

The tunnel turned back on itself, defying physics, winding about in impossible ways. He found himself in a small pocket of bright red walls, so thick with vines, they covered nearly every square inch, and, to his horror, Milo realized there nowhere left to go.

I must've missed a branching passageway.

He turned to find his way back, but the way he'd come from was gone.

Impossibly, Milo was surrounded by vine-infested walls.

He spun in a circle, panic swelling as he realized that he'd somehow gotten himself trapped.

The vines were brightest here, and that heartbeat the loudest.

Something wet slapped his face from above.

At first, he thought it was bat shit. But when he wiped at it and pulled his fingers away, he realized it wasn't black, but red.

He slowly looked up and his heart stopped.

Katie was some forty feet above him, entwined by those same red vines. Her eyes were wide open, her mouth forming words he couldn't hear above the hum. Her arms and feet dangled, reaching out to him.

Behind her was a bright red glowing ball, big enough to touch the walls on both sides, a sac of membranous glowing crimson flesh, the body from which the vines had descended, nestled in the space above, like a bat clinging to the ceiling.

Something red hit him again.

The red vines had pierced Katie's chest, and it was her blood dripping down on him.

Her mouth kept moving as if she were trying to say something, so she must still be alive.

A voice that wasn't hers came from Katie's mouth, and seemingly the walls around him, speaking in the same tone of the hum.

"Miiiiilllllloooooo."

Milo screamed.

Chapter 5 - Sarah Hughes

Sarah paced her cell, watching the windowed door across the way, hoping the light would come on soon so she could confirm Emma was in there as Blake had said.

She wouldn't rest without being certain that she was there and not somewhere being "tested."

Sarah hated Roger for selling her out. Now that Blake and the doctor knew what Emma was capable of, what other things would they have her do? How would they monetize her abilities? Or, worse, weaponize them?

Conway Industries developed biotech, implants, and even weapons technology for the military. What would they do with a girl who could teleport people to her?

The thoughts themselves were a holocaust.

She needed to get her daughter off of the space station, but now the enemy knew of her best chance for escape. They'd either stop Jon from coming or wait to imprison him as well. She'd hoped to talk some sense into Blake but had failed miserably. Was he so far gone that he refused to see his insanity?

She supposed that last question was redundant.

There was muffled excitement outside her door, and a

raised voice, though Sarah couldn't make out who spoke or what was said.

Then she saw Billy approaching the door. Closer, she could make out his words, him yelling at one of the guards to open the damned door.

Thank God!

The door slid open, and he stepped inside. "I'm so sorry, dear. Did they hurt you?"

"No. They put Emma in that room." Sarah pointed across the hall.

"What happened?" He took her hand and led her from the cell.

The guard stopped them, rifle at the ready. "If you want to talk to her, you have to do so inside the cell, Mr. Conway."

"What?"

"Orders of the doctor and Mr. Conway."

"Blake is not the boss here. I am! Now stand down."

"I'm sorry, sir, I can't let her leave without permission from Blake."

"Fine!" Billy said, stepping into the cell, "we'll talk here. Meanwhile, get my damned son down here."

"Yes, sir."

Sarah followed Billy into the cell.

They sat on the bed. "What's going on? I saw on the monitors that you and Emma were locked up in here."

Sarah told him everything, knowing full well he might not be any happier than Blake to know his son was coming and possibly bringing others to liberate them.

His frown confirmed her suspicions.

"You don't want me to go, either, do you?"

Billy took a long moment to respond, giving her stomach enough time to fill with dread that she truly had nobody on the ship who cared about her or Emma's best interests.

"What we do here is very sensitive. If word got out, if people knew you and Emma were alive, it could destroy so much of our work. Maybe even most of it. The government might very well shut this down."

"I understand. But there must be some way we can live on Earth without attracting attention. You have enough money to hide us away forever. We don't have to be up here. I want my daughter to live a normal life. I want us to be a family again, with Jon."

This last part was part lie, to gain some sympathy, but also part truth, as so many of Cassidy's memories and feelings were bleeding into hers. Sarah found herself surprised at just how much she felt for Jon when he appeared before, how much love was still in there.

But is it my love for him, or Cass's?

It didn't matter now. Sarah would say whatever she had to in order to get off the space station.

Billy was quiet until he finally said, "You're right."

"What?"

"You're right. We can hide you just as well down there as we can up here. You don't *need* to be up here. I will talk to Blake immediately."

"I disagree wholeheartedly, Father," Blake said from over the intercom.

"Son, end this madness now. Let Sarah and her daughter go home so they can be a family again."

"I'm sorry, but that isn't going to happen."

"Excuse me? You don't call the shots around here, Blake. I do!"

Billy stood, went to the door, and commanded the guards to open it.

But the door didn't budge.

And Sarah was going to be sick.

"Open the door!" Billy demanded.

"Sorry, Father. But you're no longer in charge."

"What? You can't do that."

"Don't take it personally," Blake said. "It's only business."

Chapter 6 - Cassidy Hughes

"Fucking rent-a-cops," Cassidy growled as she pulled over.

She wished Paladin never evolved into a private force with the powers of law enforcement, including pulling people over for no reason at all. Just like real cops.

Cass waited for the asshole to run her plates or whatever the fuck they were doing behind their tinted windshield. She hadn't been in any rush to reach Jon's house, but now she felt urgency.

The door swung open, then the freakish robotic-eyed Kaiser walked toward her.

He came into Shipwrecked a lot about a year or so ago and had always been a mean drunk. She'd hated waiting on him. He gave her the creeps with his weird-ass eye, and she wasn't sure if he could see through clothing or not, but the way he looked at her sometimes, it sure as hell felt like it. She wondered if he'd stopped drinking or was being a mean drunk somewhere else these days.

Why the hell is he pulling me over? I thought he was Emperor of the Rent-a-Cops or something.

She rolled down her window.

"License, registration, and proof of insurance, please."

"Really, Carl? You know me."

"License, registration, and proof of insurance," he repeated with a dead stare.

Cassidy sighed as she fished through her bag, searching for her wallet.

She found the license and insurance card, but not the registration. She leaned over and opened her glove compartment. It was filled with papers, condiment packs, an extra shirt, some underwear, napkins, tools, and a bunch of other shit. But no registration.

She handed him her license and insurance card. "Hold on, I'm looking for the registration."

She kept digging, pulling stuff out and putting it on her passenger seat, deliberate and slow, with a lot of passive-aggressive sighing to let Carl know what a pain in the ass it all was.

As she was looking through a stack of papers, her eyes seized on the pill bottle still lying on the floor.

Fuck.

She kept her expression calm, and continued as she had been, but instead of putting stuff from the glove compartment onto the seat, she started dropping it on the floorboard to cover the bottle.

She'd emptied it entirely. But no registration.

What the fuck?

She turned to Carl with a sigh. "I can't find the registration. But come on, Carl. I've been driving the same piece of shit forever. You know my car."

He still held her ID and insurance card. He looked her up and down.

Her heart raced as she wondered if he'd seen the bottle.

Fuck, can that stupid eye of his register my tension? Fuck. Fuck.

She tried to calm herself, but that was easier said than done.

"Do you know why I stopped you?"

"No." She tried to be a little more civil.

"Broken taillight."

"What?"

"Yeah, left taillight is broken."

"Fuck. I mean, I'm sorry. I didn't know. I'll get it fixed today."

He looked past her, to the mess on her seat and all over the floorboard. "Still didn't find the registration?"

"No, I probably left it at Viv's. Tell you what. I'll go get it and bring it to you if you need me to."

"How 'bout I take a look?"

Fuck. No.

She gave him her best phony laugh. "That's not necessary. This car is a mess. I'll find it and bring it to you."

"I don't mind." Carl walked around to the other side of the car.

Fuck.

Her heart raced faster. She imagined him finding the bottle on the floorboard and arresting her.

Then she'd be fucked. She'd probably do time. But even worse would be Vivian finding out. And Jon. Along with the all the Conways.

Fuck. No. Fuck.

What the hell do I do?

He was behind her car, about to turn.

She had seconds to think. Cass looked back, and saw that his head was out of view. Maybe behind the car where he couldn't see her.

At least she hoped so.

Cassidy ducked down, grabbed the bottle, and palmed it.

Then she sat back up as Carl came around on the passenger side.

She slid the bottle between the console and the seat where belt met buckle.

He knocked on the window.

She unlocked the passenger door.

Carl knelt down, started pushing papers off the seat one at a time, slowly, looking each one over, until they were all on the ground.

Then he took a seat next to Cassidy, putting his feet all over the stuff on the floor, not even caring that he was crushing stuff or getting dirt on it.

He closed the door.

He started pushing his foot back and forth, moving the pile of stuff on the floorboard as if looking for something, or deliberately trying to make Cassidy's mess even messier.

What the fuck is he doing?

He let out a long sigh.

"What's in the bottle, Cass?"

"What bottle?"

"The one that was on the floorboard."

Fuck.

No use playing dumb. He'd either seen it to begin with or he'd seen her grab it.

"Pain pills for my back."

"And why did you hide them?"

"I don't know." Her voice cracked, betraying the fear she was usually so good at masking.

He leaned over and put his hand on her leg, moving it up, patting as he went. "And where are they hiding? Here?"

He kept patting upward until he reached her crotch, then slid his hand over it.

She swallowed her bile.

"Or maybe here," he said, reaching up, grabbing her right breast, squeezing it hard, then pinching her nipple.

She fought the urge to cry out.

Cass stared straight ahead, pretending this wasn't happening, trying not to think about what might happen next. Would he really rape her, right here on the side of the road?

Carl grabbed her other breast, this time more gently, squeezing it, teasing her nipple.

"Hmm, not here either." His voice grew huskier.

He reached up, caressed her cheek, then ran his fingers over her lips before spreading them open.

She let him slide his fingers into her mouth. Fought the urge to bite them off.

He slid two fingers in, pressing down on Cassidy's tongue, going slow, then deeper down her throat.

She gagged, tears burning her eyes.

He laughed as he pulled his fingers from her throat, then smelled them, like he got off on whatever she gagged up.

She refused to wipe the tears brimming at the corners of her eyes.

"Where are the pills?"

She reached between the seat and the console, grabbed the bottle, and handed them to Carl without saying a word.

He held them up. "That's odd, no label. Don't prescriptions usually come with labels?"

"It came off."

Her lie wouldn't hold water if Carl checked to see if she had a valid prescription, but the way he was acting, he wasn't looking to bust her so much as coerce something from her.

And, in the moment, as much as the idea repulsed her, she would probably rather suck him off or fuck him than suffer an arrest.

She kept her mouth shut, waiting to see what he would do.

He shook the bottle. "Yeah, label just came off, eh? Usually they're on so tight, they're a bitch to get off. But yours just slid right off, huh?"

She nodded. "I guess."

He opened the bottle and shook one into his palm. "What are they?"

She told him the brand.

"They work?"

"They help with the back pain."

He popped it into his mouth.

Then he reached down to the water bottle in the center console, "You mind?"

She shook her head.

He took a drink, washing it down.

Then he looked at her, "Oh, I'm sorry. Would you like one?"

"No thank you. I'm not in pain right now."

He looked at her, quiet for a long moment. "I insist. I hate to take pills alone."

Fuck. Is this his idea of foreplay? Get me high then fuck me?

"I'm good."

He grabbed her hand, squeezed it tight until it opened. He poured pills into it. Five of them.

"Take them."

"That's *five* pills!"

"Five won't kill ya."

"No, I can't."

He dropped the bottle, rounded on her, grabbed her by the mouth — hard — and forced it open.

"Take the fucking pills." He shoved them down her throat.

No, no, no!

Cass struggled, but he was too strong.

The pills slid in.

Noooo!

She tried to spit them out, but he yanked her chin upward, shoving the back of her head into the car seat "Swallow."

"I need water," she gasped.

He lifted the bottle to her throat, pouring the water into her mouth, and then all down the front of her shirt.

"Swallow."

She did.

Fuck.

"Jesus Christ, never knew a junkie so afraid to take some fucking pills."

"I'm not a junkie." She glared at him.

"Oh? Not what I heard. What's that saying? *Once a junkie, always a junkie?* You think fucking Jon Conway and living in that big ol' house changes you from what you were? I sure don't."

He laughed.

Cass said nothing.

She hoped he would leave so she could make herself vomit the pills.

But he wasn't going anywhere yet.

He looked down at her wet shirt. "Touch your tits."

"What?"

"Touch your tits."

She met his eyes, doing nothing to disguise her disgust, then she reached up and touched her tit, feeling her nipple hard through the shirt.

He smiled, looking down at the outline of her nipples.

"Let me see them."

She shook her head.

"Let me see them, or I will haul your ass in right now."

She lifted her shirt and lowered her bra.

Carl stared at her tits, eyes wide, pupils dilated. Then he grabbed her hand, put it on top of his dick, hard in his pants.

"Pull out my cock."

She reached over, unzipped his pants, and pulled out his hideously engorged dick.

"Stroke it."

She didn't take her eyes off of his. He seemed to like that, meeting her stare with his own.

Cassidy rubbed the shaft, up and down.

He awkwardly mauled her tits with his hand, then leaned over and started to suck them.

Her hand broke free.

"Keep stroking it," he growled.

She did, though it was difficult with him leaning over like he was. But she kept at it, pumping faster and faster. The sooner he'd cum, the sooner he'd be gone, and then she could puke out all the pills.

He sucked harder, then bit her nipple.

She cried out.

But he didn't let go and kept biting.

She screamed.

"Yeah," he growled as she felt his cock about to explode. The fucker was getting off on her pain. So Cassidy screamed even louder, "Please, stop!"

And as she did, Carl came all over her dashboard.

Fuck, I'm gonna have to burn my car now.

He forced her to rub the head of his cock, getting his hot cum on her hand.

And chop off my hand.

She wanted to vomit, but she swallowed her disgust as he released his teeth from her tit.

He looked like he was dying for a cigarette.

Okay, you got what you want, now get the fuck out.

He looked at her and smiled. "You're good."

She was tempted to say *fuck you* and beat the shit out of him. If he were any other man, notably one without a badge and a gun, she might have cut him open using nothing but her fingernails and undiluted rage.

But he had the power to end her, and she didn't dare risk his anger.

"What were you doing crawling out of Stephen Anderson's house this morning?"

The question was so out of left field, that Cass felt flummoxed. "What?"

How did he know? Had someone seen her and called him? Or had he been following her? Or … was he keeping an eye on Stephen?

"Why were you crawling out of Stephen Anderson's house this morning?"

"Well, I fucked him last night and he didn't want his son seeing me in the morning, so I went out the window."

She hoped her bluntness would make Carl uncomfortable. Guys like him usually didn't like when women were vulgar. Sure they'd fuck or sexually assault you in your car, but god forbid you curse.

But Carl didn't even blink. Instead, he laughed. "*You* fucked Stephen Anderson? Wow. Didn't see him being your type ... or vice versa."

She ignored the insult. Waited for him to speak again, maybe reveal why he was asking about Stephen.

"What did he talk about with you last night at the bar?"

"You following me or him?" she asked, hoping not to set him off, nor prolong the length of time before he'd leave her alone — if he didn't make an arrest. She'd file a complaint that he assaulted her. She had his DNA all over her car, assuming his goons didn't clean it.

"That's none of your concern. Now answer the question. What did he say to you?"

"Small talk, mostly. We joked about the burgers, which he seems to like. Then I was leaving early because my back was acting up. Some guy at the bar was hitting on me, and Stephen came up and chased him off."

"Really?" Carl raised his eyebrows. "Stephen Anderson chased Craig away?"

She hadn't said Craig's name. What the hell was happening here? How much did he know, and was this some sort of test to see what she'd tell him?

"Yeah, then he started rubbing my back and said he could give me a massage if I wanted. So, we went back to his place. One thing led to another."

"And what did you all talk about?"

"Not much. He made awkward small talk. I could tell he

was nervous. Hadn't been with a woman in a while, I don't think. I'm not sure what more you want to know? Want to know the dirty things I said to him?"

Carl didn't seem amused.

He zipped his pants, got out of the car, and said, "Fix your fucking taillight." Then he closed her door and left.

Her heart pounded as she watched him get back in his truck and leave. The entire time she was afraid he'd stop, open his door, cuff her, and throw her into the back.

After he left, she opened the door, fell to the ground, and shoved her fingers down her throat to puke.

Eventually, she retched. But not much came up, and not a single pill to be found in the mess.

Fuck!

And then they began to kick in.

Cass got back in the car, feeling both revulsion over what had happened, and bliss from the pills slipping into her brain. She'd never taken five at once, nor was she sure how many might lead to an overdose.

Five won't kill you.

She hoped to God that the asshole was right.

But, at the moment, a part of her didn't care if he was wrong.

She'd never felt lower than this. Cassidy hated herself for allowing the assault to happen, and for swallowing the pills.

She should have fought him, even if it meant going to jail.

Cass looked up to get her bearings on where she was.

She wasn't too far from Jon's. She could make it there. She just had to drive slow and careful.

With her world all wobbly, Cassidy put the car in motion.

She somehow made it the rest of the way there, parked the car in the driveway, and stumbled toward the front door.

Once inside, she went into the living room and was met by a giant framed canvas print of a crayon drawing Emma had made. It read, *My family,* and hung over the sofa.

It was Emma's approximation of herself, Jon, Cass, Viv, and Sarah floating above them with a halo over her head.

Cass stared at the drawing and broke down crying.

She started to walk towards the couch so she could reach up and trace her fingers along the canvas, as though doing so would somehow transport her back to when Emma was actually drawing it.

On the way to the couch, the world fell out from under her feet.

Chapter 7 - Stephen Anderson

As the small boat rolled up on to the rocky shore of Hamilton Island's southwest side, Stephen, Talbot, Judith, and Houser hurried ashore and raced up the hill toward the van. Gibson, still on Lopez Island headquarters, had driven it remotely to pick them up.

Judith took the driver's seat while Stephen, Houser, and Talbot jumped into the back.

"Okay, you know what you're to do?" Talbot asked.

The plan was to hit the monitoring station using Stephen's access card, take out the Paladin guards with tranq guns, then get inside and expose the program. They had a few plans in place to prevent Paladin from killing them, but Stephen wasn't thoroughly convinced they'd live through the infiltration.

But he couldn't just stand on the sidelines. He'd sat by for too long and let Conway Industries destroy innocent lives, including, most importantly, that of his wife and son.

The time for sitting was over. Now was the time to fight.

But he had one demand. And he was finally delivering it to Talbot.

"Listen, I'm going to help you, but first we need to get my son out of here. I want him to take the boat back to Lopez.

Can you all arrange this, and for a fake ID and money for him to hide if shit goes south?"

"It's not going south."

"Yeah, you wouldn't be the first person to go up against Paladin to fail. I'm not doing anything unless you help my son get out of here first."

"Okay." Talbot nodded.

"He has tracking shit inside him. Are you all equipped to disable it and get it out?"

Talbot nodded again, getting on the phone and telling Gibson to set a plan into motion.

"That means I need to go pick him up."

"We don't have time," Judith said from the front seat.

"He's at school. If we fail, Paladin will be there before he gets out. They'll pick him up and do God knows what to him, even if only to punish me for betraying them."

Houser spoke, for the first time since they left the island. "He's right. We make time for the kid."

Stephen nodded in gratitude.

Judith sighed, then said, "Fine."

They drove to the school and pulled up to the visitors' parking lot. Stephen was about to climb out the back when Houser put a hand on his shoulder. "Hey, man, crawling out the back of the van at a school might look a *teensy* bit suspicious." He smiled a big grin, and Talbot laughed.

Stephen might have laughed, too, but he couldn't stop worrying about running into a problem checking his son out of school. Or one of Milo's Watchers seeing Stephen show up, which would likely trigger curiosity by Paladin, possibly fingering Stephen as a turncoat, then severing his access to the station.

So much could go wrong. The sooner he got Milo out of school and on the boat, the better he'd feel.

After climbing up front and nodding at Judith, he crawled out the passenger side.

Stephen straightened his clothes, trying not to look like he'd just spent the morning being interrogated, then casually made his way through the front doors of the school.

He approached the receptionist. "Hi, Natalie, I'm here to pull my son out of class for an appointment." He'd seen her a few times at school functions, so he didn't need to show ID or tell her who he was.

"Do you know what class he's in right now?"

"No, I'm not sure," Stephen said, feeling like he ought to.

"One sec." She pulled up Milo's name and schedule on her monitor. Her brow furrowed, "Um, hold on."

She picked up the phone.

Stephen's nerves were raw.

Something's wrong.

She's calling Paladin to tell them I'm here.

They're gonna lock the school down and descend on us all.

We're fucked.

"Yes," Natalie said into the phone, "is Milo Anderson in class? No. Okay, I didn't think so. Thank you."

"I'm sorry, Milo isn't in school today."

"He's not?"

Stephen's heart was a rusty hammer. He remembered dropping his son off this morning, but he didn't want to seem alarmed. So he smiled and lied instead.

"Oh, yeah, I'm sorry. I totally forgot that he wasn't feeling good when I left for work this morning. Ugh, the fog of constant parenting." Stephen pointed to his head and made a goofy expression.

Natalie smiled. "It's okay, Mr. Anderson.

He waved as he slowly backed away, trying not to display his alarm. As soon as he was out of her line of sight, he walked to the van, picking up his pace like a guy making a casual race to the toilet while still maintaining a calm demeanor.

Inside, he closed the door. "Something's wrong."

"What?" Judith and Talbot said in tandem.

"He's not there."

"Okay," Houser said, "so where is he?"

"I don't fucking know," Stephen said, a full-blown panic now swelling inside him.

"Maybe he's skipping school," Talbot suggested.

"No, he —" Stephen was about to object, but then thought of Katie.

"Can I have my phone? I need to call him."

Judith reached into the glove compartment and handed it over. "You're calling Milo, right?"

"No, I'm calling Kaiser and warning him that we're on our way."

She stared at him, not amused.

"Yes, I'm calling my son."

He dialed Milo and got his voicemail. "Hey, it's Dad, call me back."

He hung up, called the house and left a message there.

"He's not answering. We need to find him."

"No," Judith said. "We don't have time for this."

"Wait. Lemme log in to his LiveLyfe account and see if there's any message from Katie about them skipping."

Milo had no idea that Stephen had put a keylogger on his computer and was monitoring him ever since Paladin started watching. He'd always given his son the privacy to live his own life, but that was before they put spyware in the boy. Now he needed to stay a step ahead of them and make sure Milo didn't do anything disastrous. Mitigate the damage as best as he could, if the worst had to happen.

He logged into Milo's account and found messages between him and Katie, planning to skip school. They talked about how cool "it" was going to be, though they didn't specify what "it" was or where they'd be.

He read the messages aloud.

Judith said, "So, he's getting laid. Probably at this Katie's house?"

"Lemme call over there."

"I don't know," Judith said. "If they're not there, then suddenly we've got another worried parent, and on this island, word travels fast."

Talbot picked up his phone, and made a call. "Hey, Gibson, ping Milo Anderson's phone."

"You have my son's number?" Stephen said, on the verge of outrage.

"We have all your info," Judith said. "Don't get all bent out of shape. We didn't bring Milo into this."

"Okay, thank you," Talbot said, hanging up. "Okay, your son was exploring some caves a bit ago and his signal died there."

"Then we have to find him."

"No, we don't," Judith said. "He's a teenage boy sneaking off into the caves with a girl. He's safer there than anywhere else. And even if we wanted to grab him, once he's in the caves, he's off the grid. No telling where he is in the system. For all we know, Katie's a seasoned spelunker. In short, in case you didn't get my earlier hints, we don't have time for this shit."

"But what if we don't make it out alive?"

"That ain't gonna happen, Mr. Anderson," Houser promised. "I won't let it."

Talbot nodded. "We'll be public once we're in there. They try anything, the world is watching. It's over. Paladin can't touch us once we start this. Trust me. We've done this with bigger organizations. Remember Oliviere or Raintree? We brought those companies, and the rotten fuckers running them, to their knees. We know what we're doing. And the way I see things, this is the best shot you have to secure your family's safety."

Stephen was sick to his stomach thinking of Milo coming

home to a house full of Paladin guards, Kaiser taking him into custody, shoving him in the back of his truck, and the boy being thrown into some unnumbered room in the sanitarium.

He remembered his backup plan. Told them about his app, and asked if there was anyway Gibson could send Milo a message, tell him where the boat was, and still get him off the island, even him and Katie should things really go to shit.

Talbot made another call, then confirmed, "Milo will be safe."

Stephen breathed a deep sigh of relief, praying Talbot wasn't lying.

Chapter 8 - Jon Conway

Jon arrived in Seattle exhausted. He didn't dare fall asleep on the plane, lest there be a return engagement of *Everybody Hates and Kills Jon*.

He sat on the ferry. Nearing lunchtime, it felt like three in the morning. The overcast day only added to his fatigue. He closed his eyes.

I'll just take a little nap.

He'd read somewhere that naps of twenty minutes left people feeling refreshed. Jon thought that article was bullshit, or applied only to a certain segment of people, probably children without any energy deficit to begin with. But it wasn't true for a guy who couldn't even convincingly co-star opposite Yuna Matsui.

Jon stared out at Hamilton in the distance. Clouds were gathering over the island as if to welcome him.

He planned to catch a cab to Conway Gardens, make his way into his father's office, and find the damned portal. Would he meet any resistance? If Blake was there, he'd give Jon a hard time. But hell if he'd leave before finding the portal.

Blake was rarely home. If anything, he'd run into Warren. Did his brother know about it? How could he not? He was the

CEO of Conway Industries. Whatever shady shit Blake was involved in, Warren surely was, as well.

Jon thought of both his father and brother at Sarah and Emma's funerals. They'd sat there letting him grieve while knowing the truth. How could they lie to his face? Let him believe something so awful? Why not tell him his love and daughter were still alive?

There was no situation which they were right. And once Jon got Sarah and Emma back in his arms, he would devote the rest of his days to making them pay.

JON WAS STANDING in front of the house that he, Sarah, and Emma were supposed to start their new lives in.

The air around him was … *off.*

Still.

The clouds above him weren't moving, frozen in place, static like a painting.

No wind.

Silence — no sounds of birds, neighbors, or anything other than his breath.

The door opened ahead of him, though he had not touched it.

Jon entered the house, heart in his throat. Something was awry, and his gut wouldn't stop screaming.

"Hello?" he called out.

His voice echoed back on him.

He stepped through the vestibule, and then he saw her, lying on the ground, convulsing, choking on her vomit.

Overdosing.

Dying.

"Cass!"

JON WOKE UP, not even halfway to Hamilton. He looked at the darkening clouds over the island, about to unleash a torrent, and felt a certainty that what he'd seen wasn't a dream.

This was happening right now.

He called Cass, hoping the phone would wake her.

The call went to voicemail.

"Fuck."

He stared at the phone, then the island, wishing he could somehow teleport himself to the house. It would take forever to dock and get a car, let alone to the house.

If something was wrong, there was no way Jon could get there in time.

Fuck! Fuck!

He made a call.

"Jon?" Kevin seemed surprised to hear from him.

"I don't have time to explain, but I need you to do something right this second. You know the new house I got for me and Cass? Go there now. I think she's overdosing."

"On it."

"I'm on the ferry. I'll be there shortly. Please get there fast."

"You got it," Kevin said.

Then he hung up.

And Jon stared at the island as the clouds unleashed dozens of lightning bolts at once upon the land.

Chapter 9 - Stephen Anderson

Stephen pulled the van up to the monitoring station gate at the four-story building known as *Conway Business Center*.

To the outside world, it was a business center closed to all but one client, H&S Holdings.

Only a few knew H&S Holdings was a shell company owned by Conway Industries.

About a dozen years ago, the four stories were converted to living quarters for Watchers, who needed facilities to stay in when they were on duty. Their shifts were usually five days on followed by another three off. Same as Stephen had worked before Bea was locked away.

The real business at hand was in the underground facility known as the Bunker, accessed via the parking garage.

"One guard on duty," he said to Houser, who lay in the back beneath a black tarp. Stephen stopped, rolled down his window, and readied his security badge for the young Paladin guard.

"New vehicle, Mr. Anderson?"

"Yeah, my car is in the shop. Borrowed my neighbor's van."

"Mind if I take a look inside?"

"Not at all," Stephen said, unlocking the rear doors. "Go ahead."

Stephen watched in the rearview as the doors opened.

Houser grabbed the man, yanked him inside, and choked him out.

"Let's go," Houser said into his radio, speaking to Talbot and Judith behind them in another car.

He hopped out of the van, went inside the guard shack, and opened the gate. Then he hopped back into the rear with the unconscious guard.

Since the monitoring station's presence wasn't known to the public, the "business center" maintained minimal security topside during the day to dilute attention. Most of the guards were inside the station, and their closed-circuit feed was being scrambled by Gibson, who worked from headquarters.

Stephen drove into the parking garage and got out.

Judith strapped the weapons bag to Houser. "You get to be the pack mule."

Houser headed toward the elevator with Stephen at his heels. Talbot and Judith followed close behind, both wearing black ski masks and gear and armed with tranq guns. Houser didn't bother disguising himself, because, in his words, he gave "absolutely zero fucks."

Stephen pushed all four buttons at once, then pressed his hand against a security panel.

The elevator, instead of going up, began its descent into the Bunker.

It was a trip Stephen had taken every day for the past few years, yet never with the sinking gut and beaded brow he had now.

As they stepped off the elevators, Stephen waited with Talbot as Houser and Judith came out, took aim, and dropped a trio of guards in their way.

"Clear," Houser said.

Stephen followed Talbot out of the elevator, saw two

Paladin guards unconscious on the ground, and Houser retrieving their pistols and radios. He tossed one of the radios to Judith.

"Which way to the boss's office?" Talbot asked.

Stephen pointed down the hall.

They went, the path clear.

Outside the door marked *Director Bishop*, Stephen stopped and awaited instruction.

Houser and Judith raised their tranq guns and nodded.

Stephen opened the door.

They went in and dropped the secretary sitting behind her desk on the computer.

Stephen and Talbot stepped in after them, and Stephen closed them inside.

"Anyone else usually in there," Houser asked. "Other than the director?"

Stephen shook his head.

Houser set down his tranq gun and grabbed the pistol he'd taken from the Paladin guard. "Ready?"

Stephen's heart raced as he looked from Judith to Talbot, waiting for them to nod.

They did.

Houser kicked the door down, yelling, "Hands up, hands up!" as he stormed in with his gun on Director Arthur Bishop.

Bishop, a heavyset man in his fifties with thin gray hair and thick eyebrows, was thoroughly flustered as he raised his hands. The red door was behind him, leading to the one station in the Bunker displaying all the feeds. Stephen had never been in the room but had learned of its existence from a few overheard conversations. He'd told Talbot during his interrogation.

Bishop saw Stephen. "Anderson? What the hell is this?"

"Step away from the desk," Houser commanded. "Now, or I'll put this .22 into your fucking brainpan."

Bishop stood. "I don't know what the hell is happening here, but you are making a grave error."

"Shut up," Judith snapped. "Now open the door. You're going to show us your operation. And don't do anything stupid, or my friend here will paint the wall with your brains."

Bishop looked from Judith, to Houser, and finally to Stephen.

Stephen nodded. "Do what you're told and nobody gets hurt. Open the red door."

He shook his head. "No. You'll have to kill me.'

"Fair enough," Houser said, rushing at him and shoving the gun against his head.

"No!" Bishop cried out. "I'll open it. I'll open it!"

He started toward the panel next to the door. Stephen said, "Don't trigger an alarm, Mr. Bishop. Or I can't stop what will happen to you."

"Or your family," Houser added with a wink.

Bishop went to the door and placed his palm against the panel. The door slid open, revealing a large dark room filled with what looked to be at least five hundred screens.

"Jesus," Talbot said, stepping toward it. He turned to Houser. "Keep an eye on him while we go inside. If he so much as breathes wrong, kill him."

"With pleasure." Houser smiled broadly at Bishop.

Stephen didn't think the man was a stone-cold killer, but Bishop didn't know that. And he looked ready to piss his pants.

"Here." Talbot handed Stephen a pair of cam glasses. "Put these on."

Stephen set them on his head. Talbot pressed a button, looked down at his tablet, checking to make sure he was in frame, then hit a second button that read *broadcast*.

"This is Talbot Gray coming to you live from one of the most secretive places on earth, Hamilton Island, just off the coast of Washington, home to the most intrusive monitoring program ever initiated on American soil. Today, viewers, on Expose Them All, we will uncover and show you the most sinister spying program in history. And worse, a secret military project to control our minds. Today we expose Conway Industries."

Talbot headed into the room.

Stephen followed.

Chapter 10 - Kevin Brady

As Kevin raced to Jon and Cassidy's house with his lights on and the siren wailing through a torrential downpour, he called for paramedics to respond as well.

He also had Lori phone the neighbors to see if they could get a response by knocking on her door, but he wasn't sure if she had managed to reach anyone.

At one time, Cassidy, Jon, and Sarah had been his closest friends in the world. It was still hard to believe Sarah was gone. Same for her daughter. To lose Cassidy, too? Kevin couldn't consider the option.

He'd always had a soft spot for Cass, even though she treated him like shit the minute he started wearing a badge. Still, it was difficult to divorce the pain in the ass she was now from the misunderstood kid he'd once had a crush on.

How had her drug problem gotten so bad?

And why hadn't anyone intervened?

He knew she'd gone to an expensive rehab years ago on the Conway's dime, as a way to stay out of jail. But he'd heard rumors that she was back to using.

Maybe he should've busted her rather than looking the other way. At least investigated the rumors. But Cass had been through enough shit already without a drug conviction or jail time on her record. Kevin thought he was doing the right thing.

But what if the "right thing" cost her her life?

He wasn't sure he could live with that.

Kevin couldn't let her die. So he stepped on the gas, pushing his truck faster.

Ahead, the traffic light turned red too quickly.

And he was going way too fast.

Brake or speed up through the light and hope nobody hit him?

Kevin tore through the light.

He saw the lights too late, a car about to T-Bone him.

The car's horn blared as the lights barreled down on him.

Kevin closed his eyes and braced for impact.

But it never came.

The car zipped through the intersection, narrowly missing him.

He looked back just enough to make sure it hadn't crashed in avoiding him.

The car kept driving.

Kevin exhaled. Fear, like metal, flooded his mouth.

He continued, turning into Cass's neighborhood, blasting past signs, *15 MPH* and *Watch for Children*.

Keven turned onto her street.

The paramedics weren't there.

Damn it!

He slid to a stop on her lawn, right next to her car in the driveway.

His heart beat triple time as he hopped out of his truck and raced to her door.

He banged on it.

"Cass!"

No response.

In any other situation, he would've knocked again, but

Jon's urgency insisted that Kevin didn't have time. He might already be too late.

He tried her door.

Locked.

He kicked it in.

Raced inside.

Found her on the ground, lying face up, vomit all over her mouth.

"Cass!" he screamed as he dropped next to his knees and felt for a heartbeat.

None.

He got on his radio and screamed to Lori, "Where the fuck is EMT?"

Epilogue

Sarah paced her cell, worried sick Jon was about to walk into a trap.

Across the hall from her, the light went on. Emma crawled out of her bed, walked to her glass door, and waved. Her eyes were tired, and she was frowning. She mouthed, *Sorry, Mommy*.

"It's okay," Sarah said back.

Billy had been sitting in cross-legged meditation, leaning against her wall for the better part of an hour, if not longer.

He finally opened his eyes and looked at Emma. "She's awake."

"Yes."

"Good."

"Why?"

Billy reached into his pants pocket and pulled out a small hardcover notebook and a pen. He ripped out a piece of paper, scribbled something on it, then folded the paper and stood up with a slight groan.

She was going to offer to help him up but didn't want to insult him by presuming he needed the aid.

He held the paper to the door, nodded at Emma, then made a motion with his hand, back and forth.

"What are you doing?"

"You'll see." He smiled.

Sarah watched as Emma stared at Billy intensely, just as she'd stared at the space where Jon had appeared in the garden.

And then the note was gone from his hand.

She looked across the hall to see Emma holding the paper and opening it up.

"Did you teach her that?"

Billy nodded. "Not taught so much as helped her see the talent already inside her."

"What's in the note?"

"I told her to send the letter to Jon."

"Can she do it?"

"If she can't, then I'm afraid we're all screwed."

Sarah was about to ask what was in the note, when a sharp pain splintered through her being and turned the world black.

She couldn't see anything and reached out, grasping. Then the pain was gone, and Sarah felt nothing.

She called out, "Billy?" but couldn't feel him, nor did he respond.

Her voice felt like it was being spit into a void, not traveling any distance, nor carried to anyone's ears.

What the hell is happening?

At first, she thought the power had been cut off to the cell, but then a realization crept over her — she couldn't feel anything. Not the ground. Not even herself.

Sarah was out of her body.

"What the hell is happening?"

The pain returned, even worse, along with a blinding light as she heard a familiar voice.

She was no longer in the void. She felt her tired, aching body as if someone had cranked the pain to ten. She tasted vomit.

What the ...?

She opened her eyes to see him crouched over her, looking down at her.

No, how could he be here?

What is happening?

"Oh, thank God, you're alive, Cassidy."

"Kevin?"

Episode 18

Prologue

Cassidy Age 9

"I KNOW WHAT YOU DID!"

Cassidy's mom wouldn't stop yelling, no matter how many times Cass kept telling her that she didn't have anything to do with all the water in her vodka.

"Did you really think you could get away with that? That I wouldn't find out? That I don't know what it tastes like?"

Cassidy cowered on the floor, afraid that her mom was going to hit her. The way she was holding the hanger, it had happened before.

"It wasn't me, Mom! I swear!"

"Then who would it have been?"

Cass was desperate for an answer, any answer, because the look on Mom's face right now was a ray of hope. She wasn't absolutely totally all the way positive that Cass had done it, or she would have already taken her swing.

"I don't know, but it wasn't me!"

Her mom swung.

Cassidy rolled out of the way, leaping to her feet as her mother took another shot.

"You come back here!"

But Cassidy wouldn't, making her mom give chase from the living room into the dining room, around the table and into the kitchen, then out of the house and into yard.

She couldn't go back inside. Not until her mom cooled off. She probably wouldn't hit her once she sobered up a little. In between now and then, Cass could come up with a story. And maybe Sarah would help her, if she admitted to what she had done.

Because yes, she had been taking some of Mom's vodka, then replacing it with water so she wouldn't get in trouble. And now Cass couldn't stop. It burned her throat every time, but even the little sips made her feel all swimmy and weird. It was almost like there were two of her, and she was walking next to one of them.

Their mom was *always* drinking. And even though that was when she was meanest, it was when she was happiest, too. It's when things seemed like they didn't matter as much. She would laugh, even while complaining about things like money or the Conways. Mom also often seemed to feel awful the next morning, though not always, and that hadn't happened to Cass.

"I need your help."

Sarah looked up from her puzzle. She wanted to play outside, like she usually did when her sister and mother were fighting, so she poured all the pieces onto a sheet of plywood, and had organized her piles by color. Cassidy didn't know where the plywood had come from, or how she was going to get all the finished parts of her puzzle back into the house once she was done being a dork.

"What do you want me to do?" Sarah asked, sounding impatient.

"You have to help me make up a story. Mom doesn't believe me."

"Of course she doesn't believe you. I don't believe you, either."

"I only drank a little." But then Cassidy got an idea. "You can say you did it! She won't even be mad at you."

"Why wouldn't she be mad at me?"

"Because you can say you were doing it to *protect* her. Because you didn't want her to drink so much."

"No way. She'll still be mad at me, and this is all your fault." Then Sarah returned to her puzzle.

"Even if she's mad at you, she won't hit you. Mom only hits me. And my reason for doing it is a lot worse than yours. *Please.*"

"Uh-uh." Sarah shook her head. "You always do stuff, and then I get in trouble for it. That's not fair!"

"Fine," she said, standing. "But you suck! Sisters are supposed to look out for each other!"

Cass thought about kicking her puzzle, but didn't.

Without looking up, Sarah said, "You never look out for me."

She marched off, mumbling, "That's not true," under her breath as she went.

Cassidy stayed outside, waiting for her mom to crash. She kept looking through the window while crouching, hoping to see her sprawled on the couch. But every time she peeked, Mom was still pacing, awaiting her return.

"You're going to have to go inside sometime," Sarah said in an annoying sing-song as she stomped up the back stairs and into the house.

The yelling started immediately.

Cass crept to the kitchen door and peeked through a crack to see what was happening.

Mom was holding a hanger over her sister's head,

screaming in a bizarre aural and visual echo of what had happened just hours before.

"Tell me what happened!"

"I was only trying to help!" Sarah cried out. "I thought if I poured some water into the bottles, then you might drink less!"

The hanger fell like a hammer, striking Sarah all over her body, until she was sobbing, shielding her face with her arms, her mother yelling something different with every new blow.

You don't know better than me!

Stay the hell away from my things!

If you ever touch my stuff again, this will feel like I'm kissing you!

Cassidy had to turn away. This was too much to see.

And then Cassidy had to run. Because it was also too much to hear.

It was dark by the time Vivian was unconscious on the couch. Cass crept in with an armload of flowers, both wild and raised, gathered from a dozen yards and two empty fields.

But Sarah didn't want them.

She turned toward the wall when Cass entered the room, after muttering three words that cut her in two. *"I hate you."*

And Cassidy knew that the hanger would have hurt her less.

Chapter 1 - Cassidy Hughes

Cassidy was floating over her unconscious body, knowing this was the end.

Ironic as hell that she'd overdose when she wasn't even abusing, when that bastard Kaiser had shoved the drugs down her throat.

So, this is what it's like.

Cass had imagined dying more often than she cared to admit. From the times she felt like life was too difficult to continue, to those when she was coming down or withdrawing from the pills, she had pictured any number of ways she might go. The part that was always the most difficult was the thought of someone finding her body.

She'd always feared being discovered by someone she loved, especially after overdosing. Pain and anger would precede the resentment — *why did you do this to us?*

Maybe they'd blame themselves or wonder if she'd done it on purpose, suicide without a note. The ultimate *fuck you* to everyone who ever cared.

There were times when Cassidy hated her mom enough to almost wish that fate on her. But she never *really* wanted her to experience the sheer hell that her daughter's suicide would invite into her life.

Back when Sarah and Emma were still alive, Cassidy actively feared dying and leaving them behind to live with the pain. Or worse, stumbling onto her broken body. The thought of hurting either of them, or haunting her family with her death, was even more painful than the idea of dying too soon.

Cass could never intentionally hurt them.

But now there was nobody left who truly cared.

Sure, her mom would probably cry. But in Vivian's present state, she was more likely to hate her more than ever before. "She did it to herself. I tried to help, but you can't help someone who truly wants to die," she'd say to her friends.

She'd probably milk the sympathy for a while. Then she'd be mad that Cass's death would make her look like a terrible mother. Viv would probably assume other people casting blame.

A good mother's child wouldn't die from an overdose. She must've done something awful to her.

And that annoyed Cass.

She wondered if Jon would even care.

Would he blame himself? God, she hoped not. Would it be like losing Sarah all over? Thinking of his grief leveled Cass in a way that surprised her.

For so long, she'd hated Jon — all the Conways — and for so many reasons. Only after connecting with him in the aftermath of her sister's death did she finally realize how special he was, and how much he meant to her. All that time wasted on hate.

And now it was running out.

She wanted to float back down, slip inside her body, and finally wake up.

But Cass was floating without any ability to steer her soul back inside.

Wake up.

Wake up.

Ironic that at her lowest point, when she would almost welcome death as a release, Cassidy had never wanted to be alive more.

Wake up!

Suddenly, noise outside.

She looked out the window and saw a Paladin truck pulling onto the lawn.

Brady was getting out, running to the door.

Yes.

Come on, Kevin! Wake me up!

But now Cass was somewhere else.

She looked down and saw herself sleeping on a mat in a small all-white room with only a toilet and a glass door. It looked like some kind of futuristic prison.

Is this Limbo?

Or Hell?

She rolled over in the bed, her hair falling from her face. Only it wasn't her.

It was Sarah.

What the hell?

Oh, my God, we're both dead!

But they weren't alone. There was an old man sitting with his back to the wall, eyes closed, seemingly meditating.

He looked *very* familiar, a name or memory on the tip of her tongue or some deep lost recess of her brain, itching for discovery.

Who is he?

His eyes opened.

"Cassidy."

"Wait, you see me?"

"*See you?* I brought you here."

Chapter 2 - Jon Conway

Jon's cab pulled up to his house.

The front yard and street were filled with paramedics and Hamilton Island Police Department vehicles. He feared the worst, that he was too late.

That Cass was dead.

The notion of finding Sarah and Emma still alive but losing Cass had never occurred to him. She was tough. Sure, Cassidy had her problems, but he couldn't fathom her being gone.

He hopped out of the cab and raced toward the house.

Please don't be dead.

Please don't be dead.

He shoved his way past a cop coming out the door, and saw Cass sitting on the couch with a paramedic checking her pulse and Kevin pacing back and forth.

"Cass!" Jon said as he entered.

She looked up at him, her eyes wide and brimming with tears. "Jon!"

"How is she?" he asked the paramedic, an ex-football player they all went to school with named Eric Crenshaw.

"She seems okay." Eric ripped the Velcro strap from the

blood pressure cuff. "But I suggest she gets checked at the hospital, just to be sure."

"No," she said. "I'm fine."

Eric looked at Kevin. The chief nodded, "It's okay, we've got it from here."

"All right, I just need you to sign this waiver, saying you don't want a ride to the hospital." He went to his medical bag and pulled out a tablet and digipen.

She scrolled past all the legalese then signed.

Jon noticed that she'd started her signature with a giant S like Sarah used to, but then she scribbled through it and signed *Cassidy Hughes.*

She handed the tablet to Jon and gave Eric a *Thank you* that sounded slightly off, but in a way Jon couldn't quite identify.

Eric grabbed his stuff and left, joining the other paramedic outside at the ambulance.

Alone with Kevin, the tension was thick.

The chief closed the door, then looked at Sarah. "Okay, tell him what you told me."

Cass stood and went over to Jon. "I'm not Cassidy."

"What?"

"One minute I was up on the space station, and suddenly I felt this intense pain. Then I woke up here, in Cass's body, with Kevin kneeling over me."

"The space station?"

"Don't you remember Emma bringing you up there?"

"What's she talking about, Jon? Eric and my deputy came in right after she started talking, and I told her to keep hush until the coast was clear. What's happening here, guys?"

Jon stared at her, picking up on the little things. It was Cass's body, but her expression and body language were all Sarah.

He hugged her, tight. "Oh, my God, I thought I might be going crazy."

"Will someone tell me what's going on?"

"Wait, where's Cass?" Jon asked. "Is … is she up *there?* Did you … *trade places?*"

"I don't know. Usually, I can feel her out there. But … but now, I don't feel anything." Sarah looked down at the vomit on her shirt, and on the carpet, then shook her head. "Oh, my God, I can't feel her." Her eyes went wide, blinking back tears. She grabbed Jon. "What if she's …"

They stared at each other in silence for a long moment, so many questions, too much to say, and he had no idea where to even start.

"Will *somebody* please tell me what the fuck is going on?"

Jon turned to Kevin. "Sarah and Emma are alive, but they're prisoners in a secret space station where my dad is conducting experiments with my grandfather, Billy, who is like one hundred and seventy something if rumors are true. And they're working with these aliens called The Ones."

Kevin stared at them both for a long moment. Then he finally nodded. "Oh, of course." After another beat, he asked, "Did you *both* overdose?"

Jon laughed, then explained things further, including his near-death experience on the plane.

Sarah then told him about experiments conducted on them all as children. How Blake had been bringing them, and dozens of citizens from the island, for many, many years, experimenting on them, trying to "perfect humanity."

"*All* of us?" Jon asked. "Me and my brother?"

"Billy said all of us, but they left you and Warren out of a lot of it, per Blake's request. Plus, Dr. Engel specifically wanted twins … and children of twins. Like Emma."

"What did they do to us? What did they do to her? Did they hurt you?"

"Not in the ways you're probably thinking. It was mostly tests, to develop our abilities. Psychic stuff. Moving things, mind control, maybe different powers with other people. I don't know. Doctor Engel is some Nazi scientist or something. Like, actually from World War II."

Kevin told them about how Talbot Gray had recently approached him, trying to get information about a video Heller had shot before he died, showing another two bodies, both belonging to him. Roger, and maybe the people that snapped at the market, were part of some experiment.

"Yes!" Sarah said. "There's a Roger clone up there. And he's a teacher."

"What the hell?" Kevin said.

"He sold me and Emma out." Sarah told them about Blake locking her and Emma away, then about Billy, who was going to let them return to Earth. "Your dad has lost his damned fool mind."

"And now he knows I'm coming?"

Sarah nodded.

"What do you think he'll do?" Kevin asked. "He wouldn't kill you, would he?"

"Maybe replace him with a clone?" Sarah suggested.

"He kept you and Emma a secret from me. Fucking gave me his condolences knowing damned well that you were both alive. He let me grieve you both. My child and my—"

Jon stopped short before he finished with the words on his mind. *His one true love.*

Sarah looked at him, as if wondering what he was about to say.

Kevin, thankfully interrupted the moment. "Blake paid me to leave the police force."

"What?" Sarah said. "Why?"

"After the massacre at the market. He has enough votes to have Paladin absorb the police department, and they would fire me if I stayed. He was supposedly giving me a way out with some dignity."

"And hush money. You *took it?*" Jon asked.

"Molly just wants to get out of here. It was our chance to

just start fresh, and …" Kevin's eyes widened as if remembering something important he'd forgotten to mention. "Oh, shit. You don't know, do you?"

"Know what?" Jon asked.

"She's back!"

"*Who's* back?"

"My daughter, Christina! She showed up out of the blue a few days ago. No memories of what happened. No —"

Silence as Kevin's mind was likely going to where Jon's already was.

"You … you don't think Blake had my daughter up … *there*, do you?"

Sarah looked at Jon and then him, "She's a twin, right?"

Kevin shook his head, his eyes watering as he paced. "No, no, no."

He turned away from them screaming, lashing out and punching a hole in the wall.

"That motherfucker! I'm going to kill him. Then I'm gonna put a bullet in every one of those fuckers up there."

Chapter 3 - Stephen Anderson

Stephen trained the camera glasses at the monitors, broadcasting Expose Them All's incursion into the heart of Conway Industries surveillance program, so the world could watch Talbot explain what they were all seeing.

Judith, standing just behind Stephen, monitored the broadcast. "We're at three hundred thousand live viewers, and climbing."

"Good," Talbot said, "it's time the world see what's *really* happening on Hamilton Island. Make sure you share this to everyone who cares about the truth."

But even as Talbot spoke, Stephen's mind was having difficulty taking in the true scope of the monitoring program.

Not only was Conway Industries tracking every movement, every word, and everything more than two hundred people in the programs saw, there was so much more.

Another three hundred plus screens rotated between views inside cars, homes, and government buildings. A single monitor displayed more than thirty camera feeds, not in people, but hidden in static locations. It might have been easier to count the areas of the Island not being secretly monitored than to detail them all.

The truth had hit him in the gut with a hammer.

Stephen had been working for a company involved in some shady programs, but he always told himself that there was greater good in the works. He'd ignored the signs pointing to something more sinister. Even when they landed on his doorstep.

And now, seeing it all laid out before him, knowing how far the tentacles truly spread, and how little he actually knew of Conway's operations, after his wife and son were monitored and manipulated, the betrayal shook him to his core.

Talbot kept talking, and Stephen tried his best to focus on the right things while searching for Milo's feed. He had to find his son before Paladin came to shut this show down, waging their retaliation as they most certainly would.

Stephen had asked about the group's exit strategy while they were planning the operation. Talbot kept saying not to worry, assuring him that they had everything under control.

But now, as he imagined the forces of Paladin bearing down on them, Stephen could not conjure a single scenario where they made it out of this alive or without being locked up.

Had this been a suicide mission from the start? Was Talbot making himself a martyr? And if so, did that make Stephen, Judith, and Houser collateral damage?

Talbot, speaking to his viewers, said, "Most troubling of all of this is the fact that many of these cameras are peeking through the eyes of people who don't even know they've been infected with spyware, people part of 'scientific' programs they never signed up for, spied on by things inside them they never consented to. This from one of the largest suppliers of implants, nanobot technology, in bed with governments in the U.S. and abroad. One has to ask, what are they doing with all of this data? What is their *true purpose?* And, more importantly, what does Conway Industries have to do with the school shooting on Hamilton, or the more recent massacre at the outdoor marketplace? Why is nobody asking these questions? Stay tuned, fellow Exposers, because we're just getting started."

Talbot took off his glasses then set them on a counter, aimed at a bank of monitors, letting the livestream watch that wall as he motioned for Stephen and Judith to join him in the other room with Houser, still holding Director Bishop at gunpoint.

"No," Stephen said. "I need to find my son's feed first."

Talbot nodded, then went with Judith, leaving Stephen alone in front of the monitors. He closed his eyes to cleanse his mind. He had no problem tracking up to forty monitors at once, but five hundred, plus however many were rotating between multiple feeds? Impossible.

Fortunately, the monitors were divided, with the Watcher program feeds on the right and all the others occupying the left.

Relax. You can do this. You have to do this.

Stephen opened his eyes and took it all in, more than one hundred sixty additional feeds beyond what he typically monitored, so it took a moment to compartmentalize the individual data points in any meaningful way. He batched them, searching for his normal forty screens and immediately detuning from those.

One hundred sixty screens remained, but with people identified by subject numbers and letters rather than names, and seeing through their eyes, it would take forever to find Milo unless Stephen was looking at either his reflection or Katie.

He was about to go into the other room and ask Bishop if there was a way to see subject names, figuring the boss would have viewing options that he wouldn't, but then Stephen spotted something so freakish, and so terrifying, it demanded every ounce of his focus.

Katie, gored by some giant glowing red thing, reaching down to Milo.

Stephen screamed, "Get in here!"

Everyone came running, Houser keeping his gun trained on Director Bishop.

Stephen pointed to the screen. "What the fuck is that?"

Bishop's eyes were big and confused, shaking his head. "What feed is that?"

"It's my son's. That, right there, is his girlfriend. They're in the caves. What the hell is that thing?"

Bishop kept shaking his head. "I … I've never seen that before."

Houser put the gun against his head. "Tell us what that is."

"I swear, I don't fucking know *what* that is!"

"We need to go and get him! How can I see his exact location?"

"Press Command Shift seven on the keyboard," Bishop said.

Stephen went to the keyboard, embedded into a pedestal in the center of the room. He pressed the keys and the screens each displayed an overlay of latitude and longitude coordinates.

"I need to go there and help them," Stephen said, plugging the coordinates into his phone. "And I'm not asking permission."

Talbot nodded. "Go. Help your son. And thank you."

Judith took the backpack from Stephen, retrieved a pistol and box of ammo, and handed them to him. "Know how to use one?"

Stephen nodded.

"Good luck," she said.

Stephen loaded the pistol, then turned to Director Bishop. "Give me the keys to your car."

Bishop glared at him, but said nothing as he reached into

his jacket, grabbed the fob from his pocket, and tossed it at Stephen, throwing low just to make him bend over.

Stephen ignored the slight, grabbed the fob, then headed toward the hallway.

He froze when he saw a squad of armed Paladins.

They opened fire.

Chapter 4 - Sarah Hughes

As Kevin drove the police truck through the pouring rain toward Conway Gardens, Sarah sat in the back seat with Jon. He couldn't stop apologizing for believing she was dead, for all that his father had done, and for not being there for her in the past.

While she supposed some of the words had been a long time coming, it didn't feel right to discuss them now, not when so much was still in the air, when they didn't know what had happened to Cass or if they were going to be able to get Emma — and Sarah's body — off the space station.

This also wasn't a conversation to have in front of someone else, even if it was Kevin, one of their oldest friends. Sarah wanted silence until they got things settled, at least more than they were now.

But Jon had never been the silent type. He was more the Keep Talking, No Matter What, Until You Worked Your Way Out of a Problem type.

"They never told me about Emma. They used Cass as a pawn to keep us apart."

"You don't need to apologize, Jon. Not about the past. Let's leave the past where it belongs. And no need to apologize for your father, brother, or grandfather. You didn't know what they were doing. All I'm thinking about now is getting back onto that ship."

He nodded. "Of course."

She caught Kevin looking in the rearview, before quickly returning his attention to the road.

They drove in silence, save for the sound of the pavement under their tires and the rain pounding on the windows and roof.

Jon was staring out the window, and as much as she wanted to keep the next question inside, Sarah couldn't stop the words from escaping her lips. "Do you love her?"

He stared at Sarah, not saying a word, his silence saying more than enough.

"I know you two were dating. Emma told me." Sarah didn't bother telling him that she'd also had glimpses of Cassidy's life through their connection, and she had seen them together. That she'd felt her sister's love. It might make the atmosphere in the truck even more uneasy than it already was.

"And, before you say anything, know that it's okay. You thought I was dead. And besides, we were over a long time ago."

"Yes, I loved her."

"You *don't* love her now?"

"We ... had difficulties."

"Imagine that," Sarah said with a smile. "Two of the most dysfunctional people I know having problems."

"You sure you're not Cass fucking with me? That's exactly the sort of ballbusting she was famous for. And besides, I thought you didn't want to talk."

"You're right. Sorry."

Sarah returned to her silence, staring out the window, as fat droplets of water streaked by in the wind.

She was glad he killed the conversation this time. Because one question would certainly invite another and another and another until they were finally discussing their feelings. And then Sarah might confess something she barely wanted to admit to herself — just how much she'd missed him. How the moment she saw him up on the ship, time had folded back on itself, and suddenly they were in his back yard, lying in the grass, looking up at the stars and wondering about their futures.

And about their future together.

Sarah hated even thinking about these things now. She felt confident that with Jon and Kevin at her side, they'd be able to get Emma, and Cass — if she was indeed in Sarah's body — back. But it was far from a given. And Sarah was a practical woman. Even if everything somehow returned to normal, that didn't erase all that had happened. Or whatever Jon and Cass felt for one another.

Even if Jon had a change of heart, Cass was still holding onto some hope that things might work out. Sarah had felt it a few times. And had she been on Earth with her sister, she probably would've called and warned Cassidy not to get her hopes up. Jon had a way of disappointing a person when they needed him most. He was, like Cass, perhaps too broken to fix.

Where Cass was now and why could she no longer feel the connection to her? Was she in Sarah's body on the space station? Or … had she died from the overdose and somehow Sarah was pulled into her body?

She had never felt anything like this before. If it was one of her abilities, she couldn't recall ever using it. But then again, Sarah didn't remember much of what happened to them as kids. Nor did she realize she had any abilities, even though she was able to control people with her mind.

Or some people, some times. But not all people.

Otherwise, she might have freed herself from that prison long ago.

Sarah had tried to get into the doctor's head, as well as

Blake's and Billy's — the only people she thought would be able to free her without getting caught — but none of her attempts had amounted to anything. So how useful of an ability was it, really?

They pulled up to Conway Gardens. Kevin's radio came to life with call signals followed by "shots fired" and "terrorist threat" just as Jon's phone buzzed with breaking news.

He stared at the screen. "Oh, my God."

Chapter 5 - Cassidy Hughes

One moment Cass was waking up in Sarah's body, and the next, an old man was telling her he'd brought her there.

This has to be a dream.

I overdosed and now I'm stuck in a coma with weird-ass shit happening.

Had she in fact floated above her body? If not, that meant that she'd also dreamed, or imagined, Kevin showing up to try and revive her. And if he wasn't there, then she was still lying in a pool of her own vomit, body dying and nobody on their way.

Dying alone, a victim to drugs. Exactly as she'd feared.

She sat up.

The old man looked at her intensely, and she suddenly heard his voice in her head.

"Don't speak with your mouth. Speak with your mind. They're listening to us."

What the hell is going on? Who is listening?

"Good. You remember how to thinkspeak."

The old man looked even more familiar after hearing his voice. The déjà vu was like a wall she couldn't see behind, no matter how much she could feel the other side. Cass had no memories of this room, but it felt more than familiar. Something about the sound of the air, or maybe the smell of the place … something insisted she'd been there before. Even if she couldn't remember.

Who are you?

"*Billy Conway. Yes, that Billy Conway. You are on a space station floating above Earth where your sister and Emma have both been since they supposedly died.*"

What? Sarah and Emma are alive? Where?

"*Sarah is in your body on Earth. I called you here to help us escape.*"

Escape? Me? How?

"*This isn't your first time here, Cassidy. You and your sister have been here on many occasions over the years. This is where they tested and trained you. And in answer to your other question, look across the hall.*"

She stood. Her body, or rather her sister's, was shaky. So Cass was careful as she approached the door and looked across the hall at another room, identical to hers.

No. A cell.

Emma was standing there, looking at Cassidy. Alive.

"Emma," she said, barely able to believe that this could be real. If this was some hellish coma dream or limbo, it was far crueler than she had even imagined. It was one thing to be tortured physically in hellfire, but teasing her with something impossible as Emma and her sister still being alive was beyond cruel. "Is it really—"

"*Careful, we don't want them knowing you are Cass, or else they'll stop us from escaping. Right now, you are the only hope of saving your sister and niece. Of getting them both back to Earth, and keeping them from taking Jon, too.*"

Jon?

"*He found out Sarah and Emma are here. It's a long story, and we don't have time to go through it all. Not now. The important thing is that I need you to remember your training.*"

What training? I don't remember any training.

"Your memories have been washed. I can unlock them, but first I must warn you that it's going to hurt."

Hurt?

"We wash memories not only to keep you from remembering that you've been up here as part of these programs, but also to protect you from the pain. Some are quite difficult. And when I unlock them, they're all going to wash over you at once. I think you can handle it, Cassidy. You've always been stronger than you thought."

She looked at Emma. It was all so overwhelming, and she still wasn't sure if any of it was real, but if Cass was dreaming, she may as well follow the road to see where it led. And if that meant a little pain, well, that was the price of playing, or maybe escaping.

Yes. Do it. Whatever you have to. I'm ready.

Billy smiled, then closed his eyes. *"I'm going to knock. All you have to do is let me in."*

Knock? What do you mean?

And then she felt it in her head.

"Knock-knock, Cassidy."

She let him in.

Chapter 6 - Stephen Anderson

Stephen stumbled back into Director Bishop's office as the shots hit the wall where he'd been standing and chunks of concrete spit all around him.

"Get down!" Houser shouted. He grabbed Stephen and tossed him to the ground, back and out of the way.

Houser peeked and squeezed the trigger. "Got seven threats in the hall, coming quick."

Judith reached into the bag, grabbed a grenade and tossed it to Houser. "Flashbang."

He pulled the pin then whipped it around the corner toward the Paladin guards.

The explosion and light were loud, even in Bishop's office. Stephen could only imagine how disorienting it was to the guards in the hall.

Houser capitalized on the moment, stepped into the hallway, fired several shots, then came back in the office and slammed the door.

"Did you kill them?" Stephen asked.

Houser looked down at him. "You wanted to invite them for tea?"

"What are we gonna do?" Stephen asked. "There's no other way out of here. You all *have* an exit plan, right?"

Judith shrugged.

He hoped she was fucking with him.

Talbot went into the monitoring room, picked up the glasses, and held them out, using them as a camera so he could talk to the watching audience.

"We're under assault from the jackbooted Paladin Security thugs with rifles, trying to kill us for bringing you the truth. Hoping to stop us from spreading the truth. But we refuse to surrender or shut up. If you live on Hamilton Island, we need to see you taking to the streets. Go to Conway Industries headquarters and demand they tell you the truth! Do not take no for an answer. Let them know the time for hiding in the dark is over. We are many, and we are here to Expose Them All!"

He set the glasses down in front of the hundreds of screens, grabbed the backpack, and retrieved several square items that looked like small bricks with tape, wires, and blinking lights.

He started placing the bombs throughout the room.

"What's he doing?" Stephen asked Judith.

"It's our exit plan."

"Blowing ourselves up?"

"Relax, Anderson."

Stephen came back into the room, wearing the glasses and looking down at a device taped to his hand. "This is a dead man's trigger," he explained to everybody watching, though it seemed his words were intended mostly for Paladin. "We are leaving, heading off to Conway Industries so we can demand answers from Blake or Warren Conway. If anyone tries to stop us or takes a shot, this entire building goes boom."

Stephen stared at Talbot, hoping he was bluffing. Because he sure as hell didn't trust Paladin guards to hold their fire.

Houser checked to see if the hall was clear, then ducked back inside. "A few threats down, still several on standby."

"You all get the message?" Houser called out. "This building is going to blow if you shoot us. The place is packed with C4. You shoot, you all die, too. We're coming out now."

Houser grabbed Bishop, yanking him off the ground with surprising ease. How strong was this dude? Yeah, he was huge, but this strength seemed like something else.

"What are you doing?" Bishop demanded.

"Thanking God you're so damned fat, for one." Houser put a gun to the back of Bishop's head. "You're going to be our human shield to get us the hell out of here."

"No!" he shouted.

"You better hope these fuckers like you, boss man."

He instructed Bishop to step out.

Talbot followed, raising his arm to show the dead man's trigger. "You shoot me, you not only miss and hit Director Bishop, but I fall down and this place goes boom. Plus, just in case you haven't seen the broadcast, you're all being streamed worldwide."

"Say cheese, motherfuckers!" Houser said.

Stephen and Judith followed closely behind.

Bishop yelled at the Paladin guards, "Lower your weapons, *now!*"

Stephen couldn't see past Houser, but he heard guns hitting the floor a moment later. A hesitant sound, like maybe there was debate among the squad.

"Okay," Houser said. "Let's get out of here."

Stephen held his gun, hoping he wouldn't have to pull the trigger on guard just doing their duty — unless that Paladin thug happened to be Kaiser.

Which made him wonder where the hell the head of Paladin was.

Chapter 7 - Jon Conway

They were sitting in Kevin's police truck outside Conway Gardens, but none of them had stepped out. Their attention went back and forth between Kevin and Jon's phones, both of them showing two different but related stories playing out.

Kevin was tuned into a feed from Expose Them All. Talbot Gray was revealing a monitoring station, his cameras displaying Conway Industries illegal massive surveillance program. Jon was tuned into live news highlighting several dozens of protesters gathering outside Conway HQ, held back by a line of Paladin officers with body armor, rifles, and shields. A few people in the crowd were dressed in their own gear with ski masks and heavily padded clothing. They carried bats, bottles, and — Jon assumed — guns.

"Shit is about to pop off," Jon said to Kevin. "Do you need to go, um … like police and stuff?"

Kevin shook his head.

"No. Paladin wants to be the cops, then let them deal with it. Come on."

He got out of the truck. Jon exchanged a look with Sarah, then joined him as he ascended the steps toward the front door.

Jon rang the bell, wondering who was home, who might present a roadblock to getting into his father's office.

Madge Rasmussen opened the door, always with a smile for Jon.

He hugged her, cutting the old woman off before she could greet him as "Mr. Conway" instead of Jon or Jonny.

"Is Dad or Warren home?" He stepped inside with Kevin and Sarah following behind him.

"I'm not sure where your father is. Hope he's not stuck at Headquarters with those protesters outside."

"So, you saw it?"

"Yes." She frowned.

He'd always wondered how much she and her husband knew of Blake Conway's less-than-ethical side. Did they see him as the flawed man he was, or did they see him like a family member who couldn't stop screwing up, but who they felt sure would do the right thing in the end?

After all, they'd been with Blake since before Jon was born. They helped see him through the tragedy of losing his wife. Madge had a soft spot for Blake, always encouraging Jon to go easy on his father, even while acknowledging she saw his side on so many things.

She turned to Kevin and Sarah, greeting them each with a pleasant smile. She might have called him "Chief" under normal circumstances, but at home, Madge referred to him the same as she always had.

Then she hugged Sarah, telling "Cass" how good it was to see her. Jon didn't correct her as he didn't have time to explain every weird thing that had happened in the past twenty-four hours.

"Do you know the code to Dad's office? I need to get inside."

"No." Madge shook her head. "He is *very* private about his office."

"Warren!" Jon shouted. "Come and greet me, already."

He appeared at the top of the stairs wearing casual pants and a sweater, likely lounging around, maybe drinking at the bar as he watched his empire prepare to crumble around him on the news.

"Jon? I thought you were filming in New Zealand." He descended the stairs and gave his brother the kind of cold half-hearted hug one might offer someone they could barely stand.

He reached out to shake Kevin's hand. "Chief."

Then he gave Sarah a curt nod followed by, "Hello, Cass."

"We need to get in Dad's office."

"What? Why?"

The entire ride over, Jon had wondered what he would say once Warren asked that very question. Did he tell the truth? It was a big risk if he already knew it and was helping father to keep it buried.

But at the same time, Jon wanted to see the look in Warren's eyes when he laid out the facts, certain his terrible poker face would tell Jon all he need to know.

"Dad has a portal to a space station where he's keeping Sarah and Emma."

"What?" Warren said, laughing uncomfortably. "No, seriously. Why do you need to get in there?"

"You heard me. What's the password?"

"I don't know. And even if I did, I wouldn't let you in. That's dad's sanctuary."

"I can get a court order," Kevin threatened.

Warren's faux smile faded. "Aren't you retiring, Chief? I think you'll find it difficult, getting a judge to sign a baseless warrant to pester my family. Now I don't know what's happening, but why don't you all come back when Dad is here."

"I have a better idea." Jon pushed past his brother, headed to garage, flicked on the light, and searched for the tool cabinet.

He returned to the house with a chainsaw.

"A chainsaw?" Warren stepped in front of him. "What the hell are you doing?"

"I'm getting into that room."

Madge was flustered. "Boys. Please, calm down."

"Sorry, Madge. My father is holding two people I love very much on a space station, and I need to get to them. Now."

"Did Cass give you some of her pills?"

Sarah shook her head in disgust. "Don't talk about my sister like that."

"Sister?" Warren said, his eyebrows furrowed.

Shit.

Jon started the chainsaw, extra loud inside the house, and walked toward his father's office.

"One last time to give me the password!" Jon turned back to see Warren looking dazed.

"The password is Emma."

Jon killed the chainsaw and went to the pad beside the door.

Warren shook his head. "What the hell? What did you do to me? How did you make me tell you?"

Jon was confused, then saw by the way Sarah was eyeing him that she had clearly done something. She'd said they had been experimenting on her, trying to develop special abilities. Did she learn to control others?

Jon punched in the code and the door opened.

Warren grabbed his phone. "I'm calling Paladin."

"Put it down." Kevin aimed his gun at Warren.

Madge's face went red. "Kev. Please, put the gun away. This isn't necessary."

"Yeah, *Kev,*" Warren said with a sneer, dialing the number and turning his back on Kevin, almost daring him to shoot.

"Fuck it, let him call whoever he wants," Jon said. "Come help me find this damned portal."

Then he entered his father's office.

Chapter 8 - Cassidy Hughes

I hate this.

"I know," Billy assured her. *"But you must keep going."*

Cassidy loathed being told what to do, and she hated the way this felt even more.

It was jarring, like nothing she'd ever experienced. Memories were one thing, but walking around inside one was a bit like having someone force your eyes open while someone else beat at your head like a piñata, trying to get all the candy out from inside.

This was definitely her memory, even though it had been stolen until now. She was walking through a tall wall of déjà vu, and even transparent, the bricks were all poison.

Cass was sitting by herself, playing with blocks, when a man entered the room and filled her with chills, both now and inside the memory. The compound effect was like being kicked off a cliff, and hitting her head on every jagged rock as she fell.

"It's going to be okay."

She drew a deep breath, and it almost was.

"Come on." Dr. Engel loomed over the eleven-year-old version of Cass.

She stood from her pile and followed him like a robot out of the playroom, taking a final glance at all the other children around the room, scattered and playing with their own little mountains of blocks.

Cassidy waved goodbye as the door closed, but only her sister waved back.

In the other room, the one she hated most, she was ordered to sit in her usual chair, squeeze her eyes tight like always, and again attempt the impossible.

But like every other time, Cassidy couldn't.

"Try harder," the doctor ordered.

But that didn't help. She still didn't know what to do.

She pinched her eyes tight and tried her hardest, then she opened them back up and found herself sitting exactly where she expected, on the playroom floor inside Sarah's body, piling blocks.

He's going to be mad, Cassidy warned.

"I know."

And he was. Engel was furious, yelling at the girl as she cowered, her grown-up self reeling from that scream as it echoed through the ages.

"I said, *Not your sister!* Any one of the other girls!"

But Cassidy didn't know how to do that, and she had already tried hard so hard that half the time her insides felt like they were bleeding. It wasn't easy to do difficult things while sitting next to someone you hated.

"It's okay now ... Go somewhere else."

Cass blinked then looked around.

She was no longer eleven, now sixteen or so. She was sitting in that same room, in her usual chair, but this time Dr. Engel seemed pleased.

"Very good, Cassidy. We're already up to a week."

This was the closest the doctor ever came to a smile. He was happy, because his experiments with her were all working. He spent years frustrated with her because she couldn't jump into any bodies other than Sarah. But she could do something that no one else could, and was teaching her sister to do it, too.

The children all manifested slightly different powers, but even those who could body swap could never stay in their bodies for long. A few hours was taxing. A full day looked like it might ruin two minds. But the Hughes twins traded with ease, and each time seemed to make them both stronger.

"Eight days," Engel said, sounding almost kind. "Are you ready?"

She was. Switching bodies was Cassidy's favorite thing in the world.

Sarah's life was so much easier. Not just at school where people didn't call her a slut, even though Cass had never slept with anyone, or at home, where Mom was actually nice to her, even though she always said the same things that she would as herself.

Sarah suffered the sacrifice, living in her sister's crueler world so Cass could keep making them stronger.

There was only one rule, and it couldn't be broken no matter what.

"Never sleep with Jon."

I don't want to see this, Cass cried out to Billy.

She knew where this was going to go. The same place it always went. Because that's who Cassidy was to the core.

And then she was back in the moment, watching herself take advantage of Sarah's trust, her back against the headboard, legs spread, telling Jon with her vixen's smile she was ready.

Stop it. I can't see this. It hurts so much.

Acid rained through her insides. Through eons she cried.

Of course, her sister found out. And when she did, a planet exploded between them.

And now Engel was angry again.

That's when he wiped us for good.

The twins were broken, the blood so bad between them, their bond appeared to be severed.

Maybe forever.

I'm so, so sorry.

Then, like now, Cassidy sobbed.

Chapter 9 - Milo Anderson

Milo stared at the abomination that had spread its tentacles or vines, or whatever the fuck they were, into Katie.

He was all out of screams and had been reduced to a silent whimpering.

Because Katie was dead. There was no way she could survive all the blood loss, or those twisted gnarled vines puncturing her gut, heart, and legs, now bleeding out of her eye sockets.

She was still moving in spasms, electrical signals pumping movement into her limbs, as if the thing were a puppet master playing with its newest marionette.

It spoke through her mouth and hurt Milo further.

"Miiiilllloooo. Come, join us," it said in something approximating a whisper made of static and hums.

The vines crept in along the ground, inches from his feet. Was this how it had grabbed Katie and lifted her into the space at the top of the cave it had turned into some hideous nest, then started to feed?

He reached into his pocket, grabbed his knife and flicked the blade. "Don't you fucking touch me!"

He swung down at one of the vines and it slipped away, surprisingly swift.

If it could truly move that fast, with such precision, how could he possibly stop it from attacking with several tendrils at once?

Milo might be able to stab one or two, but then it would be piercing his flesh, lifting him up to its terrible glowing sac. Looking at the thing made him want to vomit.

He looked around. Still, he saw no escape. The vines must have moved to cover whatever tunnel he'd come through. He tried to find an interruption in the patterns snaking up the wall, but the tendrils were twisted together, one on top of another, like thick braided rope, spiraling up toward the source.

He might be able to cut his way through it, but what if his knife wasn't up to the task? Would he be forcing the thing to attack him? Maybe he could reason with it, beg it to let him go.

"What are you?"

"Weeeeeeeeee arrrrrrrrre Tttthhhe Onessssssss."

"What are *The Ones?*"

"Woooould beeeeee bettttterrrrr toooooooo shhh-hooooowwww youuuuuu."

"Like you showed Katie? You killed her!"

"Noooooo, weeeeee ddddiiiiddddnnnn'ttt. Shhhhhh-heeeee iiiisssss nnnnnowwwww onnnnne ooofffffffff uuuu-usssss. Ssshhhheeee allllllwwwwaaaaayyyyssss wwwaassss."

"I want to go home." Milo cried, hoping whatever it was would feel some sympathy for him, especially if Katie was somehow a part of it."

"You want to go?" This time it was Katie's voice, and without the whispering hum.

The effect was disconcerting.

"Katie?"

"Come, Milo. Be with us. It is wonderful. Soooo much beauty."

"I ... I don ... don't want to be with you. I want to go home, to my dad. I just want things back like they were. I want to be a normal kid again."

Silence. Then movement behind him.

Milo turned, frantically, waving the blade.

But the thing wasn't attacking. It had parted its vine to clear the exit.

He looked up at Katie, or what was left of her, and felt terrible leaving her there like that with that thing. But what could he do? Katie was clearly dead, and he had no way to save her. Milo would only get himself killed as well.

Yeah, so why do I still feel like a coward?

He started through the exit, bracing for the tendrils to collapse on him at any moment. There was nothing he could do if it wanted to take him, but he'd sure as hell make it hurt in the process.

Milo was making his first turn in the twisted path out of the tunnel when he heard another familiar voice call his name. An impossible voice. *Alex.*

No, it's a trick. Alex isn't in there.

Keep going.

Keep walking, you fucking dumbass.

"Don't you want to know what happened to me after? I can tell you what's on the other side, Milo."

It's not him.

It is not fucking him.

Keep walking.

"Remember that short story we wrote about that kid who keeps dying and going to Heaven over and over?"

Oh, my God. Alex is the only one who knows about that story. No way he would've told Katie about it because it was so cringy.

"Milo, there is no Heaven. But here's the good news —

there's also no death. Let me show you, buddy. I want to be together again. We can hang out in eternity."

"Stop it! You're not him."

"You know who else is here, Milo? Someone you've been wondering about for five years."

No.

No.

No.

And then he heard her voice.

"Milo? Baby? I've missed you so much."

"Mom?"

Even though every fiber of his being told him this was a trick, this monstrous thing trying to get him, Milo's heart said otherwise, reasoning that if the thing wanted to kill him, it could have done so at any time.

His heart told him to have faith. It told him to trust. Promised that this one time, things would work out exactly like they were supposed to.

All he had to do was believe.

So Milo turned around and followed his heart right into the creature's nest.

Chapter 10 - Jon Conway

Jon, Sarah, and Kevin were swiping books from the built-in shelves on his father's wall and onto the floor as Warren screamed, "You are all insane! Father is going to be soooo pissed. And you can kiss that retirement fund goodbye, *Chief.*"

Jon, not even looking at his whiny older brother said, "That's okay, Kev. I'll double the price he offered for you to stay on and be a pain in their asses."

Then he turned to his brother. "Why do you always have to be such an insufferable cock? I told you Father has been conducting secret experiments on Sarah and Emma — that they're *alive* — and your first instinct is to try to stop me from getting to them?"

"How do you even know what you're saying is true? Hear it on that Expose Them All channel? Those assholes are going to wish they never fucked with us."

"So, you're saying you all aren't spying on the people of Hamilton, running secret experiments?"

"Well, they're secret so far as we don't tend to publicize tests we do for the Department of Defense and DARPA. Sort of a confidentiality thing, you know? But everybody in the program knows what they signed up for. And you still haven't answered my question. What makes you think Sarah and Emma are alive?"

"Because I saw them." Jon stopped what he was doing long enough to meet his brother eye-to-eye. "I fucking saw them. I hugged them. They are up there."

"So, how did you get up there? And why do you need to find a portal to get back? Why didn't they come back with you?" Cracks were appearing in Warren's refusal to entertain facts.

"Let me ask you a question, Warren. Does Conway Industries have some secret project using radio signals or electronics of some sort that triggers an impulse to kill?"

"What?"

"You heard me. Do you all have a program like that?"

"I can't tell you what programs we do or don't have. But that sounds like some far-out conspiracy theory bullshit to me."

"Yeah, well I just had an entire plane of people try to murder me, Warren. Just to keep me from coming here. So, explain that."

"Maybe they saw your last movie."

Jon laughed. "Okay, that was a good one, brother. Props. But I'm serious. Dad is hiding something, and the only questions I have is, *are you helping him*, or *have we both been in the dark?*"

"Hey guys?" Sarah said.

Before Jon turned, he heard a faint crackling, like the air being repeatedly zapped.

Then he saw the bookcase sliding open. She'd found the secret trigger.

Jon turned to Warren. His brother seemed genuinely surprised as the bookcase slid open to reveal a giant blue glowing disk, floating in the air with arcs of blue light crackling around it.

"Now, if you'll excuse us, we're going to step through that portal that isn't there to go to the space station that most certainly isn't holding Sarah and Emma against their will. Will you be joining us?"

Warren simply stared, then nodded.

Jon approached the portal, feeling its rhythmic waves of energy washing over him, the hairs on his neck and arms standing on end.

His heart raced as he got closer, and Jon hoped to God he was doing this right, that he wasn't walking into some horrific thing that would spatter him across the room.

"Here goes nothing." Then he stepped through the portal.

Chapter 11 - Stephen Anderson

Stephen, Judith, Talbot and Director Bishop bounced around the back of the van as Houser raced through the Hamilton Island streets with Paladin cruisers following close behind.

They weren't going to shoot or surrender the chase.

Talbot was on the phone with Gibson, asking for updates. "Is it ready yet? Is it ready? Fuck, come on!"

Stephen wanted to ask what *it* was, but figured it best not to inquire in front of their hostage.

As they were jostled around the back, the screaming sirens far too close, Stephen felt like they were getting farther away from the caves. He kept flashing back on the thing that had torn through Katie. What the hell was it? Knowing Milo, his son would have undoubtedly tried to get help. But his phone had yet to ring.

So where would he go?

Or had whatever done that to Katie also gotten Milo?

He glared at Bishop. "Are you certain you don't know what that thing in the cave is?"

"I told you I've never seen anything like it. I work strictly in monitoring. You know that. I'm not involved in R&D, so even if they'd made something like that, it's not like I have line of sight into their stuff."

"Almost here," Houser said. "He ready?"

Talbot asked Gibson, then said, "Hell, yeah."

Houser made a U-Turn that almost caused the van to roll over. Brakes screeched and tires squealed. Then the big man gunned the engine and found a new path.

Soon they reached a busy intersection, right in front of Conway Industries where they saw hundreds, if not more than a thousand, citizens holding signs and chanting, "Expose Them All."

"How did he mobilize these people so quickly?" Stephen asked.

Judith smiled. "He's good at his job. We all take a special delight in sticking it to these fuckers."

The path ahead was choked off by a crowd. There was nowhere to go without running people down.

"Now," Talbot said.

The mob parted like a sea before them.

Houser drove forward.

Stephen turned to look out the back window as the crowd meshed back into a single cohesive body, blocking the Paladin cars and trucks from pursuit.

"Yes!" Houser shouted from up front.

"Okay, gang, this is where me, Judith, and the director get out. Houser, I'm patching Gibson to your earpiece. He's going to tell you where to go so you can get Mr. Anderson to his son."

Talbot opened the rear doors, turned back to Stephen, and said, "Thank you." Then he pushed Director Bishop out into a waiting crowd.

The mob seized him.

Talbot stepped out with Judith to applause and chants of, "Expose Them All!"

A red dot fell on his face.

Stephen was about yell for Talbot to watch out when a gunshot went off and a drone fell from the sky.

The crowd screamed its rage.

Talbot was spooked, but okay. He gave the world a thumbs up.

"Be safe, you two," Judith said, then she shut the rear doors and slapped the van twice.

Houser drove.

They stopped in another two hundred feet or so. Houser listened to Gibson in his earpiece, said "Okay, thanks," then turned to Stephen. "We gotta get outta here."

Houser loaded a bag with weapons and ammo, then Stephen followed him out of the van and down a side street. Houser bent to the ground, grabbed the manhole cover, and lifted. "The sewer connects to an old service tunnel which runs into the caves. From there, we'll find him."

"You're staying with me?"

"Yeah, and I'll help you both get off the island."

"Thank you."

"Don't mention it. Milo's a good kid."

Stephen stuffed the gun into his waistband, looked back at the growing throngs, and then down into the manhole.

Time to find Milo.

And so Stephen descended.

Chapter 12 - Cassidy Hughes

What if I fuck this up? Isn't there a danger in putting someone else in Sarah's body inside the cell with you?

"*I can keep them calmed for a while,*" Billy thoughtspoke. "*But we need to do this now.*"

Cassidy focused on the closest guard in the hall, a woman with a severe crewcut and steely blue eyes. She was sitting on a stool at the end of the hall, carrying a rifle that Billy had told her was a glorified stun gun, designed to incapacitate rather than kill.

She narrowed her focus on the woman just as she had in the memories of her tests. "Easy as riding a bike," Engel had told her.

Cassidy closed her eyes, pushed herself to the woman, and then opened them in her body.

Her name was Isobel, Cass learned after accessing some of her memories. She'd taken a job at Paladin, eager to make a name for herself. Got a bit too rough with an arrest and killed a woman. Carl Kaiser, because who fucking else, helped her to cover it up, in exchange for sex. Eventually, fucking him led to a promotion up here, where Isobel was bored out of her mind. What good was the pay raise without a place to spend her money and enjoy life? Now she was stuck.

Cass knew Billy would have his hands full, so she went to the cell, opened the door.

"Help!" Isobel screamed.

Cass raised the rifle and shot. An electric blast knocked her back into the bed.

"You could've killed her!" Billy shouted out loud for show.

"Shut up, or you're next!" she said, closing the door.

Cass turned around and looked into Emma's cell. The girl was looking up at her with wide eyes, screaming, "Don't hurt my mommy!"

She pounded on the door, crying, breaking Cass's heart. She wanted to open it and give her a big hug, to let Emma know who she really was, and that she was going to get them out of here.

Then she heard Billy in her head, and, as it turned out, in Emma's, like a three-way call among them.

"Emma, it's okay. Your mommy is fine. This lady is helping us, but you have to keep it a secret okay?"

"Okay."

Hearing Emma's tiny voice in Cass's head felt like being home. And made her want to get there that much more.

"Now use the call box and call for relief. Say you're sick, then take the elevator to the living quarters and go to my room. I'll show you where it is. Then get the red box and bring it back."

What's in the box?

"One thing at a time. Just get it, Cassidy."

She went to the room at the end of the hall, made a call following Billy's guidance, and waited.

Moments later, another guard came to relieve her. Isobel's memory said that his name was Lawrence.

"Thank you," she said. "I'm feeling like hell."

"No problem. Let me know if you want some company later, eh?"

She nodded, then had a few more flashes of memories of the two of them hooking up. Lawrence was apparently her secret fuck buddy on the space station.

She winked.

Then left to find the red box.

Chapter 13 - Jon Conway

Jon crossed over into a long gleaming white room with a single gray circular door at the far end.

Windows on either side showed outer space in its infinite stars and darkness. There was nobody in sight. Only the gray door.

He couldn't see Earth out either window, but Jon wasn't concerned. He waited at the portal for the others.

One by one, they all stepped through, each of them looking around, awestruck by all the outer space outside the window.

"Why aren't we floating like you see in the movies?" Kevin asked.

"I'm guessing it's all pressurized," Sarah said. "I know The Ones went through quite a lot to have environments like we're used to, including a garden with actual animals."

Warren could only stare.

Jon could read his disappointment, likely wondering why Father had never shared this place with him. Surely it was eating into his many insecurities, considering his importance to Blake Conway.

"I'd ask which way to go," Jon said, "but all I see is that door."

"If I've ever been here, I don't remember." Sarah shook her head. "I was unconscious each time I woke up here."

Their footsteps echoed in the long hall, reflections looking back from the windows as they made their way to the opposite door.

"How big is this thing?" Kevin asked. "And why has nobody spotted it?"

"Massive," she said. "I've not even explored all that much of it, but what I have seen is huge."

Warren finally found his tongue. "I can't believe he didn't tell me about this. Why?"

"Maybe because of the experiments he's doing up here," Sarah said. "He's using children and guinea pigs to advance science for your company, and … well, whatever his other goals are. Conway Industries is profiting off of the kidnapping and deaths of innocents. And, I haven't even gotten to the clones."

"Clones?" Warren repeated.

"Yes, he has clones of a lot of people. Roger Heller is up here. There are also clones of Emma. Probably of all of us! He took me to a room full of them. Hundreds, maybe thousands."

They reached the door.

It slid open automatically, the top and bottom dividing diagonally.

The door led to an elevator.

They stepped inside. A panel didn't display numbers, but rather areas of the station.

"Where to?" Jon asked.

Sarah pressed a box near the center of the diagram. "That's where they're keeping us."

The elevator door closed and the box ascended.

Then it stopped with a jarring lurch.

Sarah pressed the elevator's panel, but it did not respond.

A voice came over the speaker. "So, my sons have finally decided to pay me a visit."

The elevator began to move again, though Sarah's box had gone dark in front of another area's light.

"And I see you've brought the whore and Brady. You really should've taken my offer, chief."

Kevin was about to say something, but Jon motioned for him to keep his cool. No sense in pissing Blake off until they met face to face.

After a long moment, the elevator stopped.

They were met by three officers in sleek black Paladin uniforms, holding unfamiliar weapons. But the man in the middle, aiming an odd-looking rifle right at them, was all too familiar.

"Guns down," Kaiser said.

Kevin aimed his gun at Kaiser. "You first."

"You'd best *seriously* contemplate your next move. You are just a *wee bit* out of your jurisdiction, Chief. Put the gun down, or I will make you watch us strap both your kids to an exam table. Before I personally examine your sweet, sweet wife."

He gave Jon a sick grin that made him want to punch a hole in the man's face, so he could only imagine the restraint Kevin was mustering not to fill him with lead.

But Kevin didn't back down. Kept his gun aimed.

Kaiser said, "If you want to speak to Mr. Conway you need to lay down your weapons."

"Do it," Jon said, not wanting this to end in a massacre. Blake might be like a mad scientist, but he was still his father, and Jon could talk some sense into him. There had to be some connection, a part of him that still loved his family.

Kevin placed his gun on the floor.

Kaiser told Kevin to raise his arms. He patted him down, then Jon, Warren, and finally Sarah.

"Fancy seeing you again so soon, Cass," he said with a predator's smile. "I knew you couldn't resist me."

Kaiser touched her, and something happened.

Chapter 14 - Sarah Hughes

One moment Kaiser was calling her Cass, and then, as he touched her, she flashed back on her sister's memories of the man sexually assaulting her in the car.

Shoving pills down her throat.

He tried to kill her.

And she lost it.

She kneed him in the crotch.

Then, as he doubled over, she brought up her other knee, square into his face.

Kaiser fell, screaming.

Kevin dived, grabbed his gun, and raised it immediately, aiming it at Blake. "Everyone drop your guns, or I'm gonna shoot."

Blake nodded. "Go ahead."

Sarah, consumed with her sister's hate for Kaiser, spat on him as he stood. "Fucking pig!"

He sneered at her, wiping blood from his broken nose. "I should've killed you, cunt."

"Go ahead, tough guy, try it," she growled, motioning for him to come at her. Sarah wasn't just remembering Cass's memories, but was feeling her daring and feistiness as it flooded her system. Pure adrenaline blended with madness.

More flashes of what he'd done to Cassidy played out in her mind.

Sarah felt sick to her stomach, barely able to look at the man without taking the gun from Kevin and killing him right there on the spot.

"Kick your guns over," Kevin ordered.

They did.

Sarah bent to retrieve them, then she heard the gunshot thunder behind her.

She turned, confused as Kevin stood there, frozen, with a confused expression all over his face.

Then she saw Warren holding a gun.

He fired again, hitting Kevin in the back of his head.

The chief went down.

And Sarah screamed.

Then Warren turned his gun on her.

Her mind froze, turning everything else but the barrel into a blur.

He fired.

Chapter 15 - Cassidy Hughes

Cass had made it to Billy's quarters, where she found the red box and a stun gun he'd hidden under his mattress. The box was metal, the size of a pack of cigarettes, and heavily scratched. She couldn't see any grooves or anything indicating how the hell to open it. She considered shaking it, but given its considerable weight, Cassidy worried that maybe there was something explosive inside, and didn't want to risk anything.

She went back to the cells where Lawrence was still stationed, holding the pistol behind her back as she entered the hallway.

He looked at her, confused. "Thought you were feeling bad."

She raised the pistol.

His eyes went wide. "What—"

"Sorry, Lawrence."

She fired and he dropped, twitching on the ground and pissing himself before passing out.

She took his card and used it to open Billy's cell.

"Did you get it?"

She handed him the box. "What's inside?"

"An override." He pressed something to make it expand, revealing a smooth glass screen with a digital display.

"Get inside your body, we need to move," he said.

"But she's passed out."

"I'll wake you, don't worry."

"Okay," she said, focusing.

And then she was waking, Emma and Billy standing there.

"Mommy!" Emma cried, hugging her.

As Cass hugged her, tears flowed.

"Wait a second," Emma said. "You're not mommy inside."

"Perceptive girl," Billy smiled. "Your mommy is okay. We already got her to Earth. Now we're going to join her."

He held his hand out for Emma. "Come."

Cass followed them, holding the stun gun she'd taken from Isobel. Billy grabbed Lawrence's off the ground, then winced, nearly losing his balance before she caught him. He looked at her, his face in a grimace.

"What's wrong?"

"We have to hurry. They're here."

"Who?"

"Jon and your sister."

"Mommy's here? Why did she come back?"

Chapter 16 - Jon Conway

The world crawled as Jon saw Kevin drop dead.

It nearly stopped as Warren turned his gun on Sarah.

Jon screamed, trying to distract Warren, then dove toward him.

He fired just as his brother crashed into his body.

They fell in a tumble onto the ground, Jon screaming as he wrested the gun from Warren, then cocked him in the jaw with its butt.

He turned to see Sarah face down on the ground, blood spreading in a pool beneath her.

But Warren was already getting back on his feet. He wanted to scream "Why?" but instead, he aimed at Warren's chest and fired twice.

Warren slumped back to the ground, gasping as he watched blood pouring from the open wound.

Jon raced over to Sarah, dropping to her side, and turned her over.

Their gazes met. "I'm so sorry, Jon."

He looked up at Blake. "You have to save her."

Her eyes were already closing.

And behind him, the elevator door opened revealing Cass, Emma, and his impossibly-still-alive-and-not-decrepit grandfather, Billy Conway.

The moment they got off the elevator, Emma's face melted as she froze then broke into a run, crying, "Mommy!"

Chapter 17 - Cassidy Hughes

Cass stared down at Sarah, in her body, dying on the ground. She shook her head, but all the noes in the world wouldn't change what was happening.

"Do something!" Jon screamed.

Blake shook his head. "They won't get here in time. And they're not miracle workers."

"Bullshit! You can give people superpowers and make clones, you can fucking fix her!"

But Cass knew Blake was right.

She could feel her sister's life slipping away. She saw her soul slip out from her body, hovering above it, just as Cass had floated over her own just hours before.

Cass stared down at her own shell, bleeding out. And she suddenly remembered that she could change all this. All she had to do was return her body to Sarah, and hop back into her own.

She focused on her shell and did the same thing she'd done to enter Isobel.

But it wasn't working.

Sarah's soul was drifting away as Jon and Emma cradled her, trying to call her back to life.

Cass turned to Billy. *How do I get back in there? How do I put Sarah back?*

"No, you have to stay here. We still need you to take over one last person."

I'm not letting Sarah die. Not again.

"If you go back into your body, you will die."

I fucking know it. Now tell me how to get back!

"The other person must be conscious. It won't work. She's already slipping."

No!

Cass tried again, focusing hard enough to pass out.

And then an idea came. Cass was focusing on the body instead of the soul.

She turned her attention to Sarah's soul and began pulling her back into her own body.

As Sarah's soul came closer, she looked at Cass. "What are you doing?"

Giving you your life back. Take your body.

"No. I got shot. Not you."

I'm not taking your body.

"Yes, you are. You've done so much, Cass. You've come so far. I know you never heard it all that much from me or mom, but I'm proud of what you did. How you were there for Emma and for Jon. You deserve to be happy."

Tears streamed down Cass's cheeks as Sarah's soul faded. She could barely see her. Soon she would be gone, forever.

Cass looked down at Jon and Emma, crying over Sarah's body. God, she loved them. She didn't want to leave them. But she couldn't steal her sister's place. She loved her too much, and she wasn't going to let her take the fall yet again.

Sarah looked into Cass's eyes. "Stop trying. Take this chance. Start over in that new house like you wanted. You can all be a family. A happy family. He loves you. I can feel it. And so does Emma. Take this, Cass. For me. And know you deserve it."

Her heart shattered as Cass looked down at Jon and

Emma. It would be so easy to take the offer, and yes, they probably would be a happy family, but that would be a stolen life, one that belonged to the sister who had always sacrificed for her, taken the brunt of their punishments, been there for Cass, without ever asking for anything in return.

Cass reached out and grabbed Sarah in a hug, then pulled her back into her own body.

She tried to yank herself away, tried to resist. *"Stop, Cass. Stop!"*

But her sister refused.

And suddenly Cassidy was outside of Sarah's body, her soul standing over Emma and Jon, watching them grieve the right body but the wrong soul.

She wanted to reach out to touch them one final time, but her soul was fading too fast.

Sarah was the last thing she saw, looking at her and bawling.

Mouthing the words, *Thank you.*

Chapter 18 - Jon Conway

Jon cradled Sarah and Emma, sobbing, unaware of anything other than the moment and its loss.

This time was even worse.

Now he could feel Emma's raw heartache, losing her mommy after just getting her back.

Cass tapped Jon on the shoulder. "She took her body back."

He turned to her. "What?"

"Cass took her body back, and gave me mine."

His eyes widened, as Emma threw her arms around her mother, hugging her tight, bawling even louder. Jon joined her, holding Sarah and Emma tight, not wanting to let either of them go ever again.

Though he had Sarah back, and Emma had her mother, the loss was still deep.

Maybe deeper because of the horrible way things had ended between them.

Jon never had the chance to say he was sorry, to tell Cass that he forgave her and had never stopped loving her.

Chapter 19 - Brock Houser

As Brock and Stephen drew closer to Milo's last location, the cave system grew warmer, and a low humming echoed throughout.

"Can you feel it?"

"Yes," Stephen said. "It's that thing that had Katie, isn't it?"

"I was hoping you'd know. You're the one working for the mad scientist."

Stephen shook his head, then pointed toward an opening with glowing red vines illuminating the walls. The iridescence pulsed in rhythm, a lower hum just under the first, almost like a heartbeat.

"I think you should stay behind." Houser checked his belt to make sure he had enough ammo for his AR-15. Then he patted the grenades hanging from the belt strapped across his chest, counting six. The closer they got to the source, the more he feared they'd find Milo dead. And no father should have to follow his son to the grave. Finding another person's child dying was painful enough.

"No," Stephen said. "He's my son. I'm not staying behind. I came to save him."

Houser realized he wasn't going to change his mind, so he nodded. "Do not engage the creature until I do. Understood? Put your pistol away until you need it."

Stephen nodded and slipped the gun into his waistband.

They continued, going through an ever-narrowing tunnel as it grew brighter and the humming intensified, the pulse growing louder, enough that it felt as if it were beating inside his heart.

Houser stopped, put a finger to his lips. "Shh. You hear that?"

"What?" Stephen asked.

Houser cupped a hand to his dominant ear to amplify the sound.

"Whispering. You don't hear it?"

Stephen cupped hands to both his ears. "No."

Houser kept walking, his pulse quickening as the walls grew even tighter. The rhythm quickened, too, and the vines glowed brighter and darker, matching his humming pulse.

"Houser?" the whisper said.

"Milo?" he called out.

"You hear Milo?" Stephen asked.

"Shh." Houser moved faster toward the source.

"Houser?" the whisper came again. A girl.

Was Katie still alive? If so, how did she know his name? And why wasn't Milo talking?

The tunnel grew tighter still, not from the rock walls closing in, but rather the giant vines thickening, making movement slow and laborious. But these vines were slick, and reminded him more of tentacles than plant life.

"Houser, help."

"I'm coming!" he shouted, shoving massive ropes of red out of the way.

The vines went bright red as if in response.

The tunnel widened ahead. A dark-haired girl stood there with her back to him. She wore pink pajamas. Déjà vu rippled through him as he tried to remember where he'd seen them before.

"Katie?" he called out, even though this girl seemed younger.

She turned around and stopped his heart.

"No. It can't be."

Yet it was. Cecilia Ramirez staring right at him.

"Help me, Houser." She coughed drywall into her hand.

No, no, no.

She couldn't be real. This monster, whatever it was, had to be fucking with his mind.

But he couldn't just turn away on the off chance she was somehow here with Milo and Katie.

The tentacles relaxed, falling aside, allowing him entrance.

"Is he in there?" Stephen called from behind.

Houser didn't answer. He just kept walking, getting closer to Cecilia, standing there, somehow, alive on the floor of this cave. He was just inches away from her.

Her dark eyes met his. Sweat beaded her brow. Tiny scratches lined her face. She burst into tears. "You found me. You finally found me."

"How? You … you were dead. How are you here?"

"You found me." It was all she could say, opening her arms for him to pull her into a hug.

He did.

And then he felt the tentacles creeping up his legs.

Houser looked down to find himself holding Katie's corpse where Cecilia had been.

He screamed as his body began to rise.

He looked up to the monster's face and saw Milo floating above him, his eyes wide open and white.

"Weeeellllllllccccooooommmmeee,   Hhhhooouuu-ussssssseeerrrr."

Stephen screamed below.

Chapter 20 - Billy Conway

Billy stared at the dead bodies of Cass and the cop, then looked over at Kaiser, crying over Warren, unaware he was mourning a clone and not the man he'd known and loved, clueless to the truth that he'd already loved and lost several other clones just like him. He had probably never known the real Warren, who had died six years ago in a car accident the world had never even heard about.

"What is the point of any of this?" Billy shook his head, looking at his son.

"Don't blame *me*. You started it. Are you really going to let a few minor setbacks change our mission? We can end wars. Eliminate cancer. Live more or less forever and create a society we can truly be proud of."

"When it costs us the people we love?"

"We knew some eggs would get cracked," Blake said. "Progress demands sacrifice."

"Eggs?" Jon yelled. Then he leaped up and rushed his father, grabbing him by the throat, then by the back of his head, forcing him to look down at Cass and the cop. "Those aren't fucking eggs, you maniac!"

"It's over," Billy said. "We're going home. We're pulling the plug."

Blake shrugged Jon off, then shook his head. "We will do no such thing. I won't let you destroy everything we've built. I refuse. You end this now, and The Ones will never help humanity rise. They'll see that two of its greatest specimens don't have the backbone to follow through with the tough decisions."

"I don't care. Let these kids go home."

"You fucking hypocrite! You wouldn't be alive now if not for The Ones. They saved you. They saved us. And they will save humanity from its own parasitical nature. No more wars. No more death. A true age of wonder, Heaven on Earth without the dogma of false gods."

Billy reached into his pocket and pulled out the red box.

Blake's eyes widened.

"What are you doing?"

"Raising the anchor."

"No," Blake shouted. "Do *not* pull anchor. Somebody stop him! Kaiser!"

Jon grabbed a rifle and aimed it at Kaiser. "Stay put, doggie."

"What is the anchor?" Emma asked.

"The Ones sent emissaries across the universe millennia ago, looking for lifeforms they could help. Each ship has a pair. One stays on the ship, the other on the planet, learning, observing, hidden until the time is right. This device will recall the anchor and the ship will leave orbit."

"Sorry, son, but I'm doing this for —"

Billy froze.

His words and his body were gripped by a force. He looked around, searching for the source, as Blake certainly didn't possess any abilities of this magnitude.

Then he saw the perpetrator — Doctor Hanz Engel — stepping through the door.

"Sorry, friend, I have to agree with your father. We can't let you do that."

He reached out his hand, telekinetically calling the box to his palm.

Engel released his grip on Billy, dropping him.

"Give it back!" Billy launched a psychic attack on Engel, overwhelming his senses with agony.

Engel gritted his teeth, then pushed the pain at Billy, sending him back to the floor. How or when the doctor had gotten these new abilities, Billy didn't know. He must've been working in secret for some time, behind their backs.

Billy rose into the air.

He tried to fight it, but Engel's powers were too strong.

"Put him down!" Jon raised the rifle.

Engel knocked Jon down as well, seizing the rifle and sending it flying backward, where it landed in the elevator.

"Stop!" Emma cried.

"Foolish old man, letting petty sentimentality cloud your judgment."

Billy arms were yanked straight out in front of him as he kept floating higher, now nearing the ceiling. Engel forced him to wave like a puppet, showing off his powers and control in a humiliating display.

Blake finally spoke up. "Put him down!"

"But the show isn't over yet."

And with that, Billy's forearm was thrown backwards, snapping at the elbow.

He screamed, the pain blinding. He fought to stay conscious. He was the only one who could stop Engel … if he could devise a counter move.

"Stop it!" Blake screamed, moving toward Engel.

Engel raised him up as well, bringing him right next to Billy, the two of them suspended like a wicked child's playthings. Jon, Sarah, and Emma were huddled together. He could feel Sarah and Emma's desperation and sent a thought to them both.

Don't do anything. Wait. I will think of something.

"You're all weak. I tried to tell them that, warned them that Billy was having second thoughts, and now they can finally see for themselves."

"Who are you talking about?" Blake asked.

And then it appeared … the glowing blue orb that he'd first seen in the cave as a child in 1861, The One, floating into the long hall, slowly changing form into something resembling a human, but taller, longer limbed, and with no eyes, mouth, or features beyond the dark matter swirling inside the glowing blue light that made up its form.

Its hum was constant and low. Billy could feel its vibrations in his body and mind.

Jon, Sarah, and Emma stared in a mix of disbelief, horror, and awe. Their revulsion rolled over him in waves, rippling over his pain.

It spoke, modulating its normal speech to something approximating a human female voice. "I'm sorry, gentlemen. We've not exactly been forthright in our intentions. Your next evolution is not as we led you to believe."

"What are you talking about?" Billy asked.

This alien had not only saved him as a child, it had become his friend — hell, even family — over the many years, helping Billy grow as an individual, businessman, and scientist. He thought they shared the same desire to help humanity. Had it always been lying, or had it been corrupted by Kaiser?

"It would be easier to show you, as your words cannot fully explain."

Suddenly, Billy's mind was overtaken with a flood of memories going back thousands, hundreds of thousands of years, too many to make sense of it all, save for one thing — The Ones spreading across the universe, not to evolve lifeforms in the sense Billy had always believed.

They were absorbing them, each new species becoming part of the whole, the collective, The Ones.

And humanity was next, thanks to their work on the station.

Billy felt despair roiling within everyone else as It had shown them all the same thing.

The room was shocked into silence. Except for Dr. Engel, who Billy realized was now one of them.

Billy tried to clear his mind of the sheer hopelessness flooding it when Emma's scream cut through him like ice.

Chapter 21 - Emma, Brock, Sarah
And Jon

EMMA

EMMA WAS on the verge of exploding.

Seeing her mother die and Chief Brady getting killed, finding out her mother was still alive but Aunt Cass was, in fact, dead, and then Grandpa Billy's arm breaking before the evil Doctor Engel brought that monster out.

The bad things were winning, and there was nothing anyone could do.

Seeing what The Ones wanted to do was too much.

So Emma found a way to turn off what The One *wanted* to show her and instead peeked into what it *wasn't* wanting to reveal — the other part of it, the anchor, nesting in a cave.

The anchor that Grandpa Billy had wanted to use the red box to bring up here.

She saw it, the big ugly red thing, hiding, burrowed beneath the island for so long.

And then she saw something else, the last person in the world she expected to see — Brock Houser, about to surrender.

She had to do something.

Emma remembered the one thing she could do, the thing she'd been secretly taught by Grandpa Billy.

But she couldn't focus with The Ones' barrage of horrors.

So she did the one other thing that always worked to distract adults.

Emma screamed louder than she ever had in her life.

The One stopped its attack, and everyone looked at her.

She closed her eyes and focused only on Houser, how he joked with her, how he treated her not like a kid but like a little adult, and how he made her feel safe.

He would do anything to protect the people he loved.

Come on, Houser!

~

BROCK

ONE MINUTE HOUSER was opening his eyes to the horror of being trapped by the giant creature in the dark cave, and the next he was standing in a wide-open hallway, bright white and tall, right in front of Emma, looking up at him with her giant eyes.

"You're here!"

At first, he thought it was the monster playing tricks on him as it had presented Cecilia to lure him. But then he saw Jon and Cass. No, not Cass. She was on the ground, dead. That was Sarah.

And Chief Brady, dead.

Then the big motherfucking blue thing that reminded him of the creature in the cave.

Blake Conway and some other man he didn't know, suspended in the air like Milo had been.

He wanted to ask if this was real, but would a hallucination tell you it wasn't? Maybe he'd ask how he got here, but would it change the situation?

Emma looked at Houser's AR-15, then pointed at the man in front of the blue thing, an evil Nazi-looking fuck if ever he'd seen one.

"Kill him!" she shouted.

Houser didn't think twice. He'd seen enough to paint a horrifying picture of what had happened even without knowing the details. If little Emma said a fucker needed bullets, then Houser would happily oblige.

He fired on the Nazi.

~

SARAH

THE ENTIRE TIME that Dr. Engel had been torturing Billy and delivering his evil monologue, Sarah was trying to worm her way inside his head, find a way to control him, maybe get him to press the button on the box, or put Billy and Blake down.

Something.

But she couldn't get in. His defenses were up, or maybe he was changed by the alien in such a way that she couldn't infiltrate his brain.

But then Houser blinked into existence.

It took Sarah a moment to recognize the man since she only had snippets from Cass and remembered things Emma had said about the man who'd found her when she disappeared.

Houser started shooting, and The One stepped in to take the bullets, screeching as it fell to the ground. Waves of energy came their way, knocking them back.

Engel started running toward the door, trying to flee.

Sarah found an opening into his mind and finally got in.

She stopped him, then made him turn and lower Billy and Blake both to floor.

The One was approaching, but Sarah was only peripherally aware of it as Houser kept pumping bullets into its barely-there body.

"Get the red box!" Blake shouted to Emma, running toward them.

Emma focused on it, then the box blinked from Engel's hand into hers. She handed it to Billy.

"Here, Grandpa."

The doctor screamed and ran toward them, a blade in his hand.

Houser filled him with bullets, and he fell into a pool of red syrup on the ground.

As Houser reloaded, Billy pressed the button on the red box.

The One looked down at him, seeing what he'd done, and released an even louder shriek, lifting Billy with the force of its mind then tossing him into the air so fast that he hit the ceiling hard, bones crunching before falling to a bloody heap on the ground.

"Grandpa!" Emma shouted, running to him.

The air began to crackle around them.

And then the anchor, the other half of The One, whatever it was, appeared.

A giant red sac of light with long tentacles like vines dangling beneath it. It was carrying two people Sarah knew — Milo and his father Stephen, their eyes white and wide, bodies trapped in its tentacles.

"What the hell is that?" Kaiser shouted, running up and taking aim.

"Careful, you might shoot the Andersons."

He clearly didn't care, unleashing an electric blast at the Red One.

The creature stumbled forward with a loud shriek, a tentacle whipping by and grabbing Kaiser around the head, squeezing it tight and popping it off in a bloody, brainy pulp.

Then a tentacle came at her.

~

JON

THE TENTACLE REACHED FOR SARAH.

Jon leapt on the thing, tackling it.

The tentacle lifted him off the ground, and Jon instantly regretted his decision. It wrapped around him and started to squeeze. He'd seen Kaiser's head split like a melon and was sure it was about to do the same to his ribs.

He screamed with his last bit of air, trying to get Houser's attention as the man reloaded his rifle. The Blue One was starting to get up, turning its face without eyes or expression their way.

No!

Houser loaded the magazine and opened fire on the Red One, bullets destroying the sac, bright red goo and chunks of black spilling forth in a gushing splash.

The creature flailed, dropping Jon, then Stephen and his son, to the ground.

Houser kept firing into the sac, tentacles writhing spasmodically in what appeared to be death throes.

~

SARAH

. . .

BLAKE GRABBED SARAH AND EMMA, trying to pull them back toward the elevator.

"Come on, we need to get out of here! The station is going to leave without its anchor."

"No!" Sarah cried, not wanting to leave Jon and Houser to die.

Houser had brought the red alien down as the Blue One rose, turning its attention to them.

She could feel its rage, cold and endless, the collective pain of its alien brethren on countless other planets, in star systems far from her own, wanting to destroy everyone on the ship as its mission was ending. She felt its disappointment, years of preparing Earth to become part of it, now all for naught.

It began to change form, a black hole forming where a mouth should be, an aperture that emitted a bright white beam of destruction, ripping through walls to its left and into a room on the right, exposing equipment of alien architecture.

Smoke billowed from the demolished equipment.

The entire station lurched, knocking everyone backward, including the Blue One.

Sarah got to her feet.

Houser and Jon were running toward her, and the elevator, in an attempt to escape.

But even if they all reached the elevator, its beam would slice right through it and incinerate them all in an instant.

Sarah had to get into *its* mind.

And so she focused.

~

JON

. . .

"GO! GO!" Jon shouted, jarring Milo and Stephen from their daze.

They were soaked in crimson goo, but otherwise, both seemed unharmed.

He pointed to the elevator. "We're leaving!"

Then he reached down with both hands and yanked them up from the ground.

They ran and Jon followed, quickly getting ahead of them.

"What the hell are you doing?" Jon screamed as he and Houser closed in on Sarah, standing there, staring, dumbstruck by the giant fucking blue alien about to end them all.

She ignored him.

He pulled at her, but she refused to budge.

"It's getting up!" Houser yelled, stopping, and turning to fire.

The Blue One's hum grew louder, deeper. He could feel it trying to weaken his will.

Houser's bullets ripped into it, momentarily stunning the creature, but it wasn't as weak as the red one had been.

It raised its head, its white beam rising with it, and only a few feet from incinerating Sarah.

Jon screamed, reaching out, to try and pull her back.

Suddenly, the Blue One stopped, the beam frozen, ripping through the floor, but not hitting Sarah … yet.

The beam died on its face, but just as Jon thought it was extinguished, it surged, glowing bigger, hotter than before, like it was building up to some giant blast.

Sarah screamed, "Get on the elevator! I'm holding it back, but I can't control it forever. Go!"

"Mommy!" Emma cried out.

Blake held her, to keep his granddaughter from running out of the elevator.

"No!" Jon screamed. "We're not going without you."

"If you don't we'll all die. Save her, Jon. Save Emma! Get to the portal."

Jon couldn't accept that as a solution. There had to be something else.

But Houser ran out of ammo.

The creature wasn't going down.

It was starting to turn its head toward them, the beam building intensity. The humming turned into a high-pitched whine, like a fan motor spinning faster and faster, about to break and destroy it all.

"Go!" Sarah screamed.

Jon looked back to the elevator as Emma broke free of Blake's hold.

"No!" he screamed, turning from Sarah, running toward Emma then scooping her up.

Behind him he heard the Blue One's high pitched explosion as the beam began to unload, destroying the structures around them.

Any second now, and it would be ripping right through them.

Emma screamed as they dove into the elevator, Houser right behind them.

The elevator doors slid shut, and the last thing Jon saw was Sarah standing defiantly as the beam was about to wash over her.

The elevator descended.

"Mommy!"

And then Sarah was in there with them.

Emma had brought her, just as she'd brought Jon and Houser to the ship.

Which meant that Sarah's control over the Blue One was gone.

Explosions rocked the ship above them.

The elevator continued descending, then plummeting, fast.

They all yelled as it screamed down the shaft.

There was a squealing on the sides as the brakes kicked on, stopping the box from exploding at the bottom.

The elevator doors opened.

They ran toward the room with the portal as more explosions rocked the ship.

Jon couldn't even think of how many people were aboard the station, spaceship, or whatever the hell it was, how many people were dying in the wake of the Blue One's destruction.

He could only focus on their escape.

They reached the portal.

More explosions. The entire ship felt like it might blow up into a million pieces at any second.

"Go! Go!" Jon screamed, making sure everyone got through the portal before following them.

And then they were in Blake's secret office, all of them shaking, crying, and looking as if they'd raced through hell.

The entire room was rocked by the sound of an explosive force, and Jon felt it coming through the portal. The Blue One had found it and was coming for them.

"Shut it off!" he screamed at Blake.

Blake raced to his computer.

The high-pitched whine was winding up. He could hear it coming, though he dared not look into the portal.

"Move, move, move!" Jon screamed, shoving everybody out of the portal's path, bracing for either the beam or the alien to come tearing through it.

It was the beam — screaming through the portal and cutting a swath through space, time, and Blake Conway.

As the beam incinerated all in its path, including Blake and his computer, the portal winked out of existence.

Blake was now just a pair of feet and legs to his knees. The rest, and the wall behind it, were obliterated, the blue skies of Hamilton bleeding through the gaping hole in Conway Gardens.

Jon was too stunned to move as he looked around to make sure everyone else was okay. They were all accounted for, all of them fine. Physically, anyway.

Tears began to swell in his eyes as Emma crawled over and hugged him. "It's okay, Daddy. We're safe now."

He hugged her back.

Sarah joined them

Followed by Houser.

And then Stephen and Milo.

Somehow, Jon felt Cass with them too. He wasn't sure if it was real or imagined, and he might never understand reality again given all that he'd seen in the last couple of days.

If Cassidy wasn't there with them, she was, Jon felt certain, in all of their hearts.

Epilogue

JON

LATER THAT NIGHT ...
Seattle, Washington

JON SAT in the small mirrored room in the FBI Seattle office where he'd been brought to give his statements in the aftermath of all that had happened.

After he, Sarah, Emma, Stephen, and Milo stepped through the portal, their plan was simple. *Don't say a word to anyone.*

There were no bodies to explain, likely having disappeared to wherever the space station or UFO or whatever it was had gone. The only remains awaiting discovery would be Blake Conway's feet, which Jon buried deep in the back yard.

Eventually, *someone* would come around to ask about his father, Kevin, Cassidy, Kaiser, and the other Paladin guards. Jon and Sarah agreed that Kevin's wife deserved to know something about her husband's death, rather than having him vanish without a trace.

When FBI agents Juliette Starke and Desmond Birch arrived at Conway Gardens a few hours after their return, Jon knew the plan for silence was futile. The agents, both in their early thirties, maybe younger, invited them to their field office in Seattle to discuss "the space station incident."

Jon agreed, though he insisted that he would only talk if Sarah and Emma were left alone. They consulted out of earshot, then Juliette said, "Okay, but they can't talk to anyone until we come back."

As he got into the back seat of their car heading to the ferry, Jon put in a call to his father's lawyer, Stuart, who said he was on his way to the office and would meet up with them there.

That was more than an hour and a half ago, and he had yet to appear. The lawyer lived in Seattle, so Jon was growing more annoyed by the minute. The man was never late to anything. And this was his family's private council. He was supposed to be here to help field questions about Conway Industries — questions that Jon had no way of answering, let alone knowing anything about, even though he was about to inherit his father's company, along with all of its legal and public relations disasters.

He hated his father and brother for leaving him to clean up their horribly unethical, illegal mess. Jon intended to tell the lawyer to open access to everyone. Let the world know what happened. He didn't want anything to do with this. He wanted to take care of Cassidy and Kevin's funeral arrangements, then move on with whatever life he had left with his daughter and Sarah.

Jon looked up at the clock, one of those ancient models that still apparently belonged in police stations and interrogation rooms. It surprised him. He would have thought that was only in the movies. How long were the agents going to let him stew at his reflection before coming in to talk?

How much did they know?

And were they planning to charge him with anything? Jon wasn't sure what, but history was full of people railroaded by the powers that be. They knew about the station, which led him to believe they were somehow involved with whatever the hell his father had going on, at least to some extent.

Were they here to find out how much he knew, or to silence him?

Jon shifted in his seat, wondering if his lawyer would ever arrive. Tension knotted his shoulders. He should've waited before entering the interrogation room.

Maybe he could tell them he'd be right back, then go outside and wait for Stu. He was about to stand when the door opened and Juliette entered the room.

Where was Birch? Maybe behind one of the mirrors?

Maybe they were using the attractive female agent to loosen him up.

"Sorry to keep you waiting, Mr. Conway. Again, my name is Juliette Starke, and I'm with the Omega Division of the FBI."

"Omega Division?"

"Yes, a branch of the FBI that handles threats of unexplained nature. Anyway, I just want to——"

The door opened.

A man came in. Tall, heavyset, older, and bald. He had thick dark eyebrows and a sharp nose that reminded Jon of an eagle's beak. His frumpy gray suit was two sizes too big and had a week's worth of creases at least. He had dark circles under his even darker eyes. His frown seemed permanent.

He said nothing to Jon, nor did he sit. There wasn't another chair if he wanted to. But the man seemed content to stand in the corner, behind Juliette, watching with hands folded at his waist.

Juliette continued without any introduction. "I just want to confirm that you haven't spoken to anyone else about the incident earlier today. No friends, family, or the media?"

Jon didn't mention Houser, Stephen, or Milo. It was best if they all disappeared. "Nobody but you and your partner."

"Good. Everything I say to you from here on out is classified. Do you understand?"

Jon nodded, then said, "Yes."

"We worked closely with your family on certain technologies to help us combat some of the more sinister forces out there."

"Like giant fucking aliens?"

"*Aliens?*"

Jon told her an edited version of what had happened.

The woman had no emotional response, listening as if he were reading ingredients. Jon couldn't tell if she already knew about the aliens or if they were a surprise. Nor could he read Agent Two Tons of Gloom standing behind her.

After he finished, she said, "Let's just say we protect people from a variety of unusual threats. And your brother and father helped us."

"This have anything to do with the Expose Them All thing?"

She glanced in the mirror, looking at Tall Dark and Gloomy, then back at Jon. "We can't go into specifics, but rest assured, we will handle that."

"Handle it? I'd say the horse is already out of the barn on that one."

"We've got a narrative to spin, and the Conways will come out looking good, don't worry. What we need now is your cooperation."

Jon didn't like where any of this was going. It sounded like they were going to whitewash it all, that nobody would ever know the truth about the testing of subjects, the missing children and adults who would never be seen again, the decades of horrors committed by his family or the aliens.

"What we need now is to ensure a continuity of services."

"*Continuity of services* — what does that even mean?"

"Conway Industries pioneered some very important breakthroughs, and we need the scientists and doctors to keep doing their work."

"Who the hell is going to trust the Conways to do anything now?"

"As I said, we have a narrative. It'll be taken care of. We'll blame a rogue group within Conway Industries led by Carl Kaiser, which, as I understand it, isn't far from the truth."

Jon just stared at her. He'd known his family had worked with the Department of Defense and the Army but hadn't known about any involvement with the FBI, let alone any Omega division.

"As I understand it," Juliette continued, "you will inherit the company. We'd like you to consider naming this woman your new president. You can stay on as CEO or get someone else."

She slid him a folder. He opened it to see a woman in his father's Circle, though he didn't know her name. Only that she'd worked with him forever.

"In exchange, we'll create narratives to explain everything, including the disappearances of the dead, and we'll ensure you and your family's safety."

"Is that a threat?" Jon asked.

She finally showed an emotion, and it was discomfort. Jon thought again to how young both her and the other agent had been. They weren't calling the shots. It was Mr. Grumps, or someone he reported to.

The man finally spoke, his voice deep and full of gravel. "Not a threat so much as us being frank with you, Mr. Conway. We take care of your problems, you and yours get to live nice and comfortable lives, and important work continues to be done, work that is saving countless people."

"By abducting and experimenting on them?"

"We never approved or had knowledge of abductions, except to create clones. To our knowledge, no actual people have been harmed by the programs."

Jon shook his head, disgusted.

Juliette looked at him sympathetically. "I understand your frustration, but if you knew of the real threats facing us every day, threats your father's scientists help us fight, then you'd understand the importance of a continued partnership. Normal people, and even the conspiracy theorists like Expose Them All, have no idea how important our work is. They're quick to demonize us, paint us as some nefarious clandestine cabal."

"Maybe you should be more transparent."

"That is *not* an option," the man said, abruptly. "So, it's up to you, Mr. Conway. Do you want a narrative painted where you and your family are the bad guys, a life where your star is forever tainted, where Sarah and Emma have no hopes of a normal life? Or do you want to let us help you?"

Jon swallowed his knot. This wasn't a choice. He would love to tell the world everything but wasn't so naive as to think it was the better choice. People *would* blame his family, and Sarah and Emma's live would be tainted, and what would people even do with the truth? How would it improve their lives to know what happened? And if Conway Industries was really helping the FBI to fight *unnatural threats*, then wasn't that a good thing?

"Fine," he said. "I'll be a good boy."

~

JON

. . .

TWO WEEKS LATER …
Hamilton Island

JON APPROACHED the front of Great Endeavor Church where the empty casket stood in memoriam of Chief Kevin Brady, whom the world believed died at sea while on duty. It was only one of the many lies the FBI had developed into "narratives." But it was by no means the harshest.

That distinction belonged to the funeral they were *not allowed* to have, the one for Cassidy. As far as the world was concerned, she was alive and well in Sarah's body. They couldn't easily explain the reappearance of a dead teacher in a public shooting. Emma was easier to explain — someone made a mistake in identifying the girl fished out of the ocean.

Meanwhile, Blake and Warren enjoyed a private funeral following their supposed deaths at the hand of a disgruntled Carl Kaiser. Jon attended their services, said nothing, and didn't shed a single tear.

But now, approaching the front of the church, he was welling up. He was mourning Kevin like everyone else, but Jon was suffering Cassidy's loss as well.

Pastor Avery handed him the microphone.

He gazed at the packed church, looking at Molly, Christina, and Aidan, then to Sarah and Emma sitting beside her. They were all crying, though grieving different lives.

Jon had spent the entire night before writing the eulogy, practicing it more than any lines for any movie. He wouldn't be satisfied unless he left everyone in the church loving Kevin as much as he had. He wanted them to feel the loss of a great man, and for his family to see how much he meant to the island.

"As I look around this church, I see not only family, friends, and co-workers of Chief Brady, but I see the many lives that he touched. Kevin was more than a hero lost tragically before his time. He was someone who always put others before himself. This church is full of stories of lives changed by Kevin's heroism and how he lived each day, as a man who always had the courage to do the right thing, no matter how difficult the right thing might have been."

Jon continued, telling a few of his favorite Kevin anecdotes, painting a picture of the whole man, getting a few desperately needed laughs and earning plenty of tears.

He flipped the script a bit at the end, thinking not of Kevin, but of Cassidy. It was hard to fight the brewing tears, but he pushed through his choking for them both.

"Many of us wonder what happens when we die. I used to be obsessed with that mystery, and lie awake with the fear of not knowing. And, no offense Pastor, I'm still not sure. But there is one thing I do know, that this life — no matter how short it might be, no matter how early death takes it from us — it *matters*.

"From the most insignificant among us to the greats and the heroes, what we do with each day makes our legacy. It's in every choice we make, our every noble deed or selfless act of courage. These things live beyond us, in the wake of the ripples we create, in the lives that we change, and in the echoes that never die in the hearts of those we leave behind. Our actions matter. So does kindness. And following your heart. It is these things we will be remembered for, and these things that live on beyond us in our friends, in our families, and in every life we dare to touch. It is our legacy, and that is something death can never steal from us."

Jon had more to say, but the words were all gnarled in his throat. He stood there, gathering his strength with closed his eyes, trying to will the tears back inside.

The crowd murmured.

There was plenty of sniffling.

He heard footsteps. Jon didn't dare to open his eyes, afraid he'd just lose it.

A tiny hand slipped into his.

He looked down to see Emma looking up to him, eyes wet with tears. "It's okay, Daddy. You did good."

Then she led him back to his seat.

~

BROCK

THREE WEEKS LATER …
In New Zealand

HOUSER CROUCHED in the darkness of the garden across the street, watching as a pair of targets entered the two-story house.

He spoke into his com, Gibson on the other end. "You take care of it?"

"You're good to go."

"Copy." Houser gave a thumbs-up to Gibson's drone hovering in the darkness above.

He scurried across the street, glued to shadows, then exploded toward the guard at the front door using a non-lethal takedown. The guard wasn't part of the normal crew, so Houser spared his life.

"Going in," he whispered, not bothering to hide the man lying on the porch.

"Copy," Gibson said in his ear. "Thermal scan shows one on the first floor in the rear, three on the second — back bedroom, including the target."

Houser entered through the front door, gripping a hammer.

He found the man on the bottom floor, sitting in a recliner and watching a soccer game.

Houser sneaked up behind him.

The man never saw what killed him.

Houser smelled weed and heard laughter coming from the upstairs bedroom, one guy insulting his friend in Russian. Techno was thumping, barely drowning out the bullets on some deafening video game.

He slid the hammer into his belt loop, then retrieved his suppressed SIG Sauer P226 9mm pistol as he ascended the stairs.

Approaching the bedroom, Houser saw his target sitting at a computer, headset on, yelling at someone on the other end as he fired at his enemies online. One friend was smoking while the other was swigging his beer, both of them standing on either side of him.

The guy with the beer turned toward Houser.

But Houser fired a shot right into his head.

Before the bottle hit the floor, Houser spun and fired at the second man standing.

Both men fell, causing the target to flip off his headset and spin around, reaching under his desk.

Houser shot at his arm, hitting the man in his hand.

He screamed in Russian, holding his bleeding palm and pressing down on the wound.

Houser shoved the gun in his face, then ripped his headset and mic out of the computer and tossed it onto the floor. "Speak English, motherfucker."

"What do you want?" he yelled in broken English.

"The Jon Conway video. I want to see where it's stored on your network."

"What are you talking about? His agent paid us. It's gone. *Deleted*."

"Bullshit." Houser aimed at his crotch.

"Okay, okay," he said, spinning around in his chair and going from the game to another screen, typing and bringing up a directory.

The drone floated in behind Houser, syncing with the computer. "This what you needed, G?"

"Yeah, that's it. Just gimme a minute while I upload the virus."

Houser started whistling, causing the Russian to glare at him.

"What are you doing?"

"Just wondering."

"Wondering what?"

"Wondering how you can be so stupid to fuck with my friend? Didn't anyone tell you not to fuck with my friends?"

"I don't even know you man!"

"You're about to get to know me real well."

The man said nothing, though Houser could tell that he wanted to. He wanted to do a lot of things in that moment, including rip Houser's tongue out, but he didn't do dick or shit with Houser's barrel kissing his crotch.

"Done," Gibson said in his earpiece.

The screen went crazy. Big blocks of color and text zipping across it as maniacal laughter erupted.

"What did you do?" the asshole asked.

"Wrong question."

"What is the right question?" Now he was whimpering.

"The right question is what am I gonna do? Go ahead, ask."

The man's lips trembled, words not coming out.

"Oh, you're not even gonna guess?"

"P ... p .. please, d—"

"Wrong," Houser said, shooting him right in his face.

~

MILO

. . .

THREE WEEKS LATER ...
Tacoma, Washington

MILO DIDN'T LIKE BEING STRAPPED to the weird chair in the basement of Expose Them All's headquarters as the crazy-ass doctor strapped him in.

"Relax," Doc Jackson said. "It doesn't hurt."

His father was beside him, holding his hand. "It's okay, son. You'll be fine. You're doing the right thing."

Milo nodded. It was his idea to take the doctor up on his offer to erase Katie from his memories, along with the memories of his time under that horrible alien monster's control, a time which he'd seen and felt the nightmarish chaos of their collective consciousness.

His father's memories of that time were already gone.

For the past few weeks, they'd both been living and working with Expose Them All, monitoring people up to no good. Following the expose on Conway Industries, Jon Conway and Houser had visited Talbot and asked him to lay off for now. Explained some of the situation, and how he was planning to make things right, but they had to give him time to do so.

He'd explained some other stuff, too, which neither Milo or his dad were privy to, but he guessed since Talbot and Judith trusted Houser vouching for Jon, things were okay. Now they were turning their attention toward other criminals and politicians.

Milo enjoyed the work. He felt a sense of purpose again. It was something he imagined Alex would've enjoyed doing with him.

Nights were difficult, with nightmares about Katie being killed playing over and over in his head.

So when the doctor offered to wipe her from his memories, along with the alien, he agreed.

"Okay," Doc said as he went to the radio and started playing some jazz.

"Is this part of the process?" Milo asked.

"No, man. I just like smooth jazz. Don't you, Milo?"

"Um, no."

Doc laughed. "Someday, you'll appreciate it. If not, I can adjust your brain so you will."

"Um, no." But Milo joined his laughter.

As Doc walked over to the counter to mess with his computer, Milo turned to his father. "He wouldn't really do that, would he?"

"No. But if I could get him to make you like something where people aren't screaming, I most definitely would."

"It's not *screaming*. It's singing emotionally."

"Yeah, whatever." Stephen smiled.

It was good to see his father happy again. He was a lot more relaxed now that he wasn't living under Conway Industries' thumb. Also, there was word that the new doctors at Bea's hospital had made progress. She might be coming home to their new home in Tacoma, where Expose Them All was now headquartered. Talbot had bought an entire row of houses for his employees so they could live on the same block and be something of a family.

After everything that had happened, Milo didn't even mind Other Mother Bea so much. He wondered if Dad had secretly asked the doc to change his mind about her. He was going to ask, but Doc came back.

"All right, kiddo, you ready?"

"Yes," Milo said.

Doc prepared the needle full of nanos that would go to work at erasing the memories.

He thought of Katie and Alex, and all the times they'd spent together. How many memories they shared as a group. Then he thought of Manny.

"Doc, what happens to the memories where Katie was in them, but so were other friends? Will they be erased?"

"Some will have to go. Others we can rewrite to put other people in them. As I told you before, it's hard when we get to individual memories. We can't just erase her dying without it affecting other things in your memory. She's too much of an anchor. We'll go over it as I guide you. Now close your eyes."

Milo did.

Doc injected him, and Milo remembered the last time he, Alex, and Katie had hung out at the park together, and how hilarious Katie had been when she teased Alex about his haircut.

He began to tear up.

He didn't want to lose that memory. It was one of his favorites.

"Wait," he said, opening his eyes.

"What's wrong?" Doc asked, looking at Milo.

"Don't erase Katie."

"Are you sure?"

"Yes. I know her death will haunt me, but I can't erase that at the cost of all the good memories I have of her and Alex. I don't know if I'll ever have friends as good as those again."

Dad squeezed his hand. "You'll make more friends, Milo."

"Maybe. But they won't be Alex, Katie, and Manny."

"Okay," Doc said. "Then we'll just erase the alien garbage."

Milo closed his eyes, smiling as he returned to that day in the park.

~

SARAH

JULY ...

Hamilton Island

"CAN I OPEN MY EYES YET?" Sarah asked.

"Not yet, Mommy," Emma said from the backseat.

"And no peeking," Jon said, driving her to their surprise date.

After they got back, Sarah initially only started seeing Jon as a friend. She stayed with Vivian for a while, though she had to apologize for "her" drug use, over and over and over.

It had been weird living with her mom and pretending to be Cass. Viv was a different person to her than she'd been to Sarah, and though she'd sort of realized it before, she'd never really seen quite so well just how different one woman could be with two different siblings.

She wished her sister had known the kinder version of Vivian.

She wished Cassidy's life had been easier.

And sometimes she wished Cass had the Happy Ending she deserved with Jon. Her sister did truly love him. He might have been the only person she ever did love. Something else Sarah had realized while connected to Cass and being inside her — Cassidy had *always* loved Jon, but she never acted on it when they were younger because Sarah had *liked* him, too.

She wanted her sister to be happy, but was also thankful to Cass for letting her be a mother to Emma again. In that moment, out of her body, a part of her thought maybe Emma might be better off with Cassidy. She wasn't sure why she thought that, if she'd felt the strength of their bond after her death, or if it was how much like a family the three of them had seemed when together.

Sarah wanted that for her daughter and couldn't imagine a world where she and Jon would ever be that close again. She didn't want to deny Emma the experience of having both a mother and father who loved her so much. Despite their split,

Jon and Cass loved each other enough that they would have eventually found themselves back together.

She and Jon could only be friends.

Or so Sarah had thought.

A few months following the incident, she and Jon were sitting outside on the porch after tucking Emma in at the end of his visit. They were talking about the old times, back when they dated. Something about the moment brought her back to them as kids, hanging out on her porch, staring up at the stars and sneaking kisses.

Then their gazes locked, and she kissed him.

And in that moment, Sarah felt as if all the time, all the pain between them, was finally erased. She'd never stopped loving him, either.

Nor had he stopped loving her, despite his feelings for Cass. Sarah thought it possible that someone could love two people at once. Maybe it was rare, or she might have been delusional, but one thing she knew for certain was she'd never been happier with him than she had been in these last few months.

She and Emma moved into the house where he and Cass had planned to start their makeshift family.

And that same thing felt right for Sarah.

"We're here," Emma said, clapping from the back seat.

"But keep your blindfold on," Jon said.

"You better not be taking me to that awful burrito place you both love so much."

Emma laughed. *"Nooooope."*

They held her hands, walking Sarah carefully onto a sidewalk and then through grass. The wind in her hair, the sound of running water, other people walking and talking.

They started to ascend a hill.

"Watch your step, Mommy."

"Okay."

They stopped.

Jon took off her blindfold.

They were in the park where they had their first date as teens.

"Oh, my God," she said, looking around. It felt like forever since she'd been here. "This is where your daddy and I had our first date."

Emma smiled. "Did you kiss each other?"

Jon pointed at his feet. "Yes. Right here on this spot. Your mom and I were lying down, holding hands, looking up at the stars and talking about our futures. I kept wondering if I should kiss her. I was sooooo scared, but then I took a chance and did."

Sarah said, "Awww, you were scared? That's so cute."

"Hey, let's all lie down and look up at the stars together," Emma said.

Sarah thought the grass might be damp, but she didn't care. "Okay."

Emma lay in the middle, all of them holding hands, staring up at the stars. The little girl definitely had a case of the giggles.

"So, what do you want to be when you grow up?" Jon asked her.

"I wanna be a detective like Uncle Houser. Or a teacher like Mommy."

"I wish I could teach again, but it'd take forever to get certified all over as Cass."

"So, what do you want to do, Mommy?"

"I don't know. Maybe volunteer at a shelter."

"What about you, Daddy? Are you going to be in any more movies?"

"I dunno. Right now, I just want to spend time with my ladies. Actually, right now, I'm kinda hungry. Anybody got anything to eat?"

Emma giggled as she sat up. "I have cookies in my pocket."

"What?" Sarah sat up and looked at her. "Where did you get cookies?"

"When we visited Mrs. Rasmussen earlier, she gave me cookies."

She dug into her pockets and pulled out a small, carefully wrapped bundle.

Sarah looked at Jon, who also sat. "It was nice seeing Melinda today. Glad she's keeping Madge and Xavier and the rest of the staff on."

"Well, *she* certainly isn't going to cook or do anything by herself."

Sarah raised her eyebrows, motioning to indicate that Emma was listening. He needed to set a positive. "We say nice things only, remember?"

Jon grinned. "Sorry."

"Yeah, Daddy, nice things only."

"Hey, she only did that rule because of you calling those boys in school buttheads, you butthead!"

"Hey!" Emma said. "That's not nice! Now I'm not giving you a cookie."

Jon batted his eyelashes and made a puppy dog face. "Pretty please?"

"Okay, you can have one. Here."

Emma handed him the bundle, still wrapped.

Jon opened it and looked at it with an odd expression. It wasn't cookies. No, it was … a small box.

"What's that?" Sarah asked.

Jon stood, looking down at it with that same face.

Something was wrong.

Jon got down on one knee.

Oh, oh, no. He isn't!

Sarah had never imagined Jon proposing. Not after he went Hollywood, and especially not now. Yes, things were great, but she could tell he was scared of messing everything up.

Jon opened the box, revealing a diamond engagement ring that sparkled like a prop.

She gasped and covered her mouth.

"Sarah, from the first time we lay here under the stars thinking about our futures, I knew you were the only future I wanted. Will you be my future?"

Her heart raced.

Tears welled.

He pulled the ring out of the box and slid it onto her finger.

"Sarah Hughes, will you marry me?"

Emma yelled, "Yes!" before Sarah could. She was jumping up and down, *sooooo* excited.

But not nearly as excited as Sarah felt.

"Yes, Jon Conway. I will marry you."

He swept her up into their second most memorable kiss on this hill as Emma threw her hands around both of their waists.

As they all hugged, Sarah looked up to the stars and whispered, "Thank you, Cass."

THE END

Fourteen years ago on a parallel Earth, a mysterious alien species turned most of the planet to uninhabitable Ruins where the rules of nature were drastically altered and caused almost everyone to disappear.

Get Tomorrow's Gone Today!

A Quick Favor...

Thanks for reading *WhiteSpace Season Three.*

If you liked this book, please leave a review on your favorite bookselling site so others can enjoy it too. Just a couple of sentences would be great.

Thanks!

Sean & Dave

From the authors:

I'd like to start by thanking you for joining us on one last trip to Hamilton Island — especially those who have been waiting very patiently (six years!) for us to finish *WhiteSpace*.

And I'd like to apologize for the wait.

When Sean and I started writing books, we had no idea what we were doing. Not really. We thought, *Hey, wouldn't it be awesome to have four serials going at once?*

Did I say four?

Yeah, about that …

Because of the success of our serials, we got noticed and signed to our first traditional book deal with 47North to start *another* two series, *Monstrous* and *Z 2134*.

Suddenly we were juggling *six series*, plus our Dark Crossings shorts, which, as it turns out, is kind of freaking hard.

It's easy to *start* a series. We could probably start twenty new ones without even coming close to running through a tenth of the ideas we want to explore.

But to actually maintain six series running at the same time as each of the worlds and stories grew bigger?

That stuff is hard — especially when you're writing at the pace we write.

Turns out, we couldn't keep that engine running.

So some of the stories got finished while others went into limbo. We finished *Yesterday's Gone* (our most popular series) and *Z 2134* first. Then we had to figure out how to finish the other series — *Available Darkness*, *ForNevermore*, *Monstrous*, and … *WhiteSpace*.

The problem was some of the series never sold all that well. And taking months to write a new book in an underperforming series, not to mention the costs to bring that book to market, was a juggling act. We needed to balance writing books we thought might sell enough to offset the losses we might take on finishing up the other series. As an author, you have to sometimes make business decisions if you want to keep writing.

Still, we owed a proper ending to every series we started, no matter how many readers it had. I hate investing in a new show only to have the network cancel it before it had a chance, or before the stories were finished.

We never want to do that to our readers.

So we spent the past couple of years closing all our open boxes, finishing the stories we'd started back in 2011 and 2012. We finished *Available Darkness* and brought in a couple of writers to help us finish *Monstrous* and *ForNevermore*.

Then suddenly, *WhiteSpace* was all we had left.

The hardest of them all.

WhiteSpace has always held a special place in our hearts, and based on the email we get, in a lot of our readers' hearts, too. It's our cult classic, I guess you'd say.

And we wanted to do it justice.

We wanted to make the wait worth it.

And we wanted to give proper closure to our characters, people who have been with us for seven years.

As we plotted *Season Three*, we knew some of our characters would die. Hell, after reading *Season Two*, I still hate us for killing Alex and his mom! If I could go back and change one thing in Season Two, I might have kept Alex alive.

But, we can't retcon the story just because we like a character.

I do wonder if we killed a few too many people in *Season Three*, though.

We had some meetings — and some debates — with Sean arguing, "Come on, we can't kill Kevin. He's been through Hell, and he dies in such an unceremonious way."

I agreed.

But it also felt right for the story.

In the end, I told Sean it was up to him.

And he agreed, Kevin had to go.

Cass was even harder. She was the main character for this series, and we both hated to see her go. But it also felt like a noble end for her character — sacrificing her life for Sarah.

Also, Sean pretty much decided she'd die in the beginning, so if you want to send an angry email — blame him.

In the end, we hate to see these characters go, but we're glad to finally close this one last box.

It's the end of an era at Collective Inkwell, and the beginning of some new ad-ventures.

We've got a lot of cool stuff planned for you in the coming months, including standalone stories, more of our thrilling new vigilante series, *No Justice*.

And something I thought we'd ever do.

Something we thought long and hard about.

Something we're revealing here for the first time — a return to the world of *Yesterday's Gone*.

As always, thank you for reading,

Dave (and Sean)

About the Authors

Sean Platt is an entrepreneur and founder of Sterling & Stone, where he makes stories with his partners, Johnny B. Truant, and David W. Wright, and a family of storytellers.

Sean is the bestselling author of over 10 million words' worth of books, including the Yesterday's Gone and Invasion series. Sean is also co-author of the indie publishing cornerstone, Write. Publish. Repeat. and co-host of the Story Studio Podcast.

Originally from Long Beach, California, Sean now lives in Austin, Texas with his wife and two children. He has more than his share of nose.

~

David W. Wright is the co-author of edge-of-your seat thrillers including the best-selling post-apocalyptic series *Yesterday's Gone*, the paranoid sci-fi *WhiteSpace* series, and the vigilante series, *No Justice*, as well as standalone thrillers *12*, and *Crash* which was recently optioned for a movie.

David is an accomplished, though intermittent, cartoonist who lives in [LOCATION REDACTED] with his wife and son [NAMES REDACTED.]

He is not at all paranoid.

He is "the grumpy one" on the *The Story Studio Podcast* with fellow Sterling and Stone founders, Sean Platt and Johnny B. Truant.

You can email him at <u>david@sterlingandstone.net</u>

We swear, he almost never bites. Unless you feed him after midnight.

Also By Sean Platt

The Dead World Series

Dead Zero

Dead City

Dead Nation

Dead Planet

Empty Nest

The Beam Series

The Beam Season One

The Beam Season Two

The Beam Season Three

Robot Proletariat Series

En3my

Robot Proletariat

The Infinite Loop

The Hard Reset

Cascade Failure

Reboot

The Tomorrow Gene Series

Null Identity

The Tomorrow Gene

The Tomorrow Clone

The Eden Experiment

Karma Police Series

Jumper

Karma Police

The Collectors

Deviant

The Fall

Homecoming

Yesterday's Gone

October's Gone

Yesterday's Gone Season One

Yesterday's Gone Season Two

Yesterday's Gone Season Three

Yesterday's Gone Season Four

Yesterday's Gone Season Five

Yesterday's Gone Season Six

Tomorrow's Gone

Tomorrow's Gone Season One

Tomorrow's Gone Season Two

Tomorrow's Gone Season Three

Available Darkness

Darkness Itself

Available Darkness Book One

Available Darkness Book Two

Available Darkness Book Three

WhiteSpace

WhiteSpace Season One

WhiteSpace Season Two

WhiteSpace Season Three

Stand Alone Novels

Burnout

The Island

Crash

Emily's List

Pattern Black

Devil May Care

The Secret Within

Also By David W. Wright

Cold Justice

Cold Justice

Cold Reckoning

Hidden Justice

Hidden Justice

Hidden Honor

Hidden Shame

Hidden Virtue

No Justice

No Justice

No Escape

No Hope

No Return

No Stopping

No Fear

Karma Police

Jumper

Karma Police

The Collectors

Deviant

The Fall

Homecoming

Yesterday's Gone

October's Gone

Yesterday's Gone Season One

Yesterday's Gone Season Two

Yesterday's Gone Season Three

Yesterday's Gone Season Four

Yesterday's Gone Season Five

Yesterday's Gone Season Six

Tomorrow's Gone

Tomorrow's Gone Season One

Tomorrow's Gone Season Two

Tomorrow's Gone Season Three

Available Darkness

Darkness Itself

Available Darkness Book One

Available Darkness Book Two

Available Darkness Book Three

WhiteSpace

WhiteSpace Season One

WhiteSpace Season Two

WhiteSpace Season Three

Stand Alone Novels

12

Crash

Emily's List

Threshold

The Secret Within